THE TALE OF THE LAZY DOG

Charles Pol Thrillers Book Two

Alan Williams

SAPERE
BOOKS

THE TALE OF THE LAZY DOG

Published by Sapere Books.

20 Windermere Drive, Leeds, England, LS17 7UZ,
United Kingdom

saperebooks.com

ISBN: 978-1-913335-91-5

For my wife

PROLOGUE: THE MAN ON THE ROOF

Sgt Don Wace came on duty at 1900 hours, just as the rain started. Over the few yards between his canvas-hooded jeep and the shelter of the hut door he was already splashed to the skin. He stood loosening the strap under his jaw and tipped the black and white M.P.'s helmet forward, wiping his hand over his straw-coloured crewcut and around his sticky neck to the Adam's apple that jumped in his throat like a yoyo every time he swallowed.

After a moment he unslung his M16 carbine, snapping it on to semi-automatic, then settled the helmet back above his eyes and stood surveying the scene of his night's vigil. Rows of breezeblock huts, skeleton shapes of watchtowers, rain bouncing off the mud-baked tracks and turning to steam in the hot stagnant air, thick with fumes of burnt kerosene and the long scream of jets that was like hundreds of feet of tearing paper.

With the rain came darkness, as though the lights were being turned gradually down in a giant auditorium, and soon it was only by leaning out and peering through the vertical spears of water that Wace could make out the shapes of his two colleagues, each only fifteen feet from him at the corners of the hut. Wace himself guarded the doors — two broad double sheets of grey steel with the white stencilled words: **U.S. GOVT PROPERTY — KEEP OUT**.

Wace was in a bad mood. He and his two colleagues were usually detailed to guard duty at the central air-traffic complex or the main gates, where there were canteens, PX facilities, plenty of action: streams of local girls on bicycles who had to be stopped and checked, sometimes even searched, as they left in time for curfew. There were even a few round-eyes with sallow skins and skirts half way up their thighs, who worked for the Military Assistance Command and knew all the M.P.'s by name.

But this hut here was out in the boondocks. And like the others all around, it was locked and lifeless, with no windows. Wace's geography of the airfield was muddled, even after several months of duty here. There were no stars to go by; but taking his bearings from the brownish glow to the south where the city lay, and the red-hot streak of after-burners across the sky to his left, where the fighter planes were taking off every few minutes from the military airstrips, he reckoned he was somewhere near the heart of the vast supply and ordnance depot to the east of the main traffic complex. And to his right, beyond the watchtowers and high-tension wire, he could just make out, against the arc-lights above the minefield, the rows of high-tailed, heavy-bellied transport planes — C 123s and Hercules, and the lighter twin-engined Caribou that can lift five tons of dead weight and land in just over three times its own length.

Wace cursed again, wondering what the hell he was doing by this lone hut. If they were going to knock out anything, they'd go for the planes — as they always did, putting in mortars and rockets first, then sending in waves of human mine-detectors, screaming like monkeys and hurling satchel-bombs as the M.P.'s gunned them down at the wire. So what was so goddam important about this hut that he and his colleagues had to stand here wet and bored for four black hours without even the chance of a coffee?

The rain was letting up and far out beyond the perimeter the flares began to drop, bursting in a neon glare that drifted slowly to earth, like phosphorescent shapes sinking through water. He watched them go out, when suddenly to his right a pair of headlamps swung into view, approaching fast down the waterlogged track. He straightened up with his carbine in both hands, holding it slightly upwards from his waist, its fluted muzzle tracking a line just in front of the lights, ready to jerk back and rake the vehicle from end to end — thirty rounds in one second, on fully automatic.

It was a long black Fleetwood sedan with smoked windows so he could not see who was inside. He watched tensely as it bounced to a standstill in a whoosh of mud and an officer in combat fatigues leapt out, reaching him in two strides, his words coming in a breathless rush: 'Sergeant Wace, detail from ATCO Three?' Wace stood to rigid attention and saluted. 'How many you got here, sergeant?'

'Three men, sir.'

'Only three? Christ!' The man rubbed his hand over a sweaty dark-skinned face: 'This the official detail from headquarters — just three men?'

'That's all they gave me, sir.'

'What orders?'

'Stand guard till twenty-two-thirty hours, sir.'

The officer paused, working his jaw muscles as though trying to dislodge something from his teeth. 'O.K.,' he said suddenly, 'you do just that till we come to move this stuff out to Number Four transport runway. We'll be using a forklift truck for the job, and there'll be an armed patrol under Colonel Miller. Codename *Happy Hound*. Got that?'

'Yessir.'

'Meantime I'm sending an extra detail. And I want you up on that hut roof with your eyes in the back of your head, Wace, and not let anyone near this place till the patrol gets here. Not anyone! O.K.?'

'What about the extra detail, sir?'

'What about it?'

'How do I recognise it, sir?'

The officer looked at him sharply, then nodded: 'I'll be back with them myself. I'll flash my lights twice at the end of the track. Now get on the roof!' He turned and jumped into the jeep, and was already backing it round as Wace shouted, 'McCulsky!'

One of the men at the end of the hut came lumbering through the mud, not bothering to salute. 'What's the beef, sarge?'

'You heard the man. They're sending up an extra detail. Maybe they don't trust us.' He looked at the steel doors behind him and shrugged: 'What the hell they got in there, anyway? He said a full colonel and a forklift truck to move the stuff! Must be something mighty special.'

'Maybe it's the latest issue of *Playboy*?' McCulsky's grin was invisible under his helmet.

'Yeah, so why they flyin' it out then?' Wace said irritably. He glanced up at the roof: a good twelve feet high, with no parapet, no cover of any kind. Those motherin' big brass-arses from MACV! he thought sourly. Someday he was going to get even with some of the officers that ran this airfield. He turned to McCulsky. 'Help me up,' he said, putting the gun on to safety and slinging it round his neck. McCulsky cupped his hands into a stirrup and Wace sprang on to his shoulders, almost snapping off a length of guttering as he pulled himself up over the edge.

He knew at once that the roof was not safe. It was a rough concrete surface, slightly convex to allow the rain to drain off, but so badly built that more than half of it was under at least an inch of water; and as he took a step forward he felt the whole structure give under his weight like a diving board. Wace had lived long enough on a farm to take a simple pride in a job well done, and his anger switched now to embrace the whole local population. Good Federal taxes handed out in subcontracts to these goddam gooks! he thought. The concrete had been so watered down that it was more like plaster.

He took another step and there was a dull cracking sound under his boot. He flung his arms out with a yell, as a great slice of roof came away with him, and he fell into darkness.

He landed half upside down, looking up at McCulsky's big helmeted face hanging above in the jagged frame of what was left of the roof.

'What happened, sarge? You O.K.?'

Another set of flares had burst in the sky, this time very much closer, and in the few seconds of livid purple light, Wace was able to sit up and take stock of his surroundings. His first impression was that the hut was empty, the rectangular walls of the same featureless breezeblock as on the outside, the floor spattered with loose concrete and a slush of rainwater.

'You O.K., sarge?' McCulsky called again.

Wace made an effort to haul himself up, wincing with pain. 'Get a light, will yer?' he shouted, 'I think I've gone an' busted my foot.' He sat back and began to swear, his legs stretched in front of him, his weight supported on his hands. 'Motherin' gooks!' he groaned, listening to McCulsky scrambling down the wall outside. He looked down suddenly. His hand had slipped under a sheet of torn paper. The flares were dying slowly and in their flickering glow he noticed now that the whole floor seemed to be covered in paper — uneven black rectangles of it, stretching away like badly-laid flagstones. He examined the torn sheet under his hands. It was stiff and charcoal-grey with a slightly furry texture like sealskin, which he recognised as the waterproof wrappings they use for ammunition cartons.

But these were no ordinary cartons that Wace was lying on. He had only a glimpse of what lay underneath, before the flares died altogether; and for several seconds he just sat there in the dark, his hand still holding the torn paper, his ears beginning to sing.

A powerful torch beam came on above, dazzling him. Instinctively he pushed the flap back into place, as McCulsky called: 'Can you make it to your feet, sarge?'

Wace put his hand across his eyes. 'Just drop the light.' It fell a few feet from him, rolling away into a corner, and he began to crawl painfully after it, his fingers tracing the tight-packed edges under the paper, each about the size of a small brick. He was panting when he reached the torch and turned the small square of light on to the wrappings under his hands. 'Hey sarge!' he heard McCulsky cry, but the voice was a long way off. Wace's fingernail was already sawing through the stiff silken paper.

'Sarge, it's the extra detail!'

But this time Wace did not even hear. He was kneeling now, staring at the fresh slice he had just torn in the package under him. 'Jesus,' he muttered. 'Jesus H. Christ on a bicycle!'

PART 1: 'IN A COUNTRY THAT NEVER WAS'

CHAPTER 1

Murray Wilde was almost the last passenger to leave the plane, followed only by an old woman with blue-black hair and a pig, which had spent the two-hour flight strapped upright with an extra seatbelt, its nether quarters wrapped in sackcloth.

He was a long-limbed man of about thirty-five in a biscuit-coloured suit, carrying a canvas grip-bag and a Leica in a scarred case round his neck. The airhostess, bowing in her skin-clinging ankle-length *sin*, looked at him with more than usual interest. Westerners were something of a rarity on this airline: schedules erratic, safety record poor. (Its maiden flight had vanished without trace over the jungle, with the loss of all twenty V.I.P.'s.)

Near the foot of the steps was some sort of policeman with plimsolls and a revolver, who was too preoccupied watching a dog licking its private parts to take much notice of Murray as he stepped out into the hard yellow sunlight and began ambling across the tarmac, but not immediately in the direction of the terminal.

It was late afternoon and very hot. The windsock at the end of the runway drooped like a burst balloon. He passed two more Dakotas similar to the one he had arrived in, both bearing the name of the national airline in curly Sanskrit lettering. A tiny brown-faced mechanic, working on one with a hammer, looked up grinning as he strolled by. He went on past a row of white prefab huts and reached a shed with a sign: **HI-LO SNACKBAR. OPEN 0500-2100 HRS. AIR U.S.A. PERSONNEL ONLY. KIPS ACCEPTED**. He had crossed into alien territory. But still no guards, no floodlights, watchtowers, electrified fences, minefields round the perimeter. Just one lewd policeman and a happy mechanic.

He paused, sweating. The airfield was more than a mile across, the far side lined with arc-roofed hangars and rows of silver transport planes drawn up on the shimmering tarmac like shoals of fish. Nothing stirred. Even the snack-bar seemed deserted. It was the lull before dusk, when the last flights would begin returning, and there would be a couple of hours' busy activity while the planes were serviced and refuelled in readiness for the first missions at dawn.

This was the quietest corner of the airfield — the part that handled only civilian traffic. The terminal looked like a provincial French railway-station; there was an old-fashioned clock on the control tower and a wrought-iron balcony for spectators, which was empty. A couple of black-clad women with pigtails squatted by the entrance, not even looking up as he passed inside, under a notice in four languages: *'Hatred Never Ceases Save by Eternal Love'* — *The Lord Buddha.*

The last passengers had already gone through Immigration. He went up to the desk where three very small officers with white piping on their shoulders pored over his green Irish passport, with the gilt harp and Gaelic lettering worn off, most of its pages stamped and overstamped with visas and immigration seals of four continents. They went into a huddle over the page listing his personal details, until one of them cried, *'Professeur!'* and they all gave him wide smiles as they waved him through.

In the Customs hall there was a noisy argument going on about the pig who, divested now of its sackcloth, had already fouled the floor in several places. The officials looked bored as they chalked Murray's grip-bag without asking him to open it, and he walked out through the scrum of half-naked children fighting to carry the bag for him, under a notice across the door: **50 KIP PER BAGGAGE. MERCI**.

The taxi was a brand new Toyota, and its driver, in a drip-dry shirt with gold cufflinks, kept their speed up around a hundred kilometres an hour, driving in the middle of the road with his hand down on the horn. Streams of acrobatic cyclists flicked past; cars swerving to avoid them like dodgems through the dust; off the main airport road with its rows of shanty-huts raised on stilts above pools of stinking water, into the sudden shade of tall planetrees down an unpaved boulevard. Faded, rusting shop signs: *Coiffeur de Paris, Le Jockey Tailleur, Cafe Tout Va Bien, Tiger Beer*. The spell was momentarily broken.

They crossed the only traffic light in town — still not working since his last visit here just over a year ago — and turned into the main street. Single-storied, open wood-frame shops heaped to the roof with the bounties of Big Power aid: American detergents, French cosmetics, Scotch, gin, bourbon, king-size cigarettes, cocktail biscuits, electric shavers and hairdryers, washing machines, watches, cameras, transistor radios, even portable TV sets, although the nearest transmitting station was more than six hundred miles away.

And gold. Gold laid out like fruit on market stalls. Gold from pale yellow to deep bronze; slim bands, chunky signet rings, bangles, bracelets, earrings, pendants, chains, lucky charms, ornate statuettes, plates, cups, bowls, whole tea sets of gold.

The taxi pulled up in front of one of the town's most imposing establishments: a three-storey stucco building with balconies and a red awning marked *Bar des Amis*. Just above, almost illegible on the peeling yellow paintwork, was the word HOTEL. Murray paid the driver one dollar, stepped over an uncovered drain and through the open door into the bar.

It was very dark after the sunlight, with the air stirring from some unseen fan. A boy in a smart white tunic was behind the bar, doing the crossword from a French newspaper. Murray spoke to him and he nodded towards a girl sitting further along behind a cash register. She was small and plump. Murray went over and told her in French who he was — that he had cabled for a room from Phnom Penh.

'*Monsieur Wilde?*' She reached behind her and handed him a big iron key and a vellum envelope with no stamp, addressed in typescript to *M. Murray Wilde, Hôtel des Amis, Vientiane, Laos*. Inside was a gilt-edged invitation from the Canadian Embassy, one of the countries on the International Control Commission, asking him to a reception that evening to celebrate National Independence Day.

He turned it over, frowning. It seemed his had not been the only cable from Phnom Penh warning of his arrival in Laos. On the back was scrawled: '*See you there. G.F.*' He looked at his watch; almost five o'clock. The reception was for 6.30. They weren't leaving him a lot of time.

'When did this arrive?' he asked the girl.

She shrugged and slid off her stool, almost disappearing behind the bar, and went and whispered something to the boy. 'Before yesterday,' she said, coming back. 'Monsieur Georges brought it.'

He nodded, conscious of a faint irritation. The fat French man in Phnom Penh was moving fast — perhaps too fast. Murray had come to Laos to make his own arrangements, in his own time — although he had to concede that a top diplomatic reception was not a bad place to start. Vientiane, administrative capital of Laos, was a small parish-pump town where the one sure way for a stranger to attract attention to himself was to lie low.

The girl had moved away to serve a little man who had just trotted in and ordered a Pernod. Murray put the envelope away and was picking up his grip-bag, when a voice, oddly familiar, cried: 'Murray Wilde? Long time, no see!'

He blinked at the sunlight from the door. The man was short and bald with pebble-glasses and fluffy white hair round his ears; he looked and sounded like an English tradesman, slightly run to seed in a rumpled off-white suit and open-necked shirt.

'I'm sorry —' Murray began.

'Napper,' the man said: 'Hamish Napper. Drink?'

'Thanks — a beer.' Murray climbed on to a stool beside him and was still trying to place him when, in a most untypical English gesture, the man shook hands. It was then that Murray remembered him. An awful evening just over a year ago in the garden of the British Embassy, his nerves shot to shreds, ill with no sleep and too much drink, the two of them propped up under a frangipani tree, arguing wildly about the war, Murray claiming recent experience, blind with rage and whisky, the old man gibbering with the wisdom of age and hindsight. He had been in Indo-China for more than twenty years, and now held some ill-defined post with the Political Section. It was said that he had once played football against Ho Chi Minh during the visit of the British Mission to Hanoi in 1954 — nine men a side, and Great Britain had lost, since no one had dared tackle the President for fear of upsetting the negotiations.

Murray had remembered him again because of his hands. For it was on account of the symptoms they betrayed that Napper's career had hung in the balance. Now, in the half-darkness of the bar, the man's touch was peculiarly repulsive: a moist swollen hand, with the cushions between the joints soft and puffed up like marshmallows.

'So you're still here?' said Murray. 'They didn't give you the push?'

Napper gave a little throaty chuckle and shook his head. 'Must have chattered a lot that night. We were both a bit under the weather, I think. Yes, I'm still here — though I've had to give up a few of the old habits. Weaned back on to the bottle, so to speak.' He pushed his empty glass across at the girl. 'Takes a bit of time though — and real hell for the first few weeks. The docs got me down to only two pipes a day, but the swelling in my hands and feet still hasn't gone down.'

'When are you leaving?'

'End of the year. I'll be at the statutory retiring age, y'see. I must say this, they've been damned decent about it at the Embassy — even joke about it, saying they can't start sending old junkies back to the U.K. Bad for the Service.'

'What will you do?'

'Full pension — bungalow near Godalming — bit o' fishing. Might even write my memoirs. I've got a few tales up here,' he added, tapping his bald pate, 'that would make a bit o' hair in Whitehall stand on end. Trouble is, I don't think I could do it.'

'The Official Secrets Act, I suppose?'

'Oh, bugger the Act. It's just that when I sit down and try to write it, I can't remember anything.' He smiled into his cloudy drink. 'What are you doing in Laos?' he added suddenly.

Murray shrugged: 'R-and-R. Rest and Recuperation, shall we say?'

'I-and-I, I call it. Intercourse and Intoxication.' Napper chuckled, sipping his Pernod. 'On to any good stories?'

'No. Should I be?' Murray was wary now, remembering that behind that jaunty, short-sighted, rather sad little face was a mind that had once held a position of some delicacy and importance on behalf of Her Majesty in this corner of the world. He said casually: 'Is there anything I should know? Any coups brewing?'

Napper shook his head. 'They've actually banned the coup, you know that? *Le coup d'état est inter dit au Laos.* It's an official Government decree.'

'It's a lovely country.'

'The best,' said Hamish Napper. 'You get to love it — softens everyone, even the Russians. Everyone except these bloody Americans! Interfering buggers. First they had the casino closed because it was on the second floor of the girls' lycée. And it wasn't even as if there were any classes going on — it only opened in the evenings. And now you know what they're trying to do? Get the Government to ban pot. Just think of it! About the only staple product this poor bloody country's got, and they want to stamp it out, all because the families of these damned American military people are frightened their teenage brats — teeny-bops, I think they call them — are going to start getting hooked. And you know how many military attachés the American Embassy's got in Laos at the moment? Eighty-five! *Eighty-five* military bleeding attachés!' he cried, beside himself with rage. 'And we and the Russians have only got two between us — officially. God rot the lot,' he muttered, gulping the rest of his Pernod.

A girl had come into the bar, strolling towards them. She was European, tall and very dark, dressed in trousers and a leopard-spotted combat jacket. Hamish Napper looked round and greeted her in faultless French, his good humour rapidly recovered. He introduced Murray: 'This is Jackie. Mrs Jacqueline Conquest,' he added, with rather less enthusiasm. She and Murray shook hands. She had a round, pretty face, calm and unsmiling.

'What will you have?' Napper asked her in French.

'I can't stay,' she said, her eyes straying round the dark corners of the bar. 'I have to meet someone.'

Napper's pebble glasses gleamed slyly; the French language had sharpened his manner, giving him an almost predatory cunning. 'So it's someone else, is it?'

The girl gave the nearest thing to a smile and hunched her shoulders: '*Tu penses!*' She turned to Murray: '*Bon soir, Monsieur Wilde. Salut 'Amish!*'

They watched her leave, stepping gracefully over the drain and out of sight. 'Who is she?' Murray said, calling the bar-girl's attention to their glasses.

'Jackie? French girl, married to a shit. American chap called Maxwell Conquest — ridiculous bloody name! — seconded up here from Saigon. I don't think they're happy. She spends half her time wandering round in a dream. She wasn't looking for anyone in here — she just didn't have anywhere else to go. She wouldn't be seen drinking in here with us — her hubby wouldn't like it. Hubby's a good clean all-American boy who has three showers a day and never takes a drink unless the ice has been made from chlorinated water. Bastard.'

'What does he do?'

'Spook. CIA. Spends most of his time closeted with Colonel Buchbinder's boys in the American compound, hatching plots against the Lao politicians. He's supposed to be my opposite number. We don't get on.'

'And you do the same thing — hatch plots?'

'Me? Bah!' He chuckled again — just a little too easily this time, Murray thought. 'Usual odds and sods — they wouldn't put an old crock like me on to anything important.' He finished his drink and struggled off his stool. 'Still, must be toddling along now. H.M.G. calls!' He pulled out a fistful of large tissuey hundred-Kip notes — delicate pink and mauve like the old French franc notes, with the chateaux and cardinals replaced by pagodas and dancing girls — and before Murray could stop him, had thrust them across at the bar-girl. 'On me, old man. See you before you leave.' He gave a little wave as he went, moving in a kind of crab-footed shuffle, punctuated every few steps by a quick hop.

Murray felt he should have been amused by the man; yet he wasn't. Vientiane could never be described as a first-grade diplomatic posting, but while Britain remained a co-signatory of the Geneva Agreement on Laos, it still mattered; and Murray was beginning to wonder whether even the British Foreign Office would continue to tolerate an ageing, heavy-drinking, garrulous ex-opium-addict, unless he was of some real worth. For Hamish Napper was still employed — and had probably been so for more than two decades — in what is loosely called 'political intelligence', which can be a sensitive area of work, especially in South-East Asia. Yet instead of putting him out to pasture long ago, they were allowing him to reach full retiring age at the end of the year. And the year, Murray reflected, as he started up the stone steps to his room on the first floor, still had several months to run. He hoped he was not going to regret Mr Hamish Napper.

CHAPTER 2

Murray walked the few hundred yards down to the river where the reception was being held at the Lang Xan Royal Palace Restaurant. The sun had gone down and an astonishingly large amount of traffic had appeared, roaring in both directions down the pitted main street: a ceaseless gleam of chromium, with headlamps on high-beam — Chevrolets, Citroëns, VWs, dozens of little Japanese models driven ferociously in the middle of the road. Murray, hesitating under the awning of the Bar des Amis, remembered wondering, on his last visit to Laos, at this phenomenon of Vientiane. For where did all these cars come from, and where did they go? The road south, following the Mekong down to Savannakhet, was passable in the dry season only by large buses or vehicles with four-wheel drive; while the old *Route Nationale Treize* up to the Royal Capital of Luang Prabang had long been cut by the Pathet Lao forces and was open for only thirty kilometres. There were no other roads out of Vientiane — only the laborious and infrequent ferry that plied across the river to Thailand.

But then nothing in Laos, Murray reflected, was quite as one expected. Visiting wits on sabbatical from the State Department dubbed it 'Laos-Chaos'. A war had convulsed its jungles and mountains for a decade; had on at least two occasions sent shockwaves through the Chancelleries of the Free World; had caused the 7th Fleet to be alerted and hasty conferences convened between Moscow, London and Washington.

Yet here, in the eye of the hurricane, the Communist Pathet Lao still maintained an official headquarters in the centre of town — a well-appointed French mansion hung with bougainvillea and the portraits of Mao and Ho, and boasting a beautifully-tended vegetable garden that faced the Morning Market where raw opium and cannabis resin were on sale alongside dyed silks and fresh fish and ballpoint pens. Murray Wilde, grown cynical and tired of the silliness and cunning and brutal charm of this continent, had once written of Laos, '*The war that never happened in a country that never was*'. It was as near the truth as he ever hoped to get.

He had reached the river swelling through the soft twilight, with the din of traffic drowned by the sustained screaming of cicadas in the high grass by the water. The Lang Xan Royal Palace Restaurant stood in its own grounds, behind a gate supported by stone elephants and a driveway crowded with a fleet of Government and Corps Diplomatique limousines. The place had been originally conceived, on the departure of the French, by some visionary Lao princeling who had planned it as a vast tourist hotel in preparation for the day when Vientiane played host to the Olympic Aquatics on the Mekong. But the princeling was swept aside by a coup, the money ran out, and the tourists and the Olympics never came. All that was built of the Lang Xan Palace was the restaurant, bar and ballroom: a curious blend of stunted Corbusier and Cecil Beaton — shards of glass and rusted steel entwined with wrought-iron arabesques and gilded egrets perched on the steep half-completed pagoda roof rising from the river like some surrealist ski-jump.

The entrance was jammed with *cyclo-pousse* drivers, curled up in their passenger seats, smoking or asleep. An officer of the Royal Lao Army collected Murray's card and showed him across an unswept cement floor to the folding doors into the ballroom. The Ambassador and his wife greeted him with rigid smiles, welcoming him aboard the bandwagon of international diplomacy. For while the Cold War might be fought out across the world with propaganda, trade embargos, troop movements, threats and blackmail, here in Laos, under a pair of triple-tiered chandeliers — not all of whose bulbs worked — the conflict was joined over stiff drinks, the bitter ideological platitudes dissolved in preposterous offstage buffoonery. Murray had heard many stories of these diplomatic gatherings in Laos, which rarely ended without some *incident*. An impeccable Indian member of the Control Commission had once slapped a Pole's face after an argument about seats on the ICC plane to Hanoi; and after one particularly boisterous do at the Danish Legation a distinguished member of the British Embassy had spent the night on the Chinese Communist chargé-d'affaires' sofa.

There were about fifty people in the room, half of them in uniform, standing in neat groups according to nationality and rank. Murray calculated that they must be only on their second round of drinks, served tirelessly by tiny men in white mess-jackets and embroidered slippers. It would take at least another hour before international protocol began to collapse. He was on nodding acquaintance with perhaps half a dozen faces; but for the first time in many days he at last felt no need to hurry. The man he had come to meet would make himself known to him in good time.

He helped himself to a drink and began to circulate. The Indians were there in a tight circle — surprisingly large, Sandhurst-built men in white-laundered uniforms, talking solemnly over whiskies and soda. In another corner were the Poles, conspicuous this time for their ungainliness: squat pale men with wide nostrils and slack mouths, their dove-grey uniforms with shelves of épaulettes and silver eagles hanging awkwardly on them, as though fashioned for a more gallant generation.

A resident French journalist, who had attached himself to Murray, began to explain, in the side-of-the-mouth tones of the well-informed, that since the Czechoslovakian crisis the old Polish delegation had been withdrawn, and replaced mostly by Russians or Russian-born Poles. It was not a detail that Murray paid much attention to at the time. He was looking at a predominant group of Americans in the centre of the room. Among them was the girl he had met that afternoon in the Bar des Amis — Mrs Jacqueline Conquest. He recognised her only at a second glance; the floppy camouflage jacket and trousers were replaced with a sheath of tight-fitting deep blue silk, tracing a profile of long legs, high hips, large fine breasts; her hair scooped up from the nape of the neck, making her face seem more slender, her eyes larger, darker, even across half the length of the room.

He began to move towards them. He knew at least one of the men in the group — a pleasant gangling young man called Luke Williams who was in charge of the U.S. Information Bureau — and Murray's present occupation as an author and freelance journalist afforded him the excuse to introduce himself.

Luke Williams already knew him by reputation, and the build-up he gave him was almost embarrassing. The two other men in the group nodded gravely; but the girl stood by with the same unsmiling calm she had displayed in the bar that afternoon, and something warned Murray that it would be unwise to let on that they had already met. One of the other two was her husband: a slim tight-faced man with a buttoned-down shirt, buttoned-down mouth, and grey arrow-shaped eyes. Murray distrusted him on sight. He noticed that neither he nor his wife were drinking.

The other man was the new head of USAID in Laos, Colonel Buchbinder — muscular and close-cropped with the handshake of a stevedore and horn-rimmed eyes that never shifted nor blinked as he spoke: 'Pleased to meet you, Mr Wilde! Sorry I wasn't here on your last visit but we're gonna make up for it this time, I'm sure, giving you plenty of opportunity to see our economic assistance programme in action at all levels of national life, getting things really moving in this country —'

The girl's gaze had fixed on a point somewhere above their heads, beyond the shabby damp-blotched walls — a gaze of total boredom.

'Luke here will fit you up with our information kit,' Colonel Buchbinder went on, 'every detail of our aid effort right up to date. And for any other details you want to know' — he swivelled his owl's stare on the tall smiling boy on his left — 'Luke's your man!'

Luke Williams beamed back at Murray: 'Anything I can do to be of help, sir. You know my office, opposite the main Embassy compound?'

Murray thanked him, while Colonel Buchbinder and the Conquests moved off to join their Ambassador. The girl had turned away without a gesture, even a nod. Neither she nor her husband had spoken a word — though Murray was aware all the while of the CIA man's cold stare, and was glad when he was gone.

He turned gratefully back to Luke: 'Listen, there is something you can do for me. I'm only in Laos for a few days — a kind of stopover between assignments — but I'd be very interested' — he had unconsciously dropped his voice so that the

American had to lower his head to hear — 'in doing a rice-drop.'

Luke straightened up, smiling brightly: 'Sure. No problem. It's been done, though.'

'Everything's been done,' said Murray. 'I'm interested in some special camera effects, early morning stuff — sunrise on take-off — and as far north as possible. The highest drops you do.'

The American's smile had changed to a slow frown. 'That's very high, and very north. Nearly nine thousand feet if you want the limit, which is where it begins to get rather close to Chicom territory.'

'So? You fly up there — I want to see it.'

'You never done a rice-drop before?'

'No. That's why I'm asking you.'

'I gather it can be pretty hairy up north. Specially if the weather gets bad. And it's all the same in those mountains — high or low. We do a pretty simple drop just forty minutes from here, over Xieng Khouang. You'll get your kicks there if a storm comes up.'

'No good,' said Murray. 'I've had all the kicks I want in life — I'm getting old now. I want a genuine drop as far north as you can get me cleared for, and taking off as early as possible in the morning.'

Luke Williams nodded dubiously. 'I'll see what I can do. They may insist on a personal liability disclaimer, and that takes time.'

'Why? I've signed plenty of them before — in much worse situations than this. Unless, of course, you're going to tell me that you lose too high a percentage of your rice-drop sorties over north Laos —'

'Oh no, don't get me wrong, it's just a formality. You know what civilians are! We're not dealing with the military up here.'

'I'll sign whatever you give me,' Murray said.

'No other family — wife or kids?' The boy spoke as though he were personally concerned.

Murray shook his head: 'Nobody you'll have to worry about if anything happens to me. You or Air U.S.A. or anybody else. With me it'll be like a stone in the ocean.'

The American stood turning his glass slowly round in his hand; he was drinking iced tea. 'If there's any trouble,' he said at last, 'I think I can fix it through Colonel Buchbinder. He has the last word on all aid flights.'

Murray shot him a quick, reassuring smile: 'Thanks, Luke. But try and see if you can do it without Colonel Buchbinder. I want it official, of course — but not too official. I don't want to find myself doing a straight PR job for Air U.S.A. — "Hands Across the Sea" and all that crap.'

'I know just how you feel,' Luke said, full of earnest understanding. 'I think I can get it fixed on the level, Mr Wilde. You're staying at the Friends' Bawdy House, I guess?'

'Certainly.' They grinned at each other, man-to-man. 'When do you think you'll know?'

'If it's on, I should know by tomorrow noon.'

'Just call the hotel bar and leave a message.' Murray hesitated a moment, reaching out for a fresh drink off a passing tray. 'By the way, Luke, do you know someone here called George Finlayson?'

'You mean, Filling-Station?'

'Who?'

'That's what he's known as here — never without a drink in his hand, and no one's ever seen him drunk yet. He's a Britisher, you know. The man with the best job in the world.'

'He works for the International Monetary Fund, doesn't he?'

Luke laughed: 'Well, IMF pays his salary, if that's what you mean. He's actually employed by FARC — Foreign Aid Reserve Control. One of these crazy outfits that try to keep the Laotian economy going. The IMF backs it, with most of the funds coming from the U.S., Britain, France and Japan. The idea is to stabilise the kip by buying it up with foreign exchange at a free rate of five hundred to the dollar.'

'And what exactly does Finlayson do?'

'Finlayson is FARC — literally. Sole employee, along with a very dishy little Vietnamese girl who's supposed to work the telex. Once a week the National Bank of Laos sends him a note of how much the kip has dropped through the floor — usually about ten to fifteen million — and Filling-Station gets off a telex to the IMF man in Bangkok who arranges for the deficit to be made up in hard currency. After that, his only job is to drive down to the Bank on Fa Ngum Street — a little villa with two rooms and a vault — and collect the money in sacks which he takes back to his own house and burns in a special incinerator we built for him in the garden.

'To tell the truth,' he added, 'when FARC first started operations, they were dumping the money in the Mekong and the fishermen were catching it as far down as Thakhek. What was known as "keeping the kip afloat". It could only happen in Laos.'

'How come they gave the job to an Englishman?' (All Murray knew about George Finlayson's past was that he had been a banker in Hong Kong.)

'I heard he got it through an ad in the *London Times*. Anyway, he sure landed himself a deal — one hell of a salary for about half a day's work a week, with no tax — and not paid in kips either! But you've never met him?'

'Not yet. Although he did invite me here this evening.'

'Uh-huh.' The American was smiling again, adding in an undertone: 'He's standing right behind you.'

CHAPTER 3

'Ah, how d'you do, glad you could make it. Sorry I was late showing up — pressure of work. Got in safely? No crash-landings or anything? And your room at the hotel all right?'

George Finlayson was a stout man with a large sombre face, nicotine-stained moustache, hair receding from a broad damp brow. His manner was deadly earnest, his voice low and measured, with the slightly off-course accent of the expatriate. He reminded Murray of one of those melancholy weathermen on British television. Except that weathermen do not wear heavy chain-bracelets of 24-carat gold.

'The electricity's cut off every night at nine, you know,' he went on, staring gloomily into his champagne. 'It's the old French generator — packed up completely after the big flood last year. The Russians promised us a new one, but it hasn't arrived.'

There was an awkward pause, in which Murray was uncomfortably aware of the tall stooping figure of Luke still between them. 'So what happens?' Murray said at last.

'No light, no air-conditioning. Except for the Americans — they've got their own generator.'

'But what about before nine o'clock?' Murray asked, glancing up at the half-lit chandeliers.

'That comes from the Thais — cable across the Mekong. Only the stuff's rationed, of course. Lot of trouble up in north-east Thailand at the moment. Communist insurgents, opium wars. Usual bother.'

'It's a damned scandal,' Luke broke in: 'The Russians got the deal all lined up, then they welshed because they said

Souvanna's Government's been leaning too close to the Free World. They were supposed to deliver two months ago.'

'So what about the Free World?' said Murray. 'Can't we afford a generator?'

Luke Williams laughed and wagged his head: 'Oh, we're doing better than that, Mr Wilde! We're building them a dam. Fifteen million dollars' worth of construction at Nam Ngum, just twelve miles north of here. Nearly five hundred feet wide and a reservoir more than two hundred feet deep when it's finished. It's going to transform the whole economic structure of Laos, believe me!'

'I do,' Murray murmured, but he was thinking of more than the economy of little old Laos. The American's words had planted in him the seeds of an idea. 'How far have you got with this dam?'

'They've been at it for three years,' said Finlayson: 'It's a question of the jungle versus the mud versus inflation. At the moment all three are winning.'

'The main barrage's already complete,' Luke said defiantly, 'and the reservoir's up to a hundred feet deep since the rains. It'll only be a few more months before blast-off.'

George Finlayson made no comment, for at that moment the band of the Royal Lao Army which had been drawn up in darkness outside the French windows, looking like a cross between bell-hops and miniature Napoleonic hussars, broke into a chaotic rendering of what sounded like 'Colonel Bogey' — until Murray realised that the room had grown very still, everyone standing rigidly with glasses raised. They were listening to the Lao National Anthem. It seemed to go on interminably, a monotonous, toneless blaring and booming, while Murray noticed a Laotian in a smart business suit mounting a rostrum at the end of the room, followed by the Canadian ambassador.

The anthem was over at last. Finlayson, who had been standing as stiff as a sentry, hurriedly consulted a huge gold watch. 'Speech time,' he muttered. 'Only half an hour and they'll be cutting the lights. We've paid our homage — how about slipping out for a spot of dinner?'

Luke had moved away, and above the flutter of applause there was a sudden disturbance by the rostrum. In the centre of a growing crowd stood a diminutive, barrel-chested Laotian in a scarlet and green uniform ribbed with gold braid and oversized medals. He was shouting, in a high sing-song voice, eyes glaring red, gums flashing gold. The ambassador had paused on the steps of the rostrum, listening gaunt and stricken.

'Trouble,' Finlayson murmured. 'That's General Oum Rattiboum, commander of the Northern Province. He had one of his opium factories burnt down last month by the Chinese Nats — the Kuomintang mob who stayed on after Chiang Kai-shek pulled back to Formosa. Some row about paying Oum too high a levy after the last harvest. Oum's answer was to send in a squadron of T-28's of the Royal Lao Air Force and bomb the hell out of them. There's talk of five hundred dead. The Americans and the ICC are bloody furious. They've been trying to get the Government to sack him.'

They were making their way towards the door now, while across the room a chorus of voices — shrieking Lao and plaintive European — was swelling dramatically.

'It's always like this,' said Finlayson. 'There'll be more whisky and champagne, speeches and toasts, and it'll quieten down — for the moment. But I wouldn't be surprised if Oum attempts another coup — waits until Souvanna goes to Paris for his operation next month, then moves his troops down from the north.'

'I thought they'd banned the coup?' said Murray. They had crossed the cement lobby, down the steps past the *cyclo-pousse* drivers who were awake at once, running at them like dogs after a bone.

'That won't stop Oum,' said Finlayson. 'He's already tried two coups in the past four years. And the last one damned nearly came off — except he wasted six precious hours at a dinner party with some Frenchmen up in Luang Prabang, when he should have been marching on Vientiane.'

'What sort of coup — right-wing, left-wing?'

Finlayson shook his head. 'Neither, old boy. With Oum it's strictly personal.'

Murray grinned. 'Are you a friend of his?'

'Nodding acquaintance, shall we say? We have a few things in common,' he added mysteriously, as they reached his car — a big dusty Mercedes, its leather seats shrunken and cracked like a weather-beaten skin. 'Hop in. There's a little French place along the river where they do one quite well — for Vientiane.'

Murray climbed in beside him and the car started with a long wheeze. 'So Oum Rattiboum's engaged in an opium war up north — besides the other war, of course?'

Finlayson shrugged, jarring the gears. 'Anybody's guess. No one really knows what goes on in this country — not even the generals. The Royal Lao Army's supposed to be fifty-thousand strong. All balls of course. Lucky if it's got fifteen thousand. Oum and the other generals simply draw pay for thirty-five thousand non-existent troops,' he added, as they accelerated away in a swirl of dust and gravel.

'So there's no trouble bribing them?'

'Bribing them? More difficult offering sweets to a child!'

They had reached the gate between the stone elephants, driving on the wrong side of the track, when a long black car flying the Royal Lao flag swept round in the opposite direction, missing them by inches. Murray realised that had either car been on its correct side there would have been a head-on collision.

Finlayson drove with disconcerting calm, the car clanking and careering over the potholed mud along the margin of the broad dark river. After a moment Murray said: 'Do you know Mrs Jacqueline Conquest?'

'Jackie? But of course! Lovely creature, isn't she? Poor fish.'

'Oh?'

'Out of water, old boy. Married to the CIA, so what can you expect? You met the husband?'

'I didn't talk to him.'

'Not Vientiane's most engaging citizen. Fortunately he's going back to Saigon soon. You've come from there yourself, haven't you?'

'Via Phnom Penh.'

Finlayson raised his eyebrows: 'I didn't think journalists were allowed into Cambodia? — ever since one of your chaps wrote up Sihanouk's mother as running all the brothels?'

Murray smiled, watching the track curving away in the headlamps. 'I've got "University Professor" down in my passport.'

Finlayson nodded: 'Ah yes, I think Charles Pol mentioned it. You lectured in Vietnam — up at Huế, didn't you?'

'That's right. Reading, writing, and rioting.'

'What made you pack it in for journalism?'

'I didn't. The university packed it in after the Tet offensive. They closed the Foreign Language Faculty.' Finlayson swerved violently to avoid a dog — a mangy, crouching creature — and for a moment Murray was back on that morning in the low damp streets of Huế when they'd just mortared the university buildings and he'd run out, dodging, limping, his buttocks torn by shrapnel, and been driven away in a jeep through the warm rain by a white-faced Marine corporal who'd gone on mouthing the same prayer over and over again, with the streets crackling with gunfire and Murray sitting up beside him, awkward and bloody, when they turned a corner and came on the dog, lean as a greyhound, ribs clear through the skin, its head down gnawing at the belly of a corpse — swollen Vietnamese in wet grey trousers, one hand flung out in the mud like a bunch of over-ripe bananas. Then the smell had reached them, cloying sweet and sour in Murray's throat with the taste of bile clinging to his hair and clothes, while the Marine drew up and shot the dog with one burst from his M16, swearing with tight-lipped puritan anger, as Murray leant out and vomited into the mud.

'So you're a chum of Charles Pol?' Finlayson said suddenly, and Murray shook himself back to reality. 'How's he getting on in Cambodia?'

'He makes a living. When did he get in touch with you?'

'About ten days ago. Said you needed someone to show you round, make contacts, meet people — that sort of thing.'

'Hence the reception? Couldn't we have met in some quiet bar instead?'

'There aren't any quiet bars in Vientiane at night, old boy. Much better to have it out in the open. And you did get the chance to meet Luke Williams and Buchbinder — not to mention Mr and Mrs Conquest.'

Ahead a light glimmered through some trees and Finlayson swung the car off the road, up on to a sandy verge beside a low brick building with a verandah and a red neon sign: '*La Cigale — Genuine Cuisine Française*'. Finlayson led the way in, his gold bracelet glinting like handcuffs under the light.

It was still fairly empty inside, with candles on the tables and rows of multicoloured bottles behind the bar. Finlayson chose a table in the corner and began to consult a large handwritten menu. 'They do very good deep-fried prawns,' he said. 'And there's a wine that's surprisingly good — young and very fresh.'

Murray let him order from the waiter, noticing that he spoke French with the same colloquial ease as Hamish Napper; and in the same way as with Napper, this oddly altered his character, making him seem more serious, less the comic Englishman abroad — a man of substance, yet of some mystery. He ordered Ricard as an aperitif, fish soup, white wine and river prawns; then sat back facing Murray, solid, complacent, filling his whole chair. 'Ah well. So you met old Charles Pol down in Cambodia? You don't mind telling me how?'

'He didn't tell you himself?'

'Not the details. Only the more important matters. But the details are important too, I think — if we're to be entirely in each other's confidence.'

'Quite so. Well, I was down in Phnom Penh last month, on a sort of unofficial working holiday, and ran into him in a restaurant. It was a late lunch — we were the only Europeans in the place — and he asked me to join him for a drink.'

'And you confided in him then?'

'No. Not until a couple of days later. He'd hired a car to go up to Angkor Wat and asked me to join him. I accepted.' Murray paused, reflecting now — as he had done so often in the last month — that the decision to go on that trip, taken so casually at the time, might yet prove the most fateful of his whole life.

'And what was your impression of him?'

'Fat.'

Finlayson chuckled: 'Yes, my God he's fat!'

Murray thought Pol probably the fattest man he had ever seen: the Michelin man alive, tyres of fat squeezed into a damp ill-fitting silk suit with huge thighs sagging over the edges of his chair — a flamboyant, garrulous gourmet of a man with a goatee-beard and a preposterous kiss curl plastered down over one eye; his talk, erudite but funny, punctuated by a shrill, almost girlish laugh.

At first Murray had likened him to one of those joke-professors in a nineteenth-century farce; but over the next couple of hours of that first meeting — and the best part of a bottle of excellent cognac — he had learnt that Charles Pol had fought as an Anarchist in Spain, had been a double agent for the Free French during the war, and two decades later had reappeared in North Africa during the death-throes of *Algérie Française*, working for the Gaullist secret service against the O.A.S.

Pol had refused to specify what he was doing in Cambodia; but from a few unguarded hints Murray guessed that he was working as some kind of 'adviser' to Cambodia's volatile ruler, Prince Norodom Sihanouk — the all-purpose dictator, film director, actor, clarinet-player, poet, pop-singer, and political one-man band who went so far as to edit his own opposition newspaper in which he attacked himself once a week. Murray approved of Sihanouk, and he was intrigued by Pol. He had decided to stay close to the Frenchman for the next few days, which was one of the reasons why he had joined him on that trip to the ruins of Angkor Wat.

Finlayson, who had the habit of breaking off the conversation and relapsing into long silences, was now busy lapping up his soup. Murray finished his Ricard and tasted the wine, thinking: How fitting that it should have been in Angkor that the whole idea had taken root — that vast sunless place full of temples of leprous stone rising out of the jungle like some deranged Versailles. For here, resting on a terrace overlooking a lake of dead water, Murray had told Pol the story. He hadn't thought it particularly important at the time — just an interesting anecdote out of a war that was full of anecdotes, funny, brutal, absurd. This one had been a straight recitation of fact as told him by a lonely American boy over too many drinks in an R-and-R bar in downtown Bangkok. Murray had repeated it just as he had been told it himself; but the Frenchman had been panting and sweating so much that Murray thought he hadn't been fully listening.

Only later, as they drove back through the darkening countryside, did Pol bring the subject up again. And what he said had brought Murray bolt upright in his seat, hardly knowing whether the Frenchman were joking or not. Of course he was joking — it was madness, a fantasy inspired by the weird wonders of Angkor, followed by too much wine at the tourist hotel. But somehow there had been something in Pol's manner — some hint of secret authority, of hard practical ruthlessness — that gradually made it seem neither mad nor fantastic. From that moment Murray had thought of little else. At work, in bed, in restaurants, aircraft, talking, drinking, doing nothing, his mind had been turning over, exploring every possibility, probability, until gradually the whole crazy scheme had begun to come alive with a dangerous reality, like suddenly finding oneself living — in detail — an obsessive, recurring dream. He only wondered how much Pol had confided in

George Finlayson. And if he had, just how seriously Finlayson had taken it?

The banker was now getting to grips with his plate of deep-fried prawns. Murray took a drink of white wine and said: 'And how did you get to know Charles Pol?'

Finlayson sat chewing thoughtfully. 'My business takes me down to Cambodia from time to time,' he said at last. 'I ran into him first at the *Cercle Français* in Phnom Penh.'

'What exactly does he do in Cambodia?'

'He didn't tell you?'

'He was evasive, shall we say?'

Finlayson shook his head glumly. 'He's a cagey devil. To tell the truth I've never fathomed the French. They're all for wine, women, good food, the intellectual life — then you scratch the surface and what d'you find? Cloven hoof and hairy heel, that's what. Anyway, I've never been able to trust a man with a beard.'

'He trusts you.'

Finlayson's eyes bulged across the table, solemn and slightly puzzled. 'Go on.'

'He was the one who put me on to you. I don't know how much he's told you, but he wouldn't have even mentioned your name if he hadn't had a good deal of confidence in you.'

Finlayson paused, his fork in mid-air. 'Yes, I must admit, in one way and another Charles and I've got to know each other pretty well. White men sticking together, you might say — especially when it comes to doing business with these Asians. They can be damned slippery sometimes.'

'I thought you said you didn't trust him?'

'No further than I could throw him — and that wouldn't be far!' He allowed himself a faint smile. 'But you can't always work on your own — trust yourself and no one else. Can you?'

He thrust his face forward, his brown-stained moustache twitching as though to communicate some message of special significance. 'I have to confess,' he added, 'I've done a couple of deals with old Pol. When it comes to business we're as thick as thieves.' Again the hint of a smile played across his gloomy features.

'And he told you everything?'

'He told me what he said you'd told him. The bare bones, I'd call it.'

'And how much was that?'

'You want me to go through it?'

'Please.' Murray finished his prawns and drank his wine, listening to Finlayson's low monotone repeating almost word for word the tale Murray had heard from the young American all those weeks back in the Bangkok clip-joint. When it was over he smiled and called for a second bottle of wine. 'So what's your opinion — professionally? Do you believe it?'

Finlayson stroked his moustache and gazed across at the bar where a noisy group of Americans had burst in and were ordering Jim Beam bourbon on the rocks. 'Well,' he said slowly, 'it's a very plausible theory.'

'But is it true? Could they really have had that amount at one time in one place?' Murray was leaning forward now, his eyes trying to hold Finlayson's across the dim candlelight. 'Is it *possible*?'

'Oh certainly. Of course, I don't deal with Vietnam as such. Most of my work's tied up here in Laos with foreign aid. But I do get a peek at some of the gold figures. And they're pretty staggering. As you know, since the gold crisis in fifty-seven most of the big trading's shifted from up here down to Saigon. It's now one of the biggest gold markets in the world — the Chinese Reds are buying it up through the London Gold Pool.

And by international law all gold buying must be transacted in dollars — U.S. of course. And if some of the figures I've seen are correct, it amounts to a very fair sum.'

'How much of it is hot money?'

'A lot of it's warm, shall we say.'

'And all in dollars?'

'Indeed. Who wants to deal in a load of old Vietnamese piastres when there are greenbacks around?'

'So what happens to these greenbacks?'

'They try to get them out of the country. A flush-out, they call it. It's done about every six to eight months. They fly the stuff out to some safe place, usually the Philippines, then ship it back to the old U.S.A.'

He was interrupted by one of the Americans at the bar, who had caught sight of him and now came lurching over: 'Hi George! How's the kip keeping?'

'Quite satisfactory, thanks.' He made no effort to introduce Murray. 'And how's the flying?'

'Up and down, like always. We lost another last week — C 46, had an engine go and went smack into a mountain. One helluva life, at four hundred bucks a week, and you finish getting burned up on a stinking mountain in Laos! Well, see you around, George.'

'My pleasure,' Finlayson murmured. 'Air U.S.A. pilots,' he said to Murray when they were gone. 'It's a CIA outfit. Quite a joke really — the only charter airline in the world that carries no passengers, but will fly anywhere and drop anything.' He took a deep drink of wine, while Murray sat studying the crouched backs of the pilots along the bar, thinking hard but saying nothing.

'What about this American sergeant chap?' Finlayson asked. 'How much have you discussed with him?'

'Nothing — directly. He's an M.P. for a start, and he doesn't want to spend three years in the stockade, plus a dishonourable discharge. All he said was he might be able to get me on to the airfield to have a look round — might even arrange for me to wear an M.P.'s uniform. But that's not your side of the business.' He leant forward again across the table. 'Let me ask you something personal, George.'

'Fire away.'

'Have you ever done anything illegal in your life?'

Finlayson's pale eyes bulged back at him. 'Illegal, old boy? Perish the thought!'

Murray smiled: 'What about the Lao National Lottery last year? The first and only one of its kind in the world — the only one that never paid any prizes?' He peered at him closely over his glass, but the large melancholy face across the table was giving nothing away. 'I suppose Charles Pol told you about that?'

'Isn't it common knowledge? You advised the Lao Ministry of Finance — told them it was a good way to raise a little extra revenue — then took a small cut of the profits?'

Finlayson nodded slowly, gazing into his wine. 'Fair's fair,' he said. 'It was rather underhand, I grant you. But I still don't think Pol should have let on.'

Murray smiled: 'You may not have done anything very illegal in the past — but that's all going to change, if we go through with this. Understand?'

'Understood.'

The pilots at the bar were beginning to sound drunk, throwing dice and shouting. Murray envied them. Four hundred dollars a week, with the spice of danger thrown in, and no moral obligations.

Finlayson said quietly: 'So what do you want me to do?'

'Find out the time, date and place of the next flush-out. Can you do that?'

'I'll keep my ear to the ground. One sometimes picks up a clue here and there.'

'It's got to be more than a clue, George. If you're going to be cut in, it's got to be all or nothing. What about the previous flush-outs?'

'Oh, one heard about them, but usually only after they'd happened. I remember, because they're always given the codenames of weapons. The last one was *Happy Hound*, the ones before, *Mighty Mouse* and *Bullpup*. Like children with important toys, don't you think?'

'Find out the name and time and place of the next one, George.' Murray sat very still, waiting for the banker's reaction, while the Americans at the bar argued over a bet.

Finlayson spent some time wiping his mouth with his napkin, then twirling his wine glass in the candlelight. 'If I may be so judiciously indiscreet,' he said at last, 'I must have some guarantee as to your own integrity. I mean to say, if something goes wrong —'

Murray nodded: 'So something goes wrong?'

'I mean to say, old boy, what are your actual plans to date in this matter? I know Pol's behind it, probably putting up the cash and so on. But what are *your* plans?'

'I need two pilots,' said Murray. 'The best two pilots in South-East Asia, with a lot of nerve and not too many scruples. I want two pilots who can get a medium-sized transport plane — Caribou or C 123 — off the ground in a hurry, in darkness and flying several hundred miles at treetop level without radar or a radio compass, and can land it under the same conditions — blind.'

'And what about you?' Finlayson did not sound worried, just healthily suspicious.

'Me?' Murray grinned and finished his wine. 'I'm just the ideas man — a displaced intellectual. If it all falls through, don't worry about me. I won't blackmail you to the IMF. I'll just write it up afterwards — as fiction. It ought to make a good yarn. But for the moment I'm the only one of us — as an accredited journalist — who can walk in on Air U.S.A. and ask to go on a rice-drop; who can wander on to an airfield with no special permit; cross frontiers without too many tricky questions being asked; get thrown out of unauthorized areas without arousing too much suspicion. All right?'

Finlayson nodded, signalling for the bill. 'Let me just ask you one thing, Wilde — if it doesn't sound impertinent. What did you do before you came out to Asia?'

'Lived off a rich wife.'

Finlayson nodded again, without comment. The pilots at the bar had made up their quarrel and were bawling for more drinks. As Murray and Finlayson passed them on their way out, the one who had come up to their table turned on his stool and shouted, *'Cheer-io Gee-orge old chep!'* in a grotesque mimic of the English accent.

'Good night to you all,' Finlayson answered, with resolute lack of aggression. The rest of them watched with glassy grins — a row of big, well-scrubbed, all-American boys of forty-five who'd seen it all, resting now on their wide wallet-bulging butts, pissed and far from home.

Christ, thought Murray, as he stepped out into the tepid black night: No wonder they flew into mountains! He wondered if they got danger-money as well.

CHAPTER 4

'Hi there, we're in luck, sir!' Luke swung his long legs off the desktop and sat forward with his boyish grin. 'You're off the launching pad — got you fixed for a drop tomorrow morning at sunrise. Weather permitting of course.'

Murray sat down opposite, buttoning his jacket against the icy air-conditioning. The room was of bare weatherboard, with a physical contour map of Laos and North Vietnam covering most of one wall. A framed photograph of the U.S. President watched over both of them with a look of funereal responsibility.

Luke had managed to get his pipe going at last and it was giving little puffs like a toy steam-engine. 'You have to check in at the airport, Air U.S.A. Gate Two, at five-thirty tomorrow morning. Take-off's scheduled for six. It's a two and a half hour flight north of here, and the weather begins to get bad about mid-morning, so take-off has to be timed so you reach the drop zone around when the sun's burned off the mountain fog. O.K. with you?'

'Fine. Where is the drop zone?'

Luke spun round in his chair and jabbed at the top of the map with his pip-stem. 'It's a numbered grid reference, but we won't know what it is till just before take-off. All I can tell you is it's way up north, not far from the North Vietnamese border. It'll be rice and cornmeal, in triple-sacking, for the use of anti-Communist cadres among the Meo tribesmen. It's all here in our leaflet.' He spun back and thrust a heavy folder across the desk marked **KINGDOM OF LAOS — YOUR INFORMATION KIT**. 'And here's your clearance pass. You hand that to a Captain Gaccia at the Air U.S.A. traffic manager's office. Anyone'll tell you where it is when you get inside the gate.'

'Any trouble getting through the gate?' Murray asked casually.

Luke shook his head, laughing: 'No, no, we're everyone's friend here in Laos! Dropping rice is the way to win 'em. You know we even drop whole school kits? — blackboards, textbooks, even the funnies with the captions translated into the local dialect. That's the way to victory — words, not guns!'

And so say all of us, thought Murray, as he stood up and shook hands across the desk. Luke followed him to the door, stepping with him into the aching afternoon glare. 'Remember to wear something warm,' he called: 'couple of newspapers and an extra undershirt. It can get darned cold up in those planes. And don't forget your passport — just in case.'

'Thanks.' Murray waved cheerfully, thinking, Nice helpful Luke, we ought to cut him in, give him something for his trouble. But Luke Williams did it for love — love of liberty and a brave new world where mountain tribes read 'Peanuts' and ate rice that fell from heaven.

Murray walked away to where he had left the hired Willys jeep, parked in the shade of a mouldy phallic-shaped wat, out of sight of the Embassy compound. The canvas flaps were drawn shut on both sides, and he was just climbing in when he saw the girl come round the wall of the temple. She was wearing trousers again, with a dark Chinese tunic buttoned to the throat and a conical straw hat that covered her face in a pool of shadow. She paused by the jeep. 'Mister Wilde? We met yesterday with Mister Napper, and again at the reception.'

He stood up, smiling uncertainly. It was the first time he had heard her speak English: correctly, but with a marked French accent, as though defying the infectious drawl of her husband's tongue. 'Can I give you a lift anywhere?' he asked.

'No, I am going just to the American Embassy. Thank you.'

Murray held his hand to his eyes, squinting down the hot sleepy street, thinking of some excuse to delay her. Lunch was over, cafes closed for the siesta, and it was too early for a respectable drink; only the dark air-conditioned clip-joints down the main street were open, and he did not want to risk a refusal.

'Yesterday I did not realise,' she said suddenly, 'that you are the Mister Wilde who taught at Huế University. *Faculté des Lettres, je crois?*'

'That's right. Do you know Huế?'

'*Bien sûr!* Or perhaps I should say I used to know it — before they destroyed it. It was the most beautiful city in the Orient. It was a crime what they did!' Her voice had risen to an unexpected note of passion, subsiding at once into neutrality: 'You were there when it happened, weren't you? It must have been very disagreeable.'

But Murray said nothing, and there was a heavy pause. He suddenly had no wish to talk more about Huế: it was too painful for preliminary small-talk. For several seconds they stood facing each other in the silent shade of the temple. 'How long are you staying in Vientiane?' he said at last, a little desperately, remembering Le Bar des Amis — quiet and cool at this hour, the fans still working by courtesy of the Thai cable across the river.

'My husband's stationed most of the time in Vietnam. We've been here for four months, but we go back next week.'

'You live in Saigon?'

'The Americans give us a house there. It's not very amusing, but at least it's better than this village. I hope we'll be sent some day to Hong Kong.' She gave a small despairing shrug: '*Mais on ne sait jamais.*'

'Come and have a drink at the hotel. Something to remind you of France,' he added, with forced enthusiasm; and for the fraction of a second she hesitated.

'No, I must go to the Embassy. Thank you.'

He watched her longingly out of sight, her body moving elusively under the loose Chinese tunic — wondering how long it had been since he'd had a girl like that? Perhaps never. He had not even asked her where she came from.

It was stifling inside the jeep and Murray's hands left wet marks as he unfolded the French roadmap, *Croquis Routier de L'Indo-Chine*, which he had bought second-hand that morning from a local bookshop. There seemed to be no up-to-date maps of the country: the Americans inhabited a land made up, it seemed, not of towns and villages, but of numbered grid references, drop zones and radio-compass bearings. He had also found one sketchy map of Vientiane — a largely useless document marking only 'friendly' embassies, the Post Office and the USIS library. But it did show the road out to the airport — and, even more important, where it joined the long-neglected *Route Nationale Treize*, now Highway Thirteen, up to Luang Prabang.

It was for this road that Murray Wilde now headed — first checking the exact time and mileage, writing both down in his notebook. He avoided passing the American Embassy, in case he ran into Luke who would almost certainly want to know where he was going. Instead he made a detour round the deserted Morning Market, past the guards at the Pathet Lao vegetable garden, up the broad dusty avenue towards the Monument des Morts — an impressive imitation of the Arc de Triomphe, plastered with lavish gold-leaf and still unfinished after ten years, straddling a road that had ceased to exist, commemorating the dead of wars that had not yet happened.

It was impossible to drive through it because of some innovations that had been started inside on a row of golden Buddhas. Murray had to mount the muddy track round the side, driving on past the embassies of Laos. Solid stone residences set back in luxuriant grounds where the French *colons* had once held court were now peopled by random groups of international squatters. Weary, womenless men, dried up by the heat, their livers in disrepair, their political alignments warped by the daily task of fighting the Laotian telephone service, enraged by the gay corruption of the Lao leaders, and by the maddening problem of countering rumours of battles, both past and impending, with the reality of a largely non-existent army whose few indolent officers spent most of their time smuggling gold and drugs.

Only the Americans, in their hermetically sealed hygienic compound, with its own plumbing, water-purification plant and closed-circuit television, lived in happy expectation of Laos surviving the twentieth century. They, after all, had something to offer — not only rice and blackboards and comics, but also a dam. The High Dam of Nam Ngum.

About a mile beyond the Monument he passed a forlorn signpost marked, RN 5. HANOI 579 Kms; and a few hundred yards on came another, almost equally futile: RN 13. LUANG PRABANG 224 Kms. From here the road began to deteriorate rapidly — a humped deep-rutted track raised slightly above the level of the rice paddies where water buffalo wallowed up to their necks and wattle-roofed huts squatted on their stilts, their doors crammed with naked children who waved and howled with pleasure as he passed. But Murray scarcely noticed them; his eyes were on the details of the road, noticing now the modern steel telegraph poles on one side, carrying just a single wire.

After another couple of miles he came up behind an elephant that filled the whole road, with two small boys on its back. He had the jeep grinding in bottom gear, his view dominated almost entirely by the slow-heaving wrinkled grey rump above him. The French map said the turning was some twenty kilometres out of town; he had gone more than half of that now, but the road was still too narrow to pass the elephant. The sweat was itching down his face, stinging his eyes, his shirt soaking against the seat. He tried hooting once, but the boys took it as a salute and returned it with waves and smiles, while the beast continued its dogged, lumbering pace. He kept cool, remembering that patience was the great secret, the supreme advantage of this country. Only the Americans stayed on the ball, keen and bustling, and there weren't enough of them. At least he hoped there weren't.

The rice fields had ceased. There was high jungle ahead, and Murray took advantage of a slight widening in the track to swerve round the elephant into the tunnel of trees. The road was climbing now, clogged yellow mud stamped with the deep-ridged tread of enormous tyres and caterpillar tracks, like the trail of some prehistoric reptile. The turning up to Nam Ngum, though unmarked, was unmistakable: the tracks turned abruptly to the right where the trees had been hacked down, their stumps half buried in banks of fresh mud pushed up by bulldozers; while ahead the old *Route Nationale Treize* to the north had shrunk to no wider than a footpath, soon swallowed up in bamboo forest.

Murray put the jeep into four-wheel drive and began the twisting climb towards the dam. The steel telegraph poles had turned with him — that single wire that even the most incompetent Pathet Lao guerrilla could have snipped through at almost any spot on the twelve-mile drive. But Murray was beginning to work on another idea: telephones could be confusing instruments, especially in a country like Laos.

He was thinking hard now, checking the time against distance — fourteen miles in just over fifty minutes, taking into consideration the elephant — all the time concentrating his sweat-stung eyes on the deep, deceptive shades of the jungle. Then suddenly he was there. A last steep turn and the track had flattened out on to a broad road laid with strips of steel mesh used for emergency airfields. He felt the dawning of great excitement.

The trees on one side had thinned to a screen of limp palms, drooping in the damp heat like broken parasols. Beyond them lay the chasm of the dam. Luke Williams had said it was nearly five hundred feet wide and two hundred deep. To Murray it now looked more — a slender curving span of marble-white concrete on one side, shelving away between cliffs of rainforest down into the uncertain darkness below the sunline.

He had stopped the jeep at the end of the steel road and got out, taking his Leica and notebook. Above the ticks and hummings and snuffles of the jungle he thought he heard the throb of an engine. Otherwise it seemed unnaturally quiet. He snapped several frames of the approach road to the dam wall, noting the spongy surface underfoot — how the mud squelched up through the mesh and over the soles of his shoes — coming to a guard-house on his left where the Lao sentry bobbed out and saluted, his helmet just a little too big for him, a child dressed up as a soldier. There was a second, larger building beyond, with an air-conditioner grill built into one of the sealed windows. Murray noticed that the telephone wire, which had followed him up from Vientiane, ended here on the roof. There was also a powerful radio-transmitting aerial.

On the right, just before the dark pit of the reservoir, a wide clearing had been made in the jungle — a terrace of churned mud cluttered with miscellaneous hunks of machinery: caterpillar tractors, tip-trucks, bulldozers, mechanical diggers and grabs, all like giant bright yellow toys, their wheels and flanks splashed a duller yellow by the mud — except for the sharp metal of the grabs and digging scuttles which flashed in the sunlight, their jaws hanging open with the mud lodged between their teeth like lumps of half-chewed meat.

He counted five trucks, each with a load of at least ten tons. And the bulldozers could shift a medium-sized house. The Americans didn't do these things by halves, he thought. God bless America! He began to walk on up to the edge of the dam wall. Perhaps there was work going on somewhere — he thought he could hear the thump of the engine more clearly now — but otherwise there was this weird, shut-in stillness.

The last twenty yards of the approach road were of concrete, broad solid slabs laid out as wide as a three-lane highway. As he walked he went on snapping the camera, at various angles and speeds, until the film was finished. He paused, groping in his pocket for a new cassette. There was no barrier across the beginning of the wall, not even a parapet. And no sign of arc-lights, hurricane lamps along the edge of the dam — none of the essential paraphernalia for a crash-programme of night work to meet a deadline. At night, he decided, it would be as quiet as a sepulchre.

He reached the edge of the wall and looked down into the reservoir. At that moment a cloud passed in front of the sun and a deep shadow fell across the whole dam. Murray gave a little shudder. The reservoir was like some monstrous well. It sheered away into damp lichen-veined darkness lapped far below by water as black as ink, stirred by no ripples.

He took a couple of steps forward and aimed his Leica down at the water-level — calculating that it must be still at least a hundred feet below the top of the wall. But he never snapped the shutter. A hand gripped him from behind and held him.

CHAPTER 5

He was a heavy man with a bare red face under a safety helmet painted the same bright yellow as the digging machines.

'Excuse me, sir.' The voice was slow and not impolite, but his arm — thick and short-sleeved, covered in pale hair and mottled brown like tea stains — still held him just above the elbow, and only a few inches from the edge of the dam. 'Whatcha doin'?' he said again, harsher this time, as Murray lowered the Leica with his free hand.

'I'm taking pictures,' he said, beginning to lean against that hairy grip.

'You been takin' one awful lot o' pictures,' the man said, suddenly releasing him. 'Who are you?'

Murray was careful not to hurry. He stepped away from the edge and took out his wallet with its folder of Press cards. The man studied these with a frown, then nodded: 'O.K. You're a newspaper man, that's all right by me. But you're supposed to get a permit to come up here. We got a security problem.'

'Problem?' Murray said innocently, edging still further from the dam.

'Commies. The whole country's crawling with 'em.'

'And you think I look like a card-carrying Pathet Lao?'

The American shook his head. 'I don't mean gook commies. Plenty o' those around, but they don't bother us. I mean guys like Polaks, Rooshans — come up here snoopin' with cameras, and you can't tell the difference till you challenge 'em.'

'Any reason why they shouldn't come up and take a look round? It's a fine piece of construction you've got here.'

'It's government property.'

Murray forced a smile: 'Whose government? And whose property?'

For a moment he thought the man was going to hit him; but instead he smiled, hangdog but friendly: 'Aw hell! Want a beer?'

'I could do with one,' Murray said, genuinely grateful, as they walked back to the building next to the guardhouse where the Lao sentry still stood, staring at them without expression.

'That little bastard should'a checked you,' the American said, nodding angrily at the toy soldier who nodded back and grinned. 'I don't mean no offence,' he added, kicking open the door and releasing a blast of cold stale air; 'but I got my instructions.' He waved Murray to a plastic-covered swivel chair and walked over to a refrigerator, taking out two cans of Schlitz beer. 'Personally, mind, I don't give a sweet motherin' hell if they come and steal this whole dam piece by piece and take it into China. Chicoms'll most likely get it anyway in a year or two.'

As he talked Murray ran his eye quickly round the room. Desk with telephone, filing cabinet, wall-safe, pin-up calendar of a dusky Polynesian girl with breasts like swollen gourds — although the nipples looked suspiciously pale for the rest of her colouring. No doubt some tactful adman not wanting to upset the sensibilities of these randy defenders of the Free World, he thought, noting the VHF set in the corner, battery-operated.

His host had slumped down in the chair opposite and began cranking open the beer cans. 'Name's Tom Donovan. You're British, aren't you?'

'Irish — at least most of me is. Born in Ennis, County Clare. Murray Wilde. Here's to you, Tom!'

The American gave a mighty grin, and soon the two of them were deep in shop-soiled blarney about names and places and whose ancestors had gone where, and what great Irish names had done what to where; then Murray was treated to most of Tom Donavan's pitiable history — Pittsburgh engineer, Marine Corps, Sicily, Naples, bad conduct discharge for a minor currency infraction, divorced, three children, two grown-up girls and no idea where they were, his son dead in a car smash. And here he was 'out in stinking Asia helping Uncle Sam build a dam in a country that wouldn't know the Aswan Dam from its goddam arsehole!'

At the end of half an hour Murray had managed, by a combination of patient listening and careful prompting, to find out as much as he could about the Nam Ngum Dam without arousing Donovan's suspicions. Ninety per cent of the labour was Lao, and ninety per cent of that was mostly absent or stoned on pot or the local firewater, known as lao-lao or 'white lightning'. No, there were no U.S. guards — the country's neutrality forbade that — there was just the local sentry, and he went off at sundown. If anybody really so cared, he could come and help himself to just about as much loose supplies as he wanted. Only most of the time there weren't any supplies. He thumped his furry paw on the desk: 'Five weeks now I've had in orders for a new turbine shaft. Does it come? *Shit.* This place is even worse than Veetnahm — here the stuff gets stolen even before it gets into the country! Three years we've been working our arses off for these Laotians, and for what? They don't have no use for a dam — most of 'em don't even have use for a toilet seat!'

'I was told it would be finished in about three months?' said Murray.

'Three months — horseshit! We'll still be working on it when the Chicoms get here.'

Outside there was the sudden drumming of rain. Murray got up to go.

'Any time, Mr Murray, it was a pleasure! I'm here most days 'cept weekends. And I tell you, it gets mighty lonesome up here. But there's always beer in the icebox if you're passing again.'

Murray thanked him and ducked out into the rain, running with his head down towards the jeep. The lone Lao sentry had disappeared, as he turned the jeep round and started back to Vientiane.

PART 3: THE DROP

CHAPTER 1

Murray drew up outside Gate Two of Vientiane's Wattay International Airport at a few minutes past 0500 hours. The sky was already like the inside of a seashell, the air calm and warm; but heeding Luke Williams' advice, he wore two undervests and carried, besides his camera, a spare sweatshirt wrapped in two back-numbers of the *Bangkok World*.

No one challenged him. The wire-net barrier was already swung up under a brightly-lit billposter: AIR U.S.A. — HANDS ACROSS THE SEA. The airfield beyond was a vast pool of mist humming with distant engines. Murray followed a sign, *Air U.S.A., Traffic Enquiries*, to a door with an engraved plaque: *Major W. Y. Gaccia — Traffic Manager. Please Enter.*

A dark clean-shaven man in a floral shirt and blue slacks rose and held out his hand. 'Morning sir! Mister Murray Wilde — I'm Bill Gaccia. Luke Williams sent me up your flight papers. You're a little early.'

'I thought I might get a chance to watch the rice being loaded. And get a cup of coffee. My hotel sleeps late.'

'Sure thing, Mr Wilde. Let's just get the formalities over.'

Murray handed him the pass Luke had given him yesterday, and Major Gaccia gave him the familiar Xeroxed slip for 'notification of next-of-kin in case of accident'. As usual — or in want of anyone else — he filled in the name and office address of his literary agent in London, a pretty, alarmingly efficient young woman whom he had occasionally considered on his rare visits home since his divorce.

'Right, I'll take you through,' the major said, leading him out into the corridor, and Murray wondered what the Y in his name could stand for (Yuri? Yorick?), as they entered a long, low-ceilinged room full of glaring neon and the chatter of teleprinters. It was bitterly cold. A number of casually-dressed men in early middle age, all looking very fresh and clear-eyed for the hour of the morning, strolled in front of maps fixed with coloured pins and plastic numbers. No one was in uniform, Murray observed: this was the generation that was past Korea and Vietnam, but still too young to drop the kicks, or the idealism.

'We have two categories of rice-drop,' Major Gaccia was explaining, 'milk-run and rollercoaster. The first's a cinch, just a fun-ride round the hills, but on the second — what we call the rollercoaster — you get into those high mountains, electrical storms, no visibility, and up there, sir, you keep your safety-belt fastened!' He grinned: 'You're booked on the rollercoaster, Mr Wilde.'

On the walls were aerial photographs of some indefinable terrain; weather charts, a great sign IN GOD WE TRUST, and a smaller one by the door as they went out: *'No transistor radios or battery-operated shavers to be utilized during any flight. Your safety is our safety. Thank you.'*

'How long does the loading last?' said Murray. It was already 5.15 and scheduled take-off was for 6.30.

'Shouldn't take more than forty-five minutes. You've got time for a coffee and a chance to meet your pilots.' They had entered what Murray recognised as the 'Hi-Lo Snack-Bar'. It was again very cold, with soft piped music — Ray Conniff against the rising scream of a turbo-prop. Major Gaccia led him to a table where two men sat in flying-suits drinking black coffee.

'Gentlemen, may I introduce Mr Murray Wilde, a writer and newspaperman from Great Britain. Mr Wilde, your chief pilot,

Mr Samuel Ryderbeit. Your co-pilot, Mr Jones. Mr Wilde will be joining you gentlemen on Flight Applejack Six.'

The men at the table nodded without a word. Murray examined them both with the stirrings of misgiving. Unlike the men in the operations room next door, neither looked in the least fresh or clear-eyed. The co-pilot Jones, the older of the two, had not shaved and was wearing dark glasses. He was a grizzled pale-grey Negro with sunken, almost wasted cheeks and a hand that made the coffee lap over the edge of his cup.

The other man, Ryderbeit — perhaps because he was designated as chief pilot — was even more disturbing. A very tall man with a hooked, hairless face of slightly greenish hue and long yellow eyes of astonishing brightness, but with a hint of orange at the edges. He was wearing under his partially unzipped flying-suit a black silk turtle-necked shirt, and black suede flying-boots. Both men wore on their wrists identification discs of solid gold.

Major Gaccia was saying to Ryderbeit, 'Sammy, Mr Wilde here is anxious to watch the loading. Perhaps you could take him out and show him, after he's had his coffee.'

Sammy Ryderbeit nodded again, not looking exactly enthusiastic at being cast as Murray's guide.

Major Gaccia turned and said, 'I have to get back now, Mr Wilde — there's another passenger due on your flight, checking at my office at five-thirty.'

'Who is it?' said Murray.

'Some photographer, I think. In your line of business, anyway.'

Damn! he thought: So it threatened to be a P.R. outing after all. He sat down opposite Ryderbeit and for a moment the two of them scowled at each other across the stainless steel table.

Jones had loped away to an iced water tank in the corner where he was helping himself to a relay of paper cups.

'You ever done this before, Mr Wilde?'

'No.'

'Takin' pictures or writin'?'

'Both.' A Lao waitress had come up to him and he ordered black coffee.

'You use a typewriter or work in long-hand?' Ryderbeit said, leaning across the table leering.

'Typewriter,' Murray said blankly, and looked back into those yellow eyes, dilated like a cat's — puzzled now by the man's accent.

'I once knew a scribbler,' Ryderbeit went on: 'Mad poet bastard — used to grow his fingernail long then slit it up the middle and use it as a quill. You ever heard of such a tactic in your trade?'

'Never,' said Murray, irritated that he could not place the accent. It was almost American, yet not like any American he had ever heard. Australian perhaps? It was a hard accent, aggressive yet curiously clipped, almost prim.

'If you're coming on our ride you better have some of this,' Ryderbeit called suddenly as the waitress came back with Murray's coffee. He had pulled a stout pigskin flask from inside his flying suit, and without asking permission, poured a generous spout into Murray's cup. 'That's good Napoleon brandy! Don't sneer at it, soldier. You'll be glad of it in a couple of hours. You haven't seen the weather reports. Not like me and No-Entry Jones here — we're privileged.'

His co-pilot had returned, settling down with a sigh, and Ryderbeit leant over with his arm round the Negro's scrawny neck: 'Isn't that right, No-Entry? We have seen the reports and we are not afraid! We do our sacred duty for the honour of peace and freedom in this best of all possible worlds.' He smiled at Murray with a double row of very sharp white teeth. 'Mister Wilde, let me introduce you to No-Entry Jones, one of the unsung heroes of the struggle against Communism!' He shook the older man in a rough affectionate way, still watching Murray with his leering stare; and suddenly Murray recognised the accent — slightly distorted, like that of so many expatriates, but still unmistakable. South Africa.

He sighed, thinking, That's all I need! Mad white mercenary and a middle-aged Negro who looked as though he had a hangover: both armed with Napoleon brandy at 5.30 in the morning, all ready for a flight over high mountains near the Chinese and North Vietnamese borders. He decided that either Air U.S.A. were out of their minds, or that Sammy Ryderbeit and No-Entry Jones must be very good pilots indeed.

Ryderbeit, after their first encounter, had now become surprisingly genial: 'Mr Wilde, do you know why they call this old soldier here No-Entry?' — and Jones shook himself free and growled, 'Aw come on, Sammy, give us a break!'

'No, no, I'm telling Mr Wilde. After all, his life's going to be partly in your hands, No-Entry.'

Murray looked at his watch: only about twenty minutes left for the loading.

'Jones was doing a reconnaissance flight in an L 19 spotter-plane down over the Plain of Jars last year — one of these flights we're not supposed to talk about out in Laos, Mr Wilde, because the Security Council would get all hot and bothered, because it's naughty you see —'

'Ah shut up,' Jones groaned, but without effect.

'Anyway, the Pathet Lao took a pot-shot at him, and because an L 19's got a floor like paper and old Jones was being careless and not sitting on his groin-protector, he got a bullet through his guts.' He clapped his hand back round the Negro's neck, who seemed too exhausted to resist. 'And because this old soldier here does not believe in dyin' nor fadin' away, he floated that little plane down over the mountains and brought it in at Luang Prabang, so perfectly no one knew anythin' was wrong till they pulled Jones out and the floor of that plane was sloppin' an inch deep in blood — not countin' what must've already dripped through the floor. And you know, Mr Wilde?' — he leaned closer to Murray, still shaking the grizzled Negro beside him — 'when they got Jones to the hospital they found an exit wound in his belly the size of this coffee cup.' He gave a sudden ferocious cackle: 'But the funny thing was they couldn't find the entry wound. They searched and they searched — but that Pathet Lao bullet went up and out of old Jones and it left never an entry wound.'

His co-pilot muttered, 'Aw leave it, Sammy, it's an old story.'

Murray smiled and stood up. 'How about a look at the rice loading, Mr Ryderbeit?'

Ryderbeit rose slowly, supple and sneering half-humorously: 'Don't worry about the loading, soldier. It's the unloading that should be troubling you.'

Outside the light was coming up fast. Ryderbeit climbed into an Air U.S.A. Mini Moke parked outside. 'You're bloody keen, I must say,' he said, starting the engine. 'Not many journalists would bother to get on a rollercoaster for the first time, then worry about the loading. Any ulterior motive?'

He drove very fast across the wide empty apron towards the arc-shaped hangars on the far side that showed through the dawn like superstructures out of science fiction. Murray glanced at him sideways, and found to his consternation that Ryderbeit was doing the same.

'Eh soldier?'

'I don't quite follow you.' Murray was worried by Ryderbeit — far more than by the prospect of the rice-drop ahead. 'I'm doing a story.'

Ryderbeit's cackle carried even above the drone of the Moke. 'Come on, soldier, I'm not an infant in arms, and nor are you. I read, you know — and more than just the local rags.' He nodded at the bundle of *Bangkok Worlds* Murray was still gripping foolishly under his arm. 'You're a serious writer. I know your type — you want to record history in the making, witness a rice-drop, get all the details down in your notebook — bit of experience off from the usual bloody little chores of going to Press conferences and hearing about poor sods getting sliced in half by fifty-calibre machineguns while they're walking through elephant grass. Two paragraphs, O.K.?'

Murray sat very still, watching the gaping rear-ends of the transport planes forming out of the gloom. His fists lay clenched in his lap; it did not seem a good idea to punch his pilot on the snout before they'd even taken off.

Ryderbeit had turned the Moke left, driving under the wing-tips that swished over them like a fan. 'I'm not trying to be rude or anythin',' he added, 'I just want to know why you want to see a lot o' bloody rice being loaded off a truck on to a bloody plane?'

They had stopped. The plane ahead was not one of the high-tailed modern transports, but a stout clumsy-looking machine with its tail near the ground and a big open side-door through which the rice was being loaded off a forklift truck by two khaki-clad Laotians.

'Recognise her?' said Ryderbeit: 'C 46 — one of the veteran warriors of World War Two and still flying. Like the old Dak she's about the toughest plane ever built. Only she's well past middle age now, and like all the Daks she'll have to go sometime.'

'Don't you use any of the modern ones — C 123's or Caribous?'

'Not on a high drop. I tell you, that old crate there wouldn't fetch much, even as scrap metal. They can't afford to lose the modern ones.'

Murray nodded, watching the tip-truck move out from one of the hangars, back up against the forklift and deposit its load of sacks with an almost soundless slither. The forklift then slid forward, raising its flat spatula lift like a great spoon and pushing the sacks through the side-door of the C 46, where the two Laotians rolled them away on a track of steel rollers, up into the belly of the aircraft.

'You lose a lot of those planes?' he said at last.

'We lose 'em, but it's not policy to talk about it. Not to journalists, anyway. I don't know how much I can trust you — do I, soldier?' He was sitting behind the wheel, watching Murray with a funny crooked smile. Murray wondered if this was just his usual way of welcoming inquisitive journalists — or whether there were something more conspiratorial in his manner? He decided to change the subject. 'You're from South Africa?'

'Rhodesia. A bloody rebel.'

'They ran you out?'

Ryderbeit started the engine. 'Soldier, they've run me out o' practically everywhere. Jo'burg, E'ville, Brazzaville, Rio, Caracas, Genoa — you name it, and you'll find three dirty words — Samuel David Ryderbeit. South-East Asia's about the only place that'll still have me. Here, Bangkok, and old Saigon.' He was driving back, more slowly this time, towards the snack bar. 'Funnily enough, one of the few places I haven't been thrown out of is Rhodesia,' he added. 'I'm right behind old Smithie, don't get me wrong! I may be a Jew, but I'm not one o' your soft-bellied white liberals. No-Entry back there's about the only kaffir I've ever had any time for. Anyway, he's only small part kaffir. His grandfather came from a very old Welsh family.'

'So what happened in South Africa?'

'Trouble. Domestic trouble — twice. You married, Mister Wilde?'

'Not anymore.'

Ryderbeit gave his low cackle: 'I've been married three times — the only man in the world who makes wedding bells sound like an alarm clock! And all three times to real rich bitches. First one divorced me after six months for extreme cruelty. Second one lasted nearly a year, then again I got the bounce — same thing again, hit the bullseye. That time I got out and made for the Congo. Third wife was the richest of 'em all — Venezuelan oil up to her nostrils, and lovely with it. It was third time round the track for me — but it wasn't that that worried her. Trouble is, y'see, I've only been divorced once.'

Murray grinned: 'So you came out here? Where did you learn to fly? Rhodesian Air Force?'

'Who else? Taught me to touch down a Piper on a cricket pitch and take off again without knocking off the stumps. That was a good place, Rhodesia — except it's too small, too many bloody little cocktail parties round swimming pools. Know what I mean?'

'I haven't been there, but I think I know.'

Ryderbeit had pulled up in front of the Hi-Lo Snack Bar and opened the door of the Moke, taking out a clipboard of weather charts. He paused. 'I think you know a lot o' things, Mister Wilde. What I want to know is why a celebrated scribbler like you should be so interested in some little old rice-drop over north Laos?' He slammed the door and walked away towards the snack bar.

Murray sat for a moment, wondering if this was what George Finlayson meant by 'finding two of the best pilots in South-East Asia'. With growing doubts he began to follow Ryderbeit into the shed, then stopped dead.

No-Entry was sitting where they had left him, opposite a figure whose back was turned to both of them — a figure in a loose leopard-spotted combat tunic, sitting over a cup of coffee, drinking with both hands. She turned as they came up, smiling briefly at them both, with no surprise at all.

CHAPTER 2

Murray and Jacqueline Conquest sat side by side, strapped into the canvas-webbed hammock seats just inside the open door. The eight tons of rice, in three layers of sacking stamped '*Donated by the United States of America*', lay piled along the roller-tracks that ran up the aircraft floor like a miniature railway, round and back again, ending at the open door.

From the roof hung a number of parachute harnesses. The six 'kickers' — handpicked Thai paratroopers on loan to Laos — sat on top of the rice bags, wearing quilted uniforms but no safety belts. The inside of the aircraft was dim and oily and smelled of hot oven plates. It was impossible to talk above the rattling roar of the two massive prop-engines, as Sammy Ryderbeit and No-Entry Jones manoeuvred the machine round and lined her up at the end of the runway.

Great gusts of smoke blasted back past the door. Murray caught a glimpse of the three Ilyushin bombers — part of Russia's ambitious aid programme in the early sixties, later abandoned when the spares failed to arrive — their gutted brown carcases lying in the long grass at the edge of the airfield. There were a few violent jolts, the port engine in front of the door coughed a couple of times like a huge beast in pain; the whole plane shuddered, howled, then began the lumbering run for the take-off.

The girl beside him sat calm and upright, eyes front on the dangling rubber boots of one of the 'kickers' sitting up on the rice sacks. Murray had recovered from the shock of seeing her. At first he had stood in the Hi-Lo Bar and gaped at her, while Ryderbeit wasted several minutes' flying time leering solicitously and offering her his brandy flask, which she had declined. Murray was now trying to work out the implications. The reason for her being here was simple enough: she fancied herself as an amateur photographer, had heard from Luke at the Embassy yesterday that there was a fairly hairy rice-drop fixed up, and having nothing else to do, had decided to come along for the ride. Murray should have recognised the type earlier. South-East Asia was full of them — bored girls trailing round the trouble-spots, all rigged out in man-sized paramilitary kits, working off their various neuroses by being right there where the action was.

The only difference was that this girl, apart from being a great deal more attractive than most, was married to a man in the Central Intelligence Agency. And this, on Murray's present mission, was something that could — to say the least — prove embarrassing.

They were off the ground at last, wheeling over the town, away from the great looping brown river, the sun coming up over the rim of the earth, glinting off the mosaic of rice fields that looked like fragments of a shattered mirror. The Thai paratroopers began to smoke — one of them offering his packet of king-size filter-tips to Jacqueline Conquest, but she shook her head with a small artificial smile. A girl that didn't drink or smoke or smile, thought Murray. What did she do? The camera in her lap was a massive Japanese device, with telescopic lens and grip-handle like a miniature bazooka. He noticed that she carried no extra clothing, and her combat tunic, open at the neck, showed only bare lightly-tanned skin. The slip-stream from the door was no longer warm. He unfastened his safety belt and began unwrapping his extra sweatshirt, then paused, considering whether to offer it to the girl. There would be complications here, with the six Thai paratroopers watching them with inscrutable intensity. Instead he offered her the two *Bangkok Worlds*, shouting to make himself heard.

She accepted, and began unbuttoning her tunic without any ostentation, folding the newspapers across her flat belly, under an amply-filled unboned bra of white silk, while the six kickers went on smoking and watching, expressionless.

A moment later Murray's attention was distracted by the appearance of the Nam Ngum Dam passing far below in a great fold of rainforest — the scarred earth and tiny yellow machines scattered about like the playground of some bored child. The reservoir, hidden beneath the slanting sun, was as black as ever. Nothing would ever show in that water, he thought — unless it were floating. He stood in the open doorway, one hand gripping one of the parachute-lines, the other snapping away at the Leica slung round his neck. They were flying at perhaps four thousand feet, climbing hard. The dam was gone and he sat down again, shivering.

'What do you hope to get out of this trip?' he yelled at the girl in French: 'A few souvenir photos of the Chinese border?'

She shrugged: 'We don't go that near China.' She spoke less loudly, leaning very close to him, and for the first time — above the oily stench and icy slip-stream — he caught a drift of delicious perfume. 'I should ask the same of you,' she added. 'You're not a photographer, are you? So why does a well-known writer want to take pictures of one of these rice-shits?'

The phrase, *shiage-de-riz*, surprised him; but not as much as the content of what she said. And he thought, Here we go again! First this frightful Rhodesian Jew, and now this unsmiling graceful-limbed French wife of a CIA man, both wanting to know what an Irish journalist was doing bumming a ride on a rackety rice-drop over north Laos. He wondered if he had been just unlucky. Most of the time a journalist could wander round this country and no one asked a question from one day to the next. Perhaps he was being over-suspicious — as well he might. He shouted back at her: 'I illustrate my own articles. American magazines pay money.'

'Are you interested in money?'

'Like everyone else. Aren't you?'

She shrugged again, with that curious disdainful boredom he had noticed at the reception in Vientiane; then leaned back against the canvas webbing and closed her eyes.

It was getting very cold in the aircraft. Murray put on the extra sweatshirt under his jacket and began to pick his way up between the rails of rice-sacks to the pilots' cabin. It was much warmer here than in the body of the plane, with ventilators under the seats pumping out blasts of hot metallic air that joined with the rich fug of Havana leaf from a Romeo y Julieta cigar jammed between Ryderbeit's teeth. Everything in the cabin seemed very old and worn and dirty; there were cigarette ends and crumpled paper cartons on the floor, and a lot of naked dangerous-looking wire spilling out of a panel in the wall like a bunch of entrails.

No-Entry was at the main controls, still wearing his dark glasses as he held the stick back, climbing over ridges of jungle into a mauvish mottled sky. Ryderbeit glanced up at Murray. 'And how's our lovely fellow-passenger?' he cried, taking off the earphones.

'Asleep.'

Ryderbeit shook his head: 'We got her up too early — out o' bed with that sodding husband of hers!'

'You know him?'

'Too bloody right I do! I once had a fight with the bastard. Accused me of being arseholed after a crash — I'd raised the undercarriage before take-off. He was right. I had been drinking a bit — but it wasn't my fault. The contraption folded up because of hydraulic failure. Could happen to the soberest of us.'

'And where was Maxwell Conquest?' Murray asked, wondering how much of the pigskin flask had been drunk this time since take-off.

'Conquest was on the plane. It was a two-seater job and I was supposed to fly the sod up on one of these hush-hush missions to one of the U.S. forward bases near the Ho Chi Minh trail — where officially the only Yanks are seed-experts trying to diversify the local agriculture, or some such cock-rot. Some bloody seed-expert is Maxwell Bloody Conquest — unless you count what he does to that lovely lady we have in the back!' He broke off with his wild cackle. 'Anyway, we went down on the runway with rather a bump and Maxwell hurt his arse somewhat — bruised his coccyx, I think it was. But that didn't stop him telling me I was a crazy alcoholic, or words to that effect, which didn't really disturb me too much — I've been called lots worse than that in my time. But then, when I'm helping the bastard out, he says he's going to report me and see I lose my pilot's licence. And that's the kind of talk that Samuel Ryderbeit has to take rather seriously. So I hit the little shit a kind o' mild slap across the chops, and he has the impertinence — even with his bruised bum — to hit me back. It appears he knows some rather nasty tricks in the unarmed combat line. Anyway, I lost two teeth and he broke my cheekbone, which was just as well, because I was able to lodge a complaint against him with the American Embassy — G.B.H. with an offensive weapon, namely karate — and I even got a personal apology from the Ambassador. I also kept my licence.'

'Conquest should be delighted you're taking his wife up on your flight.'

'Yeah, it worries me a bit too. If I'd known I wouldn't've let her on the plane. I just hope nothin' happens on this ride.'

'You'll be all right, he's going back to Saigon next week — and taking his wife with him.'

Ryderbeit gave his crafty leer: 'I might try looking her up some time — when her husband's not around.'

'How do you mean?'

'I'm going down to Saigon myself next month.'

'You mean you operate out of there too?' said Murray, as a number of thoughts began flashing through his mind — and none of them to do with Jacqueline Conquest.

'Sure I do — part of my contract with Air U.S.A. We're a busy international airline, Mr Wilde. As the ads might say, we provide safe and reliable service to the latest three States of the Union — Laos, Thailand and South Vietnam.'

'It doesn't worry them, you're not being an American citizen?'

'It doesn't worry 'em in the least. None of the hush-hush flights carry any markings on their planes, and if I go down and fall into unfriendly hands, no one knows anything about me. That's the one advantage of holding a Rhodesian passport. What do the Reds do? Kick up one hell of a fuss at the UN, parade me through the streets of Hanoi? And what do the Yanks do? Shrug their shoulders and say I'm just another poor white African outcast, shot down on some smuggling run over South-East Asia. And there are enough of us doing it, I can tell you — boys out o' the Congo, Algeria, the Yemen, Biafra. Now Vietnam. All the fun-spots of the world!'

'And you do it just for the money — four hundred dollars a week?'

Ryderbeit looked up, frowning: 'You seem to be very well informed?'

'It's the going rate, isn't it?'

'More or less. Sometimes more, for the hush-hush ones — the spotter-flights over the Ho Chi Minh trail where No-Entry here got it up the rear passage.'

The co-pilot, his grizzled head encased in earphones, did not hear. Ryderbeit's voice had suddenly lost its matiness: 'You're anglin' for somethin' out here, aren't you, Mr Wilde? Now come on, quit stallin'. I've been talkin' eagerly enough — too bloody eagerly to a journalist, for that matter. But since I've got a pretty keen idea you're not goin' to write any of this, I'm prepared to oblige. Now how about you returnin' the compliment?'

Before attempting to reply, Murray did some rapid thinking. Unless Ryderbeit had a sixth sense, or was pathologically suspicious, it seemed almost inconceivable that he would have been talking like this, had he not been tipped off. There was also the matter of Air U.S.A. The activities of this airline were ambiguous, to put it mildly. It was a registered commercial company, operating largely on a charter basis; but it was no secret that most of its custom, as well as backing, came from the CIA. And if Murray were to quote even half of what Ryderbeit had just been saying, the Rhodesian's job would be worth about as much as a post-dated cheque after a poker game with strangers on a train. And Ryderbeit — unless he were mentally deficient, or slightly mad — must be well aware of this.

There could be only one disturbing explanation: Sammy Ryderbeit knew what Murray was doing in Laos. He had been told. And the only two people who could have told him were George Finlayson and Charles Pol. Murray was just wondering why either of them would have done so, when the plane began a violent shuddering. No-Entry was easing back the stick as high coils of cloud climbed darkly above the windows.

'How long till the drop?' Murray asked, playing for time now.

'Long enough.' Ryderbeit unfastened his belt and stood up, taking Murray by the arm. The floor was sloping dangerously and Ryderbeit's fingers, which were lean and supple like the rest of him, felt very strong. 'Let's go back and have a little chat, soldier.'

Jacqueline Conquest was sitting up again, staring out into the cloud. Ryderbeit shouted some gallantry at her, in fluent appalling French, then signalled Murray into one of the hammock seats a few feet away from her along the wall. Murray was beginning to regret having given her both his *Bangkok World*s. Ryderbeit, on the other hand, gave no sign of feeling the cold, which was becoming intense. Instead he took out his flask, offering it to Murray who accepted gratefully this time, then took a long drink himself, smacked his lips and grinned: 'Well, what's it all about, soldier? There can't be much loot in working for a few crappy newspapers.'

'I do all right, thanks.'

The Rhodesian shook his head: 'Don't waste my time, Murray Wilde, sir. What's the game? Gold, guns, opium? Come on, you wouldn't be the first to try and con a poor innocent Air U.S.A. pilot into running an unscheduled flight over some remote territory where the rule of law's not too strong, and drop a few rice-bags that don't necessarily have to contain rice, *n'est-ce pas?*' And he gave Murray a hard slap on the knee.

'I'll have some more of that brandy,' Murray said, as the floor began another series of shuddering bumps.

'Don't drink it all. We may need it before we're down.'

Murray drank, screwed the top back on and waited. It was now quite clear how things stood. Finlayson, having sounded him out that first evening at the Cigale, and presumably been impressed, had acted swiftly; having found out that he was planning to go down on a rollercoaster, he had managed to arrange — probably through the obliging Luke Williams — that Murray's chief pilot should be this Rhodesian mercenary, who gave every promise of being prepared to do anything for anybody, providing the price was right.

When Ryderbeit continued to say nothing, Murray decided it was time to get the matter settled, one way or the other. 'You've been talking to George Finlayson?'

'Old-Filling-Station! Well o' course I know him. Vientiane's a small place. Everybody knows Filling-Station.'

'What did he tell you?'

'Ah now!' — he raised his forefinger as though administering an oath — 'I quote the Fifth Amendment on that one. On the grounds that it might incriminate our good friend George Finlayson. Shall we just say, he dropped a number of oh-so subtle hints? Filling-Station, as you may have already realised, Mr Wilde, is an English gentleman. At least he tries bloody hard to be. And in his imaginary armchair in White's or Boodle's — or wherever the British banking aristocracy still hole up in these dark days of Socialist rule — George Finlayson insinuated that you, an honourable British writer with a commendable career behind you at a Vietnamese university, might be interested in a certain business venture. O.K.?'

The floor slumped sickeningly like a lift going down too fast. Ryderbeit said, 'Better strap yourself in — I'm going back to give Jones a hand. The drop'll be coming up soon.' He glanced across at Jackie Conquest and murmured, 'I suppose that beauty realises there's no toilet on this crate? We just hang on out of the door holding on to the parachute-lines. She might find that a bit awkward.' His grin darkened to a frown: 'What's she doing on this plane, anyway?'

'You tell me. Joy-riding, I should think. At least I hope that's all it is.'

Ryderbeit stood considering Mrs Conquest with more than his usual lecherous leer. 'Yeah, I hope so too.' He paused. 'We'll have our little business talk later. Be seeing you, soldier!' He turned and said something to the Thai kickers, who put out their cigarettes and began clambering off the sacks.

Sammy Ryderbeit walked back up to the cabin.

CHAPTER 3

Murray and Jackie Conquest hung over the edge, their wrists wrapped securely round the parachute-lines, and watched northern Laos move slowly below them. It was a landscape that changed with disconcerting rapidity, one moment a rumpled carpet of rich green mohair, suddenly moulting into bone and gristle carved with deep crevices and waterfalls spouting from immense heights. And now cloud — freezing, drifting through the door like smoke, leaving little beads of moisture on the metal fittings and parachute buckles. Then suddenly it would be clear again, but with a diffuse yellow light that gave the ground a strange shadowy effect, like looking down from a bathyscope on to the floor of the ocean — deep-green rocks overgrown with seaweed, full of hollows of purple darkness. The height — or depth — was also disconcerting. One moment they seemed to be flying at several thousand feet, then a shelf of mountain swept up so close that they could see the leaves on the treetops, a jumble of tiny huts, a path hacked out of the jungle.

The time was 8.40. They had been airborne for just over two hours. One of the kickers had a clasp-knife out and was slicing through the ropes that fastened the first batch of eight sacks to a wooden sledge, which the others now began to ease up towards the door. Murray and the girl stood back. The sledge reached the sharp bend in the roller-tracks; the Thais braced themselves, holding the load at the very edge of the floor while one of them wedged a block of wood between the sledge and the rollers. They were small men, but immensely strong. The load must have weighed nearly half a ton. The plane was now banking steeply, turning round the side of the mountain until the trees seemed to be growing outwards, almost horizontally. Murray saw the jumble of huts again, and the yellow track on the mountain top. More cloud, for a moment so dense that he could hardly see the girl leaning back against the inside of the door; and when it cleared he recognised the beginnings of an excited fear in those dark sullen eyes.

The same mountain top came round again, for the third time. A bell rang just above his head, with startling shrillness. One of the Thais screamed something and whisked the wood from under the sledge. The others heaved all at once, and the whole load of sacks went over the edge, very fast, tumbling, then slowing, it seemed, as they drifted out towards the ground. Murray could see figures moving out of the trees like ants. The sacks fell in a straight line along the edge of the track. The Thai paratrooper who had given the shout, and was obviously in command, looked up with a grin and made a thumbs-up signal to Ryderbeit, who was peering back down the length of the plane.

The second sledge-load was already being wheeled into position. The operation began again. This time it took four turns before the drop could be made. Twice the cloud closed in, and the third time the kicker was just a fraction late; but he had the wit to hold his hand and wait for the fourth run. Murray caught his eye and for a moment thought the little man was going to burst into tears. On the fourth turn, the sacks again fell in the same straight line just outside the trees, the rice protected from spilling by the three layers of sacking.

Murray was beginning to get the hang of it now. The track was not a marker-zone, but a dangerously short airstrip, suitable only for a helicopter or the tiniest one-engined aircraft. If the sacks landed near the middle, their impact could put the strip out of action for perhaps several hours. On the other hand, if the load fell into the trees, the branches could split the triple-sacking and that would be the end of several hundredweight of rice — or anything else that happened to be inside.

What Sammy Ryderbeit and No-Entry Jones were doing — in an antiquated aircraft, and in bad weather — was the equivalent of low-flying, high-precision bombing. At these heights, in strong wind, a parachute drop would be less accurate: the rice could be blown off-course and fall miles away, down into some inaccessible gulley that would take days to retrieve.

A freefall drop required skill. A not unbelievable skill — there were plenty of pilots in the world who could no doubt accomplish the same feat without much difficulty. But they might not be the kind of pilots that Murray had in mind.

On the fourth drop the last few sacks hit the trees. It was only a marginal miss — perhaps a gust of wind, a split-second error of judgment — but Murray saw the sacks explode in little white puffs. The head kicker gave Ryderbeit the thumbs-down signal this time, then gestured Murray and the girl back to their seats, and told them to strap themselves in.

During the next few minutes the ride became much rougher. Half the load had now gone, and the rest of the sledges were being rolled down the floor from behind the cabin and jammed with extra wooden slabs. Murray realised they were climbing steeply, his ears cracking with pain. It became very dark in the aircraft. He wondered for a moment about oxygen masks. There were none in evidence. He shouted fatuously at the girl, 'Ça va?' but she said nothing. The plane began a new swaying motion, followed by a change in the engine pitch. Even to Murray's untrained ear, he knew they were losing power. The first flashes of lightning came a moment later. Ryderbeit had appeared in the door of the cabin and was yelling, 'Cut loose! — the bloody lot!'

The Thais went into action again, slicing the ropes of the remaining sacks, rolling the last half-dozen sledges down the floor at terrifying speed; but this time there was no question of wedges, calculating the drop, waiting for the bell. The sledges tippled out of the door, one after the other, and vanished into cloud. Almost at once the pitch of the engine improved, and there was a slight, perceptible lift.

The six kickers — still moving with a panic-free precision that would have aroused the admiration of the roughest British paratroop sergeant — took their seats along the wall and for the first time began strapping themselves in. Murray also noticed that at least two of them were sweating — no more than a delicate row of beads across the brow — but his experience of the East had taught him that Orientals do not sweat easily, particularly in a temperature barely above zero. And these men were hardened paratroopers. They knew the form, and the form was not good.

Fifteen minutes passed. It was almost 9.30, but there was no sign of the sun burning off the mountain mists, as Luke Williams had predicted. The sun showed only at long intervals, in an ugly crepuscular glow that had nothing to do with daylight. Thunder crashed distantly through the weakening roar of the engines. Lightning lit the oily darkness inside the plane. It was like the studio effects of some horror film.

Murray found himself gripping Jackie Conquest's hand in a spontaneous gesture which was reciprocated. The port engine had begun to cough again; but this time it was a long angry sound, as though desperately trying to clear something from its twin-throated exhausts. Murray gave the girl's hand a last squeeze, then unclipped his belt and started to climb precariously towards the pilots, ignoring the vague gestures of warning from the row of kickers.

It seemed quieter up in the cabin, like a dim cramped office with the instrument panel glowing behind greasy dials. Ryderbeit was back behind the main controls, while the Negro co-pilot worked on a soiled one-millionth-scale cloth map with the contours drawn in mauve for red night-sight reading, occasionally mumbling into the mouthpiece of the R/T set in front of him and jotting down figures with a wax crayon on a celluloid chart. Suddenly the floor keeled over and Murray nearly fell across Ryderbeit's lap. The dials began spinning crazily and the cabin was suddenly filled with light. He looked up. There was something wrong.

The cloud had broken, too late. They were flying down below the level of the mountains, as though into a cave. Mist hung from the banks of jungle like shrouds, coming closer and closer — suddenly racing past, and Ryderbeit was making a number of rapid movements that were at the same time curiously delicate, like a pianist executing a complicated trill. Or a surgeon. A surgeon slicing quickly, ripping at the entrails of the aircraft, tearing it apart — thousands of hours of stress-torn machinery howling as the mountains came rolling over towards them and the cloud burst round them again, and Murray found himself lying on the filthy floor among the cigarette ends and the crumpled paper cups.

Ryderbeit had pulled off his earphones and they were dangling down from his seat, giving out a squawking crackle of voices that Murray found all too familiar. Jones was talking into his mouthpiece when Ryderbeit suddenly shouted, 'Cut that out, you bloody idiot — *cut it out!*'

No-Entry switched off the set in front of him and slowly removed his dark glasses; his eyes were small and raw, his face like clay.

Murray got to his feet and picked up the earphones, recognising now a few garbled words and numbers — '*nah-cha-bam-quouc-lim-chi-quouc…!*'

'Understand it?' Ryderbeit yelled, not moving his eyes from the instrument dials, which seemed to have settled down slightly.

Murray nodded: 'Vietnamese.'

'North Vietnamese,' said Ryderbeit.

'Who are they?'

'Dien Bien Phu control tower. They've got a military airfield there. We're getting a direct signal. According to my calculations we're at least ten miles inside the border.' He gave a savage laugh: 'Ten miles inside North Vietnam, soldier. That's trouble.'

CHAPTER 4

'What happened?' Murray asked.

'We missed the second drop zone,' Ryderbeit told him.

'Second?'

'They gave us two — second one at the last moment, even after the weather reports had come in and I told 'em I couldn't lift four tons o' rice an extra thousand feet through a probable flamin' occluded front. But don't let's get too technical. We missed the pass, that's all. I couldn't get her over before we had time to jettison the load. The bastards'll probably try to eat my arse for getting rid of it — but if I hadn't we'd have crashed.'

'Where are we?' The altimeter was wobbling at around eight thousand feet — which was still not above the highest mountains. Ahead there was again nothing but dull yellow cloud.

Ryderbeit said: 'We're heading due north for a second pass that should get us back into Laotian airspace. If not, we're screwed.'

'How far is that?' The speedometer showed only about two hundred knots.

'Five, six minutes,' said Ryderbeit. 'We're flying blind now — I daren't try for a radio bearing or they may pick us up — and what's more, the NVA have got radar down there. Only while we're still in the mountains there's just a chance they won't spot us.'

'What's the worst that can happen?'

Ryderbeit grinned: 'You're a bloody optimist, aren't you! The worst is several things. They can blow us out of these filthy skies with a SAM — Surface-to-Air Missile. Or they might have Migs down there — but I doubt even those little buggers would try to chase us through this muck. Or we can just crash.'

As he spoke the port engine failed. A couple of splutters, a quick rattling sound, and the prop swung to a standstill. Ryderbeit's hands worked energetically at a row of switches. Nothing happened. His eyes were on the static gyro-compass now, unblinking, as he moved a lever to the left; then said to Murray, in a voice grown small and tight: 'Better get back and start putting on parachutes. The kickers'll show you. And hold the little girl's hand for me.'

Murray staggered back down into the hull of the aircraft; but when they counted up they found there were only seven parachutes for the eight of them. Murray gave one to Jackie Conquest and made some miserable joke about first-class passengers on the *Titanic*. The chief kicker tried to sacrifice his own parachute, but Murray declined it with mock-heroism; he was not exactly afraid of having to jump — it was just that he had a feeling that while he kept faith with the plane and its pilots, they might still get through. Putting on a parachute which he'd never used before, and jumping into some unknown crevasse of jungle, seemed the final surrender.

He knew they were losing height fast now. A series of lurching drops that jerked at his guts, wrenched his neck back, made him giddy and muzzy-eyed. The Thais were standing round Jackie Conquest, strapping her into the harness, securing the line to the steel bar along the roof, explaining that the parachute opened automatically. One of them began to demonstrate how to fall, elbows pressed to his sides, knees jack-knifing under him, until he looked like a foetus.

At this moment Jackie Conquest vomited — a spew of instant coffee, quickly swept across the floor and into the cloud. She straightened up at once and glared at Murray with a look of embarrassment and rage. 'I am sorry!' she shouted, in English.

He gave a dim smile: 'It's the least of our troubles!' — reflecting, almost sadly, that this physical act had been the first really human thing he had seen her do since they had met.

The Thai kickers throughout had maintained an impeccable inattention, like waiters during an ugly scene in a restaurant involving valued customers. Murray meanwhile decided on a discreet withdrawal, making his way again towards the pilots' cabin, the floor rocking downwards this time, as the one engine struggled bravely to hold them out of that final, fatal spin. He found Ryderbeit working frantically at the controls, exchanging gestures with No-Entry Jones who was still bent over charts, checking dials — a wordless exchange of hand signals that was meaningless to Murray, yet wonderfully calm. He stood propped against the back of Ryderbeit's seat, watching the finger of one of the altimeters creep back round the dial, anticlockwise, the 1,000 feet digits recorded in decades — 80, 70, 60 — falling fast, while the second dial, recording the hundreds of feet, was now beginning to spin. The view through the windshield was still of dull blind cloud. He waited — ten, fifteen, thirty seconds. Then suddenly Ryderbeit relaxed: 'How are the passengers, soldier?'

'The girl's been sick. She could do with some brandy.'

'You scheming bastard!' He laughed as he handed up the flask: 'But no smoking back there, right?'

'Right. Where are we?'

'Where are we?' Ryderbeit yelled at No-Entry who called back, 'To my estimation, we're down to five thousand, on a zero Gee-Bee, which would indicate we're down through it, and that the Lord has been pretty damned generous!' He sounded like the popular idea of how brave emancipated Negroes in the American Armed Forces are supposed to sound.

Ryderbeit nodded grimly. 'This boy Jones is what we in the flying business call a navigator. There is no navigator in the world like Jones. He has just got us through the pass, blind. But then of course, he has the advantage of voodoo.'

The joke was obviously stale on the Negro, who merely shouted at Murray: 'I advise you, Mr Wilde, to get back and strap yourself in.'

Ryderbeit added: 'We're going to try and land on a strip that was not built for any kind of aircraft like this. Send my compliments to the lady, and don't both o' you drink all the brandy. I'm goin' to want some myself, if we get down.'

They came down on what Murray had come to think of as a sentimental cliché — '*On a wing and a prayer*'. The port wing with its dead engine went down over a field that looked like a layer of rusted corrugated iron. Everyone in the back — Murray, Mrs Conquest, the six Thais — were strapped in, parachutes cast off, hunched forward with knees and elbows gripped close to their bodies, waiting for the bone-crushing impact. The rollers on the empty rails began to turn on their own momentum.

Then a sudden, awful quiet.

The second engine had cut out. There was a rattling of loose gadgets and rice-rollers, the soft roar of the slip-stream that had fallen to less than forty knots. The floor sank lower, to meet some uncertain surface of mud and water and half-grown rice shoots that could scarcely bear the weight of a big greedy insect.

Wild thoughts careered through Murray's mind: Were things prearranged? The meeting with Sergeant Wace in the Bangkok bar; accepting a drink from the fat friendly Pol in the little restaurant in Phnom Penh? There was a truth somewhere — not God necessarily, but a kind of rhythm of reason. Or of non-reason. If there was any God — or perhaps two of them — they were up front bringing down this great hunk of metal, slowing her down with a sudden scream from the starboard engine, then a whirring roar as they touched the ground, lifting and hitting again much harder this time, with a thick sloughing sound as the port wing went down and cut deep into the ground so that the whole weight of the plane began to turn as though on a wide pivot — a plough biting into the earth, grinding and bumping and biting still deeper, its wing tip snapped off, its engine gone too, the whole wing crumpling like silver paper, torn from the body of the plane as the machine seemed to settle for a moment, solid and perplexed but still in control — then started to bounce with a beating of the head, limbs numb but feet shocked and thudding against the steel floor, the whole world going round and round and people and metal all screaming round; then stillness.

They hung in their safety belts at an odd angle, and there was blood on one of the Thais' faces. Jackie Conquest sat upright, quiet and gentle and very beautiful, Murray thought, hanging in her seat like a doll with her uniform bulging under the arms with the newspapers he'd given her, and the heavy camera swinging from her neck.

The plane had stopped. He found he was sneezing violently, his whole body shaken, eyes watering and nose blubbering like a baby. Afterwards they told him it was because of some cornmeal that had been spilt in the back of the plane during a previous flight and that on the sudden dive and impact of landing, it had blown back up the plane. Murray suffered from mild hay fever, but he was not entirely happy with this explanation. As had happened several times before, he was terrified of being seen to be terrified. Was this one sign of courage, or just the hangover from a comfortable over-educated background?

He was still wondering and muttering to himself when Jones dragged him out of the plane. They walked side by side, unplugging their boots from the mud, and he kept looking back at the cracked silver tail of the plane, while the Negro jogged his arm and said, 'C'mon, man, it's O.K., it's O.K.'

He had no idea where he was.

PART 4: THE SERGEANT'S TALE

CHAPTER 1

They found themselves in an odd little town, grey and wretched, but still bearing the imprint of French civilisation. There was a tiny square surrounded by flaking colonnades; and the legs of some statue — a general or perhaps a poet — standing in the middle of the cracked concrete, its jagged shanks sprouting some rich ugly weed.

The Americans — in the singular, as it turned out — had their USAID headquarters in one of the old French houses, freshened up with paint the colour of flesh. The one American inhabitant was even larger and more close-cropped than usual — a lanky raw-boned man with a big white smile called Wedgwood. The walls of his office were papered with enormous crude paintings of men in uniform — squat brown-faced men with square shoulders and straight arms, very badly drawn, as though by a child. Under each was printed: KNOW YOUR ENEMY: NVA REGULAR. NVA IRREGULAR. PATHET LAO REGULAR — etc; then a detailed list of the weapons these men might be bearing. There was also one corner devoted to the fold-out pin-ups of at least six months' issues of *Playboy*.

Murray stumbled over to the iced drinking water tank and helped himself to a couple of paper cupfuls. There was a dull throbbing in the side of his head, yet he seemed to notice things with a heightened awareness. He noticed, when he sat down again, a tiny mole just behind Jackie Conquest's left ear where her hair broke forward across her cheek. She was sitting next to him beside a furled *Stars and Stripes*, and now that she had removed the copies of the *Bangkok World*, her combat tunic was draped loosely over her breasts.

Wedgwood called to a Lao assistant who went away to brew up some coffee, while Ryderbeit and No-Entry began a long, but not quite complete account of their aerial mishap. They made no mention of having transgressed North Vietnamese airspace, concentrating only on a failed port engine and how they'd feathered the plane down through eight thousand feet of mountains, over-running the airstrip and finishing up in an untilled rice-paddy.

Wedgwood took notes, shaking his head wonderingly and saying he couldn't understand how any of them came to be alive. When the Lao assistant came back with the coffee Ryderbeit gave his most engaging smile and said, 'Could we possibly have something stronger, Mr Wedgwood, sir?'

'Why sure, boys!' And a moment later the American was back with a full quart bottle of Four Roses bourbon, plus the inevitable paper cups. They all drank, except No-Entry, while Wedgwood began to make plans to fly them back to Vientiane. He might be able to lay on a chopper before nightfall to get them down at least as far as Luang Prabang. It might take longer to find transport for the Thai kickers, who had mysteriously and discreetly disappeared.

The bourbon had begun to deaden the throbbing in Murray's head. Later Wedgwood, taking the bottle with him, led them all out into a narrow muddy street, to a house with arches and ornate balconies which he said was the nearest thing to a restaurant in town. He wouldn't stay because he had to get back and send some radio messages; but he left them the bourbon.

It was very hot inside, full of slow fat flies and the foetid smell of fish. After a moment they moved out to the back where there was a small patio with a shallow pond and three goldfish flicking about in the dark water. The proprietor, a polite Tonkinese, brought out chairs, a table, and four glasses. The meal he served was peculiarly vile, but none of them had any appetite. After a second glass of bourbon Ryderbeit contented himself with sitting back with a hunk of stale bread, rolling little lumps between his fingers and dipping them in his bourbon, then tossing them into the pond, watching the fish dart up and swallow them. Each time he gave a low mirthless laugh, waiting intently for their reactions. One of the fish rolled to the surface, its mouth out of the water, gasping; the other two, after a couple of bites each, sank to the bottom, twitched for a moment, then lay still.

'There you are!' he cried, swinging his chair round: 'There you have the whole human predicament — the ones that float and the ones that sink. I think we're the ones who float — wouldn't you say so, No-Entry? You're not drinkin', No-Entry, you miserable bastard!'

The Negro lifted his head wearily from his elbows, his eyes wrapped again in their dark glasses. 'You know I can't drink, Sammy.'

'After a flight like that one, you bloody well drink!' Ryderbeit roared.

'Cut it, Sammy. I'm tired.'

Ryderbeit scowled, splashing more bourbon into his glass. 'The rest o' you're drinking?' he said, turning to where Murray and Jackie Conquest sat nursing their glasses in the shade of the wall. 'C'mon, those need freshenin' up,' he added, leaning across with the bottle.

'We're doing fine,' said Murray, not liking the look of Ryderbeit at all. The bounce and gaiety he had displayed back at the USAID headquarters was dissipated now into a sour, needling moodiness, as the level of the bourbon dropped and the other three spoke less.

'Tell us about the Congo,' Murray said wearily. It was Ryderbeit drinking in silence that worried him most.

'I'll tell you all you want to know about the Congo, Murray boy — but later. First I'd like to hear what lovely little Mrs Conquest here was doing on my plane. You come to spy on me, darling? All rigged up in yer battle kit like some bloody film extra, with her bloody great camera thrown in for the act — then back you go runnin' to Mister Bloody Maxwell Esquire and tell him that Samuel D. Ryderbeit just happened to wander a few miles over North Vietnamese airspace, then went and flipped his plane down in a rice-paddy — all because he'd been takin' a few sniffs at the old brandy-flask! Isn't that right, darling?'

'Take it easy,' Jones murmured from the end of the table.

Ryderbeit grinned. 'I'm takin' it nice and easy, No-Entry. Just want to know what this sweet little married lady's been doin' on my flight.'

'You know what I was doing,' she said stiffly. 'I got the official clearance, just like Mr Wilde here. I came to take photographs.'

'Photographs of a load o' bloody cloud — or the mountains of North Vietnam? How many frames did yer take?'

'That's none of your business!' Her eyes had high dark lights in them, emphasised by the sudden parched whiteness of her cheeks. 'Just because you've saved my life doesn't mean you can order me around like a servant!' she cried. 'I can look after myself very well — don't worry, Mister Ryderbeit!'

Ryderbeit gave a crooked, downward smile at the fishpond. 'I'm sure you can look after yerself, Mrs Conquest. Bein' married to the Central Intelligence Agency gives you rather an edge over the rest of us. As for me, I expect to die every day of the week.' He rolled another pellet of bread, dipped it in bourbon and this time put it in his mouth. 'I just want to know what you were doing on my flight, that's all.'

'I've told you. I came to take photographs of a rice-drop. Anyway, what concern is it of yours?'

'It's every bloody concern of mine, Mrs Conquest. Because I'm the chief pilot — I was in sole charge o' that plane — and it's of the greatest concern to me who comes on my flights, and why.'

'I've told you why.'

'Cool it, Sammy,' said Jones again; and Murray began to stiffen in his chair, watching Ryderbeit closely now, knowing the man was spoiling for trouble. Ryderbeit's glass was empty. He reached out for the bottle and refilled it; then, tilting his chair perilously far back, he decanted a cigar from a pigskin case, getting his lighter out and grinning at Jackie over the flame like a snake with a bird. 'So what yer goin' to tell that bastard hubby o' yours when yer get back, Mrs Conquest?'

'He doesn't even know I've come.'

'Doesn't even know!' Ryderbeit brought his chair down with a crash, sounding genuinely surprised. 'Why the hell not?'

'Leave her alone,' Murray snapped. 'She's told you why she came — to take some photographs, enjoy herself on a dull morning. Now just leave it at that.'

Ryderbeit turned, cocking one eye with a slow enigmatic smile. 'O.K., soldier. O.K.! If you say so, I'm not goin' to argue. Your business here is my business. If you're not worried havin' along the wife of the Central Intelligence Agency, then I'm not worried either. But' — and he swung back to Jackie, jabbing his glowing cigar at her like a gun — 'if you breathe one word to contradict the official report that that boy

Wedgwood's sending out — one little whisper about us transgressing North Vietnamese airspace — I'll take your pants down and give your pretty little backside such a thrashin' you'll be takin' your meals standin' up for a week!'

She flushed darkly, and Murray closed his fist. But before either of them could speak, Ryderbeit suddenly laughed and sat back again, breathing smoke up at the square of grey sky above. 'You wanted to hear about the Congo? I'll tell you about the Congo — the best days o' my life I spent in that lovely place.'

Anything, Murray thought, to kill time till the chopper arrived to take them to Luang Prabang. Ryderbeit's mood had become more mellow, as he talked of his light twin-engined Piper Comanche and how he'd flown over the elephant grass with the other mercenaries going through like beaters after game, and how the Simbas had come running out in their lion-skin head-dresses, howling like dogs while he shot them down in rows with his fifty-calibre machinegun — sometimes splitting them almost in half, sometimes letting one run free for a mile or so, teasing him with low passes, waiting till he tried to dodge back into the bush, then knocking him flat with one short burst.

Some of his tales were scarcely credible for their horror; it was almost as though he were taunting them for some violent reaction, although he got practically none. Even his constant references to 'munts' and 'kaffirs' seemed to leave Jones totally unmoved — dozing with his head on his arms, as though he'd heard it all before, and didn't much care anyway. Jackie sat pale and very straight in her chair, smoking and sipping her drink, without any discernible expression except mild boredom.

With more than half the bourbon gone, Ryderbeit seemed to tire of atrocity stories — torture, rape, cannibalism — and now moved to a lengthy dissertation on his fellow mercenaries in the Congo. Murray was scarcely listening, enjoying his bourbon and the relative peace of the hot sticky afternoon, thinking that the worst was over with Ryderbeit — just a nervous tantrum following the crash perhaps — when something rather odd happened.

Ryderbeit had admitted he wasn't too keen on the Belgians: they were smug and fat and ran too fast when the going got rough. There were also a few Britons, mostly poor whites who'd run out of Kenya and Nyasaland; and a couple of public school boys who wanted to be heroes and were about as much use as two left boots on a one-legged munt. And some of the South Africans and his fellow Rhodesians weren't much cop either — unemployed layabouts who wanted to earn an easy buck shooting black men. No, the ones he admired most were the French — the ones who'd come down from Algeria. 'Especially the Legion. Those Legion boys were bloody good!' He sat back, sipping his drink, sounding almost tearfully nostalgic. 'Rough but good. Lots o' Krauts among 'em, o' course — and real bastards they were! But good soldiers. No parlour-pink nonsense about the Geneva Convention with those boys. They really knew what fightin's all about.'

Suddenly he stopped. Jackie Conquest had begun to cry. It was a stiff soundless weeping, two tears rolling out of her large dark eyes and dripping on to her tunic before she had time to catch them, then recovering almost immediately, with that look of embarrassed fury she had shown when she had been sick on the plane. For a moment Ryderbeit hesitated. Then he stretched out and touched her hand. 'What's the matter, darling?' He sounded almost gentle.

'Nothing. Nothing at all!' She sat shaking her head violently, reaching for a handkerchief.

'Something I said?' he asked: 'Something about the Legion?'

'*La Légion*,' she repeated, in a curiously wooden voice. 'My father was a *commandant* — twenty-two years with the Legion. He killed himself in 1961 after the uprising in Algiers. He preferred to die rather than face the shame of selling out to that long-nosed traitor, de Gaulle!' She sat glaring round the table, her eyes suddenly dry again and very bright. 'You see, I'm from Algérie. I was born in Oran — what we call a *pied-noir*, a "black-foot".' She gave a harsh laugh, her eyes grown wild now, and Murray wondered whether she were slightly drunk, or perhaps suffering from delayed shock. 'You don't have to tell me anything about *La Légion*!' she went on; and Ryderbeit leaned over and refilled her glass. He was looking faintly confused. At the end of the table No-Entry Jones watched and listened behind his dark glasses. Murray felt a certain grateful confidence in him, sitting there still and quiet, and dead sober over a bottle of mineral water.

As for Jackie Conquest, her outburst had explained everything. The bold Mediterranean beauty, the unflinching devil-may-care attitude with which she'd boarded the C 46 — and now this sudden passion about her dead father, lost son of a lost empire. For after the final collapse in Algeria, it was not hard to see why she had fallen for marrying an American. But instead of the Great Society, she had found herself back in the wreckage of France's previous colonial disaster, living in the claustrophobic squalor of an American Saigon. The only mystery was how she managed to be there at all. Wives of U.S. personnel were rare in Vietnam. Murray wondered how old Maxwell had swung it? Or how his wife had stuck it? Perhaps it was simply because she had nowhere else to go. For a girl reared since childhood on the beaches and boulevards of French Algeria, to have to resign herself, still in her twenties, to become a grass-widow of the CIA — inhabiting some neat little American suburb among the lawn sprinklers and two-car garages, bumping trolleys with the permed housewives in the local supermarket — must have been a dismal prospect indeed.

Ryderbeit was tossing more bourbon-soaked morsels to the fish — one of whom to his annoyance appeared to be stirring to life again — and was now telling about his ill-fated adventure in Europe. 'I tried to sell an aircraft carrier in Genoa to the Syrians. Just imagine a Jew selling arms to the Arabs!'

Murry smiled bleakly: in Ryderbeit's case he had no trouble imagining it at all. 'What sort of carrier was it?' he asked.

'One o' the big Yank jobs. Beautiful deal. I had it goin' for only forty million bucks, on a two and a half per cent commission. Trouble was, y'see, the bloody carrier didn't exist. I was sweatin', I can tell yer — on speed-and-stress pills for a whole month until the deal fell through. Only that's the last one that does fall through for Samuel D. Ryderbeit. The very last.' His eyes, with their ugly glare at the edges, swivelled round and met Murray's, holding them with a slow leer.

Murray did not look away; he remembered, through the miasma of bourbon, that back in the plane, before the final crisis, Ryderbeit had promised that they would talk more about their 'business proposition'. How much, he thought again, did the man really know? How much had Finlayson told him, before arranging to have him contacted through Luke Williams? And supposing Finlayson had told him everything — as much as he knew himself from Pol — how much was Ryderbeit to be trusted?

Murray was feeling almost too drowsy to care. No-Entry had gone to sleep again, and Ryderbeit was regaling Jackie with more tales of adventure — this time in South America where he'd got a job catching snakes. If Murray had been more alert he would have read the danger signals in Jackie's dark brooding stare. Her expression was not just one of dislike for Ryderbeit, but of deep, uncompromising, contemptuous loathing. But the Rhodesian — with less than two inches left in the bourbon bottle — seemed blissfully innocent of her reactions. Perhaps the knowledge that she was a Daughter of the Legion had blinded him to her more sensitive emotions. She would not quickly forget that coarse, evocative threat to thrash her — and she was not going to let him forget it either.

He was now telling her: 'I used to sell 'em for two dollars apiece — not for their skins but their meat, which was canned as cocktail delicacies. I'd creep up behind the little bastards and snatch 'em up by their tails, then crack 'em like whips so their heads came off.'

Jackie Conquest interrupted: 'May I ask you a question, Mr Ryderbeit?'

'Anything you like, darling — providin' it's not hush-hush stuff for old Maxwell.'

Jackie stubbed out the cigarette she had just lit, and from the fixed look in her eyes Murray knew there was going to be trouble. 'Mr Ryderbeit —'

'Sammy to my friends, darling!' He emptied his glass, still oblivious.

'Mister Ryderbeit, are you a sadist?'

He looked at her dead straight, with his bloodshot cat's eyes, and said, in a dangerously soft tone: 'I don't know, Mrs Conquest. You tell me.'

Murray broke in: 'Come on, that's enough.' But she ignored him.

'If you are not a sadist, then you must be a pathological liar. A psychotic, I think they call people like you. What is your opinion?'

'Come on, that's enough!' Murray said again, feeling absurdly British and inadequate.

'Keep out o' this,' Ryderbeit said, in the same soft voice. 'This is strictly between me and the lady.' Very deliberately he poured himself another drink — the last of the bottle — and sat for several seconds squinting at the dark golden liquid, his head half turned towards the girl as though waiting to catch her next words. Then, with a smooth sweep of his hand, he emptied the entire contents into her face.

She gave a short scream and Murray hit Ryderbeit across the table. He hit him hard on the nose and mouth, feeling the skin of his knuckles split; then again very hard in the left eye, with the rage rising uncontrollably within him as he looked into the girl's face, wet and white with fury — springing round the table and trying to strike him again, a final blow on the jaw to silence the drunken lout, but instead the thin figure of Jones loomed in front of him and something collided with his head, carrying on through like the point of a spear to the back of his skull, and he went out cold.

He came to, looking at a confusion of legs — chair legs, trouser legs, legs in black suede — as he started grappling his way slowly up the side of the table, trying to mumble something, worrying about the girl, when someone hit him again — a low, nasty, calculated blow that made him think of Ryderbeit and his smashed cheek at the hands of the karate expert, Maxwell Conquest.

This time he took a lot longer to get to his feet, blinking through warm blood as he was helped down some steps past a row of foul-smelling vats of food, to be sick over a wooden parapet into a cesspool full of bubbles that were like pustules on a wet black skin, and he was sure he could hear them popping as he stood retching down at them. He had no idea how long he stayed there. He stood up at last, still heaving and blinking through blood. All in the cause of chivalry, he thought. And at the end of it all he somehow had the vacant, dismal realisation that Mrs Jackie Conquest had disappeared.

CHAPTER 2

On the steps Murray found he was still being helped, slowly and steadily, but he could not quite see who it was. Some things he saw very clearly indeed. He passed the boiling vats and saw a gibbon on a chain sitting astride a very thin cat. The gibbon looked up at him with bright button-black eyes, furtively, as though it knew it were doing something it shouldn't.

He was led up more steps, into a stone room and was sat down on a bed. It was a low double bed covered with one grey sheet, under a mosquito net that had holes in it that would not have kept out a fairly large rat. The walls were bare and peeling, and there was a rusted iron bidet and a huge armchair in the corner under the half-shuttered window.

In the armchair a man was sitting. The door closed and Murray looked up and saw No-Entry Jones. He guessed it was he who'd helped him up the steps. He looked back at the man in the armchair. He recognised Ryderbeit — but he looked different now, like a photograph of someone in a newspaper that's been badly folded. The lean satanic grace of the features was gone, oddly misshapen, and one side of his face was swollen the colour of a plum. 'Hello soldier! How d'ye feel?'

'Fine. But you look bloody awful.'

Ryderbeit tried a lopsided grin. 'You should see yerself!'

'Is there anything to drink?' said Murray: 'Something quickly medicinal?' The pigskin flask plumped on to the bed beside him.

'Help yerself. Cognac on whisky — not the best combination, but it'll have to do.'

Murray took only a sip and had to go and retch again into the bidet. When he got back to the bed he felt slightly better. 'Did you know there's a monkey downstairs trying to screw a cat in the kitchens? Seriously. I've just seen it.' He nodded at Jones by the door, feeling slightly light-headed.

'Disgusting,' said Ryderbeit. 'Throw us the brandy.'

Murray tossed the flask back, surprisingly accurately, and Ryderbeit fielded it low in the slips. 'Soldier, you're doin' fine. In a moment we can get down to serious business.'

Murray sat for a moment, breathing hard. 'Did you do this to me?' he said at last. 'I don't mean old Muhammed Ali here. I mean the second job?'

Ryderbeit nodded. 'That was me. Real mean, eh soldier?'

'Why didn't you try it on Maxwell Conquest? Why me?'

'Perhaps because you're not as good as Maxwell Conquest.'

'Perhaps not,' said Murray thoughtfully. 'Where's the girl?'

'She's gone back to the USAID office to wait for the chopper. We've still got about half-an-hour.'

'You shouldn't have thrown that drink in her face,' Murray said.

'She insulted me. You heard what she said. I don't usually waste good bourbon, even on a bitch like that.'

'That's no excuse,' Murray said lamely. 'No bloody excuse at all. I have no apologies' — remembering vaguely that he still owed his life to Ryderbeit and the Negro by the door.

'You're doin' fine, soldier. Better and better! Another nip of the hard stuff, and we'll be able to start talking turkey — as they say in the great big country across the water.'

Murray took a second, longer sip from the flask, and this time there were no ill effects. He looked at Ryderbeit, crooked-faced under the light from the window, and suddenly it didn't seem to matter anymore. Nothing mattered. Like after Huẽ when he'd got drunk at the base camp in Da Nang and insulted two Marine Colonels — hard bitter men who looked as though they wanted to use their fists in the long slack of the evening after the day's fighting — but instead had suddenly turned all reasonable, realising he had been through it too, and wanting to quieten and comfort him. That had infuriated him even more — just as Ryderbeit, all bruised and soft-voiced, was doing now. He said slowly: 'When I get you outside alone, Sammy — without your bodyguard here — I'll break your back legs!'

Ryderbeit smiled: 'We'll keep the courtesies for later, soldier. First I want to hear a little story — the one you told our mutual friend, Mr George Finlayson — who, as we both know, is an upstanding English gentleman with a responsible position with the International Monetary Fund, and is conning 'em rigid.'

'I didn't tell Finlayson anything.'

Ryderbeit spread his hands out, palms upward: 'All right, so you met some Frenchman down in Cambodia, and he told Finlayson. Correct?' Murray said nothing. A fly droned and bumped against the ceiling. 'I just want to know what Finlayson knows,' Ryderbeit went on. 'Just as you told the Frenchman, and the Frenchman told him.'

'Why don't you ask him yourself?'

'Because he won't tell me. Says it's none of his business. He's a man of honour, is our Filling-Station.'

'I should try twisting his arm. He's a big chap, but he doesn't look all that fit to me.'

Ryderbeit unscrewed the brandy flask. 'Look, soldier, I'm as patient as the next man. But we're a long way from home out here — in what the Yanks call the boondocks — and there aren't many people to shout for — unless you count Mrs Conquest and that sap of a USAID man.'

Murray stared dismally back at him. Two of them, one of me, he thought. Negro heavy by the door and the man in the chair putting a proposition backed up by an unspecified threat. He was curious to know the precise nature of the threat, and asked.

Ryderbeit chuckled: 'Murray old soldier, you went and got footless pissed just now and got into a fight. The owner saw it all — I even had to give the little bastard five thousand kips to soothe his feelings. Doesn't like his place being turned into a rough-house by a lot o' drunken round-eyes — 'specially when one of 'em damn near falls into that sewer at the back. Because if No-Entry here hadn't held you up, just as sure as Moses wasn't conceived on the Sabbath, you'd have fallen in. And you'd have had no one to blame but yerself. No one.'

'There's still Mrs Conquest.'

Ryderbeit shook his head: 'She didn't see a thing. She ran out so fast she didn't even see Jones helping you outside. That's how bloody loyal and helpful is your Mrs Bloody Conquest!'

Suddenly Murray felt very frightened. It was always possible that Ryderbeit was bluffing, and was hoping he'd talk because he'd had a few drinks and been badly knocked about — not counting the crash. But it was also quite possible that Jackie Conquest had been right: that Ryderbeit was slightly mad, a sadistic psychopath who might dump Murray in the bubbling black sewer at the back just for the hell of it. He looked helplessly at No-Entry Jones.

'Why don't you just tell us, Mr Wilde,' Jones said, in his gentle drawl. 'After all, there's no real harm done — just a few bumps and scratches. Sammy and I don't bear you no malice, and you got nothing to lose. Nothing, that is, if you tell us.'

This sounded like good sense to Murray. At least better sense than anything he himself could think of for the moment. After all, the story was sufficiently fantastic for there to be always the chance — a dangerous one perhaps — that they wouldn't believe it anyway. 'I'd like some more brandy,' he said, settling back against the bolster on the bed.

Ryderbeit tossed him back the flask. 'We've got about forty minutes, soldier. Take yer time.'

'Well, it was like this. I was in Bangkok a couple of months ago, in an R-and-R bar on the Strip down Petchburi Road, and I got talking to a young sergeant in the M.P.'s stationed in Saigon, at Tân Sơn Nhất Airport. He does regular guard duty, mostly on the main gate and the traffic complex. Then, about four months ago, he had a funny experience. He'd been posted one night to guard a hut inside the big ordnance depot there. A perfectly ordinary hut, about three times the size of this room, with no windows and a double steel door. There are hundreds of them all over the airfield — but with this one there was a difference.'

The room had become very quiet. Murray took another sip of brandy and went on. 'Just after he came on duty that night a civilian car drove up and a major got out — very flustered, he said — and asked him how many men he'd got in his detail. He said three, which was normal, and the major ordered it to be doubled. He also told him to get up on the roof and keep an extra lookout for the next three hours — till a special detail under a colonel would arrive to take whatever was in the hut out under armed guard. Well, the major went off and the sergeant climbed on to the roof, and went through.'

'How d'yer mean, through?'

'The roof collapsed. A gimcrack Vietnamese job where they'd watered down the cement. The usual story. Anyway, he just turned to me in this bar — a kid of about twenty-two who'd had a few drinks over the top — and showed me his foot. It was still in plaster after his fall. That's what had got him his R-and-R. Then he said, "You know what I fell on to?" And I said no and he said "Four feet of money."'

He paused. Neither of the other two said anything.

'I asked him what sort of money and he said greenbacks — just like that. I asked him in what denominations and he said, "All of them — fives, tens, twenties, up to C's."'

'He had time to count 'em?'

'Only a few packets. But enough to see what was inside.'

'So how did he know it was all greenbacks? Did he check it all? How was it packed?' Ryderbeit was sitting forward now, greedy and impatient.

'In packages of waterproof paper. His boot went through one of them, which was all twenties.'

'Used?'

'Used. Then he got curious, even with a broken ankle, and slit open a couple of others, and it was all good U.S. currency, mostly in high denominations — fifties and hundreds — and again mostly used.'

'He was taking a risk, this boy, opening 'em all?'

'He said some of them were torn anyway, from the roof falling in. And his fellow M.P.'s were more concerned with getting him out of the hut than checking what was inside.'

'And how much did he help himself to?'

'Nothing — so he said. There were too many other men there. And they could always have searched him.'

'Did they?'

'No. In fact he told me he was pretty sick he hadn't. The stuff was packed as thick as dictionaries and he didn't think Uncle Sam would miss just a few inches of it.'

'And how much was there?' Ryderbeit's breath was coming in short gasps, his fingers gripping his knees. 'How much?'

'Four or five tons. It had to be moved out on a forklift truck, and they loaded it on a plane that night and flew it to Guam in the Philippines. Then it was shipped back to the States. From there on it's all high finance.'

'How high? Just how much in the kitty?'

Murray stared at the ceiling. He had only the sergeant's word for it — and the gossip that had followed in the M.P.s' guardroom. 'About one billion,' he said slowly: 'With a big B. That's to say, an American billion — one thousand million in good legal Treasury bills.' He closed his eyes. 'Give or take a few million,' he added. And Ryderbeit, through his broken lips, gave a stiff laugh: 'That's very nice, soldier. Very nice indeed! Except how does this young sergeant pal o' yours know it was a billion, unless he counted it?'

'He just looked at it. He said that after a bit you get an eye for these things. Just a month before he'd been on guard one evening at the central traffic complex when a Ford panel-wagon drove up and two Treasury guards got out and told him to keep an eye on the truck while they went and got a cup of coffee from the canteen. The doors weren't even locked, and while they were away he took a look inside. The floor at the back was piled with stacks of greenbacks, all new this time, and still in their bank wrappings. When the guards came back he asked how much was there. And they told him — eight million dollars.'

Ryderbeit gave a long whistle: 'It sounds as though they got a security problem on that airfield.'

'He said they handle money like that every day of the week. And it was no more than the equivalent of one suitcase full. But in that hut there was enough for at least a hundred suitcases.'

Ryderbeit sat with his dark hooked face set back in shadow now. 'One billion,' he breathed: 'Holy Moses!' There was a long pause. 'Holy Moses in hell!' he cried, 'they'd never have that amount in the country at one given time — it's crazy!'

'Not crazy at all. They were getting rid of the stuff — what they call a "flush-out". Total currency recall. They work it in any country where there are too many Americans and too little economic stability — two things that often go together. And what certainly go together are American troops and American dollars. You can bring in all the currency regulations you want — circulate military Scrip money, make the possession of greenbacks illegal — but the greenbacks are always there.'

'Like lovely spring weeds,' Ryderbeit murmured, 'shooting up in all the wild places of the world. Flush-out — currency recall. Yeah, I've heard of it. I've even dreamed about it. Every few months you gather in all the cash from all the bank vaults and private safes in the country and ship the whole load back to the States, print the equivalent in Scrip, and hope the black market and the rackets stop.' He was leaning forward again, pressing his hands together, giving his swollen smile. 'But they never do, do they? Like the old problem of disease versus antibiotics. In Vietnam it's the same with Scrip and the black market as it is with penicillin and the clap. And you know how bad the clap's got in that poor bloody country? — so bad you hardly dare masturbate.' He began to sway back and forth as though in a rocking-chair. 'But one billion U.S.' He shook his head: 'That's too much. Too much even for my imagination.'

'Why? Just forget your home-spun venereal philosophy, Sammy, and look at some simple arithmetic. The Americans are fighting an expensive war out there. About thirty billion dollars' worth a year, on the recent average. So what's so odd about finding three per cent of that money circulating inside the country itself?'

No-Entry interrupted suddenly from his motionless place by the door. 'Mr Wilde, any G.I. serving in Vietnam who's found with even one George Washington on him goes straight to the stockade.'

Murray nodded. 'Quite so. On the other hand, in nearly two years in Vietnam I've never played in a poker school with American troops where I wasn't offered the option of being paid my winnings in greenbacks, if I asked for them. They've all got greenbacks, because outside the PX nobody's interested in anything but dollars — and that goes for everyone from the Prime Minister down to the shoe-shine boys. You know that even the B-girls down Tu Do Street won't take anything but greenbacks now — even in tips?'

Ryderbeit shook his head: 'Poor bloody soldiers. But half a million G.I.'s can't account for one billion dollars.'

'It's not the G.I.'s that have to account for it. I'm thinking of big business — U.S. construction corporations getting some of the fattest engineering contracts in history, building airfields and artificial harbours and whole new towns, all with a ten per cent kickback from the Federal Government. And those boys don't get paid in piastres or Scrip, or any other kind of Monopoly money. Then there are the other companies — French, British, Thais, Japs, Indians, Chinese, Aussies — not to mention the gold traders and opium smugglers, and those patriotic Vietnamese with numbered Swiss bank accounts, all busy making an indecent, dishonest living till the referee blows

114

the whistle in Paris and the war's over. Don't worry, there are probably more greenbacks at this moment in Vietnam than in any other part of the world, outside America itself. And as far as the U.S. Treasury's concerned, a dollar bill's a dollar bill — even a dirty one.'

'Even if Mao Tse Tung's wiped his arse on it,' Ryderbeit said, standing up suddenly and fingering his wounded face. 'But one billion — that's about four hundred million Sterling. By my reckoning one hundred and sixty times more than your Great Train Robbery. And those poor sods are rottin' away in jail for thirty years, and all they did was pick up the petty cash!' He stood in front of the half-shuttered window, staring at a corner of the hot little town outside. 'I suppose, according to the legal computer, we ought to get about five hundred years each? Under British justice, that is. Or even American justice. Only it wouldn't be American, would it?'

'I haven't consulted senior counsel on the matter. It might be a tricky point in international law.'

'And rather an important one too — if we look on the gloomy side o' things. For instance, if we were arrested here in Laos —' He turned, still stroking his jaw, but smiling now: 'You know there was a big dollar heist at Vientiane Airport about a year ago? A gang o' Frenchies grabbed three million bucks as it was bein' loaded on to one of our Air U.S.A. planes for Bangkok. But they made the mistake of not bribin' the local police and got picked up at a roadblock. They were tried by Lao law, and d'yer know what they got? Three years each, with permission to go out at weekends — providin' they don't leave town. You can sometimes see 'em drinking in the Bar des Amis. Not a bad life — considerin' half the money still hasn't been recovered. I mean, if we did get caught, it would be a help if it was out here —' He had turned back to the window, his voice trailing into thought. 'What puzzles me though, is why these Yanks are so bloody keen to ship all this money back to the States. Why don't they just burn the stuff — like Filling-Station does in his back yard?'

Murray had been worried by this too, until Charles Pol had given him the answer. 'It costs a lot of money to reissue four tons of cash — especially when it's an international currency. If it was in thousand dollar bills there wouldn't be so much problem, because they're all registered. But not fifties and hundreds. Far cheaper and easier to spare one plane and a cargo fee to San Francisco.'

'And riskier.'

'So maybe the U.S. Treasury are just mean? Sammy, you and I were both married to rich girls, and you know that rich people have funny ideas about little details. They'll think nothing of a few Rollses and Renoirs, then they go and economise on cheap sherry.'

Ryderbeit's face was still turned to the window, but his shoulders were hunched in a curious way so that Murray could see he was laughing silently. 'I like your reasoning, soldier. It's so bloody fantastic it might just be true. But what I'd like to know is how many other journalists has this Yank sergeant boy o' yours told?'

'He said I was the first journalist he'd ever met.'

'All right, so he talked to some of his mates in the Military Police, and they talked to their mates, so now it's all round town — several towns. Bangkok, Saigon, Hong Kong, Vientiane — probably even Tokyo and L.A. and the Bronx. So why haven't we heard about it before?'

Murray shrugged. 'Maybe it's classified information. Maybe he didn't talk about it.'

'He talked to you about it.'

'He'd had too much to drink.'

'And how often does he have too much to drink?'

'How would I know? Maybe he's talked about it before and nobody took much notice. Maybe they were too busy worrying about the war.'

'To hell with the war! If this sergeant wasn't just shootin' his mouth off, and there really is this kind 'o money passin' through Saigon, why hasn't some genius thought of knockin' it off before?'

'You might ask why some bright boy in Ancient Rome didn't invent gunpowder or the Greeks think of the typewriter. It's true that in Vietnam they'll steal anything and sell anything. Weapons, whisky, cigarettes, petrol, spare parts, trucks, jewellery — even furs, if they wore them out there. From time to time you may get a million dollar PX racket, or some joker like the American quartermaster down in the Delta recently who went and got a hundred grand timber contract for Army billets, and spent the lot building a string of brothels. But it's still small short-term stuff. There's a war on, and everyone in a war like this — except the motivated idealists — grabs what he can while the going's good. No one thinks of the real big time. Like selling aircraft carriers that don't exist' — he nodded deferentially at Ryderbeit, who nodded back — 'because that sort of crime is out of focus in a war, it's in the wrong league. Really big organised crime's a peacetime occupation. It needs leisure and stability. In war people just don't have time to think of it.'

Ryderbeit nodded, still gazing out of the window. 'And you're the genius who has?' He suddenly spun round, his thin strong fingers flexed at his sides, and took a step forward. 'You're a bloody conman, Murray Wilde! You're smart and full o' fancy shit, but you haven't told me one thing. Nothing but a spew o' gossip from some pissed little sergeant in a B-bar in Bangkok.'

Murray braced himself against the bolster, half watching the immobile form of No-Entry Jones by the door, preparing to deal Ryderbeit a fast kick in the groin the moment he came within range. 'So what else do you want to hear?' he asked, with feigned weariness.

'How you propose to walk on to the most heavily guarded airfield in the world and hijack a planeload of one billion dollars, without some M.P. saying "Excuse I..."'

'We'll be the M.P.'s,' Murray said quietly. 'My sergeant friend has already offered to show me round — unofficially. He's even agreed to lend me an M.P. helmet and gun and take me out to the hut where it happened. You're quite right about Tân Sơn Nhất being the most heavily guarded airfield in the world — but it's guarded against the Viet Cong, not against people like us. No Vietnamese is going to have a chance in hell of getting within a mile of that money. But that's just the beauty of the thing. They don't put the stuff in an armoured compound, which is just inviting a V.C. rocket attack or a suicide raid. They put it in some shed out in the back, and nobody bothers. As for us, a journalist or Air U.S.A. pilot can wander in and out of that airfield, just flashing his card at the gate. And dressed up as M.P.'s we can probably get right up to the plane. The only problem is finding out the exact time and place of that plane.'

'And how do we do that?' Ryderbeit still stood tensed and aggressive, but he had moved no closer.

'I'm working on it.'

'Through old George Filling-Station?' he sneered. 'Or your Frenchman down in Cambodia?'

'Perhaps — if you give them time.'

'I see. So your sergeant friend's all ready to risk his stripes smuggling you round his precinct impersonating an M.P.? That doesn't sound like any M.P. I ever heard of.'

'So perhaps he feels he owes me a few drinks. He's also got a grudge against his superior officers. When we last met I suggested a little scheme by which I and a couple of journalist friends try to stay on the airfield patrolling the perimeter after curfew — just to see how good the security is, and write it up afterwards. My friend liked the idea — thought it might make a good story, at the expense of H.Q.'

'Like hell it would. And while we're patrolling the pitch, we just happen to stop at a plane with one billion aboard and tell the crew to step down?'

'You got any better ideas?'

Ryderbeit sighed and sat down again. 'Gimme the brandy.' Murray threw it to him and he took a long drink. 'It's crazy. It's so bloody crazy it might just work. We grab the plane and get it off the ground — and then what? You think they're not goin' to have their whole air-screen up there lookin' for us?'

'That's another thing we're going to have to work on,' said Murray. 'But the Cambodian border's less than fifty miles direct flying from Saigon. They're going to have to move fast.'

'Did your sergeant mention what sort o' plane they use?'

'A Caribou.'

Ryderbeit nodded. 'Beautiful plane. With a full payload, top speed of around a hundred and eighty to two hundred knots. That's goin' to give us about fifteen minutes from take-off. And then what? We land at Phnom Penh and declare it all to Customs?'

'We fly up to Vientiane. You know the Nam Ngum dam just twelve miles north of the city?' Ryderbeit nodded. 'It's the perfect spot. About five hundred feet long, and just about wide

119

enough to take a heavy plane — with a bit of luck and a bloody good pilot. If you can land and pull up in time, there's a whole range of earth-moving machines and tip-trucks right there to shift the cargo, and bulldozers to push the plane into the reservoir. And that's the most important part. We've got to keep that plane hidden for at least forty-eight hours. And the reservoir up there looks deep and dark enough to hide it for maybe weeks.'

Ryderbeit was sitting very still. Murray knew he had his interest now, completely.

'We load up a ten-ton truck and drive it down to the airport before dawn. From then on you know the form. We swap the cargo over into rice-sacks, load them on to one of your Air U.S.A. charity flights, and take off just like we did this morning. Only we don't come back.'

Ryderbeit's face cracked into a painful grin. 'I like it, soldier. I like it a lot.' He looked round at Jones. 'What d'yer think, No-Entry?'

The Negro nodded. 'I think it has great potential, Mr Wilde.' Somewhere in the distance they heard a dull clapping noise.

'That sounds like our helicopter,' Murray murmured; but no one moved.

'So we disappear on a rollercoaster up north,' Ryderbeit said at last. 'Another crew of poor bloody Air U.S.A. boys written off without mention. Then what?'

'We're in wild country up here. Where there's not too much rule of law — to use your own words this morning. We could try a lot of things — providing we make sure the price is right. The opium trails, for instance — through Burma and down into India. With that sort of money we could buy the whole Burmese Government. How much do you think U Thant gets paid?'

Ryderbeit chuckled softly. 'Yes, I like it. More and more. I suppose your French friend's got some ideas in that line?'

'He's working on some. All you've got to worry about is flying that plane.'

'And landing it in five hundred feet. Let's just hope to hell it is a Caribou. With a plane like that I'm happy. They call it the "flying wing" — it's got so many flaps I've seen one land across the width of a runway. But if they're using something heavier —' He shook his head and looked at his watch. 'Well, children, time for the chopper.' He stood up and came across to the bed, smiling. 'No ill feelings, soldier? Because I've enjoyed our little chat. A lot more than I thought I would.' He took Murray by the arm and led him past No-Entry Jones, who held the door open for them both, closing it behind them. 'In fact,' Ryderbeit added, as they started down the stairs, 'I think we can consider ourselves in business.' He squeezed Murray's arm. 'A fifth share of one billion U.S. — that's what I call a couple o' bob to be gettin' on with!'

CHAPTER 3

They had some explaining to do at USAID headquarters, in the little water-logged French square where the rain had just started, and they were already fifteen minutes late. The helicopter had struggled all the way up from Luang Prabang to get them out, and the pilot, an elderly man with a balding crewcut, was silently furious that they were not there on time.

Their appearance did not help. Wedgwood was aghast, clearly imagining some terrible incident with the local populace with whom his job was to live in peace and harmony until his year was up. But Ryderbeit's explanation was so disingenuously true as to be totally disarming. They'd had a touch too much of Wedgwood's bourbon which had led to a slight fisticuffs in which Murray Wilde had come out the winner. (This was just plausible, since Murray's injuries were abdominal rather than facial.)

Ryderbeit was in good form. He offered his empty flask to the helicopter pilot, laughed and apologised; then offered to pay Wedgwood for the bourbon, but the American refused, with big helpless gestures. Jackie sat all the while quietly in a chair against the wall, with no more emotion than a look of boredom, and perhaps faint disgust. Murray tried once to catch her eye, but failed, and thought it better not to try again. The pilot then led the way, in single file, to the helicopter — a slim steel skeleton with a glass bubble for a face. There was still no sign of the Thais. Poor bastards, he thought. What it was to be privileged!

Later, as they whirled up through the cloud with a strange tranquillity after the poor dead C 46, he found that Jackie had taken hold of his arm. No one else noticed. Ryderbeit and Jones were slumped in deep sleep, and the pilot was intent on his instruments.

She said, 'Thank you for what you did. It was very gallant.' Then added: 'I caused you a lot of trouble, didn't I?'

'No, it doesn't matter. It was nothing serious.'

'They hurt you, didn't they?'

'Not badly.' He nodded at Ryderbeit's slouching puffed face. 'I hurt him too.'

She squeezed his arm: 'He's mad. And dangerous. They should not permit him to stay in this country. He has no principles, he is just a killer. He talks about the Foreign Legion, but he knows nothing about the Legion. Only about the worst of them, the scum of the earth — Germans and people from the east of Europe who cannot remember anything except how to kill. I despise those people. I hate them.'

Although she spoke quietly and close to his ear, the passion in her voice had an intensity that cut above the clattering roar around them. Murray kept glancing at Ryderbeit, wondering if he heard — even with his mongrel white African French. But Ryderbeit slept on —dreaming of what horrors? Murray wondered.

She kissed him, softly, bumping against him with the motion of the helicopter. 'I'm sorry,' she murmured again. 'I should have stayed.'

'There was nothing you could do.'

'But there were two of them — that Negro as well. I should have stayed.'

'No. No.' It seemed a pointless argument: she hadn't stayed, and there was nothing more to be said.

Then she surprised him: 'What were you all talking about after I left you?'

He pulled away from her, studying her solemn unsmiling face. 'Talking about?' he repeated.

'You were there so long — you must have been discussing something.'

'Just patching ourselves up. I didn't feel too good.' He tried to smile, but something must have showed.

'You look worried,' she said. 'Something is wrong.'

'Nothing.'

'You talked about something and it's worrying you.'

'*Merde!* We didn't talk about anything. We'd had a fight, that's all. A fight over you.'

She clutched him, with sudden violence, and kissed him again, her teeth touching his through her soft cold lips. He tried to swallow, his throat dry and tight. He wished to God he hadn't had that brandy. She held on to him, in the gently vibrating machine, and would not let go. There was a quiet frenzy about her now, a hint of hysteria. He tried to pull away and she murmured, in a quick whisper: 'Don't go, don't leave me!'

He didn't move; he couldn't move; if he had wanted to leave her, the only place to go was a few thousand feet down into the jungle. It occurred to him that she might have conceived some wild unreasoning passion for him. He began to grow wary. He preferred to make the running in these matters. Girls who took the first step were usually bad news — especially one who was unhappily married to an American agent.

She was still clinging to him, rocking next to him in her hammock-seat while Ryderbeit and No-Entry slept on. It was nearly five o'clock. It wouldn't be long now till they landed at Luang Prabang; and he wondered, with some apprehension, whether there would be further transport down to Vientiane that night. There was only one place to stay in the Royal Capital, a tourist hotel built by the French, and he had visions of the night ahead. Another quart of whisky scrounged from the local Americans; three men and a girl; trouble. And Maxwell Conquest was going to want to know what had happened to her.

Then another theory occurred to him, something even less comforting. Was it possible that her husband had sent her here — sent her on this rice-drop to watch him, cajole and spy on him? That these clutching hands and quiet passion were all an artifice of the Central Intelligence Agency? That Maxwell Conquest had somehow learnt something, and was anxious to find out more?

'Why did you come on this trip?' he asked her.

'I wanted to.'

'But *why*?'

'I had nothing to do, I was bored.'

He could feel her breath, warm and clear of whisky, stirring against his cheek; and he remembered her standing in the reception that first evening, her tall body in the sheath of deep-blue silk; and he hoped there would be no plane that night out of Luang Prabang.

PART 5: THE NIGHT OF SISERA

CHAPTER 1

Murray locked the door on the inside and put the key on the table by the bed. The fan from the ceiling swung with a faint clanking sound; the air was cool and the hotel quiet. It was almost dark.

He turned and looked at her. She was still standing with her back to him in front of the window, looking out across the sharp black banana leaves. The window was open and in the stillness insects went on pinging against the wire mesh. He moved across to her without switching on the light. Her face was a shadow under the black hair, her body firm and mysterious as he took hold of her arms just below the shoulders, feeling her quiver through the coarse combat-tunic. He had known how it would be the moment they began the bus ride from the airport, round the hill in the centre of the town with the little pagoda at the top, glinting in the dying sun like a golden dagger.

There had been no plane on to Vientiane — nothing until noon next day. The hotel was a shabby concrete building with a live bear in a cage in the garden and two French pilots drinking Pernod in the bar. The only other guest was a thin grey Dutchman who was in Luang Prabang compiling a dictionary of local dialects and roamed about the lobby, grumbling about there being no plug for his electric shaver. There was also no free whisky, but after a thrifty dinner Ryderbeit had got into conversation with the pilots, who bought him and Jones a bottle of rusty wine. Murray and Jackie evaded them with care, and managed an early unobtrusive escape upstairs.

He kissed her now on the neck and she said, 'Is the door locked?'

'It's locked,' he whispered, without moving his lips. 'They'll be downstairs drinking for hours, if I know Ryderbeit.'

She nodded: 'French pilots — in an empty hotel — drinking bad French wine. Don't you think it's sad?'

'Why should it be? They chose the job — they weren't conscripted.'

'Undress me,' she said, without moving.

He started on the five olive-green buttons and the tunic dropped to the floor. Her body was very dark against the white bra, which he snapped off, feeling her shiver all over now.

Smooth lean shoulders and rounded belly with the neat diagonal fold of the navel, which is the symbol of French surgery. Breasts plump and stiff-nippled as he gripped them and squeezed her to him, turning her round, feeling himself harden against her, ripping skilfully at the zip of her trousers, peeling them off her buttocks and down her long legs, thinking wildly, It's too good, too soon — the girl's crazy, I'm crazy — lying with her now on the bed, kissing the triangle of dark deep-scented hair, feeling her writhe and arch her spine, while the insects pinged and the fan swung with its slow clanking swish.

He made love to her in rhythm with the fan, until the sound was lost in her sighing and moaning, and a final long cry that carried into the night of Luang Prabang, in the jungle-heart of Laos. He lay limp and giddy, growing slowly conscious of the burning of her fingernails in his back and shoulders, remembering stories that Charles Pol had told him of these girls from French Algeria who would sit in the pavement cafes and laugh at some Moslem lying lynched at their feet. Beautiful black feet.

'Why did they call you "*pieds-noir*"?' he asked.

She whispered something he didn't catch, still holding him to her, gripping him with her thighs, trying not to let him escape out of her; and when he did, she gave another small agonised cry and her nails bit into him again, painfully this time. '*Pieds-noirs*,' she murmured: 'It was the name the Bedouins gave the first settlers who came to Algeria because of the black shoes they wore.'

They lay on top of the sheet listening to a breeze stirring the banana leaves outside the window. 'I wonder if the bear will wake us,' she said suddenly: 'Wake us with his growling?'

'It'll be more likely Ryderbeit growling.'

'*He* should be in a cage. He's a terrible man — *un affreux*.'

Murray smiled. *Les Affreux*, the Terrible Ones, had been the nickname given to the white mercenaries in the Congo. 'He isn't quite as terrible as he makes out,' he said. 'He plays the comedy a lot of the time.'

'You think so? Just because he saved our lives? *Ah!*' She made an angry gesture in the dark and sat up. 'He was saving his own life. You talk about him as though you were friends.'

Murray shrugged: 'That Negro Jones puts up with him. I don't suppose they have to fly together. Ryderbeit may be *un affreux*, but he must have some qualities.'

She leant down and kissed him, wide-mouthed, her tongue rolling luxuriously round inside his mouth. 'You have qualities,' she said at last, allowing him to breathe again. 'Magnificent qualities.'

He pulled her on to him, pressing her breasts hard against him, his hands sliding down her long back, over the soft curve of her buttocks, feeling her warm and wet between the thighs

— this strong, dark, beautifully-made *pied-noir* who belonged to him, in that moment, completely. And he thought, with uneasy satisfaction, I've cuckolded the CIA. He wished to God he could hate the CIA — that they had done him some irreparable wrong so that he could hate them as much as he could love this girl. And he realised, with a catch of misgiving, that he could love her very much.

Sometime later he asked her: 'Do you love your husband?'

'Don't talk about him. Please. Not now.'

They slept heavily after that, for several hours, before Murray woke suddenly. There was a confusion of voices outside, muffled and heavy, then a banging on the door. '*Murray Wilde, you evil bastard!*'

He sprang up, putting himself between the girl and the door. A French voice broke in, quiet and rapid; then came a crash on the door, low down as though someone had kicked it. 'Get out o' there, you sneaky copulator!' Ryderbeit yelled, hammering with both fists. 'You selfish thievin' bastard!'

One of the French voices began again, '*Alors mon vieux, vas te coucher.*' And Jones repeated, 'C'mon Sammy, let's go to bed.'

Jackie had woken too and whispered, between the hammering, 'What's happened?'

Murray stood naked in front of the door and said loudly, 'Ryderbeit, go to bed, as Jones tells you. Go to bed and shut up, or I'll set the bear on to you.'

There followed what sounded like a scuffle, then a great howl of anguish: 'I wanna talk, I wanna drink, I wanna talk t'yer Wilde, you greedy thievin' copulator! And I'm all 'lone…!' His voice receded with a shuffle of feet and muttered voices.

Murray went back to the bed. 'You're right,' he said, 'he should be in a cage — with the bear.' He lay down and kissed her on her mouth and cheek and under the ear. 'He's just drunk.'

'He knows I'm in here. How do you think he knows? He looked in my room, I suppose. He's a pig.'

'He's only drunk.'

'It's not good, if he talks — if those pilots and the Negro talk — and my husband finds out. There are no secrets in this country.'

'It'll be all right,' he whispered, without conviction. 'He probably won't even remember in the morning.'

They lay as they had slept, his arm round her shoulder and hand between her legs. Then, in the dark silence, he felt her sobbing. 'It is so humiliating! It's always the same,' she cried, 'hiding away, in dirty hotels in this dirty continent, full of dirty drunken *misérables!*'

He held her tightly, beginning to rock her like a child: 'Don't worry, just sleep. Sleep and forget.'

But he could not forget. What had she said, *always the same?* How many times the same, in how many hotels? — dirty furtive hotels in Vientiane, Bangkok, Saigon? Couldn't he take her away, rescue her from the whole ugly scene, run like hell with her? What was there to stop him? His job as a writer allowed him almost unlimited freedom of movement, his talents were not exclusive to one organisation. He could run faster and further than Maxwell Conquest.

There was nothing to stop him, except a mythical fifth of one billion U.S. dollars.

CHAPTER 2

They woke early, with the light splintering through the banana leaves outside. The fan had stopped sometime in the night and already they were beginning to sweat. They did not speak at all as they came together again, with a steady synchronised passion that left them drained and happy, sweating freely now, their minds still empty of the hard realities ahead. Ryderbeit and Jones. The plane at noon. Vientiane and the mean-mouthed husband in the CIA.

They stood together under the shower and in the shafts of sunlight Murray studied her in detail, then began systematically to kiss her whole body from her mouth down to the inside of her thighs, with a deep mute passion this time, while her fingers held his head. As they stepped back into the bedroom, their skin already drying in the heat, he pressed her back across the bed, becoming suddenly greedy and desperate, because this might be the last time: there would never be another forced landing and forced night in a distant hotel behind the lines. She protested at first, feebly murmuring that she must go, it was getting late; then surrendering as totally as before — perhaps sharing his own desperation, because she must have known too, far better even than he, what the chances were — how hopeless they were. Afterwards she wept, quietly, without hysteria or embarrassment; and he could only comfort her with the promise that he would try to help her. (Help her with two hundred million dollars?)

It was crazy, of course. He should run away with her now — today, this week, before she took that plane to Saigon.

She wiped her eyes and stood up to dress. 'We must go and buy toothbrushes and dentifrice,' she said, with startling practicality. She looked at him with her large eyes and smiled: 'I'm sorry, but you taste a little bit of whisky. Only a very little, and I don't mind. Really I don't mind. I probably taste too. But we mustn't be like Ryderbeit. He must taste disgusting this morning!'

They laughed at Ryderbeit's expense, as they crept down the stairs and out of the empty lobby. The hotel was still asleep. In the main street there were a few Laotian schoolchildren on bicycles, and long-haired beggars sat in the shade of the pagoda roofs, listlessly offering their wooden bowls. Between the pagodas were long flights of steps down to the river where naked children were preparing sampans for fishing.

They found a tiny shop that sold a few Western pharmaceutical goods, alongside the more traditional healing herbs and potions. Jackie also bought a comb, and Murray a razor. Afterwards they climbed a steep shaded path to the top of the hill in the centre of the town, to the little golden-spired pagoda which had a terrace with white stone balustrades and a small ivory buddha set back in a shrine full of strong-smelling flowers. From here they could see the whole town and the great brown Mekong winding deep between the hills, past the Royal Palace, which was like a miniature French chateau with long windows and a lily pond in the garden. Then the tiny airfield with its rows of helicopters and the T 28 fighter-bombers, lined up like bumblebees; while somewhere to the north, beyond the layers of dim blue hills, was a muddy little square with a lonely American called Wedgwood and the broken body of a G 46 transport plane. It seemed very remote now, very unreal.

He stopped and looked at her carefully. 'What will happen, Jacqueline, when we get back to Vientiane?'

'I will see you perhaps.'

'It won't be easy.'

She shrugged. 'No, of course not. And I go to Saigon next week.'

He took her arm and led her back to the zigzagging steps down into the town. It was breathlessly hot, even in the still shade. Halfway down she turned to him: 'You don't want to see me again, do you? You don't want the complications. Why should you?' She started off again, walking fast now until she was almost running down the last few terraces of steps. He began to run too and almost collided with her in the steel light of the street. For a moment they walked together, out of breath and in silence. Then she said, without looking at him: 'We'll see each other in Saigon, perhaps?'

'How do you know I'm going back to Saigon?' he asked sharply.

'You have to go back — you have your work there.' She began to walk away again, briskly down the middle of the street. The few pedestrians avoided her, strolling in the margin of shade. Murray followed, but did not try to catch her up. Outside the hotel they were waylaid by a line of little girls who leapt up from their haunches, trying to sell them lengths of embroidered silk. Jackie brushed past them, but Murray was inveigled into a shrieking, giggling argument which he could not comprehend, and missed her as she entered the hotel.

When he got inside, she had already disappeared. There was only Ryderbeit, sitting alone in the restaurant, sipping a glass of milky liquid. He looked up at Murray with eyes like bruised fruit. 'Hello soldier. How are the tubes?'

Murray sat down reluctantly. 'Where are the others?'

'Sick as dogs.' He grinned through his cracked lips, his smooth greenish complexion sprouting only a fringe of black stubble. 'And how was the long night with you, Murray boy?'

A waiter in shorts and singlet came and poured Murray some coffee. 'Fine except for you. What the hell did you think you were doing?'

'Drunk. Smashed into small pieces. And how's the lovely Mrs Conquest? Playin' it pretty close there, aren't you, soldier?' He leant closer across the table, breathing the sweet aniseed odour of Pernod. 'Come on, Murray boy, credit where credit's due. If you didn't screw that lady last night, I'm a pork chop in a synagogue!'

Murray nodded into his coffee. 'What's that got to do with you?'

'Trouble, that's what. If we want to set up an operation like ours, and you go and screw the wife of a high Yank Intelligence officer, you're asking for trouble. For all of us.'

Murray began to stand up. 'Forget it,' he said. 'Forget it, I'm tired.'

'I bet you're tired. But don't forget it. Just work on it. Work on it hard, soldier — because if my reckoning's right, you're on to a good thing.'

'I don't follow you.'

'Don't you? Sit down. Sit down and finish your coffee.' Murray sat down. 'Let's talk about little Jackie Conquest.'

'Like hell we will.'

'Not about what she's like in the sack — though I can't say I'm not curious, and just a little envious. I mean, what she does *out* o' the sack.'

'What does that mean?'

'Her job.'

'She doesn't have a job.'

'Not in Laos, maybe. But back in Saigon she does — or did before they posted Maxwell temporarily up here. I knew there was something else about that girl. She used to be quite a high-powered secretary with MACV. In fact, I heard talk that she was a kind of personal assistant and Girl Friday to General Greene himself.'

'Greene?'

'That's the joker. Virgil Luther Greene, one-star Army general in charge of what is laughingly called the Saigon Precinct. Which includes Tân Sơn Nhất Airport. You beginning to read me?'

'How do you know all this?

'I just remembered. There was a lot o' sneaky gossip about it — how Virgil was hirin' a French bint and knockin' her off on the quiet. Though I didn't entirely believe it.'

'Why not? You believed it of me.'

'Ah but you're a swordsman, soldier. Virgil Greene's maybe one of the last shooting generals — believes in zappin' Charlie Cong personally from his own private chopper, usin' it like a howdah in the good old days of the Raj — though he's reputed to be not so hot between the sheets.'

'So what's this got to do with Mrs Conquest?'

'Just this. If she's still got that job, she most likely has access to the General's office, which is in the heartland of the Tân Sơn Nhất complex. In there, they've got closed circuit TV, two-way radio, alarm systems — the whole security shoot wired up direct to that one little room. And in there, if we're really lucky, sits the lovely Mrs Conquest. Reading me, soldier?'

'Not entirely.'

Ryderbeit frowned into the dregs of his glass. 'You're being dull, Murray boy.'

'I feel dull. Enlighten me.'

'Well, in my more sober thoughts this morning I've been workin' on one of the little problems that lie ahead. Now supposin' we get on to that Saigon airfield in one piece and manage to seize the plane and get it airborne. As you said, it's a pretty short run into Cambodia — not more than fifteen minutes. But these Yanks are goin' to get pretty wet around the crotch when they find they've lost a fair little slice of their Federal Reserve. So what we need is something to keep 'em busy for a few minutes. A little diversion.'

Murray nodded. 'If they send up fighters after us we're not going to last five minutes — let alone fifteen. Then there's always the danger they'll chase us into Cambodia and risk violating neutral airspace.'

'That's a gamble we'll have to take, as well as them. But what I've been thinking of is something nice and simple. Like a full Red Alert.'

'A Red Alert! But that'll have every plane on the field in the air?'

'Exactly. But they won't be after us — they'll be spottin' for a full-scale V.C. attack. And if I know the drill, the moment an alert like that goes out, it'll be followed by several minutes o' beautiful, organised chaos. Three or four thousand men grabbin' up guns and pullin' on boots and foldin' poker hands, while the sirens start up and the fighter pilots make for their planes. So what's wrong with a few more men runnin' out to that rich little transport plane and tellin' the crew to step down because the flight's postponed?'

Murray smiled. 'And you think Jackie Conquest can get into Virgil Greene's office and send that Alert?'

'She'll have to, won't she? Otherwise we're not goin' to stand a virgin's chance in a nuclear sub. You just sleep on it, soldier!

We've got to get the whole local U.S. and Arvin units thinking there's a serious V.C. Tet-style offensive taking place against Tân Sơn Nhất — and goin' on thinkin' it for at least those fifteen minutes. Then, when they've found out the plane's gone, there'll be another fifteen minutes confusion tryin' to decide whether it was the scheduled flight after all, or maybe the plane's been hidden for extra security. And even when they find out the truth, and the shit hits the fan, they've still got to work out which way their one billion has gone. And after about another thirty minutes, when the radar's picked us up over Cambodia, then poor old Virgil's hair starts turning white, and a few hours later he's in the padded cell.'

'And what happens to Jacqueline Conquest?'

Ryderbeit stared thoughtfully at his fingernails, which were immaculately kept, cut to the quick. 'She sends the alert and comes out after us. She must have every kind of pass that's needed on that airport. She has her own official car — she just drives out across the apron and gets on to the plane.'

'And you think she'll do it?'

'For love or money she will. And to be on the safe side we'd better see she does it for both.'

Murray nodded: 'All nice and cold-blooded. And supposing she still doesn't want to play?'

'Well, you'll just have to try bloody hard and see that she does. But for the moment it's not Mrs Conquest who worries me so much. It's what we do when we're clear of the dam and Wattay Airport, and on that rollercoaster up here again over North Laos. You mentioned you might have some ideas — and I don't mean gettin' that little bee-lipped bastard U Thant on our payroll, or anything jokey like that. I mean a serious business proposition.'

Murray shook his head. 'Not now, Sammy. First I have to confer with my business associates. You and Jones may have muscled in, but you're not the only ones.'

Ryderbeit gave his crooked smile: 'Still don't trust me?'

'Would you respect me if I did?'

'True. But for nearly a hundred million pounds Sterling each — who's going to start squabblin' over that?'

'The rich are greedy and mean, Sammy. We both know that. Certainly I've got some ideas, but I'm not giving them all to you now — not over a breakfast of Pernod on our second morning.' He stood up. 'First I'm going to have a shave.'

'You came all prepared for a stopover?'

Murray shrugged: 'Mrs Conquest and I went out and did the necessary shopping this morning while you were still in your pit. She's a practical married woman.'

Ryderbeit leered: 'This morning! A bit late, weren't you?'

'You're a dirty-minded aviator, Sammy. Just toothbrushes and a razor. And I don't want a single bloody word out of you, drunk or sober, when she comes down.'

'Not a bleep, soldier. Now you just run upstairs and get on with the good work!'

CHAPTER 3

The plane back to Vientiane was a DC 3 of the national airline and departed, amazingly, on time. It was only half full, mostly of sleeping Royal Lao officers and three gun-metal cases with stencilled lettering: HANDLE WITH EXTREME CARE.

Jackie Conquest, who had emerged from her room only minutes before the bus arrived for the airport, slept throughout the flight. Since coming down she had treated Murray with a studied indifference which he found perplexing and faintly ominous. In his experience adultery usually made women conspiratorial or flauntingly reckless. Mrs Conquest was being neither.

Ryderbeit and No-Entry Jones sat together near the tail of the aircraft, talking quietly; Murray still found their relationship obscure. Ryderbeit was comparatively simple: a free-booting, blood-thirsty boaster who could no doubt be dangerous — though probably not as dangerous as Jackie Conquest made out. But the quiet grey Negro was an enigma; Murray decided he must find out a great deal more about him before he committed him to Pol and the full plan.

They landed near the little air terminal with the balcony and the clocktower. This time there was no plimsolled policeman to meet them. The reception committee consisted of three Americans. Two of them were in dungarees, waiting with a trailer-truck; one jumped aboard and began handing down the three gun-metal cases, which appeared mysteriously light. The third man, in a grey suit with knife-edged creases and a narrow tartan tie, was Maxwell Conquest.

Murray felt no alarm. He realised that it would have been very odd if a husband had not come to meet his wife after she'd survived a crash-landing. But he would also have expected the man to look pleased or relieved. Maxwell Conquest looked indifferent.

He stood quite still on the tarmac waiting for them to come down the steps. His wife went first and he said something quickly to her, but she just shrugged, and Conquest turned back and looked at Ryderbeit.

'Mr Ryderbeit. I hear you lost your plane up at Phongsaly.'

'That's right, Mr Conquest. And I bloody nearly lost your wife and all the passengers with it. This airline of yours ought to abide a bit more by IATA rules.'

'It happened yesterday morning. Why wasn't I informed until today?'

'How should I know? I don't run the CIA.'

'My wife was on board your aircraft, Mr Ryderbeit. That made you personally responsible for her safety. I got a report this morning that you were heli-lifted out of Phongsaly to Luang Prabang yesterday afternoon. Why didn't you come on back to Vientiane?'

'Because there was no plane, and you know it.'

'If I'd been informed, I could have arranged the necessary transport. Why wasn't I informed?'

Throughout this exchange no one moved. Jackie Conquest stood beside her husband, looking bored. Conquest's eyes were like chips of dirty ice. 'I repeat, why was I not informed last night, Mr Ryderbeit?'

Ryderbeit laughed: 'Look, I'm not one of your bloody spooks and I don't carry a walkie-talkie tucked in my crutch. How could I inform you unless —?'

Conquest cut him short: 'I will not tolerate that kind of language in front of my wife, or any other woman for that matter, Mr Ryderbeit!' He took a step forward until they were within sparring range. 'I repeat again, why was I not informed last night that you were in Luang Prabang?'

Ryderbeit flung out his hands and said wearily: 'So why the hell didn't your USAID man up in Phongsaly inform you? You boys run this bloody country, not me. I'm just the hired help.'

'Not for much longer you won't be, Mr Ryderbeit.' Conquest's face had turned the colour of impure wax. 'You know damn well there's a USAID office in Luang Prabang. They could have radioed us here and we could have had you all back before dark.' He turned suddenly to his wife, his face tight with rage: and in that one glance Murray understood. Ryderbeit might have known about the USAID office, but had been in no hurry to get back, preferring a boozy evening with the French pilots. On the other hand, Jacqueline would almost certainly have known too — which could only mean that she had been in no hurry either to get back to Vientiane by nightfall.

Murray now acted, not out of any sense of honour because the Rhodesian was in the firing-line, but simply to intervene before Ryderbeit lost his temper. Whatever Maxwell Conquest might suspect about the lost night in Luang Prabang, he clearly had Ryderbeit in his sights, not Murray.

'Mr Conquest,' he said, stepping between them, 'I don't think you quite appreciate what happened yesterday. I mean, you should try bringing down your plane on one engine through a high mountain pass in a heavy storm and make a successful forced landing in a paddy field. By some miracle no-one was hurt. But we were all just a little shaken up — you'll understand that, won't you? You'll understand that when we got to Prabang, we didn't go racing off to the second USAID office in one day, we went to the hotel and got our heads down. So if anybody's going to get the big stick over this it should be the Air U.S.A. traffic controller who sent up a clapped-out C 46 into an electrical storm with a faulty port engine. Anyway, your wife's alive and well, Mr Conquest — and for my money there isn't one other pilot or navigator in ten thousand who could have brought that off.'

Conquest stood listening with a dull stare. 'Are you an aviator too, Mr Wilde?'

'No, but I can make a damn good witness.'

Conquest nodded. 'Excuse me.' He took his wife's arm and without another word turned her smartly away to a side-door in the terminal building. She and Murray had not even exchanged a parting glance. Murray watched her for a moment, then began to walk with Ryderbeit and Jones towards the main Arrivals door. There was to be no V.I.P. treatment for them; even internal passengers from the Royal Capital had to be checked through Immigration. Laos was a country at war, he remembered, as Ryderbeit said: 'That bastard didn't look sweet, did he?'

Murray shrugged: 'Maybe he loves his wife?'

'He sure doesn't love me,' Ryderbeit said, kicking one of the baggage-touts in the entrance hall. 'Anyway, thanks for the recommendation. I may need to quote you on my accident report.'

'Thank you too, Mr Wilde,' said No-Entry Jones: 'It's of especial help, when you lose a plane, to have a friendly, independent witness.'

'Friendly!' said Murray, smiling wryly as he waved at one of the Toyota taxis outside. 'You mean that friendly little afternoon we passed yesterday, Mr Jones?'

'I am sorry about that,' said Jones, 'but I hope it will prove beneficial in the long run.' He declined the taxi. 'I have to check in with Control. You coming, Sammy?'

Ryderbeit winced. 'What the hell for — I've had the push, haven't I? I need a drink.'

'You haven't really got the sack?' Murray said, as the taxi swung out on to the dusty highway into Vientiane. 'Conquest can't have that much influence?'

'Conquest is CIA, and CIA is Air U.S.A., and the name of Samuel David Ryderbeit is getting to be international bad news by now. It's not just Conquest, anyway. There's a whole load of other things catchin' up. That aircraft-carrier business, for instance. A lot of people got very unhappy about that.

'It's a funny thing,' he added, staring glumly at the streams of bicycles outside: 'Try sellin' a perfectly good watch to a stranger in the street, and he won't touch it. But just mention some bloody great carrier and you get every arms merchant in Europe offerin' you air-tickets to Geneva to start discussions. That's another funny thing — always Geneva.' He turned suddenly: 'Is it going to be like that with us, soldier? A planeload o' greenbacks and a lot o' nice serious gentlemen in dark suits and homburgs meetin' us at Geneva airport to discuss terms?' For the first time since they had met, Ryderbeit sounded subdued, almost sad.

'You getting sacked just now's been a great help,' Murray said brutally. 'Couldn't you have tried to smooth Conquest down? You're the hero, remember — you saved his wife's life, not me. I'm just the one who spent the night with her.'

Ryderbeit sat stroking his hairless chin. 'Yeah. She looked pretty uptight this morning, didn't she? I just wonder what young Maxwell'll do if he finds out?'

'What the hell can he do? Sue me for enticement through the Saigon courts?'

'He could try and get you run out of Vietnam. At least, that would be the more official line — the State Department way of doing it. Only we're not quite under State Department jurisdiction here, so he might try to play dirty. They have a nasty habit in Vietnam of rewarding adultery by cutting off the offending member. It depends on whether Maxwell's one of the Ivy League or not. I suspect not.'

Murray nodded. 'And all in the interests of getting his wife to send a Red Alert on Saigon airport. It looks as though I'm getting to become a different sort of hero.'

The taxi had pulled up outside the Hotel des Amis.

The girl behind the bar handed Murray another vellum envelope in which this time was a sheet of paper with the copper-plate heading:

FOREIGN AID RESERVE CONTROL
ROYAUME DU LAOS
Georges Finlayson, Directeur

Underneath, in ballpoint, was scrawled, 'Be at the White Rose at 8 tonight. Yrs G.F.'

Ryderbeit leant across and read it over his shoulder, laughing: 'Ah, he's a naughty lad, is our Filling-Station! That place, the "White Rose", is the dirtiest knockin' shop in Asia — the girls there are like tins o' worms with outboard motors! Still, you won't catch any CIA boys in there.'

Murray ordered two beers. 'Tell me about Jones,' he said.

'Jones?'

'How do you come to be flying with him? A bloody kaffir, as you call him. Or small-part kaffir — it doesn't matter. He still doesn't fit in.'

'He's the best navigator there ever was. And don't let any of those other Air U.S.A. bums tell you otherwise.'

'You like him?'

'Sure. I'm broadminded, see. And No-Entry's a good man. I'd stake my life on him — I do most times I go up with him on one o' those rollercoasters.'

'You trust him?'

'Absolutely.'

'What's his background?'

Ryderbeit drank half his beer in one long swallow. 'Background? Ralph Jones, learnt his navigating in Flying Fortresses and his manners in Virginia — the hard way. I think he once washed dishes in a bar in Richmond. He used to box too — middleweight champion for his unit in Germany. When he left the Air Force he did a whole list of jobs. His last one was disc jockey for some radio station in Miami.'

'What brought him out here?'

'Prejudice. Boredom. And money. A couple o' hundred a week with tax doesn't go too far in Florida — even when the most expensive places are barred to you. Anyway, No-Entry's a pro — he didn't want to waste his talents sittin' around in a sound-proof studio playin' late-night M.C. to a lot o' teenagers jerkin' themselves off in the back o' their daddies' cars. I mean, Jones has a certain professional pride. You follow me?'

'Partly. What I don't follow is how Jones puts up with you. Does he have any racial pride as well?'

'He has a certain sense of humour, soldier. He thinks I'm amusing. He once told me that a white African Jew and a

Welsh-American Negro adds up to quits. We've never discussed the matter since.'

'Does he have a criminal record?'

Ryderbeit's head snapped round, his eyes bright even in the dimness of the bar. 'What d'yer mean?'

'Just what I said. Does Jones have a criminal record? Something extra that encouraged him to get out of the States, and can be traced back?'

Ryderbeit sat hunched across the bar, picking his teeth. 'He once killed a man. In Karlsruhe in forty-five. He was with a flaxen-haired Gretchen in an off-limits beerhall, and a gang o' Krauts jumped him. Four of 'em had the sense to run, but the fifth tried to represent the master-race single-handed. No-Entry hit him somewhere rather sensitive just behind the ear and dropped him dead.'

'What happened?'

'Not much. In those days you could do pretty well what you liked to Krauts and get away with it. He was court-martialled on a manslaughter charge and got off with a severe reprimand. But they also shipped him back to the States where the odds weren't quite so loaded in his favour.'

'That the lot?'

'Otherwise clean.'

'As far as you know?'

'I'd know. Jones and I don't have secrets.'

'And what about you, Sammy? How's your record — apart from the aircraft-carrier?'

'Lousy. Bigamy in South America, but they'd have a problem tryin' to prove it. And the Congo doesn't count.'

'What about here — Thailand and Vietnam?'

'Clean as a nun's knickers.'

'Anything on the FBI or CIA files — apart from Conquest?'

He shook his head. 'They wouldn't have hired me if there had been. But why all the interest?'

'I should have thought that would be obvious enough. If we bring off this heist, and manage to hide that plane, there's going to be the biggest world-wide manhunt since the Creation. And the first people they're going to check on are the boys with records. A first-class pilot who's just had the sack from Air U.S.A. would be a pretty high priority.'

Ryderbeit laughed: 'But by then it would be too late, soldier. All I need to do is get on that Tân Sơn Nhất airfield, Saigon. After that I just vanish. I've done it before, I can do it again. Samuel David Ryderbeit, the Vanishing Jew.'

Murray nodded: 'And how long is this job going to last now?'

Ryderbeit looked at his watch, then threw some money across at the girl. 'We're on a six-month contract. I'm still part of the outfit, even if they stop me flying. So as long as the next flush-out comes within the next six months, I can still walk on to that airfield any time I like.' He slapped Murray on the back. 'Cheer up, soldier! I may be your weak link, but you're not goin' to find anybody better. See you at the "White Rose" at eight.'

'You think you're invited?'

'It's not a London club, y'know — you don't have to be a member to get in. See you, Murray boy!' — and he strolled out into the sunlight.

CHAPTER 4

There was nothing pretentious about the 'White Rose'. A two-storey wood-frame house with a bamboo frontage and a strong smell of drains. Murray pushed past the *cyclo* drivers, through a bead curtain into a square dark room with tables round the walls, divided by low wooden partitions. The only light came from a couple of blue bulbs which had the effect of illuminating only those objects that were white — teeth, tiny triangular pants, the tops of white socks which are the hallmark of U.S. civvies in South-East Asia.

There appeared to be a large number of girls in the room, most of them in varying degrees of undress. A jukebox was playing an unintelligible song and the smell of drains was replaced by sour cigars and insecticide. The main action was taking place in the centre of the room, where a huge American, wearing only his trousers and vest, had measured his length on the floor and lay groaning under a crowd of giggling girls who struggled helplessly to haul him to his feet.

Small hands were already grabbing at Murray's arms and thighs, and little voices called up through the dark, 'You number-one boy, you wanna massage?' It was some minutes past eight and he was peering about for Ryderbeit and Finlayson, when another voice, close beside him, cried: 'Murray Wilde — well I never!'

He swung round. The little man was leaning against the end of one of the partitions, his hands thrust down the pants of two girls who were otherwise naked. His pebble-glasses stared up at Murray under the blue light like dull metal knobs. 'Surprised to see you alive,' he said, swaying forward and steadying himself against the pair of little buttocks on either side. 'Heard you made a forced landing up north yesterday? Phongsaly, wasn't it? Must have been tricky.'

Murray nodded. 'How are you, Hamish? Come here often?'

Napper chuckled, his lips loose and wet: 'Twice a week. Can't get too slow at my age. How 'bout you? Mixing work with pleasure, eh?'

Murray frowned. He found Napper's presence faintly disquieting. He began glancing round again for Ryderbeit and Finlayson; and this time, beyond the scrum of girls who had now got the American into an upright position, he saw Ryderbeit at a table in the far corner sitting with a shadowy figure he could not recognise.

'Looking for somebody?' said Napper: 'Friend or foe?'

'Nobody. Be seeing you, Hamish.'

'Go careful!' the little man cried, still gripping the girls' bottoms and grinning beatifically now: 'No more crash-landings. Might hurt yourself next time.' Murray began to cross the floor, knowing that Napper was watching him: round the American who seemed to have had a relapse, his cropped head sunk between his knees, bawling dismally, 'I weigh two hundred and fifty pounds without a hard-on!'

Ryderbeit was lying back along the partition bench, wearing a cream slub-silk jacket over his black shirt. His companion was one of the house-girls sitting astride his knee, wearing nothing.

'Hello there, soldier! Filling-Station with you?'

'No. He's not here?'

'Not yet,' said Ryderbeit, patting the little brown belly on his lap. 'Sit down and order yourself a girl.' But one had already perched herself against Murray's hip and began listlessly fluttering her fingers between his legs. He brushed her away, saying: 'You know Hamish Napper? — works with the British Embassy?'

Ryderbeit nodded. 'Old fellah who smokes.'

'He's over by the door. And he knows about our crash yesterday.'

'So what?'

'He's with the Political Section, that's what. Intelligence — D.I.5. I thought Air U.S.A. weren't too keen to publicise their failures?'

Ryderbeit shrugged: 'Damn right they're not. But in a place like this' — he began patting his girl's rump as she wriggled further up his thighs — 'you don't keep any secret for long out here.'

'There'd better be one that is kept,' Murray muttered, watching Ryderbeit's girl writhing with routine enthusiasm. Her companion took the cue and nimbly unzipped Murray's trousers. He zipped them up again and Ryderbeit laughed: 'Shy, soldier?'

'I thought this was going to be a business meeting with Finlayson?'

'Business with pleasure,' Ryderbeit said, pinching the pair of nipples in front of him. 'By the way, I had an interesting afternoon. Took a little trip up to that dam o' yours. Pretty spooky place.'

Murray glanced at the two girls. 'Can they understand what we're saying?'

'Sure, they both got Ph.D.'s in English Lit. Haven't you, darling!' he cried, giving his girl a sharp smack on the buttocks that made her squeal. 'You're being over-sensitive, Murray boy. Relax.'

Murray looked round the room again. Still no sign of Finlayson, although it was now nearly half-past eight. 'So what do you think of the dam? Could you make a landing on it?'

'For one billion greenbacks I could! Though I don't say it's goin' to be a nice easy pitch. Especially in the dark, with no radar. The length's about all right — always providin' she's a Caribou. But the width's nasty. It's not the curve I mind — that could even be a help, if I bring her down on a left torque, featherin' the port engine just before touch-down, which means correctin' a slight drift to the left. But even with a Caribou, I'm not goin' to have more than a couple o' feet to spare on each side. We'll have to have strong flares — Finlayson can arrange that — and somehow we've got to fix that bum overseer, Donovan. He's a nosey bastard, said I was the second person coinin' up for a snoop round in three days.'

'A few thousand dollars should square him.'

'It's not the money that's the problem — it's havin' an extra person in on the know. Personally, I'd be in favour of disposing of Mister Donovan as quietly as possible.'

Murray peered at him through the half-light. How did you rate a man's life against a billion dollars? Even a dull broken life like Tom Donovan's? The second girl was crooning in his ear: 'You wanna whisky, Johnny?'

'Beer,' said Murray. Across the room the drunk American was being dragged by two compatriots towards the door where Hamish Napper still stood propped immobile between his two half-naked acolytes. 'Our friend Finlayson's taking his time,' he murmured.

'Not like him at all,' said Ryderbeit. 'He's reputed to be the last punctual man left in Laos.'

Murray's girl came back with his beer, looking plump and bad-tempered. 'Five hundred kip,' she said, without sitting down. He paid her, looking hard at Ryderbeit.

'If we're going to start talking about murdering people, you can count me out, Sammy.'

'Now, now, soldier, nobody said anythin' about murder. Nothin' specific, that is. Just a gentle hint. Because for a share of one billion you can't expect it's goin' to be all kid gloves and satin slippers, can yer?' He stood up suddenly, toppling the girl off his thighs like a doll. 'If Filling-Station's goin' to keep us waiting, I'm goin' to enjoy myself.' He started to walk round the table, leading the girl who reached no higher than his waist, then paused, leering back round the partition. 'What about you? Blown yer head o' steam with that lovely French round-eye, I s'pose — you lucky bastard!'

Murray watched them disappear together through a curtain at the back of the room. His own girl began murmuring about the price of a massage, but when he shook his head a third time, she walked away. He made his beer last ten minutes. When it was finished there was still no sign of Finlayson. He got up and crossed to the door. Hamish Napper had disappeared — whether outside or through the back, Murray had not seen. There was no telling how long Ryderbeit took to be pleasured; and the atmosphere in the room was stifling, making his eyes smart. He wanted fresh air, and time to think. It had been naive, he realised, to have assumed that Ryderbeit's talents could be purchased merely with the promise of money. The man's experience had probably convinced him that a plan on this scale was not complete — or at least not adequately insured — without the odd necessary killing.

He began to walk down towards the river, shaking off the egregious *cyclo-pousses*, thinking now of Jacqueline Conquest.

She had left him with a Saigon telephone number on the U.S. military exchange *Tiger*. As for her last week in Laos, she had told him only that she might contact him at the hotel. It had all sounded uncompromisingly vague. Perhaps she too was taking refuge in the fear of complications, the memory of a spontaneous, carnal, fruitless liaison.

He reached the corner of the street where there was a little French cafe with a couple of iron tables set out on the dirt pavement. There was only one person inside, besides the Laotian waiter. Hamish Napper. He stood with his back to the street, talking into a wall-telephone behind the bar; but at the moment Murray passed he turned and saw him. He spoke hurriedly into the phone and hung up, giving Murray his floppy wave. Murray went in.

'Hello again!' Napper cried. 'So your chap didn't turn up?'

'What chap?'

Napper beamed up at him: 'Thought you were waiting for someone just now?'

'I told you I wasn't,' Murray said, trying to sound offhand. He smiled, nodding carelessly at the phone: 'And what are you up to? Running out of the cat-house to tell tales?'

'Now steady on, old boy.' Napper stood wagging his bald pate: 'I'm not that bad, y'know. As a matter of fact, I was just ringing the First Secretary to say I'd be a few minutes late for his dinner party tonight. You're not going? Oh of course not — he wouldn't have known you were going to be here, would he? Well, sorry we haven't time for a drink.' He started towards the door, then turned, with a suddenly sober, set expression. 'Just one thing, Mr Wilde. That Rhodesian chap you were in there with just now. You want to go careful there. He's a trifle tricky, from all I hear.'

'In what way?'

Napper shrugged lazily. 'Not the sort of chap you want to get involved with if I was you. I don't know too much about him, but from what I do — well, you know —'

'I *don't* know,' said Murray.

Napper looked at his watch. 'Can't stay talking, old chap. First Secretary'll bite my head off. It's just that while you're not actually a British subject, you do, as an Eire national, come under our diplomatic charge out here. Our responsibility, you see — if you should get into any kind of jam, that is. I was just mentioning it. Well, so long. Take care.' He crossed the room with his little shuffling hop, turning to wave from the door, then climbed into one of the *cyclo-pousses* that had followed them down from the 'White Rose'.

Murray watched him lurch out of sight, then went behind the bar to the telephone where the waiter was already pumping up a stirrup-lamp in time for the nine o'clock blackout. Murray first dialled the number at the bottom of Finlayson's notepaper. All he got was a long whine. After three attempts he tried the Bar des Amis. A girl's voice chirped at him, first in Lao, then French. No, Monsieur Georges had not called — there had been no messages for Monsieur Wilde.

Just then the lighting in the cafe failed. He tossed some notes at the waiter and hurried out, breaking into a run up the last few yards to the 'White Rose', where he ducked under the bead curtain into the candlelight, elbowing his way through the T-shirts and naked flesh to the table in the corner. Ryderbeit was back, alone with a cigar and looking sour.

'And where the hell have you been?'

'Where's Finlayson?'

'You tell me. He didn't show up, the idle bastard!' He turned a jaundiced eye on Murray and grinned: 'But I got my two thousand kips worth upstairs. These girls must have been trained by the French.'

Murray sat down. 'Now listen, Sammy. I've got a feeling that things aren't quite right.'

'Huh? Just because Filling-Station stood you up?'

'I just met Hamish Napper again up the street. He was making a phone call. It could have been nothing — he said he was ringing his First Secretary about a dinner-date. But then he warned me against you.'

'*Me*? Cheeky old bastard. What did he say? Anything nice and slanderous?'

'He told me not to get involved. Didn't say how. Any ideas?'

'Perhaps he thinks I'm bad company — doesn't want respectable journalists associating with nasty white Rhodesians with illegal passports. Bad form and all that.'

'Even worse form to have one of his flock getting involved in the biggest robbery in the world — especially if it's been planned and executed on Napper's home ground. He was warning me off, Sammy.'

'Was he high?'

'I don't think so. He also seemed to think I'd been waiting in here for someone — someone who hadn't turned up.'

'Filling-Station?'

'He didn't mention any names — except yours.'

Ryderbeit stood up. 'Let's check on old Filling-Station.'

'I've already checked. His FARC number's out of order and he's left no message at the hotel. Does he have any other number?'

'Not that I know of. He said eight sharp in his note. It's now gone nine. Let's take a little walk round.'

Finlayson's house faced on to the Mekong, about ten minutes' walk from the 'White Rose'. It was a low wooden building in the traditional Lao style, raised on stone piles for coolness and to keep out snakes and scorpions, with a wide roof like a chalet and a verandah behind windows of wire mesh. There were no lights — only a dim moon under which they could just make out the dark shape of Finlayson's Mercedes parked inside the gate. The only sound was the scream of crickets down by the river.

They pushed open the gate and walked round the car, pausing at the steps up to the verandah. 'George!' Ryderbeit shouted. There was no answer. He bounded up the steps and unlatched the verandah door. 'George?' he called again, quietly this time; then crossed to the main door and turned the handle. It opened. He and Murray stepped together into a wide dark room. 'Does he always leave his place open like this?' Murray whispered.

'He did tonight,' Ryderbeit said, snapping his lighter to a paraffin lamp on a side-table. He seemed to know his way around.

The room looked comfortable and expensive: open-plan chinoiserie, in teak and bamboo, with glass-topped coffee tables, rough silk sofas, handwoven wall-screens. Ryderbeit moved quickly across the rush-matting and threw open an inside door. There was a passage beyond with doors leading off on both sides. One was half-open. Murray had a glimpse of a bathroom as Ryderbeit put his head round the door and came out again, holding the lamp above his head. He nodded at a second door which was closed. 'Try that.'

The knob was of solid cut-glass and would not turn. Murray leaned against it and it slipped open on a ball-catch. The room was much smaller and hotter than the last. For several moments the two of them stood under the lamplight in silence. Then Murray murmured, 'Good grief,' and took a step forward.

A green filing cabinet, reaching almost to the ceiling, had been emptied, drawer by drawer, its locks wrenched open, the steel split and buckled, the floor heaped several inches deep with papers, folders, bound documents, great coils of telex tape like unrolled toilet paper. A desk lamp had been dashed to the floor, typewriter turned upside down, the desk itself cleared of everything, its drawers smashed open and spilled, the telephone ripped from the wall and lying tumbled among a stack of reference books. The one object that seemed to have escaped all damage was the telex machine in the far corner.

Murray stepped over the mounds of paper and peered down at the keyboard. The machine was dead, with the current cut off; but the last incoming message had arrived complete, timed 1750 HRS. In the wavering light from Ryderbeit's lamp Murray read: FINLAYSON *** LAOFARC *** INSTRUCT * CONFIRMATION * MORNING * FULL * INVENTORY * RE * LAZYDOG *** ENDS * BANG-FARC. He frowned, checking back along the spool for the last outgoing message. It was timed nearly three hours earlier — a routine bulletin on the dollar-kip par when the *Banque du Laos* closed that afternoon.

Ryderbeit, who had been reading it beside him, suddenly turned and reached the passage in a couple of leaping strides, stopping at the door opposite, next to the bathroom. It was shut. He kicked it open and went in at a run with the lamp swinging wild shadows round the big silent room. It was very calm and ordered after the shambles across the passage. A lightweight grey suit was folded over the back of a chair, along with a freshly laundered white shirt. Underneath was a pair of big black shoes with a flower-pattern punched into the toecaps.

The bed was set against the far wall — an enormous double bed under a high tent of mosquito-netting. The windows were closed, and with the air-conditioning cut off the room had a hot clammy smell. But there was something else too — something Murray was conscious of at once, but unable to identify. Something about that smell: something rancid, human.

Ryderbeit had stepped up to the bed, drawn back the muslin drapes, and stood looking down. Finlayson lay on his stomach, his face pressed into a blue-striped pillow. He was dressed in white pyjamas and his arms were drawn up at his sides, the fingers sunk deep into the matching blue-stripped sheets which were soaked brown under his head and throat. Ryderbeit leant down and tugged at one of the shoulders. It stirred only slightly, as though very heavy. He tugged again, harder this time, and still the body scarcely moved. He stepped back, frowning, and felt one of the big grey feet sticking out from under the kimono. It was cold, but not yet stiff.

Murray had come closer, noticing now a very small dark hole in the centre of Finlayson's neck, just below the hairline. His first thought was that it was a bullet hole — small calibre, possibly a .22, fired point-blank while Finlayson lay asleep. That would account for the bleeding under the throat. Then he noticed that there was no trace of scorching and the hairs at the back of his neck were quite unsinged. A heavier calibre, he wondered, fired from a few feet and throwing Finlayson face down on the bed?

Ryderbeit had grabbed the shoulder again and wrenched it back, and this time the body rolled over with a nasty tearing sound that made Murray shudder. Ryderbeit appeared unmoved. The eyes on the bed were glazed slits, the face turned mauve with the texture of greaseproof paper. He had bled heavily through the nose and mouth, and his moustache had sopped the blood up like a sponge, still tacky and glistening. In the centre of his throat was a sharp point about an inch long which had torn a slit in the sheet when Ryderbeit pulled it free. The body now lolled on its side, its teeth showing through the clotted gap between the lips. Ryderbeit held the body only a moment, then let it roll back on to its belly. 'Holy Moses,' he murmured: 'Six-inch nail, straight through the neck into the mattress. Severed the spinal cord and probably touched the windpipe. Nice oriental touch, eh?'

Murray shook his head. 'Biblical. Jael and Sisera — your Old Testament, Sammy. You ought to know that.'

Ryderbeit straightened up and stood with his head tilted to one side. 'I don't quite follow,' he said in a thin voice, almost a whisper.

'No? "Then Jael, Heber's wife, took a nail of the tent and a hammer in her hand and smote the nail into his temple..." Or something like that. One of the brighter bits of the Good Book. Only whoever this joker was went for the neck, so perhaps he wasn't a Bible-boy after all. As you said — a nice Oriental touch. Either that, or a European trying to make out it was an Oriental.'

Ryderbeit took a step forward, breathing hard. 'Just a moment, Murray boy.' He held the lamp higher, and in the raw light his eyes had a dry yellow glitter. 'I'm not that well-educated, and I'm not even a good Jew, so I can't quote chapter and verse. But as I read you, are you saying I did this?'

'You could have done. You knew his routine and the layout of the place. You also knew he had an appointment with me

160

tonight. You might even know what that appointment was about.'

Ryderbeit nodded. 'Go on.'

'Did he live alone?'

'As far as I know.'

'Servants?'

'Houseboy. And his secretary. Nice little Vietnamese number he used to knock off in the afternoons. She could have done it. Vietnamese women have some nasty habits in the *crime passionnel* line — doin' things with razors and hatpins while their lover-boys are tucked up asleep.'

'And tear his office to pieces afterwards with a crowbar?'

Ryderbeit shrugged: 'Cover-up — makin' out it was a simple break-in.'

'Heavy work, even for a Vietnamese girl.' Murray turned and walked over to the chair with the suit folded over the back. Using a handkerchief he felt inside the jacket and lifted out a fat snakeskin wallet edged with gold. The leather compartments bulged with credit cards and cash. He rifled through a sheaf of brand new 500-kip notes, a wad of well-thumbed U.S. twenty and fifty dollar bills, then tossed the load down at Ryderbeit's feet.

'And take another look at the bed, Sammy. He's still wearing his bracelet and watch — another good five hundred dollars' worth. Funny way of trying to pretend it was simple robbery. A jealous mistress might just drive a nail through his neck — and if she was really cunning she might try to cover her tracks, like pulling out the telephone so that anyone trying to contact him this evening or tomorrow morning would think the line was out of order. But that would only make sense if she was planning on an early getaway — either the ferry across to Nong Khai to catch the overnight train down to Bangkok, or the first plane out in the morning. What doesn't make any sense at all is killing him and systematically ransacking his office, but touching nothing else in the house — not even his wallet and watch. She didn't do it, Sammy. For that matter, nor did you.'

'Oh no?' Ryderbeit had leant down and was holding the wallet open in his hand.

Murray nodded at it: 'You'd have gone for the petty cash, at least. His jewellery could be traced, so you'd probably have left that — but not those nice old Andrew Jackson and General Grant jobs. Those you couldn't have resisted, could you?'

'You bastard. First you have me nailin' him down to his cot — and now I'm robbin' his bloody corpse. You must think I've got the morals of a snake's belly!' He grinned, beginning to fold the dollar bills from the wallet into his trouser pocket. 'But since I stand accused, I might as well cash in. If I don't, others will.' He counted out half the dollars, then tossed the wallet back at Murray.

'I don't want it, Sammy.'

'Take it, you scrupulous bastard! At least let's make it look like a break-in. You can always get rid of it outside.'

Murray dropped the wallet reluctantly into his jacket pocket. 'And we'd better wipe off everything we've touched.'

'What! — for the Royal bloody Lao Police? You think they'll bother with prints?'

'They will on this job. They'll call in the old French Sûreté boys who stayed on as advisers. And later the Americans'll want to check up too, because FARC's in their sphere of influence.' He glanced again at the bed and winced. 'Come on, let's get away from here!'

Outside he wiped the office doorknob, trying to remember if he'd touched anything else, while Ryderbeit wiped off the lamp, after replacing it on the table in the main room. Then he turned down the wick till they were in darkness and Murray, still using his handkerchief, opened the verandah door.

They stood outside for a moment, listening. The moon was gone and there was a dead hush all round; even the crickets seemed to have grown quiet. Murray started across the verandah on the balls of his feet, groping for the latch of the door to the steps. He found it and rested against the frame, his whole body covered in a thin oily sweat. Ryderbeit, trained with a pilot's night-sight, led the way unerringly down the steps, round the Mercedes and out of the gate. The track back into town was empty. He took Murray's arm: 'We've got to work something out, soldier — and fast! You go back the way we came, I'll take a short cut, and we'll meet at the hotel, up in your room. It'll be all right there — nobody ever notices who comes and goes in that place. Just as long as we're not seen leaving here together. What's your room number?'

'Two. First floor.'

'I know it.' His smile shone through the dark: 'See you there!' — and he vanished like a cat into the trees.

CHAPTER 5

Murray was not at all happy as he started on the short jogtrot back into Vientiane. His eyes had still not adjusted to the dark, his knees felt weak and his guts were like water. A car distantly grating gears made him jump. He blinked, trying to pick out the dim line of the track. On his right lay the river, flowing huge through the cathedral of the night, silently and very fast. On the other side were the trees, full of soft rustlings where Ryderbeit was creeping silken and sure-footed, back to their rendezvous at the hotel.

But why the hotel? Murray suddenly wondered. Didn't Ryderbeit have a place of his own? Or perhaps it wasn't that kind of meeting he'd had in mind? He broke into a run, beginning to wonder if he could have been wrong about Ryderbeit after all. Then he remembered the heavy bulge of Finlayson's wallet bumping against his hip, and he felt the panic hit him in a rush. It had all been very clever. They'd probably never find out why a respectable Irish journalist should break into an Englishman's house in Laos, nail him to his bed, strip him of a few hundred dollars, then run amok in his office and finish up floating in the Mekong. Perhaps they'd write it off against drink, drugs, the climate, a bout of madness induced by yesterday's crash.

He had the wallet in his hand, and without hesitating over whether to help himself to a few dollar bills, flung it far out into the river — not even waiting for the splash, as he headed into the trees where crashed blindly about for a few moments before coming out again with a stout shard of bamboo. He stayed for several seconds on the edge of the path, crouched forward with elbows raised, the bamboo held across his palms like a long knife, listening. But there was nothing above the din of the jungle and the soft swish of the river.

He began to run again, head down, dodging, holding the bamboo stave low, ready to jerk it up into Ryderbeit's groin the moment he was jumped. Napper had warned him less than an hour ago to keep away from Ryderbeit; yet how much did Napper know? Could he really have known that Finlayson was in danger — was even dead — and still done nothing about it?

Murray turned a bend in the track. Ahead were pricks of light between the trees. Paraffin lamps in open doorways; jangle of a transistor radio. He sprinted up a stinking village lane and suddenly came out into the main street, not thirty yards away from the Hotel des Amis.

He slowed and dropped the bamboo, feeling limp and a little ridiculous as he started across the street, into the dark bar under the red awning. A glance round showed him there was no one he knew. He walked up to the girl at the cash register and asked for his bill for the four nights, telling her he would need a taxi to the airport in the morning to catch the 8.30 flight down to Bangkok. He settled the bill in dollars — beginning to regret now that he hadn't held on to at least some of Finlayson's pocket money — as the girl handed him a lighted candle. Up in his room he opened a new bottle of Scotch, poured half a tumblerful and swallowed it straight; then he began to pack. Shaving tackle, dirty shirt, socks and underwear, notebook and half a dozen cassettes of undeveloped film. He was stuffing these carefully down the side of his grip-bag when there was a quick rap on the door. Ryderbeit came in, rubbing his hands and grinning.

'You got something to drink up here, soldier? I could do with a couple!'

'So, it wasn't me and it wasn't his mistress. Who does that leave?'

They sat facing each other on the twin beds, stripped down to their vests in the hot airless room, sharing the whisky warm and neat out of the single tumbler.

'It leaves a few of the teeming millions of South-East Asia,' Murray said at last, feeling the sweat itching down through the hairs on his chest. 'Did he have any enemies you know of? Jealous husbands? Anything political? CIA? Or the other side?'

Ryderbeit spread his hands. 'Nothing. He was just a friendly old legalised crook running his own show. Sure, he did a few deals on the side — everyone out here does, but it's all aid money so there are no real losers — except the American tax payer. Nobody disliked old Filling-Station. It doesn't make sense.'

'Unless it was a maniac, it has to make sense.'

'Yeah, but why the nail? That's really kinky.'

'Or a professional speciality. Professional killers prefer their own tools. Ice-picks were quite a favourite in the thirties and forties in the States. Trotsky was even done in with one. And a hammer and nail's not so different. Quick and neat, especially if you know your victim's going to be asleep.'

'So you think it was a hired job?'

'What does it look like? Someone who knew Finlayson's habits well enough to get in while he was having his late nap — and someone who knew what he was after. Something in the office. Some correspondence, document, notebook — but certainly not money. And probably someone from outside Laos — hence the trick of cutting the phone to give him time to get away. He was probably gambling on no one calling round tonight. And unless he took the train to Bangkok, he's almost certainly still here. Which means we ought to report it. Now.'

Ryderbeit gave a twist of a smile. 'And help the police with their inquiries? Sorry, soldier. Where the police are concerned Samuel Ryderbeit is strictly one o' the boys who walks by on the other side.'

Murray shrugged. 'If it was a real professional, they probably wouldn't spot him anyway. He may even lie low here for a few days before getting out. It's just that I feel we ought to do something for old Finlayson, instead of just washing our hands of him. After all, we're partly responsible for what happened.'

Ryderbeit's head jerked up from his drink. 'Responsible? For what?'

'For his death,' Murray said calmly, reaching for the tumbler in Ryderbeit's hands. 'He was killed because of us, Sammy — because of the operation.'

Ryderbeit brought out his cigar case and tapped a Romeo y Julieta into his palm, biting the end and spitting delicately between his feet. 'So you think he was killed because he knew too much — was planning to run to teacher and tell tales out o' school?'

'It's possible. Only it doesn't have much scope. It would give both of us a motive, as well as No-Entry and Pol. There aren't any other candidates I know of — unless you do?'

Ryderbeit sat turning the cigar slowly round in the candle flame. 'I don't know quite what you're getting at, soldier. If somebody else is interested in our little plan, why go and kill Filling-Station? He was the vital link — the one who was goin' to put the finger on the next flush-out. And he's not goin' to be much use to anyone now.'

'Precisely. That's why I think he was killed.' Murray took a long pull at the whisky. 'No Sammy, I'm thinking of another possibility. And if I'm right, we're both in bad trouble. Let's look at it from the other side. If you're someone with a special interest in stopping this operation, and you somehow get to hear about it from the Laos end, what are you going to do? You get a tip-off that a gang of Westerners are planning a huge heist of U.S. greens in Vietnam. What you also know is that part of the operation involves Laos — which is going to mean a security problem, to put it mildly — and that one of the conspirators is none other than trusty old Finlayson of FARC — which is going to be an embarrassment. You can't have him arrested because he hasn't done anything. You could perhaps try and pull some strings to get him sacked. But then maybe Finlayson can pull strings too — he has a lot of important friends here in Laos, which is one of the reasons why Pol chose him in the first place. So if you push it you may find yourself with an international crisis on your hands.

'But your alternative — if you work by the book, that is — is to sit back and pray it won't happen, at least not right here under your nose in Laos. On the other hand, you could inform Saigon and the U.S. Treasury, and let them get on with it their end. In which case,' he added, taking another gulp of whisky, 'we're blown.'

'We don't know we are,' Ryderbeit snarled.

'Probably we're not. Because again — unless they tortured Finlayson before they put the nail in — they may not know exactly what he did know. And that's important. They may not have known about the Vietnam angle at all — just that Finlayson had become bent and was going to move in on something big. So they skip the polite diplomatic courtesies and take a short cut. They arrange — in the official CIA jargon

— to have Finlayson "terminated with extreme prejudice". A little unofficial dirty work. They have him removed.'

'The CIA? Conquest and his lads?'

'It depends how seriously you take them.'

'They're serious. But how would Conquest have heard about it? Unless through his lovely little wife, who just happened to hear someone mutterin' in his sleep about one billion dollars!' He was sitting on the edge of the bed now, smiling brightly through the smoke. 'Eh soldier?'

Murray sat as relaxed as he could, watching Ryderbeit's long thin hands under the candlelight. 'She doesn't know a damned thing,' he said at last. 'And even if she did, he'd be the last person she'd tell.'

'Oh yes?'

'She doesn't like him, for a start. And as for talking in my sleep, there was no sleep.'

Ryderbeit knocked a finger of ash on to the floor, crushing it under his suede boot. 'You'd better be right, Murray boy. For your sake as well as Mrs Conquest's. As for Filling-Station — well, so it was the spooks put the nail into the poor sod. But where does that leave us?'

'Washed up. The show's over, Sammy. Let's cut our losses and clear out before they start sending little men with hammers and nails after us while we're asleep.'

'Now wait a minute. You're being selfish, soldier. You're not the only one, y'know. There's still me and Jones —'

'I'm not stopping you. I'm just passing.'

'Passing *applecrap*!' Ryderbeit roared, slamming the tumbler down on the table and dashing the candle over into darkness. 'We don't know they know anything. We can't prove a bloody thing.' He got the candle going again with his lighter, then looked across the flame with his mean, crooked smile: 'Shall I tell you what's wrong with you? You think too bloody much. There's more than one thousand million bucks sitting somewhere out there waiting for us — remember! And you're trying to funk out on some lousy half-baked hunch that Finlayson blew us. How could he? What did he have to tell them? — that some nutty scribbler's dreamt up a plan to knock off a billion of Uncle Sam's greenbacks? Don't make me laugh! You think they'd take it seriously?'

'Finlayson's dead — they're going to have to take that seriously. Besides, even if we aren't blown, we can't act without Finlayson. We can't even find out the time of the next flush-out.'

'To hell we can't! What about this Frenchman o' yours down in Cambodia? He's on the inside, isn't he — just as much as Finlayson ever was?'

Murray hesitated. The truth was, he did not quite know how far Pol was on the inside. 'All right,' he said, 'supposing you do find out, and manage to seize the plane at Tân Sơn Nhất — how are you going to get rid of the stuff? Fly it up here into Laos, transfer it to a routine rollercoaster, and then what? Sit with five tons of dollars on top of a mountain for the rest of your life, just looking at the stuff and watching it turn mouldy in the rainy season?'

Ryderbeit sat stroking his long throat. 'We'll think o' something. Fly into Burma maybe, or up to Kathmandu. Use one o' the opium trails down into India. As you said yourself, with that kind o' money you can buy a whole Government.'

'You go ahead, Sammy. You can have my films of the dam, for what they're worth, and I'll put you in touch with Pol, and with young Sergeant Wace of the U.S. Military Police. As for Mrs Conquest — well, you'll have to chat her up yourself, if you still want that Red Alert. You're on your own now.'

'And you?'

'Me? I think too much.' He grinned and poured more whisky. 'Sorry, I've got the wind up and I'm taking off — on the morning plane to Bangkok.'

'You booked?'

'No.'

'It's a crowded flight down to Bangkok. Might not be a seat.'

'Don't be so optimistic. I've learnt at least one truth as a journalist — there's no such thing as a full airplane or a full newspaper. Only don't worry, this is one frontpage story that's going to remain between just you and me, and Filling-Station's grave. Cheers!'

CHAPTER 6

The morning was damp and heavy, with a curtain of rain creeping across the fields towards the edge of the runway. Murray stood at the airport bar, past Police and Immigration Control, and risked a beer before take-off, casting a sore sleepless eye over his fellow passengers. Mostly Laotian and Thai businessmen, a couple of families, a few French traders. Nothing out of the ordinary; nothing to suggest the presence of a hired assassin. But then nothing, he remembered, was quite as you expected in the little Kingdom of Laos.

The loudspeaker was jabbering, passengers beginning to move towards the departure doors. A hostess greeted him with a brilliant smile, despite his morning stubble, and gave him his boarding card. Halfway across to the Royal Thai Airways plane a tiny old Laotian lady walking just ahead of him suddenly swayed and crumpled on to the tarmac. He went to help her, taking hold of one frail arm, then paused, astonished at her weight. Under her silk blouse and ankle-length sin she must have been wearing her 24-carat gold like a suit of chainmail. She began shrieking angrily in Lao as another old crone hurried to her aid.

Murray moved on, thinking, And the best of Lao luck to her! She'd be a rich little old lady at the end of her journey; whereas what did he have to show for his four days' trip? A few cuts and bruises, and a hangover.

A moment later the rain hit the tarmac and he began to run.

PART 6: THE FAT MAN

CHAPTER 1

'Monsieur Pol. Please.'

The eyes behind the desk slid sideways and a fine-boned man in a dark business suit moved out from a glass partition, bowing with fingers steepled under his brow in the traditional Thai greeting.

'Yes sir?'

'Charles Pol. The King Rama suite. He's expecting me.'

'Your name sir?'

'Wilde.'

'Yes sir. One moment please, Mister Wilde.' He bowed again and glided back behind the partition.

Murray spoke to the first man at the desk, leaving his canvas grip-bag with him; then stood in the big cool lobby and waited. It was crowded, mostly with American tourists — slouched grey creatures in expensive casual clothes, with that tired baffled look of people worn-out by too much leisure. Several minutes passed. He bought a copy of the *Bangkok World* and scanned the foreign news. Finlayson's death was on page one, in a boxed paragraph datelined AFP Vientiane, under the headline: *Mystery Slaying of British Banker*. The Laotian police were stepping up their hunt for the killers, believed to be bandits. But there were still no details as to how he had been killed: only that he had been murdered during the previous day at his riverside house in Vientiane.

The Thai receptionist had moved soundlessly up to him. 'Mister Wilde. Please, this way.' Murray followed him across a quarter of an acre of carpet that lapped round the soles of his shoes, up some shallow stairs past the Rama Coffee Shop and

Cocktail Lounge, shelves of gifts, magazines, jewellery, down a long cool corridor, stopping at a varnished door. 'Please sir, enter!'

Murray stepped into damp scented heat. A girl rose from behind a desk and led him over to a sheet of plate-glass, like an observation window. Inside, under stark strip lighting, sat a row of girls, all identically pretty and expressionless, in short white hospital coats. Murray pointed to the nearest one to save time, and she came out with fingertips touching, smiling as she took his hand and led him down a linoleum passage to a second door. From inside came the thump and splatter of hands on wet flesh. She was already helping him off with his jacket when a voice called through the discreet nightclub lighting: '*Ah mon cher Murray! Comment ça va?*'

'*Ça va,*' said Murray, unbuttoning his shirt. 'And you?'

'Ah, this city! Too many Americans in too many cars. I'm not used to it. *Ayee!*' he cried, as the girl over him began a rapid drumroll on the back of his thighs.

Murray looked across at the adjacent bench and could just make out a mountain of flesh lolling on its belly, all pink and shiny like a giant fresh-peeled shrimp, buttocks divided into confusing folds of fat, his huge shoulders creased down the middle like more buttocks, the whole body topped with a great egg-shaped head on which the hair grew in damp spirals, signing off with a kiss curl draped over the dome of his brow. His little goatee beard was dripping sweat steadily on to the floor.

Murray stepped out of his clothes and lay down on the bench beside Pol. Murray's girl had unfastened her coat, letting it hang open as she went to work. Like her partner she wore only a pair of navy-blue pants underneath. Murray relaxed under the tiny strong fingers which started first on his shoulders.

'You had no trouble getting in?' Pol asked: 'No complications downstairs?'

'I was kept waiting for some time at the desk,' Murray said, still speaking French, which is not widely understood in Thailand.

'*Bien*. But you had no trouble?'

'No. Why?'

The Frenchman's eyes were closed, his cherry lips parted in a half-smile as the masseuse bent over him, kneading the deep mounds in the small of his back. 'A little matter of security, that's all. This morning someone tried to kill me.'

Murray went rigid under the girl's hands. 'You're joking?'

'Joking!' Pol gave his peel of high-pitched laughter. 'My dear Murray, I have a sense of humour — but I trust not a gallows humour. I still enjoy life.'

Murray lay with a dull lump growing in his guts. 'What happened?'

'They sent me a bomb for breakfast. *Plastique* in a brandy bottle. Imagine the impudence of it.'

'You know who it was?'

'*Eh bien* —' he shrugged a shoulder like a side of beef — 'not precisely. But I have my ideas. They were professionals, for a start. The explosive was packed in a carton with the detonators primed to go off as I opened the lid. Simple, but subtle. In fact, if it hadn't been so subtle I'd be dead now. You see, they exaggerated on the details. Always a mistake — especially when the details are good. It came up beautifully wrapped, with a typed note saying "compliments of the management". And as I'm in the best suite, right up on the roof, at eighty-five dollars a day, I was only agreeably surprised — until I noticed the label. *Hine VSOP* — my favourite of the ordinary brands.' His red lips opened slyly: 'And in Bangkok of all places! I was more than surprised now — I became curious. You see, I have a nose for these things. I got a knife and slit the box open from the bottom. The wiring and detonator were an excellent job. They knew what they were doing.'

'The same people who killed Finlayson?'

'Ah! There we can only guess. And guesswork in these matters, my dear Murray, can be a dangerous occupation. What do they say in the papers — that he was killed by bandits, don't they?'

'If that's what they want to believe.' Murray glanced across at the glistening pink face on the bench beside him, wondering for a moment if Pol's tone were just a little too casual for the occasion? 'Whoever killed him was looking for something — and it wasn't money.'

'*Ah oui?*' The Frenchman had hauled himself on to one elbow, blinking through tears of sweat. 'How can you be sure?'

'I was there — I found him. And his wallet was still in his pocket, stuffed with money.'

Pol grunted and rolled on to his back. He said nothing, and for a moment there was just the smack of hands on his loose trembling breasts.

'How did they find out you were staying here?' Murray said at last.

'Oh I didn't make it a secret. Perhaps I should have done, as it's begun to turn out.'

'And who pays for the King Rama Suite?'

Pol tittered, his eyes still closed: 'My dear Murray, that's not very delicate of you!'

'Nor of you, Charles. If someone's trying to kill you, you're making it pretty easy for them.'

'So what would you have me do? Seek asylum in the French Embassy?'

'Move into another hotel.'

'And risk even less security, for less comfort? The arrangements here are as good as I'll get anywhere — unless I choose to involve the police, which I don't! The management is most discreet. Besides, I like it here. And a man must live.' He smiled luxuriously as the girl's hands crept round his groin where his genitalia sprouted beneath his Buddha belly like a second umbilical cord.

'You're not afraid?' said Murray.

'Afraid! *Ah mon cher*, the string of my life is by now so long that when I pull it, I can't feel the end.'

'You're in great danger.'

'Perhaps.'

'They'll try again.'

'We shall see.' He relaxed happily as the girl worked in vain to coax the turtle-head out of his loins. 'I shall be leaving Bangkok late this afternoon — but first we have some business to discuss. What progress have you made in Laos?'

'I found two pilots,' said Murray. 'Or rather, they found me. Through Finlayson's agency, I suspect.'

Pol nodded, still without opening his eyes. 'Americans?'

'One is a Negro — a navigator who seems about as good as they come. The other's a Rhodesian — a mad Jew who's been run out of his own country, out of South Africa, South America, and almost every other trouble-spot you can name. This is about the last place that'll have him — outside the Communist bloc.'

'Ah. Is he a man of the Left?'

'Slightly to the Left of Genghis Khan, I'd say' — and he sensed Pol wobbling with silent laughter beside him. 'He fought for Tshombe in the Congo.'

Pol's laughter went on for several seconds, while he wiped the sweat out of his eyes and beard. 'To the Left of Genghis Khan,' he repeated: 'Oh that's good, Murray, that's very good!' He chuckled away to himself for a few more moments, then added: 'And what sort of pilot is he?'

'The best — when he's not drunk. The trouble is, he's just got the sack from Air U.S.A.'

'That's no problem. We can't use him anyway for the second flight. That will have to be a regular, scheduled rice-drop, everything above board. Two other pilots, and a team of kickers. Otherwise they'll immediately smell a rat.'

Murray swung up on one elbow, staring hard at him: '*Two more pilots?* And where the hell do we find them?'

'I'll find them. Don't worry, my dear Murray, Air U.S.A. doesn't employ men of such great integrity, as you know yourself. There are pilots — and pilots.'

'And the kickers?'

Pol shrugged an enormous shoulder. 'Thai paratroopers, aren't they? Mercenaries — nothing more. For a small consideration — a few dollars — they will be persuaded to walk back home. By the time they arrive, we shall be away — home and dry. But tell me more about this Rhodesian and his navigator. Are they reliable?'

'They're mercenaries — like the kickers. They'll do it for money.'

'*Bien!* And when say they're good pilots, how do you know?'

'They brought us back out of the mountains over North Vietnam on one engine in a storm, with no radar or a radio-compass, and crash-landed us safely in a field.'

179

'North Vietnam?' Pol jerked his head up several inches off the bench. 'You did say North Vietnam?'

'That's right. We strayed over the border. But it wasn't the pilots' fault — the plane was overloaded and missed the drop zone.'

Pol's girl was finishing his massage now by pulling out each of his finger joints with a slippery snap that made Murray wince. 'Does anyone know about this?' Pol asked.

'Only myself and the two pilots. And a girl.'

'A girl?' The Frenchman's voice had hardened as the masseuse knelt down and started on his toes — *sh-nick, sh-nick!* 'What girl?'

Murray shrugged, seeing little point in lying at this stage. 'A French girl who's married to one of the CIA chiefs presently working in Laos, otherwise Saigon.'

Pol had sat up very quickly and was staring beady-eyed at him — a bearded Buddha who was not afraid of a bomb in a brandy bottle, but was now deeply disturbed by the wife of a CIA man in an obscure corner of the earth. 'My dear Murray.' His voice had dropped several notes. 'This is not a joke?'

'No. I don't have a gallows humour either.' Pol's girl had stood up and went over to run him a bubble bath. 'She's an amateur photographer, and just happened to come along for the ride.'

'Just happened?' Pol's tone was rich with Gallic irony: 'Just happened to be there when you made contact with the two pilots?'

Murray sighed wearily. It seemed he had been through this scene once before. 'It's not quite like that at all. For a start, she doesn't love her husband.'

'Oh?' Pol cocked an eyebrow under his kiss curl. 'You know her very well?'

'I spent a night with her in Luang Prabang. I know her.' He used the verb *savoir*, and Pol chuckled as he lowered his weight on to the duckboards and waddled like some monstrously inflated baby over to the bath.

'There's another thing,' Murray called: 'She happens to work as secretary and factotum to General Virgil Luther Greene — the boy who's in charge of Saigon security.'

'And her husband?'

'I don't think she tells him much. She didn't even tell him she was going on the drop.'

Pol lowered himself into the bath with a great splash. 'And you think she might co-operate?'

'I think so.' He tried to recall those last private moments with her, chasing after her down the main street of Luang Prabang with the lame broken words of a lovers' quarrel, or the petty pay-off to a one-night stand.

Pol seemed to have regained his good humour, grinning again as he sank under the bubbles. 'You seem to have been well amused during your stay in Laos! And what about the other job?'

'The other job was fine. I found just the place. As perfect for security as anything in the whole of South-East Asia.' He began to describe the dam, the reservoir, the heavy digging machines — his enthusiasm gaining on him, then draining away with a sour twinge like the memory of a great passion run dry. It had been so perfect, so unbelievably beautiful — until Finlayson.

'You'll be all right,' he said sadly. 'There aren't even any proper guards up there — just two men, a Lao and a disgruntled American. The Lao goes off at night, and the American could no doubt be persuaded to take a little promenade through the jungle — if we made it worth his while.' He realised he was still speaking in the present tense, without even the uncertain use of the French subjunctive. 'A perfect set-up,' he added. 'Except that it won't work. They've killed Finlayson, and now they're on to you. They'll either kill us all first, or they'll catch us. And I'm an invincible coward, Charles. I want to go on living.'

Pol was climbing out of the bath, the soap-suds clinging round him like an incandescent gown of candyfloss. '*Ah mon cher, il y a toujours des problèmes, bien sûr!*' He came trundling back to Murray's bench, and there was now a bright cunning in his eye — a dry little porcine eye that showed through the wasted fat and gravy-bile a glimpse of the real Pol — hard and dangerous. He stood naked above him, balancing on a pair of small, surprisingly well-shaped feet. 'You must not despair over a small *contretemps, mon cher!* You do not know that the person who killed our friend Finlayson is necessarily the same person who sent me my present this morning.' The girl wrapped a towel round him and handed him some sandals. 'My friends today showed a certain sophistication. They hardly behaved like common criminals — bandits attacking me in my sleep with a ten-centimetre nail through my head!'

Murray nodded, closing his eyes and feeling the masseuse's cool manipulating fingers working down his chest and over his belly, and tried to distract his fear and disappointment by thoughts of the girl's little shadowy breasts under her crisp white coat — half opening his eyes to see that Pol had gone, and that she was smiling down at him, pearl-teethed as he lay wishing he were not so bored by these oriental girls — by their slavish charms and twittering, docile attentions. He lay erect and unembarrassed, wondering idly about the amatory arrangements of the Rama Hotel. Nothing too coarse for the grey-skinned tourists: yet nothing too pure for the high and mighty Dollar.

At the same time he was vaguely, uncomfortably aware of something being wrong. Some random word, some remark mislaid in a half-empty chamber of his mind — worrying him suddenly like grit in a shoe. He remembered Pol's earlier offer, on the telephone that morning, to have lunch with him in his suite. It would no doubt be a good lunch; and in any case Murray had nothing else to do.

The girl had run his bath, and he was just stepping in, when it came to him — sharp and sudden as physical pain, with a shock that almost had him leaping out of the water like a hooked salmon.

On the phone to Pol that morning he had said nothing about how Finlayson had died; and there had been no mention in any of the local newspapers, English or French, of the peculiar murder weapon. Yet Pol had talked of a ten-centimetre nail — of 'bandits attacking me in my sleep'.

Murray contained his urge to dress in a hurry and run. He gave his girl an ample tip; then, calculating that Pol would be already upstairs, he made his way along to the lifts.

CHAPTER 2

The light from outside was very strong, even through the half-drawn Venetian blinds. It fell in yellow stripes across the carpet and the muted plain decor. It fell on Pol, standing in front of the balcony windows in his bulging blue silk suit, striped green and ultraviolet like some psychedelic jungle creature. Pig-Buddha or sly fat cat? Murray wondered: for all associations with Pol had now become animal in his mind — even feline and soft-footed, as he stood balancing on a pair of tiny ballet slippers, smiling over his pointed beard.

'Murray, I have ordered champagne.'

Murray smiled back: 'In a carton?'

Pol shook his head: 'I don't think they'd try the same trick twice — do you?'

'No. I don't think they even tried it once.'

'No?' The smile hardened; but neither of them moved. Murray said: 'Let's see it, Charles. You didn't call in the police, so it must still be here. Where is it?'

At that moment there came a tap on the door. Pol moved with surprising speed. 'Who is there?' he called in English, and suddenly there was a gun in his hand — a small blunt weapon which he held cradled behind his back.

A voice from the other side said something that Murray did not catch, and Pol said 'Come in' — slipping the gun back into his trouser pocket as the Thai waiter appeared with a tray of champagne in an ice-bucket and two tulip glasses. Pol nodded him towards the balcony, handing him a ten-baht note as he went out again.

The door closed and Pol came across grinning. Murray stood in the centre of the room, watching him, undecided. There was always the chance of a mistake: a special report in one of the Cambodian papers, secret information that Pol might have come by in his mysterious capacity as adviser to the Sihanouk regime. He said again: 'The bottle of Hine, Charles. I'd like to see it.'

Pol sighed, his pudgy little hands swaying at his side. 'Some champagne first?'

'The brandy first. The *plastique.*'

'You really want to see it?'

'That's what I said.'

Pol gave him a quick, almost sorrowful glance; then, with a shrug, turned and padded over to a writing desk under the windows. Murray followed him. Pol was bending down with a creak of silk as Murray moved up behind him, making no sound on the carpet. Pol saw him and began to turn, one hand reaching into his trouser pocket, and Murray jumped him.

He threw one arm in a lock round his neck, jamming it up into the rolls of fat under his throat until the Frenchman began to choke, while his free hand dived down to the pocket with the gun. Pol lurched for a moment, then suddenly, with a great lunge, dragged Murray forward across his back, grabbing at one ankle while Murray's hand scrabbled down across the man's tight-stretched thighs, trying to reach the gun. Pol grunted and hissed, his neck bulging slimy with sweat, silk splitting under his armpits — until, with a final mighty heave, Murray's feet left the floor.

Together they now began a grotesque piggy-back round the floor — almost in silence except for Pol's snorting and spluttering, staggering with Murray lying almost flat across his shoulders, his trousers riding up his legs, his face pulled down against the short damp hairs at the back of Pol's neck, stifled by the sudden sweet stench of sweat and Eau de Vétiver.

He tightened his grip on Pol's throat, but it seemed to have little effect. The man's strength was astonishing; and Murray was beginning to grow desperate — thinking of abandoning what was left of the Queensberry Rules and going for the eyes — when Pol gave a short squeal and sat down with a thump on the carpet. He had let go of Murray, and now lay with one hand clutching his thigh, the other holding his throat. His eyes were closed and his face grey with pain. '*Ah merde!*' he gasped: 'It's the muscle in my leg.'

The pocket with the gun now gaped open, and Murray reached quickly down and lifted out a .22 Beretta, loaded with six rounds. A handy little gun at short-range. He wondered why it hadn't been used on Finlayson.

Pol stirred and opened one weeping eye. 'Get me some water, Murray.' His voice was a whisper.

Murray had put the gun in his own pocket and went through to a pink-tiled bathroom, noticing the rows of toilet waters, perfumes, powders, pills and medicine bottles — smiling at the thought of Pol being vain. He broke open one of the hygiene-sealed tooth-glasses and filled it from the ice-water tap. When he got back, Pol had crawled on to one knee, his kiss curl splayed out on his brow like a wet spider. Murray put a hand under his arm and hauled him painfully to his feet, most of his weight resting on one leg. 'Ah Murray — are you mad? What did you do it for?'

'The gun,' said Murray; but Pol shook his head with a sad grin. 'I was going to show you the bomb — not the gun.' He put his hand into his trouser pocket and handed Murray a small key. 'The bottom right-hand drawer of the desk,' he said.

Murray took it and went to the desk. Inside the drawer lay a long cardboard carton with the stamp of Hine Cognac VSOP, one side of which had been slit open and folded back. Very carefully he lifted the cardboard flap and peered inside. There was no bottle — just a slab of rough greyish substance, not unlike a long slice of pâté. There were two small holes in the side of it, and two metal plugs, each attached to an insulated wire, hanging loose from where they had been pulled out of the explosive. The electrical detonating device was concealed at the top, its weight counterbalanced by a battery fixed to the floor of the carton.

While he was examining it, Pol had dragged himself out on to the balcony where he now sat slumped in a cane chair, gently massaging his thigh. He nodded at the ice-bucket. 'I could do with a glass of champagne. Can you open it?'

'I owe you an apology,' Murray said, peeling the foil off the cork. 'I was being over-suspicious.'

Pol waved a hand. 'We all make mistakes, my dear Murray. But what a beautiful spectacle we must have made!'

Murray eased the cork out and shot it over the edge, turning to hose champagne into the two glasses. The air stirred with a warm breeze. They were very high, with the city spread out below in a dirty yellow glare under the monsoon sky. Pol struggled out of his chair and took his glass. 'I'm out of training for these gymnastics — getting too old perhaps. And you're getting too nervous.'

Murray sat down in the chair opposite and looked steadily across at him. 'Perhaps I've got reason to be nervous?'

Pol was staring out at the far-off storm clouds rising across the wide grey-green, canal-webbed horizon. 'You saw the bomb?' he asked suddenly. 'A fantastic job, hein? And what a bang it would have made! It would have been heard all over Bangkok.'

'It wasn't just the bomb,' said Murray. 'There's also Finlayson. You know he was killed in his sleep with a ten-centimetre nail?'

'*Et alors?*' Pol's face was rosy with innocence.

'You told me downstairs in the baths, although there was no mention of it in any of the papers. And yet you knew?'

Pol was suddenly shaking with laughter. 'Oh my dear Murray, is that why you attacked me? *Ah mon Dieu, quelle blague!*' He groped for his handkerchief, dabbing at his eyes and forehead, while Murray stared at him, beginning to feel uncomfortable. 'You don't think the newspapers are the only means of finding out how a colleague is murdered, do you?'

Murray took a sip of champagne and said nothing. 'It was a most regrettable incident,' Pol went on. 'But like the bomb this morning, it was a professional job — though in rather a different class.'

'And you still have no idea who did it?'

'Oh, I have several ideas. Not everyone loves me in this part of the world, I assure you. Politics are one of the easiest ways of making enemies.'

'Politics?'

The Frenchman gave an impish grin. 'Yes, my dear Murray. You see by nature I am a political animal — something of an idealist, even a romantic, if you like. I have a great sympathy for popular movements — especially when they involve the underdog. It is an arrogant illusion, perhaps, but I like to think that I am helping my fellow men — helping the weak against the strong. And for this reason sometimes the strong do not at all like me.' He paused, cocking his head suddenly to one side. 'You heard something?'

They sat listening, and it came again: another light tap on the outside door. Pol began to climb out of his chair. 'It's probably our lunch — but just to be sure' — and he held his hand out, with a little deprecating smile: 'I'd like my gun back.'

Murray hesitated. For some reason he was still not entirely happy about Pol: this vain, gluttonous sybarite, professing idealism as he swilled champagne in his penthouse suite — the boastful defender of the weak against the strong. Yet someone — and probably more than one — had taken the trouble to send a well-prepared bomb up to that suite; and next time they might, in desperation, try something cruder, more personal. Nor did they sound the kind of people who would think of sparing an eye-witness.

Reluctantly Murray handed the Beretta back to Pol, following him as he limped out across to the door, repeating the same operation as before — calling 'Come in,' and turning with the gun behind his back, watching as the waiter wheeled in a trolley laid with plates of hors d'oeuvres and cold meats, telling him to leave it inside, to keep it away from the flies — watching until the man had left, closing the door behind him. Then he turned, wrinkling his nose at the food. 'The usual American picnic!' he scowled. 'They have brought to this city the eating habits of barbarians. You know what they gave me for breakfast this morning? — a hamburger with *sauce béarnaise!*' He had put the gun back in his trouser pocket and was picking at some slices of dry fish.

'You're not worried that it's poisoned?' Murray asked, not quite without irony.

Pol grinned: 'If they're the people I think they are, the methods of Lucrecia Borgia are not their style.'

'So you *do* think you know who they are?'

Pol shrugged, carrying a plate of tinned artichoke hearts out on to the balcony and sinking into his chair with a loud crack of cane. 'I can tell you one thing, my dear Murray — they were certainly not the same people who killed George Finlayson.'

'How can you be sure?'

'Because for a start, as I just said, their styles are so different. Secondly, there was not the same motive.'

'How do you know?'

'I had information.'

'Secret information — through your work in Cambodia? Or am I being indiscreet?'

'Oh, there are no indiscreet questions, my dear Murray — only indiscreet answers. But for a man in my position there must be certain matters —'

Murray cut him short: 'All right, I'll take your word for it. But for a moment you had me worried. I thought it was you who'd killed Finlayson.'

Pol sat back with his champagne and chuckled playfully. 'Oh but it was, my dear Murray. Or rather, I had him killed. It was the only way.'

CHAPTER 3

Murray blinked at him, conscious of an angry pain in one eye — the glare of refracted light, the champagne burning high and sour in his throat. 'You bastard,' he muttered, in English. 'You fat murdering bastard!'

Pol shrugged lazily, putting his plate on the floor so that his hand would be free for the gun. 'It was necessary, I promise you. A necessary killing in the line of duty.'

Murray closed his eyes. It was not easy to lose one's temper with a man while you drank his champagne. Especially when he also had a gun. 'But why?' he said at last. 'What had he done?'

'He was planning to betray us,' Pol said evenly. 'To ruin our beautiful little plan, even before we had begun putting it in operation. A painless process of tipping off the British and American Intelligence Services and getting you and the others expelled from Laos and Vietnam before you could make trouble.' He sat back munching an artichoke. 'You guessed, perhaps, that George Finlayson was working for British Intelligence — what you call D.I.5?'

'I didn't know. How did you find out?'

'Oh I've known for some time — almost since I first met him.'

'And you still trusted him?'

'Not at all. In fact, I was never very happy about Monsieur Finlayson from the start. He was too comfortable — too bourgeois in his outlook. After all, twenty thousand dollars a year with no tax, and living on expenses, is a very agreeable life

— especially if you're a man without much imagination or ambition.'

'But you still told him the plan?'

'I still hoped he might be seduced — for the promise of perhaps a hundred million pounds Sterling. Even for a bored banker, that's a lot of money. And besides, at the time he was the only person I knew who was capable of finding out the necessary information.'

Murray clenched his teeth, trying hard not to lose his temper. Was this what Pol meant by 'romantic idealism'? Poor dull Finlayson, he'd never trusted Pol either. Never trust a man with a beard, he'd said — cloven hoof and hairy heel. But white men had to stick together. Couldn't go round slitting each other's throats, or nailing one another down to beds. Not a white man's trick at all. 'And who did you get to do it?' he said, his voice stiff with repressed rage.

Pol wagged his head. 'Secrets of the trade, my dear Murray.'

'And how can you be sure he hadn't already tipped off the British and the Americans?'

'I'm sure — that's all you have to know.'

'Through someone else in British Intelligence? An old man called Hamish Napper, for instance?'

'Ah Murray! Now that's what I do call an indiscreet question.'

Murray nodded, lifting his champagne. Naughty little Napper, he thought: Whitehall had left him out in the East just a little too long after all. Hamish Napper and Charles Pol — two oddball expatriates with eccentric habits and a shared dislike of the Americans, but a common love of the dollar. He looked out across the city, at the storm clouds coming closer, piling up high and dark along the edge of the sky. 'So if

Finlayson was the only person who could find out the information, but is now dead — where does that leave us?'

Pol did not reply at once. He stretched out and refilled his glass, watching the bottle bobbing back into the half-melted ice. 'Does "Lazy Dog" mean anything to you?' he said suddenly, pronouncing the phrase '*Low-see dowg.*'

Murray frowned back at him. 'Yes, it's a weapon they use in Vietnam. A beastly contraption that fires millions of needles over a wide area, destroying everything in sight.' Then he remembered something Finlayson had told him on that first night at the 'Cigale' restaurant: something about the codewords for the previous 'flush-outs' — names like *Happy Hound*, *Mighty Mouse*, *Bullpup* — infernal weapons of the lobotomised war dubbed with the jargon of the lobotomised military mind. Then he remembered something else. 'Wait a moment. It was on Finlayson's telex — the last incoming message before the machine cut off. It must have come in after he was dead.'

Pol looked interested. 'Do you remember what it said?'

'It didn't make any sense at the time — something like "*instruct inventory morning Lazy Dog,*" datelined the Bangkok office of FARC.'

Pol nodded slowly. 'If you go through to my bedroom you will find a black attaché case. There is something in it I would like to show you. You will excuse me, but this leg still gives me pain.'

Murray got up and went through to the bedroom. He found it on the bed, beside two white leather bags already packed. He carried the attaché case back outside and laid it in Pol's lap. The Frenchman unlocked it from a ring of keys, opening it delicately as though it were a display at a jewellers. Inside was a sheaf of photostats of Xeroxed files, letters, printed documents, held in place by a pair of spring wires. He riffled through them for a few moments, finally selecting the photostat of two foolscap sheets reduced to single quarto, pushing them across to Murray.

At first glance they looked like company reports: four long closely-printed columns of names and figures. He ran his eye down the first column — *Banque de L'Indochine, Federal Reserve (S.E.A.), Hongkong and Shanghai Banking Corporation, Bank of America, Chase Manhattan, Bank of Vietnam, Bank of India, Bank of Japan* — each listed against an eight-, sometimes nine-figure number. Many of the other names were of international companies with commercial interests in Vietnam; one of these — an American corporation with large Defence Department contracts, was set against the figure *159,698,727*.

Murray marvelled at the clinical accuracy of the accounting: trying to imagine what dry myopic mind could have set about such a task, so simple and definitive, right down to the odd seven. One five and two ones, perhaps? — two little old used 'greens' with the head of George Washington, traced, docketed, packed away among the stack of Lincolns, Hamiltons, Grants and Ben Franklins... Bloody bankers! he thought: mean, passionless little men sharpening their pencils, deducting interest, calculating the dividend. Money without a soul. *Banque de L'Indochine* — *125,899,600*. And he nodded his approval. At least here was someone totting up the loot, give or take a few bucks to make a round figure.

He handed it back to Pol and gave himself another glass of champagne. 'You're giving me an appetite. What is it?'

'Confidential report issued in Zurich ten days ago concerning the total American dollar holdings in the Republic of South Vietnam when the books closed on the first of the month.'

'Closed?'

'There's to be a new issue of Scrip on the first day of next month — two weeks from this coming Monday. And on the Sunday night the United States Government will evacuate' — he ran his fat finger down the rows of figures — 'precisely this amount of money in cash from Tân Sơn Nhất Airport, Saigon, to Guam airbase in the Philippines. The operation has been given the codename *Lazy Dog*, and the total sum involved is in the region — if you add those figures up — of around fifteen hundred and forty million dollars.'

Murray felt a weight pressing on his chest. It grew heavier, becoming intense, suffocating. He struggled forward, almost toppling from his chair. His ears were singing and a wild laser-gleam had come into his eye. 'Flush-out two weeks from Sunday,' he muttered, stifling a crazy laugh, knowing that the passion was alive again — all the carefully-plotted details, the hopes and frustrated lust for those greenbacks, fired again in a sudden rush of adrenalin — a fierce, greedy, physical lust that grabbed at him deep inside, pressed and pummelled and twisted at him, making him want to jump up and laugh and leap round Pol in a crazy drunken jig.

'Over one and a half billion dollars,' he added, his teeth bared over his champagne glass. 'Bigger than last time — bigger than *Happy Hound* or *Mighty Mouse*. The biggest ever, Charles!'

'To *Lazy Dog*!' said Pol, raising his glass.

'To *Lazy Dog*.' Murray relaxed with a great glowing sense of release. He had forgotten the bomb, the nail in Finlayson's neck, Pol's complicity in cold-blooded murder. The whole angry world, from Vietnam to the vaults of Wall Street, was focussed in that moment on those monotonous photostated figures, the equivalent of five — or would it be nearer six? — tons of paper money. He sat back with a long easy sigh. 'And this was all found and photographed in George Finlayson's office?'

Pol nodded cheerfully: 'Monsieur Finlayson was a very methodical man.'

'And your hired help must have been a fast worker with a camera!' But he softened the malice with a quick smile, as Pol pushed across a second photostat, this time with the seal of the U.S. Treasury — *Federal Reserve Board of International Monetary Fund, Bangkok. Most Confidential.* There followed the ugly devitalised prose of international high finance: — '*containerization dollar-par movement of FRB/VN Reserve Exchange…*' Murray looked up, frowning: 'How long did Finlayson have these documents?'

'Since almost immediately after they were issued by the Zurich headquarters. In fact, as soon as he asked for them. In his case — as head of the Lao branch of FARC — it would have been a perfectly normal request.'

'So he had them when I talked to him three days ago?'

'Almost certainly. He was getting the final confirmation figures, according to the telex message you read, the next day. But he said nothing about it when you talked to him?'

'Only that he'd keep his ear to the ground. And that he found the plan acceptable — or at least, believable. Why would he have sat on it? Why didn't he get on to the Americans, or the British, at once?'

'Ah.' Pol poured the last of the champagne into their glasses. 'He wanted to sound you out, my dear Murray. To find out just how serious the plan was — and how seriously, if at all, these two pilots would react. To wait till the plan had begun to mature and ripen before cutting it down. He probably didn't want you biting too quickly.'

Murray nodded, trying to convince himself that this was a plausible explanation. If Finlayson had been working for British Intelligence, would he really have worked alone on a job as big as this — even in a country as small as Laos? Or had he been working with Hamish Napper? And if Napper were the one who'd tipped Pol off, what percentage was he hoping to get at the end — to supplement his pension and the bungalow near Godalming? Yet there was one thing that didn't quite fit. Why had Napper, if he had known that Finlayson was to be killed — indeed already had been killed — been so keen to warn Murray off Ryderbeit? Was Ryderbeit himself some mysterious double agent? It seemed hardly likely. Yet Napper had gone to some pains to warn Murray off — almost as though he'd known what Finlayson knew, and was anxious to keep Murray out of trouble.

Something, somewhere, didn't add up. Murray would have dearly liked to talk again to little Hamish Napper. He thought of tackling Pol about it, but decided to hold his tongue. It was very possible that at the last moment Napper had got cold feet and wanted out — had been trying to do Murray a favour by hinting he should do the same. And if Pol suspected this, it was also a strong possibility he would have Napper disposed of as well. Pol's 'romantic idealism' did not stop at the 'necessary killing'. Instead Murray changed the subject, to something more academic, but which was also worrying him.

He nodded at the sheaf of photostats in Pol's lap. 'One and a half billion dollars is a fantastic sum, Charles. Isn't it just a little too fantastic? Too big for anyone to get rid of — especially when one hell of a lot of it must be in numbered, traceable notes.'

Pol gave his sly smile. 'Ah, but my dear Murray, it's just the fantastic size of it, and the fact that so much of it can be traced, that is the very essence, the very beauty of the plan!'

'I don't follow.'

'No? So what do you think the Americans will do when they find the money has gone? They'll be very upset of course — and they'll start the most massive land and sea search that the world has probably ever seen. But then what? After a few weeks — a few months — when they find nothing? After all, they will not be operating on American territory.'

'They'll alert every bank in the Western world — lean on every friendly, even unfriendly Government, to track those dollars down and hand them over — with us.'

Pol was shaking his head, still smiling. 'Oh no they won't, Murray. And I'll tell you why. At this moment approximately forty-four billion American dollars are in circulation throughout the world. When the Americans discover that nearly three per cent of that cash has been stolen, you ask me what their reaction will be? A large proportion of that money, as we know, will be in high denomination bills — fifties and hundreds. And a large amount of those, particularly the ones held by the big international banks, will, as you say, be numbered and traceable. But if the American Treasury were to announce publicly that three per cent of this money — perhaps a half per cent of all fifty- and hundred-dollar bills in circulation in the entire world — was stolen money, then what do you think would happen? The value of the dollar, particularly the high denomination bills, would slump — probably more than the three per cent lost. So the Americans will do nothing. They will prefer to have the money still circulating, hot, than have their creditors and the international dealers shying off the dollar and turning to more respectable currencies. For that is the whole point, Murray. If we make off with this money, we are not only stealing it — we are threatening to discredit the currency of the United States of America! And the dollar, at all costs, must be kept respectable!'

'And with a fraction of this sum — say ten million dollars — it wouldn't work?'

'Oh, a small sum would be useless. That is the only reason why I am so interested in this operation. Because one and a half billion U.S. is a reasonable, workable amount. It even gives us an edge over the United States Treasury!' He chuckled gaily, rubbing his hands: 'But this is all theory. What we must now attend to are more immediate, practical matters. We have the information, the two pilots, the landing-zone in Laos — and possibly the girl who could be of either great help, or great danger. We also have the small problem of the gentlemen who sent me my present for breakfast. I think we must find these gentlemen, and if possible neutralise them. Since they have already gone to such trouble to kill me — and must by now know they have failed — I suspect they are anxious to try and finish me off here in Bangkok before I get back into Cambodia.

'Now I have already booked myself out, as you know, on the same flight as yourself — Air Vietnam to Saigon via Phnom Penh, due to leave in exactly two hours. So their only opportunity will be between here and the airport. I suspect there are probably not many of them — two at the most, perhaps only one. So if you were to lend me a little assistance, Murray, the contest should be an even one.'

He struggled to his feet, wincing for a moment with the pain in his leg. 'You are all packed and ready to go? And you have your international driving licence with you? Perfect! It is now half past three. Our plane leaves at five-thirty, so we must be at the airport by five. Business hours start again at a quarter to four. Now, when you leave here I want you to go out of the hotel and up to the corner of the block where there's a hire-car firm. You will be in no danger — remember it is me they are after, not you — and in any case, they are very unlikely to know that you have been visiting me.

'You will hire a car — something small and not too conspicuous — and drive round and park just a little way up the street behind the hotel entrance, facing Kitchburi Avenue. I shall leave at precisely four o'clock, in a taxi. That will give us a good forty minutes to reach the airport — with ten minutes to spare for any eventualities on the way. When you see me leave, you will start up as well, at a discreet distance. You do not have to keep up with me — just follow towards the airport. I don't think they'll try anything as I leave the hotel — it's too public. The most likely spot is the beginning of the autoroute out to the airport. There I will tell the taxi to stop and dismiss him. Then I shall wait for you. If our friends are going to act, that will be their opportunity.'

'And if they do?'

'I shall try and kill them.'

'With a two-two pistol?'

Pol grinned: 'With something rather better. Now, everything is quite clear? All you have to do is watch for my taxi, and follow at a reasonable speed towards the airport.'

'Why bother about a taxi — why not come in the hired car?'

Pol stood for a moment tugging at his lower lip. 'I thought of that,' he said at last. 'But two of us might distract them — or him, as it may be. We want to draw whoever it is out into the open, now or never! Better to have two cars — it gives us more of an element of surprise.' He spoke suddenly with the mischievous glee of a schoolboy planning a daring and ingenious prank. As he led Murray to the door he stopped and took out an enormous wallet, counting out a number of crisp twenty-dollar bills. 'You'll need something for the deposit on the car,' he added: 'The rest is for the inconvenience.'

This time Murray took the money without arguing; it wasn't like taking money off a dead man. Not quite, anyway. Pol had taken out his little gun and stood back behind the door. '*Merde!*' he whispered.

'*Merde*,' said Murray, and opened the door.

CHAPTER 4

The corridor was empty. Murray walked to the end, round the corridor, reaching the two lifts: neither of which were at the floor. He touched both heat-sensitive call-buttons and waited. His watch said 3.37. Easy. Plenty of time.

One of the lifts stopped and slid open. It was empty. He stepped in and touched the button for the ground floor. Piped music clinked softly round him. The door began to close and a man squeezed in — a tubby little man in a porkpie hat. They started down.

'Pretty humid,' the man said cheerfully: an American.

Murray nodded. If there was one day in the year in Bangkok that wasn't humid, it was worth a paragraph in the papers. The lift itself was distinctly chilly. Murray disliked lifts; he felt the same sense of exposed privacy in them as in a public lavatory. He stood watching the floor numbers lighting up, with irritating slowness, along the panel above the door: *6-5-4* —

'You American?' said the man in the porkpie hat.

'No,' said Murray. 'I'm an Irish bum waiting for a break.' The lift stopped. 'And a good day on yah!' he added, leaving the little man gaping after him.

The lobby was less crowded now, with a dozy afternoon lull. No one even looked at him. The same clerk was on duty at the desk. Murray gave him ten baht and collected his camera and grip-bag; then at the last minute turned and started back up the open stairway to the Rama Cocktail Lounge. At the top he almost bumped into the tubby little American from the lift. The man smiled sheepishly, steering clear of him, round towards a wall of telephone booths.

Murray went into the bar and spent a few minutes sucking a long brandy-and-soda through a straw; then started down again, with his camera and holdall, across the lobby and out into the sticky, storm-heavy afternoon. Hot gusts of wind stung his eyes as he hurried up to the corner of the block. The rain would begin at any moment.

He spent an irritating five minutes waiting while two pale American youths on Rest-and-Recuperation argued with the car hire reception girl about the relative merits of five cents per mileage for a Toyota sedan, against ten cents a mile for an American convertible. Murray had finally hustled in and told them to finish their discussion while he arranged his own deal, because he was in a damned great hurry. The boys had gawped at him, mumbled their apologies and stood aside. He had felt bad about it almost at once; they looked nice innocent country boys, perhaps battle-weary after many months in Vietnam, still strange to the ways of the big city. Later that evening they'd be in some frowsty clip-joint, drinking bad bourbon and yapping of their experiences — just like Sergeant Don Wace had done — to any stranger who would stop to listen.

But he had soon forgotten about them, as he sat double-parked in a white beetle-backed Volkswagen about thirty yards up from the hotel entrance. It was raining hard now and the street was jammed with determined ranks of traffic, driven in laconic bursts of speed between shrieks of brakes. He had the windows rolled down and his jacket off, with the engine idling. Several taxis, of various makes, pulled up outside the hotel, exchanged fares and drove off. Trade, like the traffic, was brisk without being frantic.

One minute to four o'clock. Rain splashed through the Volkswagen window, bringing a freshness to the dust-choked air. Poor, frail, ancient Bangkok, he thought: its golden spires crowded in with high-rise construction, its canals and Floating Market cemented over in an arid, treeless, sprawling extension of the Great Suburb Society.

He looked up and went stiff all over.

In the driving mirror a taxi had pulled up just a few yards behind him. It was a cream-coloured Toyota, and in the rear seat he could just make out, through the rain blurred windows, a chubby face under a porkpie hat. He thought rapidly: one insignificant American tourist among thousands, who'd ridden down in the lift with him, bumped into him by the bar, and had caught a taxi outside the hotel. Only his taxi wasn't moving.

He looked away again, ahead, where another taxi — what looked like a Chevrolet — had just drawn up outside the hotel. A moment later Pol came limping out under an umbrella held for him by one of the doormen, carrying his attaché case in one hand and a rolled raincoat in the other. He hauled himself in with a great alacrity, while his two white cases were stowed in the boot. The Thai doorman took his tip through the window, stood back and bowed low, and Murray let out the clutch.

A big sedan screeched to a standstill a few inches from the Volkswagen's left bumper, but the driver seemed totally undismayed. Murray did a swift slalom between two more cars, stopping several cyclists dead in their tracks, keeping his eye on the mirror. He had lost the Toyota in a mass of swerving bumpers warped by the dense rain. He let the Chevrolet pull ahead, positioning himself near the middle of the stream of traffic where it would be difficult for anyone to pass.

Then he saw him again, about five cars back, keeping steadily to the inside lane. A lone middle-aged American tourist in the back of a taxi, among a scrum of taxis. He wondered if this might be a deliberate diversion. Pol had said there might have been more than one. A subtler sleuth, he realised, would have tried some back-tracking tactic, cutting in at a crossing further ahead — even varying the pursuit by following *in front* of the Chevrolet. The Toyota was just following the traffic. And Murray's job, according to Pol's briefing, was more or less the same. He was under no obligation to take risks; just a dependable chauffeur, a pick-up man scheduled to arrive after the lead began to fly. He wondered what Pol was carrying inside that rolled-up raincoat.

The rain was now slamming down in solid gusts of water, washed blindly back and forth by the windshield wipers. But the pace of the traffic only seemed to increase, all throttle and no brakes now, with the egregious cyclists dodging spiderlike between the cars, drenched to the skin and apparently impervious to all danger.

Murray began to watch these cyclists more carefully: mostly young men, lithe and sinewy in white shirts, jeans, the occasional solar topee. A few girls riding under umbrellas with children strapped to the pillion. And he remembered how it was a favourite trick in Saigon — rush-hour traffic in the rain, the terrorist flicking between the cars, the grenade tossed casually through an open window as the cycle vanished among fifty other cycles, forgotten in the chaos of the explosion.

He wondered whether Pol had the nous to keep his windows shut. And suddenly both Chevrolet and Toyota were lost: the traffic funnelled into a neck of road between cranes and cement-mixers, the dull crack of a steam-hammer even above the gravel-roar of the rain — *boom CRACK!* — the traffic slowing through a deep trough of water, almost to a standstill now. Then he glimpsed what he thought was the Chevrolet again, about a hundred yards ahead, as they speeded up towards a roundabout — gimcrack hoardings looming above the shanty-shops, giant skeleton beer bottles and Western sewing machines, Chinese film posters dripping blood from Mandarin hands and dragons' teeth (oh subtle mysteries of the Orient!), shops brilliant with raw silk, emerald-green and crimson and deep indigo and saffron. But still no sign of the little cream Toyota.

The road had widened now, the cars skimming the surface like motorboats. Seventy, eighty kilometres an hour — the Chevrolet pulling away in a heavy wake of water, with Murray straining forward in his seat, sore-eyed, sweating with the slow crawl of fear as he watched the Chevrolet disappear. And now he caught the flash of headlamps in his mirror, as the little cream Toyota pulled out suddenly from behind and slid past on the inside lane.

Porkpie-hat was sitting back, eyes front. Not even a sideward glimpse at the Volkswagen. So perhaps Pol's ruse of using two cars had some point. Yet the little Japanese taxi was obviously supercharged; Murray had his foot down flat on the floor, the Volkswagen straining up to a hundred-and-ten km/h, while the tail of the Toyota veered off into a fine after spray from its wheels. Other cars flicked by, travelling very fast. The city thinned into tin and wattle shacks, swamp and paddy fields blistered with rain, children squatting down with fishing rods, water buffalo and hand-carts and high bold airline hoardings. A signpost said *Don Muang Airport: 8 miles.*

The road now opened on to two strips of steaming concrete leading to the horizon. The rain was letting up and a dim sun seeped down across the fields. He saw the Chevrolet about a quarter of a mile ahead, pulled up on the mud verge. It was alone, closed, no one in sight. Murray slowed into the inside lane, watching carefully in his mirror. He let a couple of fast cars and an oil tanker roar past, his view blotted out for several seconds by their spray. When it was clear again he turned the Volkswagen abruptly off the road, swinging it round a few feet in front of the taxi, and stopped.

It was suddenly very quiet outside. A car swished past down the opposite carriageway and was gone. Murray was just about to get out, when he heard the snap of a door handle. A huge short leg appeared with a tiny shoe, a hand pointing the rolled-up raincoat at the Volkswagen, as Pol's head crept out under the Chevrolet door, his great body following, lowering the raincoat and reaching back into the taxi for his black attaché case. The Thai driver got out at the same moment and went round to the boot.

Pol came across and Murray opened the door for him, pushing the passenger seat forward to make room first for the two suitcases in the back. 'You're early,' Pol said through the window.

'I thought I'd better keep close. Nothing's happened?'

'Nothing.' He looked almost disappointed. 'And you?'

'There was another taxi. It passed me about three miles back.' The taxi driver was putting the cases in the back, while Murray described the incidents with porkpie-hat. Pol nodded and squeezed himself in with a wince of pain. 'American, you say? *Ah merde!* You couldn't have chosen something bigger than this German insect?' He pushed a twenty-dollar bill through the window at the driver, who stared at it with a big smile. 'Was he alone?'

'Alone. You know him?'

'Possibly. Start the engine, but don't move for a moment. Give the taxi time to go.' He shifted his mighty rump, cradling the rolled-up raincoat in his lap, and burped gently. The Chevrolet started up with a roar and squelch of mud, cutting straight across the road and bouncing up on to the grass verge dividing the carriageways, doing a swift U-turn as it headed back towards Bangkok. Pol watched it almost laconically.

'So we get moving?' said Murray.

'Give it a couple more minutes.'

'The American's well ahead by now,' Murray said, feeling impatient, nerves overwound, cramped with anti-climax. He glanced again in the mirror. Several big American cars stole up and hissed by, without incident. He nodded down at Pol's raincoat. 'And what have you got there?'

The Frenchman unrolled it with a mischievous grin. Inside lay a double-barrelled twelve-bore shotgun, sawn off about a foot from the breach. The mechanism was modern, unembroidered, of blue-black steel set in light varnished wood. It looked well-oiled and new. He broke it open and eased out the two cartridges. One bore a well-known British trademark — Number One Shot, the heaviest birdshot on the market. The other was an American brand, and of metal, with a blunt hard-nosed bullet that can blow a man's head off at thirty yards. Pol snapped it shut, patting it affectionately. 'My little gangster toy.'

'You still plan to use it?'

He gave a grandiose shrug that made the car sway. '*Ça dépend!* If they had planned something on the road, they would have already done it.' He looked at his watch. 'We should be getting on to the airport.'

Murray put the Volkswagen into gear and jerked her quickly back on to the road. 'And then?'

'If they intend anything,' Pol said evenly, 'they will try it at the airport. It will be their last chance.' He rolled the shotgun back inside his coat.

The first call for passengers on Air Vietnam, Flight 247 to Phnom Penh and Saigon, had already gone out. Pol was limping heavily between two tiny porters, with Murray hard behind, carrying both the attaché case and his own grip-bag, leaving Pol with the raincoat under his arm, both hands free. A blast of birdshot would be unthinkable in these crowds; his only hope now would be the .22.

They passed quickly through the Air Vietnam checking-in counter and joined a long line of American civilians — grave, loose-jowled men with the rumpled baleful look of those who spend their lives between airports and hotels.

Murray studied them more closely. These were no soldiers, no leathery acne-raw veterans of the Marine Corps or First Cav., no flint-eyed Special Forces — those 'warriors for the hearts and minds' — no pale draftees with five days' R-and-R behind them and the nagging doubt of venereal disease. No sir. These men on AVN Flight 247 were strictly civilians: Government employees, agents of USOM, USIS, JUSPAO, cost-efficiency experts, public relations officers, functionaries, fixers, desk men. The clerks of war.

Spooks? he wondered, as they shuffled through Customs and Immigration, where their cases and luggage were chalked without comment. It was a heavy afternoon and the officials were drowsy. They passed into the crowded chaos of the departure hall. Would they dare try here? Noise, swelling confusion, porters, police, miniature high heeled girls with slit skirts and clipboards, elegant finger-snapping Thais with white smiles and white holsters, bored American M.P.'s with black and white helmets, old women with pails and mops, young airmen in unzipped flying-suits chewing gum like athletes between events.

At the end of the hall a vast air-conditioner howled like a vacuum cleaner. The confusion was heightened by the TV screens, hung at regular intervals from the ceiling and relaying — between unintelligible flight bulletins — a frantic feature film in which a number of men on horseback were riding at the camera, loosing off rifles aimlessly into the air.

The entire staff paused, heads upturned, transfixed by the flickering grey actors, the ringing shots, crescendos of music. *'Will all members of Hotel Company, Jackdaw Division, please report to Gate Five!'* a Negro master-sergeant in a smart. Army suit was intoning through a hand-loudhailer.

Outside, a silver double-decker troop-carrying B 76 jet of the U.S. Air Force crept slowly past the plate-glass windows. Pol was elbowing his way towards the bar, sweat flowing in rivulets out of the folds of his neck, his jacket buttoned crookedly so that one flap hung lower than the other, covering his trouser pocket with the gun. He made a tragically vulnerable target, thought Murray: a sneak shot from any one of a hundred angles — crack of a small calibre, another .22 perhaps, lost in the whine and jabber of aircraft and loudspeakers, synchronised with the endless TV battle — and they wouldn't even need a silencer. The crowds were no help either: if anything they made the killers' job easier. Murray wondered what Pol had meant by saying they wouldn't choose a public place, like the hotel. Or was the hotel not quite public enough?

The only thing to do was keep moving. For unless Pol had a very good idea who it was who was after him, he was in bad trouble. The long string of his life, he'd said: he'd pulled it so many times and still couldn't feel the end. Was he pulling it now? He looked magnificently unruffled, pressing up close to the bar, a huge saffron bandana flourished in his free hand, mopping his face and brow, careful not to disarrange the kiss curl. 'You want a drink?' he called back to Murray.

'Brandy and soda,' Murray said. The TV screens were flashing up another bulletin: *Garuda Airlines, Flight 360 to Singapore and Djakarta, now boarding at Gate 9.* And a nasty thought came to him: Would they perhaps try for the plane? — another neat little device slipped aboard among the last-minute luggage — a phial of acid eating through a wire while the aircraft put on an extra thrust, climbing away from the mainland over the sea, with a bright flash, smoke curling downwards, metal ripping like paper — mangled machinery, seats, flesh, clothes, bones, luggage — tumbling down in a ball of blazing high-octane fuel, all over in a few seconds, lost under the South China Sea.

He looked round at the faces of his fellow passengers and felt a small ripple of comfort. If the people who were after Pol were those Murray thought they were, they wouldn't go for a plane-load of American Government officials. No, Pol had chosen his airline with intelligence — or perhaps luck?

Pol pulled him closer: 'Is anything wrong?'

Murray laughed grimly: 'Nothing at all, *mon vieux*! It's just —' and he lowered his voice, even while speaking French — 'I'm worried about the codename.'

'The what?' Pol had called for two brandies.

'Codename *Lazy Dog*. It's ominous. You know about "Lazy Dog", the weapon?'

'You told me about it. *Eh bien*?'

'It was a disaster. Heat-seeking missile designed to be fired from a thousand metres on to a lighted cigarette. Trouble is, the Viet Cong don't smoke. It used to zoom around and find some poor American platoon about five miles away, busy lighting up their Salem filter tips.'

Pol chuckled, handing him a brandy in a warm glass. 'I find it a good omen, my dear Murray — a non-motivated weapon!' A man on the TV screen, with a long scarred face, was reloading his rifle. The crowd along the bar stood watching. All but Murray, who was watching Pol hoist his drink over the head of a little man beside him. Pol was still holding his bandana. Murray looked at the little man and their eyes locked like magnets. He felt his mouth drying up. The man had taken off his porkpie hat and his head was as bald as a stone.

Pol slipped and fell against the American, splashing some of his brandy over him, his bandana flapping for a moment round the man's neck and down over his shirt. Three horsemen on the screen fired a volley of shots, the scarfaced man grimaced and began to fall, and the bald man at the bar opened his mouth, staring at Murray with a face the colour of wet sand.

Pol had grabbed Murray's arm, as the TV cut to a flight schedule: *AVN Flight 247 — Boarding Gate 6*. 'Let's go!' he said, moving with surprising speed despite his leg. Behind them, bald porkpie hat had disappeared behind a crowd of heads. Over the staccato shots and yells from the TV, someone called, 'Hey get a doctor!' There was a flurry of movement, a closing in round the bar. 'Kiss o' life!' someone shouted, as a Thai policeman hurried across the hall, hand on his big white holster.

Pol was still gripping Murray's arm as they reached the gate, handed out their boarding cards, passed through the plate-glass doors into a blast of kerosene and hot damp air, their clothes flapping in the slip-stream of a Boeing taxiing up to the Arrivals gate.

They reached the steps into the tail of the Air Vietnam Caravelle. Pol did not even glance back at the terminal as he began to heave himself up into the cool belly of the aircraft, where a slender girl in a flowing *áo dài* awaited them with a tray of hot scented towels.

'All right,' said Murray, when they were seated and the engines beginning to scream to life: 'How did you do it?'

'Do what?' said Pol, unfolding the steaming towel across his face.

'The little American at the bar — the one who followed me out in the taxi.'

'*Ah!*' He spoke with the towel still wrapped across his face like a mummy. 'Yet another indiscreet question, my dear Murray! When the hostess comes round, we'll have a bottle of champagne.'

PART 7: DATE AT THE 'CERCLE'

CHAPTER 1

Murray lay on the bed behind closed shutters, feeling the draught from the fan flutter against his body every three seconds, regular as a metronome. He lay with nerves taut, alert to every sound from outside: roar and jangle of the square, jeeps, trucks, baby-taxis, bicycle bells, rasping whine of motor scooters, boom of ships from the crowded river.

A quiet afternoon in a city at war. The other sounds — the sudden swish of Soviet 122-millimetre rockets from across the river, falling with a crack and shudder of air, followed by the panting of ambulance sirens; or sometimes the dull flashes and steady trembling of the earth as the eight-engined B-52's released their loads on the jungle north of the city — these sounds would come later, usually with the dark. They would come in time for the cocktail hour when newcomers to Saigon, along with the more boisterous of the foreign Press corps, could watch the display from the bar at the Caravelle Hotel where the windows were taped across to protect them from flying glass and the Tonkinese waiter teased up the martinis with just the right chill and twist of lemon.

God what an awful war, thought Murray. Drab, dirty, dishonest, pitiless ringside war-without-end: a PR man's war fed on cooked statistics, braced with spurious dogma and monstrous gadgets — all the beastly realities of the field compounded into sterilised logistics, the applied socio-psychology of the Madison Avenue boardroom. Murray hated the war, not out of any moral revulsion, or even intellectual judgment, but because it bored him. It bored him because he could see no respectable conclusion to it. He knew all the

215

arguments, for and against: hawks, doves, hard-nosed pragmatists, soft-bellied liberals, bomb-happy pin-heads who wanted to take out Hanoi and tell world opinion go fly a kite; the anaemic experts who argued a middle course, a phased withdrawal, dissecting the anatomy of Marxism versus Nationalist Communism versus Maoism while the planes whined low and machineguns flicked and flesh was roasted and shredded and the platoon sergeants went in to tot up the 'body-count' — taking all the hands and feet and dividing by four, as the wags joked in the Caravelle bar.

But worst of all, the world was now bored with the war. It had become smug with self-righteous indignation, with the tedious long-range censure of international pundits, of little men with big jobs and puppet minds who sat in the United Nations, sounding off against U.S. aggression while they borrowed American money and squandered it; and those respected, comfortable intellectuals — men of letters, poets, professors, leader-writers, stars of stage and screen, mummers and celluloid-snippers who led demos, waving paper Viet Cong flags and braving Mace — who had now wearied of the whole bloody business and moved on to other pastures of protest. Even Uncle Ho's wispy features had been superseded, as the middle-class revolutionary pin-up, by those of Che Guevara.

The war was not even a bonus any longer for those who covered it. The Press briefings told of new offensives, so many hundred KIA, VC infrastructure penetrated, hamlets secured and re-motivated: all reduced to perhaps two paragraphs of agency reports. For as the war escalated, its news value shrank. The real thing — the blood and mud and grief and trails of homeless people trying to rescue their ducks and rusted bicycles from some ravaged village while their children scrounged peanut butter and cream-crackers from perplexed

GI's — this story had been done, and done again, and news editors were bored too and wanted other angles. The fact that a small medieval country with a peasant economy and an ancient, fragile culture was being pounded and perverted by the richest nation on earth had been thoroughly reported, and accepted, and it had made many people very angry. But those many people were not angry or imaginative enough to realise that this was only part of the story. Murray had also seen some of the mass graves of civilians in Huế — after the Viet Cong had discovered that not all the Vietnamese felt quite as much in sympathy with the Communist cause as the flag-waving, Mace-groggy demonstrators in the world outside. And the Viet Cong had murdered these civilians with their hands behind their backs, burying them in great shallow pits by the River of Perfume. But this had provoked no demonstrations. It was not the Vietnam the world cared to hear about.

Murray had once written a story on the Saigon Zoo where there was a horse in a cage, which was a great attraction with the children. That was the other Vietnam. Like the business of British tracker-dogs that had caused such an outcry back in the House of Commons because Britain was contributing to the wicked Vietnam war effort by selling six hundred Alsatians to the Americans, who had paid gratefully for them and then given them to the Vietnamese Army who had promptly eaten them.

He sat up quickly. The telephone was purring by the bed. A woman's voice, crisp and American, said, 'Mr Murray Wilde, Hotel Continental Palace? Tiger exchange here — one moment please. Your party's on the line.'

Jacqueline Conquest's voice cut in: *'Murray — c'est toi?'*

'When did you get here?'

'Yesterday. We came back suddenly. Maxwell's been looking for you since last night. Where were you?'

'Up in Biên Hòa looking at corpses. What does he want?'

'I don't know. I want to see you too. *Hello!* You're still there?'

'I'm still here,' he said, hauling his legs off the bed. 'Any time?'

'Tomorrow at 12.30. At the *Cercle Sportif* — the bar by the swimming pool. Are you a member?'

'No. Only American generals are members these days. Why the *Cercle*?'

'It's agreeable, isn't it?'

'It's about the last place here that is. You're a member, I suppose?'

'*Bien sûr*. If I'm late, I'll leave a message at the gate for them to let you in. All right?'

'All right.' The line clicked dead. He looked at his watch. Nearly ten to five. Just time to catch the Five o'Clock Follies, the daily Press conference held just across the square in the reinforced, sandbagged JUSPAO building.

He took a quick shower, savouring with mixed feelings the separate attentions of Mr and Mrs Conquest. The husband probably meant bad news; as for the *Cercle*, ancient enclave of the Empire French whose select membership had shifted from colons and opium pirates to the American military elite, there were certainly worse spots in Saigon in which to continue the adulterous fieldwork of sleeping his way by proxy towards General Virgil Greene's Red Alert button.

He went out into the high corridor, past the rows of dark-stained teak doors to the cage-lift with its wrought-iron gates that clanked down the well of a stone staircase. One of the last of the old Saigon hotels to resist the antiseptic onslaught of the New World. Even in the downstairs terraced bar, where fans churned the thick sweet air among the potted palms and marble tables, there were not even any anti-grenade screens because it was thought impossible that the Viet Cong would commit an outrage against a French hotel.

Just outside the lift a voice whispered close to Murray's ear: *'M'sieur Wilde?'* He was a thin crooked-cheeked man in a grey shirt and faded blue trousers standing in the shadow of the stairs. Murray recognised one of the hotel *boys* — the mongrel French word applying in this case to a middle-aged Vietnamese with one blind eye, milky-white like a burnt-out flashbulb, who was usually to be seen lurking about the passages offering to change piastres on the black market. He had solicited Murray on a number of occasions and had always been refused.

Murray said briskly, in French, 'What do you want?'

'Someone was asking for you today, *M'sieur Wilde.* He came twice.'

'Who was it?'

'He was an American.'

'He spoke to you?'

'Only to reception. He left no message.' The man stood quite still, fixing Murray with his one narrow black eye; and there was something in his manner, usually so obsequious, that was now assured and faintly sinister.

Murray said: 'What has this to do with you?'

The man inclined his head a fraction, and even in the poor light Murray thought he detected the gleam of a smile in that one good eye. 'I notice things, *m'sieur.* Many things. The American was from the police.'

Murray did not move. He had never thought the Vietnamese — even the humblest of them — a stupid or unsophisticated race; but there was an unexpected authority here that was very unsettling. This man was no friend of Murray's, and certainly owed him no favours. 'Why do you tell me this?'

The *boy* inclined his head a little further, with a tiny shrug — more a movement of the wrists than of the shoulders. 'I believed it would interest you, *M'sieur Wilde.*'

'Thank you.' For a moment he considered tipping him fifty piastres, but at once thought better of it: the role of common hotel-tout had been dropped entirely, and Murray decided to play along with him. The man's French had been remarkably good, he reflected, as he crossed the noisy dust-choked square to the JUSPAO building — Joint US Public Affairs Office, set up in what had once been a cinema, its pale stucco walls now covered with a new hide of breeze block, the pavement outside ringed off with drums of solid concrete guarded by helmeted U.S. Marines, their rifles with fixed bayonets resting on their thighs like flagpoles. He flashed his MACV Press card to the Marine at the desk inside, and wound his way through the old cinema foyer which had been divided up into a maze of hardboard partitions, fresh and cold, full of short sleeved men in drip-dry slacks sitting over telephones and the mutter of electric typewriters. He was at the nerve-centre of the Vietnam Public Relations war machine. He shivered a little from the air-conditioning.

The Five o'Clock Follies had already begun and about half the four hundred-odd seats were taken. On the stage stood four maps mounted on blackboards showing the military Corps areas of Vietnam, each with red arrows stuck on to mark the latest offensives, black bombs to mark air-strikes. Today the maps were relatively bare. Any one of those plastic cut-outs could represent tragedy for perhaps hundreds of people — people in some jungle hamlet, Mid-West town, tenement in

Watts, a WASP family in Calvary, Georgia. Otherwise it looked like a dull day.

Murray collected the stapled Xerox handout, listing all operations conducted during the last twenty-four hours in the Republic of South Vietnam, and took his seat near the back, while an elderly bespectacled colonel ran through the items. Below him sat a stenographer and a young Negro working a tape-recorder for posterity.

The colonel was giving details of Operation Openhand, a Civic Action effort to assist the Montagnard tribesmen in the Central Highlands with the problems of hygiene and medicare. 'U.S. interpreters have been dispatched into the area to facilitate co-ordination with the local PAT's — Pacification Action Teams,' the colonel intoned, as a hand shot up from one of the front rows of reporters and an adenoid voice cried: 'Hey Chuck, are these interpreters bilingual?'

The colonel paused. 'I'll check that out, Jo,' he said, beginning to turn to the wings of the stage, then frowning as laughter rippled down the hall. 'They are qualified interpreters, Jo,' he said steadily, referring back to the Xerox sheet in his hand.

A moment later another hand went up. 'Chuck, on Item 47 here it's stated — and I quote — "At 0200 hours this morning the camp at Dak Phuoc was attacked and overrun for two hours. Friendly losses were heavy in both equipment and personnel." Can you elaborate on this incident? Any U.S. casualties?'

'Negative, Tom. It was an Arvin post.'

'Was Dak Fook wiped out?' Jo cried.

'It was not wiped out. It was overrun for two hours when Army gunships, assisted by Skyhawks, relieved the position using rockets and napalm.'

'Can you give us any run-down on the casualties, Chuck?' another voice called. 'How many KIA?'

The colonel rifled through some pages, sounding cautious. 'As of this time, we have fifteen Regulars, twelve Irregulars, and two local Militia.'

'All killed?'

'Correct.'

Pause. 'Colonel.' It was a slow weary voice belonging to a senior Washington columnist: 'What was the original strength of the post at Dak Phuoc?'

The colonel wrinkled his brow. 'It was a platoon, sir.'

'And what is the strength of a South Vietnamese Army platoon?'

The colonel peered up over his bifocals. 'The garrison was at U.S. platoon strength, sir.' And Jo's adenoids whined gleefully: 'What's the full strength of a U.S. platoon, Chuck?'

'Thirty men, Jo.' The laughter had begun again. The Washington columnist sounded almost sorry for the older man.

'Correct me if I'm wrong, Colonel. But as I have it here, you stated that the KIA at Dak Phuoc was fifteen Regulars?' — the colonel nodded gravely — 'twelve Irregulars, and two Militia?' The colonel stood on the stage and stared at his audience vacantly, resigned.

'According to my arithmetic that makes twenty-nine men killed,' the Washington columnist went on. 'And you still say the camp was not wiped out? So what happened to the one man, Colonel?'

As the laughter died down, and the colonel promised to check the matter out with his MACV superiors, a voice at Murray's elbow said softly: 'Mr Wilde sir.' He was a big freckled young man in a uniform the colour of dried mud. 'Would you please mind stepping outside for a moment, sir?'

Murray followed him out of the hall, down one of the hardboard passages to a door marked *Leroy — Joint Liaison Officer MACV*. The American knocked and opened it in almost the same gesture, then stood back to let Murray through. Inside, on an olive-green swivel chair, was Maxwell Conquest.

'Afternoon, Mr Wilde. Will you sit down. This is Mr Sy Leroy, my associate.'

The second man sat dangling his legs from a desk — a dark man with crimped charcoal-grey hair and a rubbery, slightly simian jaw. When he smiled, the crinkles round his eyes showed white against his tan. 'Glad to meet you, Mr Wilde. I've read some of your stuff. I liked it.'

Murray sat down in another swivel chair. 'What's all this about?'

Maxwell Conquest paused, getting out a buff folder from a pile beside him. 'You stopped over in Bangkok on your way in here, I understand. Have a good time there?'

'I wasn't there long enough.'

Conquest nodded. Sy Leroy was still smiling. 'You meet a man called Charles Pol while you were in Bangkok, Mr Wilde?' Conquest's voice was lowkey, very casual. 'Big Frenchman with a beard?'

'Yes, I met him.'

'Why did you meet him?'

'Why are you asking me?'

Conquest looked at him deadpan. 'You were booked out of Bangkok on the same plane with this man Pol two days ago. Right?' Murray nodded. 'Notice anything funny at the airport?'

'What sort of funny?'

'I'm asking you, Mr Wilde.'

223

'The plane left on time, if that's what you mean.' And Sy Leroy's smile widened. Conquest opened the folder, took out a big glossy photograph and handed it to Murray. It was full-face of a chubby bald man. 'Recognise him?'

'Should I?'

Conquest took the picture back and looked at Leroy, who sat forward on the desk, his palms pressed to his knees.

'Mr Wilde,' Leroy began, 'that man there was killed at Bangkok Airport at about the precise time you and this Frenchman were boarding your plane. Now you still say you saw nothing odd?' He had a gentle Southern voice, a touch of the Virginian gentleman about him, all velvet-gloved and still smiling. Murray looked back at him, at the tight black hair and rounded jaw and wondered if sometime, generations back, great grandad might have split black oak down there on the ole plantation.

'Yes,' he said at last, 'there was some kind of disturbance. Someone taken ill, I think. At the bar. I didn't see too clearly, because we were just leaving.'

Leroy leant back and nodded. 'And what was this man Pol doing at the time?'

'He was leaving too.'

'Had he gone to the bar first?'

'He had a drink, yes. But what is all this? Who was this man who's been killed?'

'He was a USOM officer working up in North-East Thailand,' said Conquest. 'Name of Amos Shelton. He was killed with a prick of amethine-cyanide, a highly sophisticated poison that can be administered with just a scratch anywhere on the skin and produces almost instantaneously the symptoms of a heart-attack or seizure. And we have reason to believe that

Shelton was killed in just such a way by this Frenchman, Charles Pol. We also believe that you can help us, Mr Wilde.'

'Oh? And just how?'

'By telling us what your business was with Pol. Telling us about your meeting with him in Bangkok. How and why.'

Murray sat back. 'I'm doing a story on Cambodia. Pol works in Cambodia, where I first met him, and he's promised to get me an introduction to Prince Sihanouk. O.K.?'

'Not O.K. at all, Mr Wilde.' Conquest was watching Murray with icy calculation. 'You ever meet someone called George Finlayson?'

'Yes.'

'A Britisher living in Vientiane. Murdered four days ago.'

'I read the papers too.'

'We think he was also killed by Charles Pol — or on orders given by Pol.'

Murray shrugged. 'Sounds as though this man Pol's a right villain!'

'We don't like him, Mr Wilde.'

'We don't like him at all,' said Sy Leroy, and for the first time his smile was gone. 'We have no immediate authority to arrest the man at this time, but we think you may be able to supply us with some of the relevant information that can get him arrested.'

'I don't see how.'

'What was your business with George Finlayson?' said Conquest.

'I didn't have any business with Finlayson. I just met him.'

'You had dinner with him in Vientiane.'

'So I had dinner with him. What of it?'

Conquest's face tightened. 'Let me be quite frank with you, Mr Wilde. You dine with a man a couple of days before he's killed, then you fly out and spend the day with the man who had him killed, and are actually with this man when he kills a second person. And then when you're asked about it, you say, "What of it?" I'll tell you what of it, Mr Wilde. I tell you it stinks.'

'All right, it stinks,' said Murray. 'And now you tell me how you know George Finlayson was killed by Pol.'

It was Leroy who answered: 'We picked up Finlayson's house-girl. Vietnamese from Hanoi. She was the one who let the killer in. She broke down and told everything.'

'To you — or the Lao police?'

'She was interrogated by Lao Security,' Leroy said gently. 'Maxwell was there, and so was a member of the British Embassy. It was all quite correct.'

'I'm sure it was,' said Murray, thinking hard. 'And who did she let in to kill Finlayson?'

'North Vietnamese, name of Than Thuoc Vinh. Licensed to kill, as the story-books say.'

'Or to terminate with extreme prejudice — like your man Amos Shelton?'

'What does that mean?' Conquest snapped.

'Someone tried to kill Pol the day I saw him. Sent him up a fancy bottle of brandy, only the brandy turned out to be *plastique*. He seemed to think it might have been one of your boys.' He met Conquest's dry grey eyes as he spoke, but Conquest did not look away.

'I don't know what you're talking about. But you go on making those sort of accusations and you can get yourself into a lot of trouble.'

'You mean the CIA might sue me for slander?'

Conquest swung back in his seat and gave an exaggerated sigh. 'Let's just understand each other, Mr Wilde. You've got a job to do here — we appreciate that. We also appreciate you may have to meet people who are not necessarily desirable. On the other hand, there's a war on in this country. And if we find out you're in any way — even the most indirect way — aiding the enemy in this war, we're going to come down on you and break you. We're not going to pull you in, because we can't do that, but what we can do is make sure you don't have a snowball's chance in hell of going on making your living in this part of the world.'

'How? By leaning on the South Vietnamese and getting them to revoke my visa? It won't make you very popular when it gets out that the CIA are vetting foreign journalists out here, and banning the ones they don't like.'

'We're not popular anyway,' said Conquest. 'But we're not sensitive about it either.' For a moment he almost smiled.

'All right, so what do I do to be a good boy?'

'Tell us all you know about Charles Pol.'

'There isn't much I do know. He eats like a pig, drinks like a fish, sweats like a sponge, uses expensive perfume and works as some sort of adviser to Prince Sihanouk. But then so do plenty of other people — including a former British diplomat. You want me to check on them too?'

'They're not killers,' Sy Leroy said drily. 'Besides, it's not Sihanouk we're after. He's no friend of the U.S., to be sure, but that's a State Department affair. It's this man Pol that bothers us. The fact that he's killed an American is bad enough, but when he's able to hire a professional killer from North Vietnam who can terrorize the house-girl through her family back in Hanoi, then kills an official of the IMF and disappears back into North Vietnam — well, that begins to worry us a lot, Mr Wilde.' There was a meaningful pause. 'So we'd appreciate it if you could find out just what this man Pol is up to. Who else he works for. And what exactly he's doing in Cambodia.'

'And if I don't find out?'

'We don't want to be vindictive, Mr Wilde. And I think we'll know if you're holding back.'

'So when do I report?'

'Only when you've got something. Have you planned to meet Pol again?'

'Nothing definite. Perhaps I'll be going to Phnom Penh — in two or three weeks' time,' he said carefully. 'Who do I report to?'

Conquest answered: 'Mr Leroy is here every day till five-thirty except weekends. If there's anything really urgent outside those hours you call this number.' He thrust a card at Murray with the name of Major D. Curry, and a telephone number, then stood up, nodded at Sy Leroy and left without another word.

Murray began to stand up too, as Leroy slid gracefully from the desktop and laid a hand on his shoulder. 'You must excuse Maxwell. He's dedicated, and he's good, but sometimes I wonder if the FBI oughtn't to have had him, and that he just got mixed up in the shuffle. No offence, Mr Wilde?'

'Not so far. Did you mean that about getting me kicked out?'

'Blackmail's a dirty word and all that. But you must admit, your associations with this man Pol look, to say the least, rather too coincidental?' His hand stayed on Murray's shoulder, guiding him gently towards the door. 'We're after Pol — but it's a bit more than that. Pol's got a history and it doesn't add up to anything we like. That's to say, the computer doesn't like it. You probably know it — Spain, Algeria, close to de Gaulle, now Snooky, then going in for bare-faced murder. We want to find out what he's up to in these parts — and we don't want to

228

find out afterwards by reading about it in the newspapers. You understand, Mr Wilde?'

'I understand.'

Leroy squeezed his shoulder. 'Always remember the old saying — a man who kills once will kill again.' His monkey mouth widened, the crows' feet stretched white round his eyes. 'And anyway, we'd like to hear something about Cambodia. I hear Sihanouk's just completed his sixth feature film out there?'

'That's right. He plays two parts — hero and villain. The hero's himself and the villain's employed by the CIA.'

Leroy chuckled, his manner easy and infectious. 'Sometimes I wonder if we shouldn't get him on our side — maybe teach us to keep the Communists out the gentle way. Well, good luck, Mr Wilde.'

Murray left the chilly JUSPAO building, puzzled and thoughtful. Perhaps Conquest and the civilised Sy Leroy were not the only ones who had reason to be troubled by Pol.

He wondered what Conquest would be doing tomorrow at 12.30.

CHAPTER 2

At just past noon Murray stepped out of the cage-lift, freshly shaved and wearing a tie, crossing the terraced bar to the front steps where a figure insinuated itself beside him: *'Cyclo-pousse, M'sieur Wilde?'* Murray found himself staring at that dead white eye at his elbow. He nodded, and almost at once a solar-topeed rider had slid to a stop at the pavement.

'Où allez-vous, m'sieur?' blind eye whispered behind him.

'Cercle Sportif,' Murray said, climbing in under the sun-hood. The sky was a hard blue and the heat fierce, exhausting. He heard the *boy* chattering in Vietnamese, and this time Murray passed him a 50-piastre note under the hood.

They began to wobble across the square, round the Palladian facade of the defunct State Opera House, up bustling Le Loi Boulevard with the steel shutters coming down for lunch and siesta; past the sandbagged railings of the half-finished Presidential Palace — a great husk of naked concrete and fluted columns standing back behind heavy trees. The blue shade of a French boulevard with the rumble of traffic growing muffled; áo dàis flitting like moths among the shadows. Murray closed his eyes, half-dozing as the knobbly brown legs behind peddled him along, into patches of blinding light, swerving, rocking to a halt for some diesel-belching Army truck.

He wondered how he would greet her, wine her, lunch her, talk her round in circles and lie to her. Because that was the only way unless he confided in her, and whatever else she might say, she was still married to Maxwell Conquest who was good and truly dedicated — who might blink at a million dollars but would not necessarily accept them. Or would he?

And would she? Would she believe him? Believe him after the third drink, in bed for the second time? For he knew that the second time, the disavowal of the common hasty one-night stand, was usually a critical manoeuvre. Or had she come to warn him — like Hamish Napper, the one-eyed *boy*, Conquest himself? he thought, as he shook himself awake, coughing with dust.

They were tearing down the old Saigon, replacing the soft yellow houses with modern blocks of concrete cells where the plumbing was nearly impeccable, but the children lay crammed in bundles down the corridors while tipsy GI's picked their way over them to be pleasured by their elder sisters who preened themselves in miniskirts and washed themselves in cheap scent.

He looked up and saw it was a quarter to one. The street was low and mean. No sign of trucks, jeeps, those reassuring M.P.'s with their Southern voices and machine-pistols snapped on to automatic. He struggled up and shouted at the driver: '*Cercle Sportif.*' But the words sounded so hopelessly alien — they carried no meaning. He shouted '*Stop! Halt!*' — jabbing one leg out of the cab, with the memory of those four journalists who had been gunned down brutally, stupidly while riding in a Mini Moke in just such a meagre little outlying street. He realised that he was also nowhere near the *Cercle Sportif.* The driver pulled up at last and began jabbering something unintelligible.

Murray was trying his best Vietnamese, from Huế, which is rarely understood by the lower classes of Saigon, when the explosion came.

There were two thuds and the shockwaves touched him a moment later with a ripple of air. The driver and the few other people in the street were staring back towards the city centre. A third sound — a strange crumbling growl — reached them now like the rumble of an avalanche. Murray was shouting at the driver: '*Hotel! Hotel Continental* — *vite!*'

This time the man in the solar topee seemed to pedal very slowly, as though exhausted by the long crawl out of the centre. After a couple more streets Murray gave up. The ambulance sirens were converging in a great animal howl just ahead near the Presidential Palace. American and Vietnamese M.P.'s were flagging down traffic, driving the *cyclo-pousses* and pedestrians back, as Murray scrambled out and gave the man 500-piastres — the going black market rate for the dollar — but the man still tried to whine and haggle. (Had Murray known then what he was to learn later he would gladly have paid double.) As it was, he called back a Vietnamese obscenity and began running in the general direction of the crowd.

Several Vietnamese police patrols had been set up, their jeeps stuck diagonally across the street, checking everyone who passed. Murray had flashed his Press card through three of them when the second explosion came — a huge shuddering clap, followed this time, it seemed, by a numbing stillness. He turned a corner and found himself back under the trees of the boulevard. He ducked sideways and began running between the shelter of the trees and the stone gate-posts of the old French villas on his left.

There was another road-block ahead — Australians this time, big lean men in floppy hats standing with self-repeaters field across their hips. 'Where yer goin'!' one of them yelled.

'*Cercle Sportif!*' He had his card out again, breathing fast, and one of them grinned nastily: 'Yer won't find much of it left!' His voice was gone as three ambulances screamed up, headlamps on full beam. Murray slipped through and joined a nervous crowd under the trees. Some were trying to back away, others forcing them forward.

The gateposts of the *Cercle* had been splintered and inside was a great scrum of uniforms and white shirts and howling faces. Above there were high trees with hanging branches, some of them stripped and clotted and broken. The clubhouse, pale blue and white, had been cracked like an eggshell. The steps up to the swimming pool were crammed with bodies, some of them twitching like the tails of sundered reptiles. A man's body, naked except for his blue socks, lay across Murray's path, his suntan a curious brownish-blue against the white strip of his waist. There was part of a girl further on, still wearing her bathing-top, but with no head. Flesh was spattered about like meat among the dust. He was pushed aside by two enormous Negroes carrying a stretcher.

An American voice on a loudhailer was calling: 'Stand back! Stand back! There may be more bombs! Please stand back, get clear, make way for the ambulances!'

He was shoved against a wall, face-to-face with a dazed American civilian who was gingerly stroking his crewcut. 'What happened?' Murray cried.

'Don't quite know. Was down in the men's room and ah just kinda hit mah head.' He began to grope along the wall, muttering, 'Bastards set off a second bomb, ah guess, just when the ambulances came. Lucky ah was in the john.'

Murray found a young hard-faced soldier with the shoulder-flash of the Special Forces, the Green Berets. 'What happened?' He didn't show his card this time, and the man said bitterly: 'Two charges. First under the pool, laid along the roof of the observation bar. Blew the swimmers into the air like a lot o' goddam fish out of a tank. Second charge laid in a dustbin just inside the gates. Killed a lot o' the ambulance boys and spectators. Who the hell are you, anyway?'

Murray looked down and saw a shoe lying near them with a foot in it. He groped for his Press card, mumbling: 'Were there any survivors?'

'In this mess?' The Green Beret frowned at the Press card. 'If I know these VC bastards they may have set a third charge. I should get the hell out o' here if I was you. There's nothing to see, unless you like stockyards.'

'There was someone I was going to meet here. I'm staying.'

Up the steps towards the pool and the bar he had to control himself. He had seen this thing before, many times, but this — perhaps because it was sited in such luxurious, familiar décor — was peculiarly horrible. An American in bathing trunks, his legs wrapped in blood-soaked towels as he was borne down on a stretcher, waved at him: 'Hey, you a newspaperman? Better get this. Hold it, boys! Name's Larrymore — Don Macaulay Larrymore — ex-Marine, seen it all, was up there and I saw it all. You can quote me.' He did not sound sober.

Murray had started up the steps again when the blood met him, in two snake rivulets, their noses glinting with dust as they crept across the clean concrete floor, swelling fresh and rich as they expanded and dropped their heady load on to the step below — and all Murray could do was run, toppling, staggering upwards, thinking that some of that awful blood might belong to a girl he thought he loved. An arm stopped him at the top of the steps. He recognised Colonel Luong of the South Vietnamese Third Corps, otherwise Laughing Larry Lung, so nicknamed on account of his nervous giggle while shooting prisoners. He was giggling now. 'Hello, Mr Wilde — this is very bad thing!'

'You were here when it happened?'

'Oh no, I was across the street in the restaurant. They were trying to kill General Greene.' He stood there in a short-sleeved Hawaiian shirt and drainpipe slacks, his rubber-soled sneakers sticky with blood.

'What happened to Greene?' said Murray.

Laughing Larry twitched and began flicking his tiny wrist on which dangled a heavy silver identification disc. 'General Greene not come, I think. He was late.'

'So was I,' Murray murmured. 'Are you sure it was Greene they were after?'

'He was to come here for lunch. These VC are pigs.' He giggled again, beginning to sidle away past a naked torso of no definable sex from which a blue bubble of intestine shone dully in the sun. 'Very bad here,' Larry said again, smiling, and Murray started down the steps again.

Had she been coming with Greene? he wondered, as another scream of sirens rose from the gates. A motorcade of black sedans with Vietnamese outriders bounced to a halt and American M.P.s sprang from the doors, coming to attention as a knot of officers converged on the shattered gates.

General Virgil Luther Greene was a tall handsome man with grey eyes set deep in an oven-fresh suntan. But the tan was perhaps a shade paler than usual as he walked solemnly towards the steps up to the empty, blasted pool. It was not for nothing that General Greene had the reputation of being a 'shooting general': he had killed as many men — Huns, Huks, Koreans, Vietnamese — as almost any serving officer in the U.S. Armed Forces; he was a crack-shot and when his tank had been burned out in a village near Rome in 1944 he had drawn his twin Colt .45's and dropped four SS men dead at his feet. These two Colts, with ivory handles, still adorned the belt of his plain Army fatigues. As he began to walk up the steps he was heard to mutter, in a loud Texan undertone, over and over again: 'Oh my God! My Lord God in heaven!'

There were no women present — besides a few dead or dying bathers lying flopped about on the wet concrete — and Virgil Greene stopped and breathed a good Texan obscenity. Then he saw Laughing Larry Lung, one of the few Vietnamese officers he respected, and they exchanged salutes. 'They're goin' to pay for this, Colonel! You see they pay for it.'

Larry giggled: 'Sure thing, General!'

Virgil Luther Greene nodded gravely and swung on his heel. Water from broken ducts was now mixing with the blood, washing down the steps and across the azure forecourt of the bar by the pool. Bodies were being carried out on stretchers, and Murray looked at each and saw that none was Jacqueline Conquest.

The General now stopped at the edge of the empty pool and stood gazing down through the cracked concrete, while a young officer explained how the VC had laid the first charges — strips of *plastique* round the glass ceiling of the downstairs bar where the men could sit over their drinks and watch the girls swimming above. Most of the water had drained down into the wreckage of this bar and the ground was strewn with shards of green glass and blue-painted concrete. Murray knew that if she had decided to meet him down there, and not in the bar upstairs, the night in Luang Prabang would be a lost idyll, and he'd have to find someone else to push Virgil's secret button.

The General was standing a few yards away, contemplating the body of a plump middle-aged man in the corner of the pool. Murray went up and said bluntly, 'Excuse me, General, your secretary — Mrs Jacqueline Conquest — is she all right?'

The General's fine grey eyes swivelled slowly in his head. 'Jacky?' he drawled.

'I was meeting her here about the time the bombs went off.'

'Who are you?'

Murray told him and the General nodded thoughtfully. 'Newspaperman, eh? Well, you get this straight, boy. Forget all the horse-crap about us scuttlin' outta Veetnam and leavin' it to these dirty little motherin' Commie bitches! We're stayin', boy. We're stayin' for the duration!'

'Your secretary,' Murray said: 'Is she all right?'

'I guess so. I left her back at the office when the news came through. She did say something about a lunch date she'd had to cancel.' He looked at Murray narrowly. 'You the date?'

Murray forced a tired grin. 'Strictly business, General. As long as she didn't turn up. Can I quote you on this atrocity?'

'You sure can!' And Murray was still scribbling awkwardly as the lithe little Vietnamese firemen, dressed in rubber diving suits, began to creep down into the flooded bar.

Ten minutes later he was back at the hotel, trying the *Tiger* exchange. She came on the line almost at once. 'Ah Murray! Thank God, you're alive!'

'Where were you?'

'I tried to call you, twice. Someone phoned here — I don't know who it was, but it sounded Vietnamese — and said if I was going to the *Cercle*, keep away. *N'y allez pas*, he said.'

'At what time was this?'

'About noon. I called at once.'

'You called anyone else?' He could see it all now: that dead white eye and crooked face muttering to the *cyclo*-driver, not daring to tell him personally not to go to the *Cercle*, but warning the girl anonymously after he'd heard himself that the charges had been planted... Murray wondered for a moment if he ought to go himself to the police — then recalled Ryderbeit's maxim and thought better of it. This was not only a city at war — it was a city of ancient ritual crime, gangland intrigue, political skulduggery that might have nothing to do with the temporal struggle of the Free World against the forces of Marx and Mao.

She said: 'No one. I didn't have time. And then I heard about the bomb. I was scared. Murray, who was it? Who phoned? What's going on?'

'Can you get away?'

'Yes, I think so.'

'At the hotel then. Downstairs at the bar — as soon as you can make it. I'll be waiting.'

He hung up, thinking: She had been in a state of shock the first time he had seduced her. She was in a state of mild shock now, and he'd seduce her a second time — cards on the table, their success in her hands — because if she were going to go along with them, it would have to be all or nothing.

He ordered a bottle of 1961 Chablis to be put on ice and sent up to his room.

PART 8: BAT INTO HELL

CHAPTER 1

'He won't do it. He would never do it. I know him — it's impossible for him.' She had rolled over and was now splayed out like a star on the stripped bed. Her voice was slow, broken with thought. 'He would never do anything that was illegal. He has a very respectable, orthodox outlook.'

Murray watched her in the striped light from the shutters — her short pretty features almost buried in hair, the deep curving profile of her back rising steeply into the wide-spread buttocks. He said, 'All right, we'll forget about Maxwell.'

'He won't forget us.'

'We'll have others besides him. We'll have them all.'

'And you still think you can get away with it?'

'I don't know.'

'It's crazy — you know that? You can't steal all the money in Vietnam and think they will let you keep it. This Frenchman you tell me about — this Pol, I've heard his name before. Maxwell doesn't usually talk about his work with me, but he did ask me about Pol because I'm French and my father might have had some dealings with him in Algeria. I told him the truth — I had never heard of a man called Pol. Then I asked him why, and you know what he said? He said, "*Because the bastard's working for Charlie Cong, like all the goddam French!*" (She spoke these last words in English, with a distorted American accent, smiling to herself in the half-dark.) 'He said it as though I were no longer French, but one of those horrible patriotic American wives — that I would necessarily hate this man Pol because he worked for the Liberation Front.'

'He works for Sihanouk,' said Murray thoughtfully. 'But that's about the same thing to a man of Maxwell's political subtleties. Did he say anything about me?'

'No. But I had the impression that he deliberately avoided talking about you. I think perhaps he suspects something between you and Pol.'

'Do you know a man called Sy Leroy?' Murray added after a pause.

She turned her head, beginning to frown: 'A Jew who poses as a MACV liaison officer?'

'Jew, part-Negro, Southern gentleman — some kind of social outcast.' He grinned. 'That's the one. He and your husband questioned me about Pol yesterday afternoon.'

'What did they want?'

He told her, concealing nothing he had not concealed from her husband and Leroy: he did not tell her of his discovery of Finlayson's body, nor that Pol had been responsible — only that Maxwell suspected that Pol had done it. When he was through, she said: 'You should be very careful of this man, Leroy. I don't know him well, but I do know he works for the National Security Agency. He would not have questioned you unless he considered you very seriously.'

For a moment Murray said nothing. The CIA was one problem, the NSA quite another. Jacqueline was no fool in appraising her husband's outfit and its rivals. While the CIA might be a rich, elaborate, devious freelance government-within-a-government, hatching plots, toppling regimes, tampering with the mechanics of international affairs, the NSA was a soberer, more compact, and ultimately more dangerous organisation. It had the ear of the President's closest advisers and its computerised intelligence data was treated with less scepticism than its rival's. But the even more sinister implication was that it dealt primarily with matters of internal security rather than foreign affairs. Murray supposed that his name, along with Pol's, would almost certainly have been flashed to Washington where they would join the 'grey list' — that twilight zone of suspects somewhere between the Immigration blacklist and the FBI files. The portents for the next twelve days, and the even more crucial ones that would follow, were not good.

He said: 'Jackie, when you meet the others, I don't want you to say anything about this man Leroy. Don't even mention your husband's conversation with me. It may not be important in the long run, but I'd prefer no-one knows.'

'You're mad,' she said. 'The Americans will know that you and Pol have done it. And then there's that crazy man Ryderbeit. You really think you can trust him — trust any of them?'

He paused. 'I wouldn't trust them with a million New Francs. But this is rather different — rather more like seven thousand million.' He found himself repeating, even believing, Ryderbeit's own thesis for mutual trust in a venture like this — that the sum was so vast that no sane man would be tempted to try to increase his own share by cutting out someone else's. He was not so sure, though, that Jacqueline Conquest saw it quite this way. She had rolled again on to her side facing him, her long legs pulled up under her chin, her eyes open, almost unblinking. '*Tu es fou, chéri*,' she said at last.

'You won't do it?'

'Do it? You mean look at General Greene's top secret air traffic control schedules for Sunday the fifteenth, then send the alarm? Yes, I'll do that — that's no problem.'

'So?'

'You can steal this money, and perhaps Ryderbeit is clever enough to land the plane on this dam. Pol may even arrange to get it out of Laos — perhaps into India. And then what? You think you will ever be free? Even with all that money, you think you can ever live a happy life?'

'*Ah merde!*' he cried. 'Jackie, you talk like a bad woman's novelette. You think any of us are interested at this stage in the morals of money? All right! We'll become wicked, spoilt, selfish rich shits with big cars and fancy clothes and we can be rude to anyone who matters, and even doesn't matter. Or perhaps we'll be just lonely old Gatsbys living in the big house which no one wants to go to — except for parties.'

She squeezed him close against her. 'You won't be like that. I don't want my share, anyway. Perhaps a little of yours.' She smiled. 'But only a little. Enough to buy a chateau on the Loire — somewhere between Chenonceaux and Blois. With a high wall and a moat to keep strangers out. And we'd drive to Switzerland through the Bourgogne country and drink the very best wine on our way to see our bankers once a month.'

'Our bankers will come and see us,' said Murray. 'But we could buy the vineyard, and even the chateau with it — except that we'd probably have Pol living bang next door.'

She wriggled her nose into his neck and was suddenly still. She felt no guilt nor shame with Murray, just a satisfied, dangerous happiness; she had come to him and run amok with him because she was lonely and bored and looking for adventure. But this adventure was altogether too outrageous, too tantalising for her mind to grasp seriously. *Mais alors je m'en fous!* she thought: almost anything was better than life in this drab, sandbagged, boorish city where the pavement cafes had long been closed and even the trees on the boulevards were shrivelled by fumes or bulldozed into turnpikes.

She said softly, without moving: 'I'll do anything you want, Murray. Anything.'

She was in the bathroom when the knock came. Murray got up, wrapping a towel round him, and called through the outside door: '*Qui est là?*'

A quiet cackle reached him through the panelled teak: 'Caught yer on the job, Murray boy?'

He unlocked the door and stared into the dark passage. Ryderbeit was dressed from chin to toes in black leather; his black suede flying-boots were replaced by leather ones, strapped across and buckled, with steel caps and heels; there was a mauve silk scarf at his throat and a pair of goggles dangled round his neck. In his hand was a crash-helmet. 'Can I come in?'

Murray stood back. 'And what in hell are you doing? Going to a fancy-dress ball as Marshal Ky?'

Ryderbeit stepped in and stood leering round him. 'Is the lucky lady who it ought to be?' he whispered, with a glance at the bathroom door, as the shower came on with a loud hiss. Murray told him, and added: 'Can it wait?'

'Not more than a quarter of an hour, it can't.'

'I'll talk to you downstairs.'

'Bring your passport and something warm to wear. And make sure you don't have any American or Vietnamese documents on you — Press cards or anything else. Just your passport with that lovely Irish harp.'

'What's up?'

'We're goin' on a trip.'

'Where?'

'I'll tell you downstairs.' He nodded again at the bathroom. 'Doin' all right?'

'All right,' said Murray, showing him back to the door.

'But don't spend all day kissin' her goodbye. We haven't got a lot o' time.'

Murray closed the door and locked it, turning back to the bathroom where the shower had stopped. He went in and told her bluntly what had happened. She nodded, standing naked with her back to him, scooping her hair up in front of the mirror. 'And he didn't even tell you where you're going?' she said finally.

'He'll tell me downstairs. I'm sorry, but I'll have to go.'

She shrugged rather too obviously. 'You go. I can't see you in the evening anyway. It's nearly five now. I have to be back at the villa before six.'

He left her and began to dress in the bedroom. Remembering the rice-drop, he wore three sweatshirts this time, and took a couple of newspapers and a polo-necked wool sweater he'd bought last winter when he was up in the Central Highlands. She came out and dressed rapidly beside him, without a word.

'The chateau,' he said; 'the vineyard in Bourgogne. It's not all a castle in the air, you know.'

She smiled faintly. 'It's amusing to build castles in the air, don't you think?' She'd built several in her time — playing games that could never be won. She'd already decided to play this one as long as it lasted, even if she did lose all in the end. She kissed him quickly on the mouth and he unlocked the door again.

'I don't know how long I'll be away — probably not more than a day. I'll ring you when I get back.'

'Yes,' she said, and was gone.

He found Ryderbeit down in the terraced bar drinking whisky at one of the marble tables. 'All wrapped up nice and warm, soldier? I didn't see Mrs Conquest leave.'

'She's discreet. Now where are we going?'

'Little place called Dong San. Up near the Cambodian border — a hundred and sixty miles north-west of here.'

'Never heard of it.'

'Be surprised if you had. It's not on most reference maps. In an insecure zone, as they say. Drink the rest o' my whisky — you're goin' to need it. And put your sweater on — we got to leave right away.'

'From here?'

'From right outside,' he said, snapping his fingers for the bill.

Murray still carried the sweater and newspapers as he walked, uncomprehending, out into the steaming heat where Ryderbeit was shooing away a small crowd, mostly children and youths, who had stopped to admire a huge motorcycle perched on the kerb. Ryderbeit pushed his way through them and called back at Murray: 'Get that bloody sweater on — and pull the neck up over your mouth. This beast really travels!'

Murray examined it. A 750-c.c. Honda — the whole machine painted fire-engine red except for the wheel-spokes and twin exhaust-pipes on either side, like four silver trumpets. The speedometer registered some horrible, impossible speed. 'We're not going to the Cambodian border on this?' he said, almost laughing.

'Don't argue. I've lined up some most important people for us to meet — not the least of them, your friend Pol. He's an amusing bastard, I'll give him that. I don't like his politics, mind, but he's a sound drinkin' companion — and that's somethin' I never quarrel with. Now get dressed and let's be movin'!' He yelled some obscenities at the last of the crowd, as he climbed astride the broad red leather saddle.

Murray said wearily, 'Look, Sammy, I know my Vietnam. There's no road to the border. There hasn't been since 1963.'

'There are two roads, you bastard. French roads — Biên Hòa up to Tây Ninh, then on up past An Loc. And don't tell me they're closed because no one, except for a few slow bloody armoured patrols, have ever been daft enough to try 'em. But we're not goin' to let a little thing like a war stop us now, are we now, soldier?' And he leant down grinning and patted the fat red petrol tank between his leather thighs. 'All fuelled up and ready to fly!'

Murray looked at him and thought: Jacky's right. The man is crazy. He tried a last query, playing for time: 'Where did you get this monster anyway? Is it hired?'

'Bought. By courtesy of Filling-Station — with his pocket money.'

'A bit extravagant, isn't it — if you're only going to be here for twelve more days?'

'Recklessly extravagant. But we've got to get into the habit, haven't we? Now get aboard and put your arms round me, lover boy, and hold on bloody tight!' He had pulled on his helmet and goggles and was fastening the scarf across his mouth. Conversation from now on would be impossible. Murray gave up and took off his jacket, folding the newspapers across his chest and pulling the sweater down over them. Then he climbed on the pillion and Ryderbeit kicked at the starter pedal.

The machine started first time, with a powerful snarl as they drifted away from the pavement, straight into the evening rush-hour. Murray closed his eyes. He didn't open them again until they were at the end of Tu Do Street where they swerved left along the river bank with their ankles almost grazing the ground; zipping past the old mercantile buildings of Saigon; shooting the lights right, again almost on their sides, swinging up on to the wide Tinh Do Bridge where Murray grabbed hard at Ryderbeit's belly, pressing himself forward against the hunched leather back, biting into the neck of his sweater, his watering eyes stretched half-open with the gritty slip-stream.

They stopped only once — on the outskirts of the city, at a dead railway line where Ryderbeit was forced to pull aside for a convoy of tanks. Murray's ears were numb, his groin aching; and as they waited for the tanks to pass over the level-crossing, he looked down the line, its tracks eroded by rust like strips of brown sponge, its sleepers long ripped up, the tracks warped, leading nowhere — the severed arteries of a country paralysed by war.

The last tank had clanked and scrabbled its way past them; and suddenly his spine felt as though it were being snapped in two as his hands locked again across Ryderbeit's stomach and they swept forward, zig-zagging out on to the great highway north-east to the town of Biên Hòa. The orange ball of sun was hanging low under flat clouds; then came the first dusk of the forest trees, the howl of the engine rising, becoming part of his body, part of the spine-jarring, numbing pain, his fingers frozen senseless even through the woollen sleeves of his sweater. Once he began inching his head up over Ryderbeit's shoulder to glance down at the speedometer; but when he tried opening his eyes they almost rolled up inside his head. The tears stiffened on his cheeks, the corners of his mouth dragged back under the neck of the sweater.

They reached the outskirts of Biên Hòa, twenty-eight miles from the centre of Saigon, in just under twelve minutes. So far the road had been secure. Ryderbeit now swept round the outer perimeter of the vast U.S. airbase there, with its attendant shanty town, and in less than five minutes they were back under the high trees, zooming down what the maps showed as a single green line — green as distinct to black, meaning *temporarily secure* as against *secure*. The red line for *insecure* would come soon.

They passed a couple of jeeps — no more than fleeting brown blobs in the shadow of the trees. Impossible to tell whether they were American or Vietnamese. Ahead, through his tears, Murray could just see the road straight and narrow like one of those roads in northern France, but lined with rainforest instead of poplar trees, passing in the monotonous crescendo of wind and machinery. They were swaying about rather less now, and he tried again to get a glimpse of the speedometer, but Ryderbeit's helmet was now almost level with the handlebars and covered the clock completely. Murray had the curious sensation that the top of his head no longer existed.

They were coming close to the edge of 'D' Zone, and the 'Iron Triangle' — the Viet Cong's deepest, most impregnable stronghold north-west of Saigon, where even the eight-engined B 52's could make little impact, pattern-bombing with delayed-action 1,000-pounders through the two-hundred-foot trees. They passed another patrol — a confused blue shadow that might have been one or two vehicles — and Murray wondered what kind of report the troops would send when they got back to base. Red motorcycle with black-clad rider, like some bat out of hell, heading straight into the most insecure corner of Vietnam.

The road was becoming eaten away at the edges now, its surface humped and blistered, rotted by rains, gnawed by insects — the remnants of a fine French road which few vehicles had touched for years. They were ten minutes out of Biên Hòa — almost twenty-five miles — but now there was another danger. Murray knew it well, as did anyone who had been any time in Vietnam. The question was whether Ryderbeit knew it.

Even back in the Viet Minh days it had been a favourite trick: to take a strip of highway deep in the jungle and dig it out a metre deep and a metre wide. Any vehicle travelling at a reasonable speed would jam its front wheels, snap its axle and lie prone. Then the ambush. Only Ryderbeit and his Honda were not going at a reasonable speed.

Using the top of his head as a windshield Murray began to examine the tarmac under his feet. Nothing happened for several minutes. He had seen such Viet Cong booby-traps before, up on the road from Qui Nhon west to Pleiku where the treacherous trenches had been filled in with fresh-packed sand and stones like raw scars. Then suddenly he saw it, on a sharp turn as they slid over on their sides, slowing enough for him to see the gap fly past under them without even a tremor. He wondered if there were men there among the trees, crouching one-eyed over their gun-sights in the deepening dark. But not even a crack marksman would have stood a chance.

It was the only such trap they did see, for night was coming fast now and Ryderbeit was finally forced to flick on the headlamp, its pencil-beam swinging giddily round the candle-like tree trunks. Giant trees that rose into dim-veined patterns like the roof of a Norman cathedral, the roar of the engine sounding like the toneless dirge of an organ, speed now meaningless, the invisible enemy as suddenly remote yet immediate as God to a small congregation.

Only once, on a bend where Ryderbeit leaned out almost parallel with the road, and Murray found himself leaning the other way, did he catch a sudden glimpse of the speedometer. The needle was hovering just above the 200 km/h mark. The machine had been spotlessly clean when they left, he remembered: probably not even run in. It seemed incredible that Ryderbeit had not done this run before. But as a pilot he would have studied the large-scale ordnance maps and would have memorised every turn, every twist of the road. He had worked to a careful time-schedule too: to catch the evening traffic into Biên Hòa, without attracting undue attention, then breaking through the out-of-town curfew into darkness.

They were coming into a town, a miserable clutch of hovels that was well on what the maps showed as the red line. Ryderbeit did not slacken his pace, although the road did. It suddenly swung round in a steep turn and seemed to stop. Shadows darted about among the huts. The Honda lurched, shrieked over on the edge of its tyres with a spray of sparks drifting up from the heel of Ryderbeit's boot as he crouched forward, shoulders level with the handlebars.

Murray only saw the roadblock as they were going through it. A ramshackle barricade of crates and sharpened bamboo staves arranged in a double row, overlapping with a narrow gap between the two. Ryderbeit took the gap like the finest professional rider, the machine swinging over, first one way, then the other, with a great squeal of rubber even above the roar of the engine. Small men in black with guns whipped past the corner of Murray's eye. The bat swerved through, its front wheel almost leaving the ground as it leapt back up on to the broken camber of the disused French road, heading into the Highlands a few minutes later.

They were out of the rainforest now and a last twilight remained across the hillscape ahead. Sound, blotted out by the total noise of the machine, had become irrelevant. In this sense the huge country before him seemed very quiet indeed. No Phantoms dived out of the sky: no rolling burst of orange napalm, followed by the slow sticky black smoke; no mushrooms of mortar smoke, smouldering fields, little whirring 'choppers' like dragonflies blinking death. Ahead, *Route Nationale Dix-Sept* wound like a ribbon of tinfoil up into folds of furry jungle, looping down again between long neat rows of rubber trees, broken by stretches of undergrowth — wild roots writhing on to the road, cracking the tarmac into a series of sharp, agonising bumps. Then miles of more trees, interrupted by the occasional shell of a house — derelict mansions that had once belonged to the French rubber barons, rising now at the end of overgrown drives like great hotels boarded up in the offseason.

Insects whirled in the headlamp, growing sticky on Murray's brow, beginning to gum up his eyelids. Birds and bats swept low across their path, leaping away into the shadows as they slowed into a bend. And now, with the coming of total darkness, they entered on the final fifty-kilometre burst up the road to An Loc. The road here was broad and straight and curiously unravaged, even by nature. The roots of undergrowth were gone, and the tarmac borders were cut sharp and firm with a faded yellow line on either side. A ghost road into the ghost town of An Lộc, once a bustling market-centre at the foot of the Southern Highlands, now a damp sprawl of rusting sheds, barracks and fortified towers, the remaining inhabitants living in little huts built from unrolled beer and Coca Cola cans — the excremental rubble of an industrial society left strewn about this remote and gentle province.

Ryderbeit swung up on to a smaller, scrappier road — almost a dirt track where the dust flayed their faces raw. Murray glimpsed the time on his wrist. These last thirty miles had passed in just over eleven minutes. He had no chance to ask Ryderbeit their next destination — the mysterious place called Dong San, somewhere on the borders with Cambodia — although, from its position close to An Lôc, he guessed it to be near one of the infiltration routes, part of what is known as the Sihanouk Trail.

Ahead, across the line of hills, the sky was now lit by dull flashes, soundless against the roar of the Honda, but too regular under the clear sky to be even a freak electrical storm. Either 155-howitzers, zapping everything that moved at a range of eight miles, or the B 52's doing the same with their saturation sticks of H.E., from the same distance, only vertically.

An hour ago Murray would have felt a kind of resigned anger at this grotesque spectacular — although it was not every journalist in Vietnam, let alone the war protesters back home, who had the chance to witness one of these monster airstrikes. Now, however, he felt a curious detached exhilaration, as though these man-made firestorms flaying the jungle-tops were merely part of the howling unreality of the ride — that they did not belong to the ordinary run of physical or emotional experience. If he had been told, in those last minutes before Dong San, that Ryderbeit was a demon driving into hell, he would not have entirely disbelieved it.

It was not really a town at all — even less than An Loc. The trees thinned a little; there was a stream, a patch of dark rice paddy, a small lake with huts crouched along the edge. A solitary light winked at them from the porch of one of these huts. Ryderbeit swung the great machine on to the verge of the track, cut the throttle and they bumped to a halt. Murray climbed off, stiff and bandy-legged, into the sudden silence. He pulled down the neck of his sweater and stretched the muscles of his face, flexing his fingers which were curled stiff from gripping Ryderbeit's leather suit.

Two men — Vietnamese in flimsy black pyjama-costumes — appeared from the edge of the track. Both held Chinese AK 47 machine-pistols level with their hips. One of them flashed a torch into Ryderbeit's face, muttered something, and the second walked round them both, frisking them professionally under the arms, round their waists and down their legs. He removed Murray's passport without a word, putting it in a jacket pocket. The first man now led them along a slippery track towards the light.

It was a single hurricane-lamp set on a table. A number of men, also in black pyjamas, sat on rush-matting round the walls. There was a thick cloying smell of smoke, paraffin and rotting fish. The lamplight seemed very strong. Murray stood for a few minutes, blinking through his bruised eyelids. Ryderbeit had stripped off his scarf and pushed his goggles up on to his forehead, peering quickly round the walls.

'Friends of yours?' Murray said softly.

'Friends o' friends.' Ryderbeit took a step forward towards a wattle door, but one of the two guides motioned him back with his AK 47. They waited.

'They look like Victor Charlies,' Murray murmured. 'Some sort of joke by old Pol?'

'They're members of the *Cao Đài*. Know 'em?'

Murray nodded, with some surprise. In these days, when all the excitement was about escalation and phoney peace talks, one rarely heard any more of the *Cao Đài*, that legendary gangster-religious sect, who — along with the more notorious

Bình Xuyên and the *Hòa Hảo*, both little more than licensed bandits — had long controlled what had then been Cochin-China, now South Vietnam. The *Cao Đài*, headed by warlords and its own self-appointed saints and prophets, had controlled most of Saigon's gangsterdom and vice. It had also been closely connected with the long struggle against the French, even been allied with the Viet Minh themselves, and went on wielding enormous political power until President Ngo Dinh Diem finally suppressed them in the fifties.

'How the hell did you get involved with them?' he whispered.

Ryderbeit grinned: 'I was ordained last week, soldier. I'm one of their priests — one of the beholders of the *Cao Đài* — the Supreme All-Seeing Eye.'

'It sounds wonderfully psychedelic,' Murray said sourly, wondering if it could all be worth a brand new Honda and a ride through death to the edge of nowhere. Ryderbeit went on: 'My non-Asian saints are Victor Hugo, Sir Winston Churchill and Joe Louis. All fully recognised spiritual leaders of the sect.'

'And where does Charles Pol come in?'

'He's a priest too. Has been for some time. This is the contact, y'see?'

Murray shook his head: 'I don't see, Sammy. You mean we're now in alliance with the *Cao Đài*?'

But before Ryderbeit could reply, the wattle door swung open and a very thin Vietnamese with a spine curved like a spoon came in bowing gracefully. 'Messieurs!' He motioned them through towards the door.

It was a square windowless room, dark except for another oil lamp with the wick turned down so low that it was guttering. Two men sat on cushions on either side of a round table laid with small metal cups, a pointed teapot, and an array of rubber piping, needles and shallow bowls. There was also a bottle of Johnny Walker Black Label, almost full and stoppered.

One of the two men was Pol, reclining Roman-style on a heap of cushions. '*Salut Murray! Tout va bien?*'

Murray nodded, looking at the second man. It was hard to tell at first whether he were European or Asian. A pair of slit, pouched eyes peered up at him out of a face that looked like a contour-map of the Mekong Delta. He was dressed in a white silk suit and an expensive, discreet tie. Three points of a handkerchief peeped from his breast-pocket, just below the unmistakable *rosette* of the Legion of Honour.

'Let me introduce Monsieur Banaji, my compatriot,' Pol began. 'Monsieur Banaji is a Vietnamese citizen, but is of French origin. He used to be one of the great racehorse owners of Saigon.'

The shrivelled contours of M. Banaji's face stretched into a smile: 'Ah, that was in the old days,' he murmured: 'Before the Japanese came, when my horses were stolen or poisoned by my enemies. Please sit down.'

Pol waved his hand at the whisky bottle: 'Or perhaps you would like to smoke? The two do not mix though.'

'I would advise you to smoke.' Banaji's voice was soft and bored, his face without expression. 'The *Cao Đài* do not admit alcohol, except to their most honoured members.'

Murray glanced at Pol and shrugged. 'I'll smoke,' he said. Banaji now spoke to the Vietnamese who had showed them in, and who now knelt by the table and began the elaborate preparations for the pipe.

'You have both arrived in excellent time,' Banaji went on. 'You travelled by what means?'

Ryderbeit told him, and he nodded, without any apparent surprise. 'There was a big raid tonight,' he added, 'just east of here. Perhaps you saw it? Their bombing is preposterous. There is nothing here but jungle and a few peasants. Twice a month now they bomb this region and there is never anything. Just one small hamlet. It is of no importance. Nothing in Vietnam is of any importance except the people. As the fish are to water. You have read your Mao?'

'Some of it,' said Murray. 'Textbooks for schoolboy revolutionaries.'

Pol chuckled from his nest of cushions. 'Ah but he doesn't write for sophisticates like us, my dear Murray!'

Murray turned to Ryderbeit and said in English: 'What is all this — a teach-in at the London School of Economics?'

Ryderbeit grinned: 'Have to take 'em in their stride, soldier. Just talk easy and gentle. They've been smokin'.'

'Speak French, please,' said Banaji. 'We have no secrets here.'

'Very well.' The Vietnamese was teasing a tiny brown pellet of opium into the bowl of a rubber-tubed pipe, basting it with the flat end of one of the needles. 'Why are we here, Monsieur Banaji?' Murray said at last.

'We must talk business.'

He looked at Pol. 'On whose terms?'

'The terms must be mutually agreed,' said Pol. 'There should be no problem. My friend Banaji has close contacts with some of the most influential men in this part of South-East Asia. Even with a war on, my dear Murray, basic things do not change so very much.'

Banaji spread out a pair of long chicken claws of hands. 'The Japanese,' he murmured, 'the French, the Americans — it's all the same thing. *Foutus. Le Vietnam est foutu.*'

'You know what we have to offer?' Murray asked him, and the Vietnamese passed Banaji the pipe, nimbly setting a flame to the bowl while the old Frenchman reached for the nozzle, his lips distending now like an oboe player's, sucking deeply with a long rasping sound, ending in little crackles of spittle as he rested back on the cushions and let the smoke drift slowly, almost endlessly it seemed, in three streams from his nostrils and a small gap at the edge of his mouth.

It was some time before he answered. 'You have money for us, I think? A great deal of money. For a certain consideration I am prepared to ask friends of mine to help you dispose of this money. We have many methods and great experience. In Vietnam itself we are limited. There are patrols, the bombing, the Viet Cong and the Americans together — they make business very difficult. But outside Vietnam — in Laos, perhaps...'

Murray looked again at Pol: 'Have you discussed Cambodia?'

'Cambodia is impossible,' said Banaji. 'It is too well controlled. As Pol here will tell you, Sihanouk has many problems — he plays too many games at once — to risk troubling the Americans more than is necessary.' He passed the pipe suddenly to Murray. 'But Laos is altogether another matter.'

Before accepting the pipe, Murray turned again to Pol. 'How much of the operation have you discussed, Charles?'

'I have had to be frank, my dear Murray. As Monsieur Banaji says, we have no secrets here.'

'He'd think me a damned fool if I blurted everything out on our first meeting.'

'You confided in me. And in Sammy here.'

'With you, Charles, there was no operation — just a nice fantasy by the walls of Angkor. But with Sammy and his third-degree approach I was hardly left much option. And what does Monsieur Banaji mean by a consideration?'

'Why not ask him?'

Murray asked him.

'Thirty million American dollars, Monsieur Wilde.'

Murray lifted the nozzle to his lips, nodding to the Vietnamese who put a light to the opium, and he inhaled carefully, watching the little brown kernel bubbling in the bowl, drawing the sweet smoke down past his lungs into his belly, holding his breath now like a deep-sea diver as he passed the pipe sideways to Ryderbeit who was already crouching forward, both hands eager.

'Thirty million,' he said slowly, 'is a fortune. It is ridiculous.'

Banaji did not move. 'No more ridiculous than the operation you have proposed, Monsieur Wilde.'

'I have proposed no operation, Monsieur Banaji. Everything that has happened here has been by arrangement with Charles Pol and Sammy here. I am no party to it.'

'Without my help you can do nothing, Monsieur Wilde. What use is your own share of this fortune unless you can transport it to a safe place?'

'Let's get one thing quite straight,' Murray said, relaxing a little with the quietening effect of the smoke. 'Pol has informed you of our proposed operation. This may succeed or it may not. If it does succeed we are to hand over to you thirty million dollars. Is that correct?'

'Perfectly,' said Banaji.

'We pay you in cash on some mountain-top in Laos?'

'Or an airfield, Monsieur Wilde. It is all understood and arranged. Your own plan — the plan you have devised yourself — has many intelligent qualities. I congratulate you on the details. If I have understood Charles correctly, you are to walk on to Saigon's airfield dressed as military policemen, and will then take charge of a plane carrying one and a half billion American dollars. You will fly it out of Vietnam and land it on an unfinished *barrage* just north of Vientiane, where the necessary equipment exists to move the money out and load it into sacks of rice. These will then be transported down to Vientiane's Wattay Airfield, where they will be loaded aboard a plane belonging to the Air U.S.A. line. Am I right so far?' Murray nodded. 'Only the pilots,' Banaji went on, 'will not be from Air U.S.A.'

He held up his hand to interrupt Murray: 'No please! From now on you will follow my own plans, or you will make your own arrangements. The pilots will be substitutes provided by myself — by my friends. They will fly you to an airport of our choosing in northern Laos where the money will be unloaded and the plane destroyed. Shortly before this a mayday signal will be sent on the plane's frequency, indicating that you have serious engine trouble.' He bent forward to accept the pipe once again. (Pol, Murray noticed, was sipping Scotch from one of the metal teacups; clearly he passed as one of the honoured members of the *Cao Đài*?) M. Banaji breathed out his last gasp of smoke and pushed the pipe to Murray.

'The final distress signal,' he continued, 'will be sent on a false frequency, indicating that the plane is preparing to make a forced landing on an airfield about two hundred kilometres to the west. Vientiane Control will receive no further messages. This, we calculate, should give us at least three hours to exchange the cargo.'

He paused, and Murray's pipe bubbled in the silence. Monsieur Banaji did not sound a fool.

'You must understand, however, that from this moment the cargo will have to be conveyed by the hands of my friends? They are men of professional experience. The money will be transported from Laos to India. You will each of you be paid at a slightly later date — I do not anticipate more than two months — in either gold or any foreign currency you desire. The transaction will be perfectly honourable.'

'Why?'

Banaji's eyes were sunk deep in his wrinkled, ruined face. 'Because for this amount of money it would be foolish to be anything that was not honourable, Monsieur Wilde. On the airfield we shall take out thirty million dollars. That will be sufficient for ourselves and the porters.'

Murray began to laugh: 'And the rest? You know how much the rest is?'

'They don't want to know.' It was Pol who spoke, with his impish smile: 'It would make them unhappy — greedy — they would not know how to digest such a sum.'

Murray nodded: 'So they just help themselves to thirty million dollars — in bundles of Centuries, I suppose — leaving us with the rest?'

Pol's smile grew wistful: 'Isn't it enough?'

'It's enough, if that's all they want. But how do we know that's all they want?'

'Again, you must ask Monsieur Banaji.'

Banaji lifted his head from the pipe. 'We are satisfied, Monsieur Wilde. But if you are not, then the arrangements must be annulled. We do not have the time to argue.'

Ryderbeit's hand closed hard round Murray's arm: 'Accept, you bastard! They're serious. These boys don't fool around. And they're not leaving us an alternative.'

Murray took the pipe again and this time lingered over it before passing it to Ryderbeit. 'How do you propose destroying the second plane?' he asked finally, turning back to Banaji.

'It will be burnt and buried. There will be nothing left.'

'And what about the airfield? They'll be searching every inch of landing space in South-East Asia.'

'That is true. Only they will not find the plane. We will make quite sure of that.'

'And the substitute pilots? Who will they be?'

'Men of our choice,' said Banaji softly. 'They will be our concern — paid for by us.'

'And the real pilots?'

'That will also be our concern.'

Murray smiled. 'Listen, Monsieur Banaji. Half the American Air Force, and their entire external security forces, are going to be looking for us. They're going to be looking for that plane — for an Air U.S.A. rice-drop plane that took off without the correct crew, sent a phoney mayday signal, then vanished. They've half caught us already.'

'Have you a better plan, Monsieur Wilde?'

The first sticks of high explosive landed a second later. The hut shuddered, the oil lamp almost went out. 'Ah, the B 52's again,' Banaji murmured. 'Another few thousand dollars' worth of bombs, and what do they achieve?'

The floor began to bounce in a curious, regular rhythm. They were all quiet for a moment, listening to the steady rumble that seemed to go on and on with the rocking floor, the flickering lamp, as Banaji offered the pipe again, once round the table, while Pol sipped his Scotch as it trembled and slopped over his lips.

'I don't like it,' said Murray. 'Why not pay off real Air U.S.A. pilots and have them just disappear?'

'Air U.S.A. pilots,' Pol chimed in, 'are employed by the Central Intelligence Agency. They are not to be trusted — at least, not at such short notice.'

'And Sammy here? They employed him too.' His words were gone in the long rolling explosion, creeping towards them now across the mountain tops, as the lamp guttered again and went out. They lay for a moment in pitch dark. 'Sammy is one in a million,' Pol said. 'You found him yourself, Murray. You want to waste valuable time trying to find someone like him?'

There must be others like him, Murray thought: wild men scattered across half the earth, on airfields in dark spots of Africa, doing the leapfrog run into Biafra, Angola, gun-running in the Middle East, South America. Probably a few like him, anyway — or who thought they were like him. And just eleven days to find them — a ready-made crew like Ryderbeit and No-Entry Jones.

The Vietnamese had the lamp going again, and the bombs began their thundering pattern very close now, with the wick of the lamp turned right up and the shadows flickering wildly round the low bare walls.

'And what happens to the real pilots?' Murray shouted: 'Do we take them with us?'

'They will be provided for,' Banaji replied, with ominous simplicity.

'Dead or alive?' said Murray, and Pol made a clucking noise like a hen: 'Ah, my dear Murray, you have a morbid mind! What would we do with two dead American pilots?'

'Don't be damned stupid,' Murray growled: 'We're not going to leave them lying around Vientiane Airport with their hands tied behind their backs!'

They waited for another stick of thunder to roll off into the hills. 'Murray.' Pol's voice reached him now from what seemed a great distance: 'I wonder sometimes if you are really interested in this money?'

The pipe came round to him again and he said slowly: 'I don't want them to find the plane — either plane. The plane or the pilots. They must be kept hidden.'

The earth heaved with a great roar. The lamp went out again and Murray's head was soft on the cushions, watching the darkness which was full of coloured circles swirling within triangles. There was silence now in the little hut. The air was hot and sweet with the opium, and M. Banaji's white silk arm was close to his head as he asked, in his low impassive voice: 'The girl, Monsieur Wilde. The French girl. Is she to be trusted?'

'She will do as I ask her.' He heard Pol chuckle in the dark. 'She will tell me exactly where the plane will be, and when it is scheduled to leave. Then she will send the alert. Sammy and his navigator will pretend to be my photographers. We will be doing a feature story on Tân Sơn Nhất airport. This young friend of mine in the Military Police has agreed to help me out — lend me a jeep and uniforms and take us all on an unofficial conducted tour of the airfield perimeter. All straight and above board. He's a nice simple boy who doesn't ask too many questions. Besides, like all Americans in Vietnam, he has orders to offer maximum co-operation to the world Press. And that's just what he's going to be doing on the night of the flush-out.' He yawned.

'It is very simple and very clever,' said Banaji. 'It must not go wrong.'

Murray lay on his back and smiled at the roof. The bombing was over now. The giant planes would be wheeling back down the margin of airspace just outside the Cambodian border, probably heading for an undisclosed base in Thailand.

The night was full of peace and quiet.

CHAPTER 2

Banaji was gone, as they sat on the verandah in the clammy grey dawn and sipped strong sweet tea. Murray's head felt soft as a sponge, with a dull incipient ache behind his eyes and at the back of his skull. He and Ryderbeit took a nip from Pol's Scotch, but it made them feel no better. Pol watched them, red-eyed and grinning. 'You look sick, *mes enfants!*' Ryderbeit cursed him and spat on the wooden floor.

'This thirty million,' said Murray: 'Do we really let them take it on this secret airfield? Collect it and count it there, then let them disappear with the whole load into the jungle, without even an I.O.U.?'

'There will be an I.O.U.,' Pol said smiling.

'Oh yes?' Ryderbeit sneered.

'I am the I.O.U.,' said Pol. 'I am your guarantor, your laissez-passer after we reach the airfield in Laos. I am one of the *Cao Đài*. It is an honourable sect. We do not betray each other, or betray our friends. We have rules — morals.'

'Morals!' Murray began to laugh, wincing with nausea. 'Morals of the Mafia, Charles. At least let's not be frivolous.'

Pol simpered through his beard. 'I am very serious, my dear Murray, I promise you. One does not joke about fifteen hundred million American dollars.'

'Less thirty million for you *Cao Đài*,' Murray put in.

'So what is thirty million? A *pourboire*, no more!'

'You yourself said we weren't to mention the total sum — because Monsieur Banaji and his boys might get greedy. Why did you say that, Charles?'

265

Pol belched luxuriantly. '*Mon ami*, Banaji is an old man now. He has great experience, he has seen two whole generations of Indo-China pass in violence, without hope. He is no longer interested in money. For him money is merely the pieces of a game — symbols of whether one wins or loses. He has no interest in a fortune.'

Ryderbeit was eyeing Pol with a nasty leer. Murray watched him carefully too, wondering for a moment whether he were in fact talking more of himself than of his compatriot. 'No interest in money — be screwed!' Ryderbeit snarled under his breath. 'That bastard's as interested as the rest of us. Why don't we tell him?'

'Because he will feel obliged to tell others — those who are perhaps greedier than he is, Sammy. One must allow for some small sensibilities, after all.'

'It doesn't sound sensible to me!' Ryderbeit cried, misunderstanding Pol's French. 'Looks as though I risked my neck on this trip for a bloody con! You think those boys — those porters, as he called them — are goin' to ride off with one and a half billion U.S. in sacks, and not even take a little peep inside? You think they're goin' to count out their nice little thirty million and leave it at that? Don't make me wet my pants laughin'! I'm not a bloody infant in arms!'

Pol glanced at Murray for enlightenment; Ryderbeit had spoken in English, which Pol understood poorly. Murray said: 'Sammy's right, Charles. It's all very fine after half a dozen pipes, but in the light of dawn it doesn't look nearly so rosy. What happens to the porters — and to the money?'

Pol heaved a great sigh, his fat little fingers digging deep in his thighs. 'So you want to forget the whole story? Is that what you really want?'

'Come on, you know what we're trying to say,' said Murray. 'There's no security in this deal, Charles — no security, no guarantee, nothing. Just a host of crooks waiting for us to take all the risks, deliver the goods, then disappear. You've got to do better than that.'

'Me? But I shall be with them, my dear Murray! I shall accompany the porters, I shall supervise them, command them. There will be no question of a betrayal. My interests are your interests. Why should there be a conflict?'

'Why indeed? Because you're European? A nice honourable man with a white skin who's not going to do down a couple of madcap adventurers you've bumped into in South-East Asia?' He shook his head. 'Still not good enough, Charles.'

Pol gave another sigh and filled their teacups to the brim with Johnny Walker. 'You forget that I am a member of the *Cao Đài!*'

'*Cao Đài — Hôa Hảo — Bình Xuyên* — experienced religious gangsters!'

'They are part Confucian, Buddhist and Catholic,' Pol said evenly. 'And they are experienced, certainly. But they are not gangsters — at least, not in our sense. They have run these countries for more than a century. Just because they do not have the ear of the great powers — the Communists and the Americans — does not meant they are not to be trusted. You think you could trust the Viet Cong or the Americans more?' He leant forward and patted Murray's knee. 'The *Cao Đài* are professional businessmen — but they are also honourable men. Not like some of our great Capitalist gentlemen in the West. The Supreme All-Seeing Eye is not a piece of oriental chicanery. It has virtues, standards. You talk very easily of gangsterism. But even our own gangsters — even the most humdrum of the criminal world — have their standards, their codes of honour. They have no contracts that can be signed and legally enforced, my dear Murray. It is the world of lawyers and bankers and middle-men that is often far more dishonourable. The *Cao Đài* are men of honour.'

Murray sat for some time sipping his whisky, watching the damp swamp that reached out to the elephant-grass and the scorched, misty hills beyond. Ryderbeit, who had listened only half comprehending, looked angry and dispirited. 'All right,' Murray said at last: 'Tell me about the bombing of the *Cercle Sportif* in Saigon yesterday.'

Pol looked up quickly, almost startled. 'What of it?'

'Who did it?'

'I don't understand.'

'You know what happened. The place was blown to bits. They were supposed to have been after General Greene. Perhaps they were. But a little fellow called Colonel Luong, one of the rougher lads in the Arvin, just happened to be having lunch opposite at the time — and General Greene was late. What's more, his secretary — none other than Mrs Conquest — got a phone call a few minutes before it happened, warning her to keep away from the place. How they got her number, and knew she was going, God knows — unless someone's been monitoring my calls at the hotel. What's more, they warned me too. Not directly — an old Vietnamese *boy* in the hotel told my *cyclo*-driver to take a long way round.'

'So?' Pol was looking no longer startled, but worried.

Murray gave a lame smile: 'Come on, Charles, was it the *Cao Đài*, the VC, or somebody we don't know about?'

'I don't know, Murray.'

'Is Colonel Luong a member of the *Cao Đài*?'

'I don't know Colonel Luong.'

Murray nodded wearily and reached for his drink. 'So who warned me and Mrs Conquest?'

'I have no idea, Murray. I have absolutely no idea.'

They sat for some moments in silence. It was Ryderbeit who broke it: 'When do we get out of here?'

'This evening,' said Pol: 'By the same means you came.'

Ryderbeit grinned: 'That's what I like to hear. You go back the cushy way, through the border into Cambodia, and we hit the hard road back to Saigon.'

'If you insist —' Pol began.

'I don't insist, Mister Pol. I did that run once — I can do it again.' He gave a sidelong leer at Murray. 'One thing I would like, though. More of this Scotch. Because I'm going to get thirsty before this evening.'

Pol heaved himself out of his chair.

'So, what do you think, Sammy?'

Ryderbeit curled his lip over his teeth. 'I think we're bein' bloody suckers, soldier.'

'We're in Pol's hands.'

'You bet we're in Pol's hands!'

'Think of anything better?'

'Nope.'

The insects started up in the falling afternoon light. 'He said the *Cao Đài* are honourable men.'

'Like hell. Perhaps they are. They got to be, with all that bloody money!'

'Sammy.' Murray gazed across the swamp. 'Do we have to go for so much? Does it have to be the whole damned whack in one swoop?'

'What d'yer mean?'

'Over one million quid each. What are we going to do with it? What can anyone do with that much loose cash?'

'You mean, cut them in for more? For extra insurance? Don't be bloody daft! If those little bastards are goin' to act straight, they're goin' to do it for thirty million, or they're not goin' to do it at all!'

'Why not try to be more moderate? Try for something a little more practical — manual?'

'Manual?'

'Something handy — like a few bundles of Centuries that we can carry out in a suitcase, for instance. Then the only problem's going to be Customs.'

'Screw the Customs. You know your trouble —'

'I think too much.'

'Think too much, and not greedy enough.'

'And you? What are you going to do with a hundred million plus?'

'A lot o' things. I can think of a whole dictionary o' things to do with it. It may look trouble to you, soldier, but not to me. Certainly not to Samuel D. Ryderbeit!' He gave a soft cackle in the dusk: 'You got problems, soldier. You got a hunger problem — back to front!'

PART 9: FLUSH-OUT

CHAPTER 1

SAIGON, Billion Dollar Day Minus Two

Wet afternoon heat down Tu Do Street. Children doing a brisk trade along the pavements — five-year-old boys shining Army boots; little girls running on tiptoe to pick the hip pockets of ambling G.I.'s; old men playing hopscotch in the shade of the bars and 'nite-clubs'.

Murray entered 'The Four Aces', pausing to accustom himself to the cold dehydrated darkness. A big notice inside read: ALL WEAPONS TO BE EMPTIED AND SURRENDERED AT THE DOOR. BY ORDER U.S. PROVOST MARSHAL. A girl sat at a counter underneath, busy knitting. Crew-cut men sat musing along the bar; girls in unbecoming miniskirts waddled among them, whispering pidgin promises. He found his man alone at a corner table. 'Hello Don.' He was a tall callow youth with spiky blond hair and a bad outbreak of barber's rash under his chin like a smear of red caviar.

'Hi!' The boy almost spilled his beer standing up. 'I was early. What yer have?'

'Let me get it,' said Murray, sitting down. 'Another beer? Or bourbon?'

'I'll have beer.' He leant over as Murray turned to one of the miniskirted hostesses. 'These girls, Murray, they been pesterin' me mad. One buck for a glass o' that goddam tea they drink. One buck!'

Murray smiled falsely. 'That's Saigon for you, Don. You ought to know your way around by now.'

'Ah sure. Sure I do. Why d'you think I resisted so long?'

'What would you say to a few more bucks?'

'Huh?' The boy's jaw dropped open and Murray replied with a conniving wink: 'I've got a little deal I'd like to set up with you. Sure you won't have a little bourbon?'

'Well — I guess no great harm —'

'You're off-duty, aren't you, sergeant?'

Wace hesitated, then grinned sheepishly. 'Guess I am — till curfew o' course.'

'Now listen, Don.' Murray placed both elbows on the table, his face very close to the young M.P.'s and his voice hushed, even above the intermittent blare of pop music. 'We have a small problem. About Sunday night.'

'You mean it's not on?'

'Oh it's very much on. Photographers — big coverage prepared — the real treatment. My editor's very keen, Don. He's even prepared to pay you for it.'

'Aw now! I mean, Mr Wilde —' Wace glanced up at a rouged bow-legged girl who was laying two small beer glasses in front of them. Murray paid with a fresh twenty-dollar bill from the bounty that Pol had entrusted to him after the visit to Son Lan.

'On Sunday night you've got official clearance for me and my photographers to tour the perimeter of the airfield? Correct?'

'Correct.'

'Don.' He spun the glass between his fingers, drank it down in one and sat back smiling. 'Don, I need your co-operation on this. We've talked about it a lot of times — about the airfield security and so on — and my newspaper wants to get a really full, unprejudiced story on this.'

'Unprejudiced?'

Murray nodded slowly. 'That's to say, we are not keen on a story that is obviously inspired from official sources. You follow me?'

The sergeant looked dubious. 'But it's sure hard to swing without official clearance, Murray.'

'Have you got the jeep laid on?'

'Oh, we got a pool of 'em down there on the field. No problem.'

'And the equipment?'

'That's all cleared too. Just that I can't go short-circuiting the authorities and letting you and your photographers on to the field without permission. I mean, I'd be crazy — I'd stand to go to the stockade.'

'A tour of the perimeter at curfew, Don. Ten-thirty, Sunday night. With official clearance?'

'It has to be.' The boy gulped at his beer, looking worried.

'And what about guns? M16's — usual M.P.'s issue? We'll be carrying them, won't we?'

'Oh sure thing! They'd think it pretty suspect if you walked round the perimeter without any weapon at all. Only I must have clearance.'

Murray nodded and they finished their drinks in silence.

Suddenly Wace said: 'You mentioned money, didn't you?'

'I did.'

'Okay. What makes?'

'I don't want an official conducted tour, Don. Just you and me and my two photographers. Without any MACV clearance.'

The sergeant cocked his head: 'So what's the price?'

'Now hold on a minute! This isn't a bribe. I just want you to do us a favour. If it works out, and the story comes off, we'd like to pay you — quite anonymously of course — a fair share. How do you feel about it?'

Sergeant Wace sat back and smirked. 'I'd like to see your money, sir. I mean, Murray, I don't play poker blind with no man — not even a friend.'

Murray passed him an envelope under the table containing two fifty dollar bills. 'Keep that in your socks for a rainy day, Don. My newspaper pays very well.' He stood up. 'See you on Sunday night — at ATCO Three canteen.'

Wace nodded, already ripping open the envelope. 'At twenty-two hundred hours then,' he began, then added, '*Jesus!*' his jaw dropping open even further as he gaped at the two bills in his lap, crumbling them away somewhere under the table. 'Hey, will you stay for another drink, Murray?'

Murray stood watching him with a slow smile. 'Yes, Don, I think I will.'

CHAPTER 2

Noon, B-Day Minus One.

The ice-cream parlour was full of the usual Saturday crowd — sleek Vietnamese youths with long hair and the assurance of those with no immediate fear of being drafted; snapping their fingers indolently to the jukebox and drinking iced coffees.

Murray met Jackie Conquest at a table at the back, away from the wire screens across the windows. At first he had scarcely recognised her, sitting over an untouched chocolate sundae, wearing a wide hat and enormous round sunglasses. 'I haven't much time. I've got to meet Maxwell for lunch at the Majestic in ten minutes.' Her voice was brisk, her face expressionless behind the glasses.

'Everything's still all right?' he said anxiously.

'It hasn't changed. Except that Maxwell's on duty tomorrow night at Tân Sơn Nhất.'

'And what the hell does that mean?'

She shrugged. 'He didn't tell me. He doesn't tell me much, you know. But it's a big airfield.'

'Big enough for both of you?'

'Why not? I have my job there, and I'll just be working late tomorrow night in Greene's office. There are some important papers to be cleared for Washington by Monday morning.'

'What about Greene?'

'He's going to a dinner party at the American Embassy. Quite a big occasion, it sounds — the Prime Minister's going to be there, and several ambassadors. If I know the General, he won't be back before midnight.'

'He will when that alert goes out — and fast! That's still in order, is it?'

She looked up and suddenly smiled. 'Well, of course. You don't think I'm going to change my mind now, do you?'

He took her hand across the table. In the last ten days they had seen each other only twice, briefly, in crowded places, exchanging only the barest messages. He said, squeezing her hand: 'You know exactly what you must do?'

'Do I have to repeat it again?' she sighed.

'The last time.'

'At twenty minutes to eleven I telephone down to the M.P.'s guardroom at the ATCO Three complex and ask to speak to you. If everything is all right, I tell you the surprise party is still on. If anything has changed — the schedule cancelled or put back — I tell you the party is off.'

'And if the party is on?'

'I shut off all the telex and telephone communications into the office, and at a quarter to eleven I send the alert. Then I drive out to the Caribou. And now what about all of you? No problems?'

'Not yet. Ryderbeit and Jones have been working non-stop on their homework — maps, compass bearings, weather charts, special survival equipment — you'd think they were training for a moon-flight. Whatever else you may say about Ryderbeit, he's a professional.'

'And what about the American sergeant?'

Murray paused. 'He's all right. He's young and green, but he's willing.'

'And supposing he changes his mind? — doesn't want to risk three years in a military prison, even for five thousand dollars?'

'Then I'll just have to answer that phone and tell you the party's off. We'll meet later for a drink and drown our sorrows. Remember, if Sergeant Wace won't play, we're still in the clear. We've lost nothing — except the money.'

'Except the money,' she nodded: 'Seven thousand million New Francs.' She stood up. 'I must go now. We'll see each other tomorrow night at eleven — on the Caribou.'

'On the Caribou,' he said, leaning forward and kissing her quickly on the mouth.

'*Au revoir, Murray.*'

He watched her walk swiftly between the groups of dapper Vietnamese, her wide hat swaying above their heads, out into the street where a couple of Americans stopped and stared mournfully after her.

Her chocolate sundae was still untouched on her plate.

CHAPTER 3

Sunday, 2100 hours. Brinx Square, Saigon

The olive-green military bus, with wire mesh across the windows, left on time — as it did every hour, on the hour — for the fifty-minute drive out to Tân Sơn Nhất Airport. Among the dozen or so passengers — all apparently American, and all in uniform — were three men in freshly laundered jungle-green combat fatigues and polished boots, carrying no visible luggage. They had boarded the bus separately and sat in different seats, two of them pretending to doze, the other reading *Time*.

The bus stopped at several points on the route, picking up and discharging passengers. The ride was free and there were no checks; only at the gates of the airfield did a sullen little Vietnamese M.P. peer up inside to make sure there were none of his compatriots aboard. The American M.P.'s waved them through with little more than a glance; it was usually only taxis and private cars that invited scrutiny. Most of the passengers disembarked at the main military terminal. The final stop, about a mile and a half away, and well inside the perimeter, was ATCO III compound; and for this last stretch, except for one sleepy Negro and an elderly Marine warrant officer, Murray, Ryderbeit and No-Entry Jones had the bus to themselves.

They were all sweating heavily now: their chests, under the flimsy tropical fatigues, strapped across with the twin-pack Air U.S.A. survival kits containing dehydrated chocolate, bouillon cubes, salt and water-purification tablets, magnetic compass, fishing-line, flares, torch, toilet paper, needle and thread, hacksaw blade, and a first aid pack, including Benzedrine tablets, morphine and anti-sunburn cream. Just before leaving they had each taken one of these Benzedrine tablets, and as the bus neared ATCO III their senses were already beginning to respond to the quickening flow of adrenalin, the heightening of senses compounded with a pleasant relaxation of the nerves.

No-Entry was also wearing a wad of maps — USAF one-millionth-scale charts of every area of the Indo-Chinese peninsula from the southernmost tip of the Mekong Delta up to the borders of Burma and China — and all of them carried in the deep ammunition pockets of their trousers four clips of .30 calibre M16 rounds. Ryderbeit also had two hand-grenades with three-second fuses.

It was a dark night, but the latest weather reports that evening from MACV headquarters had promised that the next twelve hours should be 'relatively clear and operational'.

ATCO III compound was a dreary sprawl of sheds, mud and metal roads, bunkers and fuel storage tanks. The only well-lit building was the canteen. At exactly 9.55 Murray got off the bus and led the way in, with the other two strolling a few yards behind. Wace was already there, his black-and-white M.P.'s helmet on the table beside him, his M16 slung over the back of his chair. He saw Murray and shuffled quickly to his feet; but he was not smiling. 'Hi Murray.'

'You're right on time, Don. Two minutes early. How are you?'

'Fine.' The boy's fingers fidgeted round his acned neck; he was paler than Murray had seen him before. 'You got your photographers?'

Murray beckoned to Ryderbeit and Jones. 'This is Mister Rogers, Don — Mister Jones. May we sit down?'

'Sure. Coffee?' Wace flicked his fingers at the Vietnamese girl behind the counter, his eyes straying dubiously over No-Entry who merely nodded, grave and untroubled. 'Well, Murray, you sure chose one helluva night!' he added, sitting down too.

Murray stared at him blankly.

'Yeah, there's somethin' of a razzmatazz on tonight, sirs — I mean, we got some kinda big bustle on the field.'

Murray's elbow was pushed across the table, his eyes hard on the young sergeant's. 'What kind of razzmatazz, Don?'

Wace gave a lopsided grin. 'Pretty big, by all I hear. Doubled security on the perimeter — whole company of Arvins posted in case there's a breakthrough. And all us M.P.'s on special alert.'

'Should make a good story,' Murray smiled. 'Especially if there is a breakthrough.'

Wace's Adam's apple jumped in his throat. 'I sure hope not, Murray! You oughta see this airfield during a real alert — during that Tet offensive. We got every pant-wettin' recruit on the field gettin' so goddam scared they was shootin' up us M.P.'s — shootin' anythin' they saw move!'

'You mean we might be in danger going out with you tonight?' Murray said, smiling; but Wace's eyes turned down and searched deep in his coffee cup.

'They got a lot of M.P.'s out tonight, Murray. And without special clearance — I mean, I don't want us gettin' pulled in by some big brass-hat for photographin' military installations or anything.'

'Don.' Murray spoke very low. 'We made a deal. Remember?'

'Sure, sure!' Wace nodded vigorously. 'I'm not wantin' to be obstructive or anythin', Murray. It's just that I don't like us to be out there too long.'

'You don't have to come at all,' Murray said softly. 'We'll do a quick tour of the perimeter — just the three of us — and be back here within the hour. O.K.?'

Wace gaped at him, his mouth open. 'Hey, I can't do that, Murray! That'd be crazy!'

Murray nodded. 'Where's the jeep?'

'Parked outside the guardroom.'

'And the ignition keys?'

'I left 'em in,' he murmured.

'Fine.' Murray smiled and stood up. 'We're wasting time, Don. Rogers, Jones — let's go through and get the equipment. Lead the way, sergeant.'

Wace struggled to his feet, leaving some Scrip money for the coffees. 'You'll get me thrown in the stockade, Murray!' he whimpered, leading the way out into a bare corridor of weatherboard, stopping at the last door at the end. The room was empty, lined with steel lockers; on the wall, crude familiar drawings of uniforms and weapons: KNOW YOUR ENEMY — VIGILANCE IS THE PRICE OF DEMOCRACY. And a desk with a telephone.

Wace went hesitatingly over to one of the lockers and took out three M.P. helmets; then moved to another and brought out three M16 carbines. 'O.K., I guess we better get movin'.' He paused, looking at Ryderbeit and Jones. 'You boys got no cameras?' he asked suddenly.

No-Entry nodded impassively. 'We got them small Japanese jobs, sergeant. Can't go flashing a lot of equipment around if we're supposed to be genuine M.P.'s now, can we?' Ryderbeit and Murray were already fitting on their helmets, slinging the M16's over their shoulders.

Wace started towards the door, not looking at all happy. Suddenly Murray barred his way, his heart beating fast. 'Just a moment, Don. You're staying here. Till we come back.'

Wace opened his mouth and shut it again. His eyes were beginning to register fear. He looked quickly at Ryderbeit and No-Entry, then at the door. 'Lemme outta here!' he cried, and his hands brought up the M16, pointing it at Murray's belly.

'You're forgetting something, sergeant.' Murray took a step forward. 'Two days ago you accepted a couple of illegal greens. Big ones. Big enough to get you six months in the stockade, Don.'

'You can't prove that!'

'I may not be able to prove it — but I can still report it. I'll tell them you agreed to take me on an unofficial ride round the perimeter in your jeep in exchange for one hundred dollars in cash — then at the last moment you chickened out. They can't throw *me* in the stockade, Don. They can't do a damned thing to me. Anyway, why would they think I'd make up a crazy story like that?'

Wace's lip began to tremble. The muzzle of his M16 had dropped several inches. 'Just for a lousy hundred bucks!' he cried, and for a moment Murray thought he was going to weep.

'Here's your five grand.' Murray brought out a fat roll of Pol's fifty dollar bills from his tunic pocket and tossed them down at Wace's feet. 'Now pick those up and get out — before one of your brass-hats walks in and nabs you red-handed.'

Wace stood looking goggle-eyed at the tight little roll of notes slowly uncurling themselves on the floor. Then suddenly he bent double and grabbed them up, pushing them deep into his back ammunition pocket. 'If one o' you bastards breathes a word o' this,' he blurted, 'I'll blow his head off, so help me God!'

'Forget you ever saw us, sergeant. Now put that money in a safe place and get lost!'

The door slammed and Wace was gone. Murray looked at his watch: 10.34. 'Six minutes to go,' he said, glancing at the telephone.

'You think that sap'll go running to the nearest M.P.'s?' said Ryderbeit.

'I don't think so. Not right away, at least. He'll sit and contemplate that money first. Then he'll probably do the sensible thing and try to forget all about it until he's on the ship back home.'

Ryderbeit fitted a clip of ammunition into his M16, handing out two more to the others. 'Just in case,' he murmured. 'From now on we're on enemy territory.' And together the three of them swung round. Silently and very quickly the door had opened and two men stepped in. One was an M.P., the other a civilian. The M.P. was an enormous man of about fifty, standing at least two inches taller than any of them, with a broad, blank, brutal face behind dark glasses with reflecting lenses. His voice was a slow Southern drawl, but with none of the Southern charm. 'Ye men got yer Ah-Dee cards?'

None of them moved. They were all looking at the civilian. He nodded at each of them, with no smile. 'Evening Mr Wilde — Mr Ryderbeit.' He ignored No-Entry. 'All got up for a nice fancy-dress party?'

Murray gave a tired smile. 'It's all right, Mr Conquest, we've got our I.D. cards.'

'I'm sure you have. But I'm not interested in your identification, Mr Wilde. I know it too well already. I want to know what you three are doing in unauthorised premises impersonating members of the U.S. Armed Forces.' As he spoke the M.P. laid a hand the size of a spade on the white flap of his .45 holster.

Murray nodded. 'Good question, Maxwell.' He looked down at the M.P.'s hand, then at Ryderbeit, both arms hanging loose at his sides, fingers flexed about eighteen inches below his loaded M16. Lastly he looked at No-Entry, whose carbine still lay on the table, his boxer's hands resting on his hips. Three against two, he thought: but he still didn't fancy the odds. If they tried shooting it out they'd alert the whole compound; on the other hand, Conquest had already proved himself in unarmed combat, and Murray doubted whether even No-Entry could make much impact on this huge M.P.

He decided to play for time — valuable, one-point-five billion dollars' worth of time. At that moment the M.P. took a step forward and Murray caught his own twin reflection in the man's dark lenses. 'Better take 'em down to Security and have 'em checked out, Mr Conquest,' the man said, moving only his lower lip; and Murray recognised the mute, dead-eyed authority of the big nation wielding the big stick — the nightstick and napalm, big boots on alien soil — of a simple man who still did not quite know the rules and was just waiting to stamp and swing.

But Maxwell Conquest was no such simple man, and although he did not always play by the rules, he at least knew them. And he would know that arresting three civilians — two of whom were not even Americans — on foreign territory could give rise to serious complications. Murray looked at him calmly and began to say, 'Are you intending to arrest us, Mr Conquest?' — when the telephone rang on the desk.

He reached it in one leap, before the M.P. could grab him. Jackie's voice was clear and matter-of-fact: 'Mr Wilde please?'

'*C'est moi, chérie.*' He looked dead into Conquest's eyes as he listened.

'The surprise party's all arranged,' she said, 'Same time, same place.'

'*Merci. A tout à l'heure!*' He hung up, sighed, and gave a small smile. 'This is a little embarrassing, Mr Conquest.' He glanced at the menacing M.P. who had taken another step forward. 'Perhaps we could have a word together in private?'

'Private?'

Murray nodded at the phone. 'That was your wife just now.'

'My *wife*? What the hell! — why didn't you let me speak to her?'

'Because she wanted to speak to *me*, Mr Conquest. A little personal matter between the three of us.' He nodded at Jones and Ryderbeit. 'Now I'm sure you'd prefer to discuss it quietly, in private?'

Conquest gave a little wince and his jaw muscles tightened. In the sudden silence an aircraft began revving up engines outside. 'Sergeant,' Conquest said at last, without moving his eyes from Murray: 'will you wait outside for a moment.'

The M.P. hesitated, then turned slowly, his hand still on his holster, and ambled back into the passage. 'I think you'd better close the door,' Murray said quietly; and Conquest glanced behind him to see the giant figure standing just outside. He shrugged, stepped over to the door, closed it and turned again. 'Now what's all this —?' he began, and his eyes suddenly opened very wide.

What happened next seemed to take place in slow motion, against the rising roar of the plane outside. Ryderbeit leant down as though to scratch his ankle, straightened up, and in one smooth motion stepped out to embrace Conquest. One hand went up over the man's mouth, as Conquest drew back his lips to scream; the other went down round his waist, slipping the knife deep under the ribs into his spleen. For three full seconds they both stood transfixed. The engines roared to a crescendo as Conquest's eyes took on a bright glassy look, his fingers twitching upwards. The noise outside dropped for a moment, and there came a long weird belching sound, a slackening of Conquest's whole body as he began to lean towards Ryderbeit, his knees buckling, hands still clawing feebly upwards, while Ryderbeit said in an undertone: 'Get the chair, No-Entry — wedge the door!' — beginning to lower Conquest to the floor, supporting him now with his hand behind his neck, the other holding him up under the ribs with the knife. 'Window!' he said softly to Murray, as the Negro nimbly slid the chair under the door handle and spittle bubbled over Conquest's rigid lips.

Murray turned and pushed up the window frame, dropping soundlessly to the ground outside. No-Entry followed a couple of seconds later. Murray did not wait for Ryderbeit as he sprinted towards the jeep, parked in darkness only a few yards from the canteen entrance; leapt aboard and found the keys just where Wace had promised, still in the ignition. He switched on and the motor fired first time, as Ryderbeit and Jones came running low down the path and bounded aboard with their carbines held across their chests.

'Take it slow and easy now, soldier!' Ryderbeit breathed: 'That boy's not goin' to make any more noise.'

Murray had the headlamps dipped, steering out into the one-way path between a double row of huts. They had each studied the plan of the airfield so well they knew every track, every turning by heart.

'Are you loaded?' Ryderbeit said at last.

'Load me,' said Murray, and felt his M16 jerked sideways, the confident touch as Ryderbeit snapped the clip under the plastic muzzle, the light weight of the strap against his shoulders. He wondered — despite the film industry — how long it really took a strong man in anger to break down an ordinary-size door wedged by a chair.

He had reached the end of the ATCO III compound and now turned towards the huge aerial transport lanes lying a thousand yards ahead in almost total darkness, under a sky ripped by criss-cross streaks of light — the whole night black and heavy with the fluctuating boom and scream of invisible machinery.

They reached the beginning of a long zig-zagging wall of sandbagged fighter plane parking bays, with the folding wing tips of the Phantoms and Thunderchiefs jutting over the top like sharks' fins. No one spoke again until Murray suddenly drew into a dark embrasure about a hundred yards from the end of the wall, stopped and switched off the headlamps. Just ahead were two long black sedans, unmarked, non-military, with no lights.

'Look like Treasury boys,' Ryderbeit muttered, glancing at his watch. 'Ten forty-three. Two minutes to go. That bitch o' yours had better be on time with Virgil's button,' he added, 'or we're going to be right in the shit!'

'We're pretty deep in it already,' said Murray.

A couple of flares burst high ahead along the perimeter, lighting them all up like sitting toy soldiers. They were now nearly half a mile from the hut where Conquest had died, and Murray was just wondering which alert would go out first, when he saw in his mirror a pair of blazing headlamps and a flashing red beacon heading straight at them from behind, along the edge of the sandbagged wall.

Ryderbeit and No-Entry slipped their guns on to semiautomatic. 'Wait for it!' said Ryderbeit, as a camouflaged jeep identical to their own came screeching up behind them and both doors snapped open.

'You men with Major Millbright's outfit?' a voice called. Two officers in fatigues and soft G.I. caps had stepped out, unarmed.

No-Entry Jones turned in his seat, beginning to stand up and salute. 'Correct, sir.'

'Then get the hell out o' here!' the officer cried: 'You know this whole area's off limits till twenty-three-fifteen hundred hours?'

'You givin' us orders?' Ryderbeit said, in a very passable Mid-West accent.

'I'm ordering you to get your arses out o' here!' the man bawled back, but even as he spoke there came two brilliant flashes about a hundred yards to their right, followed by a double ear-cracking explosion, and the two men flung themselves half sideways into the shelter of the jeep, as two more flashes burst about a mile away and the first officer was yelling, 'Get your heads down!' But the words drifted emptily into a high whooping howl — the panic-stricken howl of the Red Alert siren bouncing off more than a dozen echochambers in every corner of the giant Tân Sơn Nhất airfield.

The officer tried to shout above the sound, but another rocket swished down and burst with a shuddering crack behind the sandbagged wall, this time followed by a boom and the billowing glare of exploding high-octane fuel.

Ryderbeit yelled: 'Get goin'!' and Murray let the clutch out, the jeep jerking into the dark, its lights still switched off, heading towards the two dead sedans. But just as they drew abreast of them, two red bars of tail-lights came on and both cars started forward together. 'Take 'em, soldier — on the right!'

Murray swung the wheel over and passed both cars — long black Fleetwoods with smoked windows so that it was impossible to see how many men were inside. He had his foot flat on the floor, but the jeep lacked the power of the two big cars which were accelerating fast.

Ryderbeit and No-Entry sat twisted round in their seats, and a moment later their M16's flared simultaneously — two bursts ripping diagonally across both windshields, but without any apparent effect. Ryderbeit raised his gun and fired more carefully this time, the muzzle jumping in his hand as he lined up the tyres of the first car, while Jones blazed away at the headlamps of the second.

But the cars kept coming on, all headlamps intact, drawing rapidly closer. Ryderbeit swore: 'Bullet-proof glass — self-sealing tyres!' He laid down his carbine and now reached inside his tunic pockets, bringing out a grenade in each hand. The two cars were almost level with each other now, perhaps twenty yards behind, beginning to draw apart to cut the jeep off on either side, when Ryderbeit pulled the pin of the first grenade with his teeth and flung it, in a smooth lob, directly in the path of the car on their left.

The grenade hit the concrete almost exactly in front of the headlamps and exploded a second later, well under the long engine. There was a flash and the front wheels rose and toppled, the whole car going into a drunken slewing motion, while Ryderbeit leapt round, pulled the next pin and aimed the second grenade low and fast, like a deadly pitcher, under the belly of the other car as it tried to swerve away. Another flash — flames now coming from the first car — the second bouncing to a stop, its engine-bonnet springing open like a twisted tin can; then slowly rolling up on its side, two wheels still spinning in the swelling flames from the first car.

Murray then caught another red flashing in his mirror and a pair of headlamps glared back at him, gaining fast. Ryderbeit and No-Entry were both kneeling on the seat, facing backwards and fitting fresh clips into their carbines. Their pursuers this time were in a large yellow Land Rover, its siren blaring even above the crescendo of the Red Alert.

Murray had the speedometer touching sixty, running out across the smooth concrete apron as Ryderbeit crouched over the short-muzzled M16 and fired two more quick bursts. In the mirror Murray saw both headlamps explode and go black. Ryderbeit aimed again and this time his muzzle jerked round in a scything arc that cut upwards across the windshield and homed in on the revolving red beacon which suddenly went out, and he was yelling at No-Entry: 'Give it 'em on fully automatic!' This time the whole jeep seemed to lurch as Jones' little plastic gun emptied itself in a single roar — thirty rounds in just over one second flat. The Land Rover behind swerved blindly, then rocked to a standstill. No one got out: though Murray had noticed the long antenna swung out from the bonnet like a fishing rod, and knew that unless No-Entry's last burst had killed them all — or at least put them fully out of action — that radio was going to be critical.

He was still holding their speed at around 60 m.p.h., following the orange-painted lines and arrows that splayed out across the concrete towards the Air Freight Transport runways; while behind, over a wide horizon, several large fires were already lighting the sky and the sirens kept up their agonised rhythm like the panting of asthmatics. Fighter-jets were starting up behind the sandbagged walls; the secondary, slower siren howls of Air and Military Police were now baying out against the chaos of the night: and for the first time Murray began to take stock of what had really happened.

Less than two minutes had passed since those first two rockets had hit the field, and been followed — his mind registering almost subconsciously — by at least a dozen more explosions. He recognised them well as Soviet 122's: lethal, highly manoeuvrable weapons which are also notoriously inaccurate. And the fact that at least a dozen of them had landed inside a relatively compact area of the field indicated that they were being loosed off from unusually close range, perhaps as the prelude to a large-scale assault.

But the first two rockets had struck a few seconds before the Red Alert went off — which suggested that something very odd indeed was happening. Was it mere coincidence that Jackie Conquest had fired General Virgil Greene's button at almost the precise second that, at a mile or two away, some scrawny Viet Cong had lit his fuse and stood back? For Murray doubted even America's mighty war-machine capable devising an alarm system so exact that it could activate a Red Alert within seconds of the first explosions.

Yet this was just what had happened. And as they drove further into the dark wastes of the Air Freight Transport Area, he began to have an ugly feeling, not that things were going wrong, but that they might be going just a little too right.

They were now perhaps a quarter of a mile from the two crashed Fleetwoods and the Land Rover, when, about three hundred yards ahead, illuminated under the glow of more flares, they saw the familiar silhouette of a Caribou transport plane. It was already lined up at the head of the runway, red and green wing-lights on, facing down the lane of orange landing beacons. Around its wings and below its tail was a cluster of vehicles — a forklift truck, jeeps, several motorcycle outriders. Murray made no attempt to slow down, even for the large stencilled sign under a flashing red warning light:

AFTA / RUNWAY IV / TSN
ALL UNAUTHORISED PERSONNEL
KEEP OUT!

He almost laughed aloud. After that first numbing shock of seeing Conquest die, he now felt a heady exhilaration, the release and recklessness of a gambler on a wild streak — no road back now — all bridges burnt and the only way out down that empty runway in the slim blunt-nosed Caribou with its anus-vent closed under the tail, fuel trucks withdrawn, forklift empty, all systems go.

Some of the vehicles, dim now under the dying flares, were beginning to move away towards them, followed by the outriders.

Only the last two hundred yards now of flat oil-streaked concrete: men climbing out of the nose and rear doors of the plane: more on the ground — perhaps half a dozen in all — as Murray switched on the jeep's own siren and Ryderbeit unclipped the windshield fasteners, folding the Perspex forward on to the bonnet, his M16 reloaded and at the ready.

The forklift truck, flanked by the outriders, came grinding towards them. Murray kept up his speed, swerving round them with Ryderbeit and No-Entry still holding their weapons level with the bonnet. The motorcycles snarled past without incident. He began to brake only when the jeep was about thirty yards from the Caribou, with the siren still going and Ryderbeit yelling, 'If there's goin' to be any shootin', let's get between 'em and the bloody plane!'

Murray pulled up just behind the Caribou's port engine, which was already turning. As he did so, several men in khaki baseball caps ran towards one of the two jeeps parked behind the plane's tail. Obviously last-minute maintenance men. But Murray had his eyes on a third vehicle — another long dark Fleetwood with smoked windows parked slightly aside from the others, where two guards stood frozen under a fresh set of flares, staring back at where three more rockets had hit in quick succession, stitching the skyline like fireworks.

These guards wore no insignia, no helmets, just well-tailored uniforms of grey-green, with flat-visored caps and repeater-rifles slung over their shoulders. But for the rifles they could have been chauffeurs, or receptionists at some grimly exclusive hotel.

Murray switched the siren off only when he was well between the two guards and the plane. Then Ryderbeit whispered, 'Let Jones do the talking first — you come in only when it starts gettin' tricky!' A tall man in the same plain uniform, but without a rifle, had appeared in the forward door up to the pilot's cabin.

'Who's the officer in charge here?' Jones yelled, above the roar of the Caribou engine.

The man climbed down the steps. He had a delicate handsome face, polite and serious — the exact contrast to the hulking brute of an M.P. they had left to break down the door half a mile back at ATCO III compound. His voice was calm and unruffled: 'I'm the operation super — name's Sanderson. We have a Red Alert.' He said it as a statement of fact, without panic or concern, but moving closer as he spoke, examining each of them.

'You're to get your men out o' here, Mister Sanderson,' Jones said. 'Your flight plan is postponed — your crews are to move this aircraft, temporarily, to another area.'

'What are your precise orders?' Sanderson asked with exasperating calm, as the second of the plane's engines spluttered and swung to life. Ryderbeit's fingers tightened round the stock of his gun.

'All non-combat aircraft are automatically grounded,' Jones said; and the man just nodded and repeated: 'Where are your orders?'

'We have orders to commandeer all non-combat aircraft!' Jones shouted, jumping suddenly down from his side of the jeep and running to the forward door of the Caribou. 'Get your men out o' here, Mr Sanderson!'

The second engine had burst into a roar and Ryderbeit was saying to Murray in a shouted whisper, 'We mustn't let 'em cut those motors, soldier — let 'em warm up a couple o' moments longer!' As he spoke he too sprang from the jeep, his M16 held low from the waist, at nobody particular, but watching the two other guards whose rifles were still slung over their shoulders.

'This is Treasury property,' Sanderson began: 'I have no authority —'

'You have no authority period!' Murray snapped, not bothering to disguise his Irish intonation, as he watched, from the corner of his eye, Ryderbeit edging round towards the steps up to the pilot's cabin. 'This airfield is under attack, Mr Sanderson,' he went on, 'and I am to advise you that all military and civilian equipment is as from now under the authority of the military. Get it!' he yelled, above the scream of three fighters streaking overhead.

Time was running out. At any moment some genuine M.P. patrol might arrive, either to give Sanderson the same orders, or more probably to investigate the murder of one CIA man and the unknown fate of a number of Treasury guards in two unmarked cars and a Land Rover with a powerful radio.

Sanderson was looking worried now. 'We're awaiting two automobiles back there for emergency instructions,' he began slowly, but Murray broke in: 'Your two vehicles have been hit by VC rockets. My own orders come personally from General Greene. In the event of an enemy attack Operation Lazy Dog is to be put on ice — your personnel to be withdrawn — your aircraft to be placed under General Greene's personal guard. Which means us, Mr Sanderson — plus an extra detail arriving presently. Now let's get moving, sir.'

'If this plane gets hit —'

'If this plane gets hit, Sanderson, your arse's going to be in a sling!' They flinched as another rocket burst less than a quarter of a mile away. Murray took it as his final cue: 'The military is responsible for the security of this airfield, sir. And I am ordering you for the last time to get your men out of here!'

'The crew of this aircraft take their instructions from me,' Sanderson said calmly, and walked over to where the two Treasury guards stood beside the remaining jeep, parked just in front of the Fleetwood. He whispered something to them; they nodded, saluted and climbed aboard the jeep. Sanderson now walked back to where Ryderbeit was still standing under the forward door of the Caribou.

Ryderbeit let him pass, up the steps into the nose of the aircraft — the crew still aboard, engines still running. A moment later the jeep carrying the two Treasury men started up, followed almost at once by the Fleetwood. Murray nodded at No-Entry, who sprang up through the rear door, closing it quickly behind him.

Murray waited ten seconds, then climbed up to the forward door, kicked the steps away and slammed it shut behind him. Inside, in the sudden dark, he eased off his helmet and realised that he was leaning against the body of a man. It felt soft, swinging with the hammock-seat. As he touched it, the head lolled with a bump on to his shoulder, slid off, and the whole body collapsed like a sack down the metal steps and sagged against the door.

At the same moment he was aware, even above the roar of the engines, of a curious noise. The thumping, snorting, shuffling sound of a fight. A merciless, bone-breaking fight being fought out against the crackle of a radio transmitter: '*Control to Lazy Dog, do you read me, do you read me…?*' He looked down and saw that the body he had touched was Sanderson's, his neck twisted as though it were broken, while above, in the red gloom of the cockpit lighting, Ryderbeit and No-Entry Jones were grappling with the two men, fighting with their fists and feet and plastic butts of their M16's. They were fighting like dancers, rocking back and forward across the tiny floor, the two pilots in flying-suits and helmets, the other two dodging low and fast.

Murray was clambering up to the cabin when he saw the knife jab out in Ryderbeit's hand and one of the pilot's begin sinking to the floor. The second crew member, his helmet flopping back, earphones scrunched and awry, was trying to get away, backing up against the corner of the cabin; then he whipped round with something in his hand and No-Entry grabbed his wrist, and the roaring darkness burst round them like a paper bag. The man went over backwards, sliding against the edge of the cabin with the side of his face suddenly gone. The Negro stood with a heavy .45 automatic in his hand, shaking his head: 'What a damned mess!' he muttered. And there came a loud hammering on the forward door. Ryderbeit was already in one of the pilots' seats, running his hands over the controls, ignoring the static whine of the R/T monotone: '*Curly Mantle to Lazy Dog, do you hear me?*'

The hammering kept up on the door outside. He checked the last knob, looked through the side window and yelled back at Murray: 'There's a Moke out there — empty! See who the bastards are, and try and keep 'em sweet. If not' — and he nodded at the M16 in Murray's hands — 'blow 'em in half! I'm goin' to need a few more seconds to get my revs up. We've got a full payload back there, soldier!'

Behind them No-Entry had lowered the dead pilot, with half his head shot away, feet first down the steel steps on to the cargo floor, leaving a broad messy smear. Murray tried not to look at him. The .45 bullet had smashed the skull like a soft-boiled egg, splattering bone and brain-pulp over the floor and walls of the cabin. Jones was now dragging him across to the edge of the dark narrow hull of the aircraft on which lay two solid slabs of tight-packed, black waterproof paper laid in two piles at least three feet high, with scarcely room to squeeze down between them. But Murray did not stop to examine them. As he started towards the door he could feel his rubber soles growing sticky on the steel floor. The pitch of the engines was rising, the hammering on the door getting louder, frantic now, as he reached the double swing-lock and began to turn it.

He opened it less than an inch and saw her face staring up at him — a distraught fragment of face with her mouth open and dark hair swept down over one eye. She put her whole weight against the door and he glimpsed a Mini Moke with U.S. Army markings parked just below the wing. In the background, across the wide dark apron, a stream of headlamps and more flashing red beacons were converging towards them. He grabbed her through, slamming the door behind her and swinging the lock back into position.

She turned and pulled herself against him, arms round his neck, hair all over his face, not looking at the cargo or the three crumpled corpses — Sanderson down by the door, with his delicate features twisted sideways, the pulped head of the pilot down in the cargo bay, or the second crew member who was still up in the cabin, bleeding heavily from just under the heart. She went on holding him, as Murray yelled up at Ryderbeit: 'They're coming — half a dozen at least!'

Ryderbeit raised his hand without turning, his voice still intoning the pilot's catechism to No-Entry Jones: 'Flaps up — half throttle — check air-brakes — full throttle...' The floor lurched and they began to move. Murray broke away from her and seized hold of one of the hammock seats. He saw her look down at Sanderson, then at the pilot in the cargo bay, and her face showed an indifference that was faintly shocking.

The floor was swaying, the stacks of cargo beginning to shift and tremble under their tight wire moorings, each layer of packages separated by a plywood raft. Jackie had pressed herself down the narrow passage between them, steadying herself against the top of the left-hand pile, and now began neatly slitting the shiny charcoal-black paper with her fingernail, folding the edge back and tearing the whole sheet away as far as the wire binding.

As Murray followed her he felt the floor lift. She turned and kissed him, beginning to laugh, holding out a thick sheaf of bills bound in a wrapper with the seal of *La Banque de L'Indo-Chine*.

'*C'est épousstoufflant!*' she cried, using the old-fashioned Sorbonne slang, 'blown out in a gust of wind'. Murray peered down at them, and in the dim red light from the cabin he could just make out, under the sealed wrapper, the plump humorous features of old Ben Franklin, sitting nobly on the Century — the one hundred dollar bill. He nodded slowly, giddily. 'We had to kill at least four men to get those. One of them was your husband.'

She looked at him with mild surprise. 'Oh? Where?'

'Back at ATCO III compound — he walked in and found us. Ryderbeit did it with a knife.'

She nodded slowly. 'Well, perhaps Monsieur Ryderbeit has some virtue after all.'

Murray said nothing. He took one of the packs of Centuries and made his way back up to the cabin steps, trying to avoid the sludge on the floor. Ryderbeit sat without earphones, with the R/T turned up on the HF wavelength, droning with the weird jabber of modern warfare: '*Lover Boy to Glamour Girl, check out your five-zero over perimeter*' — '*Crackerjack to Glamour Girl, we have total alert over Gia Dinh.*' Beside him No-Entry sat marking the celluloid overlay on the navigation dial with his wax pencil, checking against the elaborate chart that had been prepared and abandoned by the dead co-pilot. Ryderbeit was saying: 'Up to three hundred feet and holding her steady — north, north-west — and keep yer eyes peeled for any low-flying Bird-dogs or choppers!' He looked round at Murray. 'And how's the cargo?'

Murray dropped the wad of bills into his lap. 'Just a random sample off the top.'

Ryderbeit picked it up with his free hand, riffling his thumb through it with a quick snapping sound, then nodded slowly and put the money away inside his tunic, while his left hand moved the stick gently forward and the jewelled pattern of lights, which were the twin cities of Saigon and Cholon, slid away on their left. 'But we're not out of it yet, soldier,' he said, with a strange lack of emotion, as he levelled the wings and headed now into the darkness of D Zone and the Iron Triangle — sixty miles of rainforest reaching to the Cambodian border.

'We're running into a rise,' No-Entry called: 'Take her up one hundred.'

'Up one hundred,' Ryderbeit repeated, moving the stick back and switching the R/T over several wave-bands until a harsh Kansas voice came ringing through the cockpit, loud and clear: '*We have five negative calls on Lazy Dog! Get a check on her and a call on Curly Mantle for immediate instructions!*' Another voice, pure mellow cotton-picker, chimed in: '*Curlay Mayntle rayports immediate ground-to-air sweep for Layzy Dawg!*'

Murray glanced back and saw Jackie Conquest busy edging herself along between the cargo, tearing open the top packages on both sides.

'We're getting 'em on radar, Sammy!' No-Entry called suddenly: 'Three bleeps coming up from near due south off the sea. Probably Navy boys off one o' the carriers.'

Ryderbeit swore in Afrikaans. 'What speed?'

'Mach One, coming into Mach Two, and closing fast. Look like Phantoms.'

Murray swallowed and glanced at the air-speed dial, the needle creeping round to over two hundred knots. 'Those Navy pilots know their job — they're the best,' he murmured. Astronaut material every one, he thought: getting their action learning to buzz Iluyshin reconnaissance planes over the Arctic Circle — and that kind of run does not allow for error. He turned to Ryderbeit. 'What can they do? Try to force us down? Or shoot us down — with the risk we make a forced landing and Charlie Cong gets the lot?'

'You're the thinking man, soldier. You tell me what they'll do.'

'Well, unless they've got close contingency planning for this kind of emergency, which is hardly likely, I'd say they'd have to get top priority clearance to shoot down one-point-five billion worth of Federal Reserves.'

Ryderbeit nodded. 'But I'll say this for the Yanks — they're bloody quick on the draw!'

Jones said calmly, watching the radar bleeps: 'They're closing at about nine hundred knots — height about four thousand feet. Can we take her down a little, Sammy?'

'What do the charts say? This D Zone's not all flat, and it's just goin' to need one little hill to have that whole load of Ben Franklins back there burnin' like a bonfire.'

'Down another fifty feet and we're under any radar they got,' Jones said.

Ryderbeit shrugged: 'You're the navigator.' His hand eased the stick forward, the tilt of the aircraft scarcely perceptible, the darkness ahead and below total.

'They'll be over us in less than two minutes,' Jones added, as the R/T crackled out: '*Lazy Dog — whoever you are — now hear this! You will identify yourself, your position and your destination within thirty seconds or our aircraft will take appropriate action!*'

Ryderbeit grinned under the red light: 'That means the sods don't know what to do — just goin' to try and bluff us out.' As he spoke he began to slow the air-speed — the needle dropping to 180, 160, holding at 150. Murray watched with the same baffled awe as when they had begun to crawl down through the high mountains west of Dien Bien Phu — wondering now, as he had then, how much of it was luck, how much sheer skill, and how much just the gambler's wilful instinct to win through.

The Phantoms closed a few seconds later and the radar screen became a confusion of spattered light. 'They've lost us,'

Jones said; and Ryderbeit chuckled grimly: 'What do they expect at those speeds?'

'They're coming round again — about five miles ahead,' Jones said, 'speeds down to around six hundred —' and the R/T broke in: '*Lazy Dog, this is Navy Phantom Squadron Silky Tawdry. We have air-to-air missiles and orders to use them.*'

'Silky Tawdry, you're full o' shit,' Ryderbeit muttered, and the R/T went on: '*We're giving you twenty seconds or the missiles go off, Lazy Dog!*'

'Sounds as though they mean it,' said Murray.

'They're bluffing,' Ryderbeit said. He reached inside his tunic and took out one of his Romeo y Julietas, biting the end and handing it back to Murray without turning his head. 'Light it for me, soldier.'

His nerve was extraordinary. Murray took the full twenty seconds to light the cigar, keeping the flame well shielded, knowing that even the flare of a match can destroy minutes of a pilot's night-sight. He handed it back and Ryderbeit said, 'Have one yourself.'

'No thanks.' The twenty seconds passed — thirty seconds — and Ryderbeit called suddenly, 'Let's try 'em with a mayday. Say we're on one of the military transport routes, coming down from Pleiku, losing height fast and need medivac choppers.'

No-Entry switched the channels over to the international distress wavelength, calling quickly: 'Mayday, mayday, eleven-nine-four-zero — Marine Transport Caribou Big Brother out o' Pleiku to Can Tho…'

Ryderbeit began to cackle over his cigar: 'You genius, No-Entry! Those Navy bastards are go in' to have to think twice before they start loosin' off any missiles when there are Marines around!'

'We have full payload of wounded men and need immediate assistance with medivac support,' Jones went on.

For a moment the Phantoms seemed to be undecided, the radar bleeps jerking about in little concentric knots in the middle of the screen. Jones had started again on his mayday call, when Jackie Conquest came up the steps and stood beside Murray, whispering in French: 'It's all there — every packet I looked at. The large ones seem to be mostly on the top — hundreds of thousands of them!'

He peered at her curiously, wondering if he were mistaken, or was there just a chance that the widowed Mrs Conquest had been bitten by the gold-bug more deeply than he suspected? While he was still looking at her, Ryderbeit suddenly swung the stick back and they were both thrown sideways, nearly falling down the steps into the cargo bay. The engines howled, the floor tilting upwards as Murray grabbed at some canvas straps behind the pilots' seats, seizing Jacqueline's arm with his free hand, while Jones yelled, 'Take her up another two hundred!'

The engines kept up their long climbing howl and through the windshield, against the deep grey night, there now appeared the still blacker shape of rounded hills. Ryderbeit was brushing ash off his lap, as he strained forward to see the treeline leaping away about a hundred feet below. 'We missed that last ridge by less than fifty feet. I guess one can do this kind o' thing once too often — and Samuel D. Ryderbeit's been doin' it for an awful long time now!'

'One thing's for sure though,' Jones replied gravely: 'Those Phantoms weren't built for tree-hopping.'

'What's happening?' Jacqueline asked, with magnificent detachment.

'Up hill and down dale, darling,' Ryderbeit said, without looking at her.

'Where are we?' said Murray.

'By my reckoning,' said Jones, 'we should be out of the country in seven to eight minutes.'

'Still no other visitors, except the Phantoms?'

'Nothing so far.'

'You brought me some dollars from down there, Mrs Conquest?' Ryderbeit asked, this time looking round at her with a bright smile.

She smiled faintly back, not at Ryderbeit but at Murray, giving him a sidelong wink as she tapped two well-padded breasts under her sleeveless dress. 'I've been more discreet,' she whispered: 'Only bills of fifty.'

Just then Ryderbeit gave a yelp and sprang forward in his seat, watching two pricks of light come looping down from the top of the sky — nose-lights blinking towards them at close to the speed of sound, as two of the Navy Phantoms converged and shrieked down above them, clearing the roof of the Caribou by less than ten feet. For a moment the whole aircraft seemed to pause in mid-air, cringing like a great beast being tormented by these two venomous bat-winged hunks of aluminium.

'Mad bastards! They're tryin' to head us off before the border.'

The third Phantom now appeared out above the port wing, flying in the same direction but at twice their speed — the glow of burning kerosene curving out of the rear-nostrils of its short fat fuselage as it turned ahead of them, rolling on its back, and suddenly came towards them like a fire-streaked dart, passing close above the starboard wing — less close than the others, and a lot slower, with its landing beacons suddenly flaring on like a pair of searchlights, long enough to spoil

Ryderbeit's night-sight, and probably long enough for the crew to read the Treasury markings on the Caribou's tail-fin.

'Less than five minutes to the border,' Jones said quietly.

'You think that'll stop them?' said Jackie.

'What sort of stuff has Sihanouk's Air Force got?' asked Murray.

'Nothing that can stop a Phantom, that's for sure,' said Ryderbeit — just as the lights of the first two fighters came swerving round again over their port wing. While almost directly below, flicking through the screen of trees, they saw a spray of lights.

'That'll be Trang Bang,' said Jones: 'Six miles to the border.' Above the shanty town, and the row of brighter lights that marked the U.S. helicopter base, more lights now appeared. Murray recognised the dim dragonfly silhouette of Huey 'choppers', flying towards them at about the level of the next rim of hills. The R/T came on again, this time on HF: '*Trang Bang base to Marine Big Brother. We have your position. Can you attempt a landing? We have all medivac and fire-fighting crews standing by. Over.*'

Jones leant out and spoke back on the HF wavelength: 'Big Brother to Trang Bang base. We've got three crazy Phantoms on our tail, trying to buzz us. Probably think we're from Cambodia. We will attempt a landing, but first get the bastards called off — or tell 'em the Marine Corps'll have their arses for breakfast!'

But this time they did not listen to the answer. For at that moment a great ball of flame burst in the sky almost directly ahead, followed instantly by a long explosion, like a giant orange caterpillar crawling down towards the jungle. In the vivid lingering glow they had a glimpse of a dismembered helicopter, rotor blades severed, spiralling to earth with flames spouting from its tail. What was left of the Phantom hit the hills a second later with a thud of exploding fuel and rockets that reached even into the cabin of the Caribou.

Ryderbeit was taking the nose up steeply now, shaving the rim of hills perilously close, even in the dying flames of the crashed aircraft; and again they heard the crackle of the R/T, and a voice, quick and worried: '*Base Control to Big Brother* — are you still receiving? Are you still receiving…?'

'Shut her off, No-Entry!' Ryderbeit shouted, easing the throttle out, with the air-speed rising rapidly. The radar bleeps from the two remaining Phantoms were beginning to draw away from the centre of the screen, becoming confused now with the myriad specks of more rescue helicopters lifting off from Trang Bang base.

Height 1,500 feet, still climbing with the hills. Speed more than 200 knots. Throttle full out, holding steady as Jones called: 'Last ridge ahead!' — and the branches swept up, seeming almost to brush the wings this time. Ryderbeit jerked the stock forward. The nose went down and they dropped like a lift.

'We're over the top,' said Jones. 'Welcome to Cambodia! And the Phantoms seem to be holding off.'

Ryderbeit let out a great sigh and sat back. 'I bet they are! The U.S. Navy's goin' to be really popular tomorrow down in Trang Bang. Murray boy, let's take a look at a few more of those greenbacks — big ones. I want to touch 'em, stroke 'em, kiss 'em. Jackie darling, you did beautifully! The Red Alert went out sweet and loud and right on time.'

'Too bloody well on time,' said Murray. 'It was only a couple of seconds late.'

'Late? What d'yer mean?'

'You didn't notice? There was a major VC attack going on down there — and those boys don't let off their Russian rockets just for fun.'

Jones interrupted: 'Steer east-south-east — one-seventy.'

'You haven't told me what you're getting at,' Ryderbeit went on, moving the controls as he spoke.

'You think the attack and the alert just coincided?'

Ryderbeit jerked round in his seat, looking straight at Jackie. 'You did send that alert?'

'*Bien sur.*' She began to frown: 'You don't think I've earned my passage?'

'She sent it all right,' said Murray. 'Only somebody also tipped off the Viet Cong — just to make it seem all the more convincing perhaps. I'm just wondering who — and why.'

PART 10: HAPPY LANDING

CHAPTER 1

Pol sat on the swivel chair, elbows on the desk, streaming with sweat despite the air-conditioner which was turned up full. In front of him were two glasses and a bottle of Johnny Walker three-quarters empty, standing beside his double-barrelled shotgun.

It was a small low-ceilinged room with sealed windows, filing cabinet, wall-safe, refrigerator, a nude calendar pin-up and a big two-way VHF set in the corner. It might have been any cheap, run-down office in any big American town — except that outside the jungle kept up its ceaseless shout against the empty night.

Across the table from him were three men. Two of them wore the silver-grey flying suits of Air U.S.A. and all were about the same age, in their early fifties. One was a tall man with a face like a pickaxe, eyes slanting above a high-peaked nose and a rigid but slightly sardonic mouth. The other pilot was short, heavy-shouldered, with wide flat features and massive eyebrows curling up from a button-nose.

The third man was slumped in the far corner from Pol, his rheumy eyes open with a pained, faintly puzzled expression, his big red face already taking on a sunken look, one short-sleeved arm in a checkered shirt flung out across the table, the other hanging at his side. He had been dead for about three minutes. It would take an experienced doctor — and there were few in the Kingdom of Laos — to separate the symptoms of death due to cardiac failure from those resulting from amethine-cyanide administered with a scratch from a sharp point just behind the left ear.

Pol poured himself another Scotch. He did not offer any to the pilots. 'I want it understood again,' he said, speaking slowly in French, 'that there is to be no unnecessary violence. No shooting, no trouble of any kind. All quiet and normal.' The two pilots nodded together. 'A perfectly routine flight according to the book. There is no reason why anything should go wrong.'

He sighed. It had been a long exhausting thirty-six hours since he had left Cambodia: crossing the border at an unofficial and uncomfortable point, making his way up to Champasak, then joining a sampan with an under-powered motor which had struggled against the heavy current of the Mekong up as far as Thakhek where he'd taken a crowded local bus to just south of Vientiane, to be picked up by the two pilots in the Land Rover which was now parked outside.

'All three men will be armed,' he went on, his eyes flicking from one man to the other. 'And at least two of them know how to shoot. The third, the Irishman, also has a knowledge of the Vietnamese language, so it is essential he has no chance to converse with the others.'

'It is all perfectly understood, Monsieur Pol,' the tall pilot said, speaking fluently, but with a thick accent. 'Unless any of these men makes problems, there will certainly be no problem from us. It will, as you say, be a normal flight.'

'I hope so,' said Pol. He looked again at the dead engineer from Pittsburgh whose life had been all washed up, with a broken marriage, one dead son in a car smash and no idea where his daughters were — a depressing man whom they'd listened to for nearly an hour, just long enough to get half a pint of whisky inside him, before Pol had killed him. He'd done it with a rare twinge of conscience, because the man had been an innocent, a sad stupid bit of flotsam washed up in Asia with the tide of a slow war. Someday, thought Pol, someday I may finish like that.

He looked at his watch. 'We have about an hour,' he said, nodding at the VHF set in the corner. 'We'll turn it on only at the last minute. If all has gone well, there'll probably be a full alert even here.' But he might have been talking to himself; the two men seemed to have heard it all before. He finished the whisky, wondering for a moment if he were becoming nervous. Or perhaps just getting too old?

The Treasury Caribou came down low over the great shallow lake of Cambodia's Tonlé Sap, which is really no more than a swollen river, flooding on either side more than twenty miles of some of the richest rice and fish country in the world.

No-Entry Jones was at the controls now, holding their speed down to a hundred knots, at a height of only fifty feet above the water, while Murray and Ryderbeit unfolded the inflatable life-raft and Jackie began snipping the wire bindings round the dollar packages with a pair of clippers from the cabin locker.

'Leave the hundreds, darling!' Ryderbeit called: 'Just the small stuff.'

'We're putting in the hundreds too,' said Murray. 'There's going to be no penny-pinching now. We can flush the Washingtons and a few fives down the toilet — but the raft has to have the big stuff. They may not be convinced, but we've got to get them suspicious at least — otherwise what's the point of coming down this far in the first place? We're going to be cutting it pretty fine as it is, if we want to make it by dawn.'

Ryderbeit stared at him bleakly. 'Oh you bloody thinking bastard!' Then he saw Jackie bringing out three of the neatly wrapped packs of notes from *La Banque de L'Indo-Chine*. 'These are twenties,' she said; and Ryderbeit cursed her softly in Afrikaans. 'I need a drink.' He caught Murray's eye and scowled. 'And don't start tellin' me that drink blunts the reactions! The only thing that ever blunted mine was knowin' I couldn't get one.'

He pulled out his pigskin flask and took a moderate swig, handing it to Murray. 'I can't watch the price of a big lovely country house in England go right out o' that bloody door without shedding a small alcoholic tear.'

Murray lifted the flask and tasted good French cognac. 'I didn't know you were sentimental about English country houses, Sammy?'

'I'm sentimental about anythin' that costs money.'

Murray nodded. 'Now let's get going.' He put the flask back in his own pocket, and they began tying the wired waterproof packages to the rubber straps of the still deflated raft. 'And we need a corpse,' said Ryderbeit. 'Sanderson'll do.'

'Sanderson, with a wad of Centuries buttoned up tight inside his pocket,' said Murray. 'Because that's one person you can be sure they are going to suspect, besides us — the Treasury official in charge of the operation who disappears with the plane and all the loot.'

'But why does he have to have hundreds on him?' Ryderbeit moaned.

'Because that's just the kind of thing they're not going to expect from a load of villains like us. Dump a life-raft and a few slicks of oil to throw the scent — O.K. They might even expect us to toss down a few bundles of small change. But throw in a corpse carrying several grand in Centuries — that's something that may make them bite. And we need them biting, Sammy. We need the time. We need them combing this lake in Cambodia before they start up on that dam in Laos.'

Ryderbeit spread his hands. 'Why not make it fifties, soldier? Just for me.'

'There's over one hundred million Sterling for you. Isn't it enough?' He clapped him on the shoulder. 'Just think of this as part of the percentage commission — along with that thirty million we've got to pay to the *Cao Đài*.'

'Those bastards. They'd better turn up trumps. And that fat Frenchman too.'

'Coming down over the fishing beds!' Jones called from the cabin.

Murray lifted one of the heavy two-foot-square packages containing mixed bundles of ones and fives from near the bottom of the stack, and started squeezing himself between the piles of money to the back of the aircraft where they had already stowed a couple of five-litre cans of oil next to a heap of emergency spare parts, tool and first-aid kits, life-jackets, the two dead pilots' helmets and papers, the Caribou's logbook and charts for its flight programme to the Philippines.

'The oil and greenbacks go away first,' he said to Ryderbeit, who stood almost weeping, watching him rip open the package, carrying the money loose in his arms over to the open latrine just behind the drop-door under the tail. Jackie, who had followed them back, sat down on the edge of one of the dollar piles, lit a cigarette and watched impassively.

'This is criminal, soldier. Bloody criminal!' Ryderbeit pleaded.

'Bring over one of the cans,' said Murray. Ryderbeit lifted the first oil can and stood peering down the open-ended tube below the toilet seat, the draught coming up cool and fresh off the water. 'Let it go,' said Murray.

Ryderbeit poured the can empty. Then Murray put the first wad of twenty-dollar bills down, watching them swirl round like water going out of a bath, and Ryderbeit said: 'Do you want me to crap after them?'

'Just the other can, Sammy.' While Ryderbeit was going back for it Murray let loose another stack of George Washingtons, beginning to feel the idle fantasy of it all now — the fragility of the monetary system, the waste, the sheer masochistic delight of defecating this money down an open toilet into an alien lake in a far-away country. 'There's still plenty more where it came from,' he grinned at Ryderbeit, whose eyes looked tortured as he brought over the second can, pouring it sadly down the chute, while Murray stood with the last bundles ready. Enough to buy a couple of Rolls-Royces, he reckoned — holidays in the sun, jewels, girls, cars, clothes… It was all quite unreal. Ryderbeit had emptied the second can and Murray lobbed the whole stack down, thinking for a moment that Ryderbeit was going to be sick.

'Now the raft,' he said. 'We'll inflate it by the door.'

They slid the big rubber envelope, with its tied ballast of notes in their waterproof packing, across the top of the cargo packs, setting it up against the rear door. 'Now Sanderson,' said Murray. He felt completely in command; Ryderbeit had become a mute, sulky subordinate as he went back and hoisted Sanderson's limp body over his shoulders, shuffling his way back between the money, dropping the corpse rudely on its back, the head clonking like a coconut against the steel hull. Jackie watched and lit another cigarette.

'His neck *is* broken?' said Murray.

Ryderbeit shrugged. 'Jones did it. But it could've happened in a crash, I s'pose.' He began unbuttoning the Treasury man's smart grey-green tunic, while Murray went to select two packets of hundred-dollar bills. When he got back Sanderson was lying like a drunkard, head sagging sideways in the dim light, his tunic stripped open to reveal a pathetic string-vest, the inside of the coat fitted with deep pockets with button-down flaps that might have been tailor-made for the job in hand. Ryderbeit unfastened the flaps, then paused as he looked at the money, and a nasty cunning look came into his eye.

'There must be at least fifty thousand there, soldier.'

'At least.'

'The fishermen'll get 'em, even if the fish don't.'

'What of it?'

'It'll be days before they catch up.'

'We're wasting time, Sammy. They're new notes anyway — in serial numbers.' He tried not to look at Sanderson's twisted head as he slipped the packets into each of the pockets, buttoning up the flaps, then the tunic-front. 'Now the raft.'

He went over and swung the lock of the door, stepping back at the chilling howl of the slipstream. The weather was clear, and below them the water shone under the moon like hammered steel. Ryderbeit punched the raft inflator and the oval tubes swelled stiff with a quick burping hiss. 'Lower him in,' said Murray.

Ryderbeit rolled Sanderson face-down on to the bottom of the raft. Murray threw in the pilots' helmets, papers, logbook, charts, the two lifejackets. And together they slid the load through the door into the wind.

They watched it hit the water in a spray of silver, the raft settling the right way up with the dollar bundles still attached, but without the body. They could just see a few papers, together with the lifejackets, floating some way off.

Ryderbeit stared slowly after them and shook his head.

'They'll never find him. They'll have to drag the whole bloody lake!'

'They'll drag the lake, don't worry — but he'll probably get caught in one of the nets before morning.' Murray was glad to see Sanderson laid to rest. He went back and picked up the tool-kits, first-aid and spare parts, shouting to Jones, 'This is the last lot — then take us up north!'

He hauled the heavy kits to the door and let them go, down into the shallows where the fishing nets were spread out in long delicate skeins of bamboo mesh, with clusters of sampans lying far to their left, their lights glowing like fireflies across the smooth water. 'At least we've got the weather,' he muttered. 'Let's just hope it holds over Laos!' He slammed the door and turned the lock.

Ryderbeit had gone back up the steps into the cabin and was scooping something from the floor with an oil-rag. He came back grinning. Murray saw that the rag was soaked in drying blood from the pilot who had been stabbed. 'Just for a bit o' extra polish!' Ryderbeit said, tossing it down the latrine and unzipping his flies. Then as he urinated he reached in his jacket and took out his 'illegal' Rhodesian passport, dropping it carefully down the chute, following it with his Air U.S.A. card.

'That'll give 'em something to think about,' he said, turning with a solemn laugh. And Murray smiled back. There was good logic in Ryderbeit's final abandonment of his official personality: the Americans must know by now that he was involved, and the fun-loving Cambodians would have plenty of scope here for teasing the CIA, even when the search was called off.

Jones now turned the plane north, still heading low over the rice fields, up towards the high jungles of Central Laos. About three hours' flying time, and just about the same till first light. But it was one of the virtues of this war in South-East Asia that the enemy held no air threat, and so almost no effective ground radar system existed anywhere in Laos, except in the immediate vicinity of the main air bases, like Pakse and Savannakhet. These they carefully avoiding, choosing the higher, wilder country closer to the Vietnamese border — using the Caribou's short-range radar now, keeping down frighteningly close to the mountain tops, but with the moon to help them and the plane's many landing flaps to carry them like a switch-back over the peaks, down into the valleys.

The R/T crackled with the quaint chirping of Cambodian voices, but none of them sounded unduly concerned. From the American wavelengths they now learned, with a certain gratification, that a high-priority transport Caribou had been skyjacked and lost, last known heading into Cambodia — that all available aircraft in South Vietnam and Thailand were to stand by to intercept, and if necessary to destroy this aircraft. There was no mention of Laos. For the Kingdom of Laos remained mercifully inside that No-Man's-Land of international politics.

CHAPTER 2

Pol lifted his head from his wet sleeves and peered at his watch. Light was coming up behind the sealed windows where the jungle was waking with a noise that almost drowned the high flat whine of the VHF in the corner. He shook his head and blinked across the table. The dead American engineer had slid to the floor and his chair had toppled back against the refrigerator. No one had touched him.

Pol looked at the two pilots and nodded at the radio. 'Still nothing?'

'Nothing,' said the tall pilot.

Pol moved his short fat arms about and yawned. 'They should be with us in a few minutes. Coming in from the north over the Plain of Jars to avoid any radar. We won't hear them until they're about ten kilometres away. Anything from Wattay?'

The tall pilot rose and switched the radio on to the UHF beam. After a few seconds of static they got an American voice, brisk but untroubled, intoning a weather report: '…*holding fair to middle cloud over central and east Phongsaly — north by north-east clear to cloudy — winds moderate south two-to-three…*'

'Are we keeping a check on those reports?' said Pol, suppressing another yawn.

'The weather is satisfactory,' the pilot said, sitting down. 'If there are complications, our control will inform us.'

Pol nodded gloomily at the empty bottle of Scotch. He disliked feeling no longer his own master — reflecting that if he'd had his own way he'd have chosen a more sympathetic pair. 'Any more news of the plane?' he asked.

'Nothing from Air U.S.A. direct,' the pilot said. 'But while you slept we picked up several more shortwave messages from north Thailand. There is a full alert. The plane is still reported over Cambodia.'

Pol mopped his face with a damp handkerchief. 'As long as the weather stays with us,' he muttered. 'We're gambling on the weather now — and the stakes, my God!'

The tall man arched his eyebrows. 'You've never done it before?'

'Oh I've done it before,' Pol said shrugging, and reached behind him into a plastic bag, lifting out a fresh bottle of Johnny Walker. 'We're also gambling on that pilot of theirs,' he added, unscrewing the top and pouring a generous couple of inches into his glass. He breathed deeply. 'Are the flares all set?'

'Everything is prepared.'

Pol looked down at his shotgun, and on an impulse cracked it open, inspecting both breaches, then looked up at the two men with his impish smile. 'One cannot be too careful in this game.'

The two did not smile back; for at that moment the radio came on with Murray's voice speaking clear French: '*Charles! Tu m'entends? — tu m'entends!*'

The three scrambled to their feet, Pol reaching the radio in two pigeon struts. '*Je t'entends bien, mon chou!*'

'*Tout va bien?*'

'*Tout va bien!*'

'Get ready then,' Murray: 'We're coming in — three minutes away.'

Pol snapped off the radio, smiling through his sweat, and waddled out into the hot night, full of the shriek of birds and the black smell of the reservoir. The two pilots, carrying flashlights, had run ahead and were lighting the string of acetylene lamps along both edges of the dam wall. Pol waited by the yellow earth-moving machine, with its low slung toothed scuttle, which was drawn up in front of a bulldozer and ten-ton tip-truck — all three vehicles at the head of the steel-mesh road leading on to the dam, their ignition wires crossed, ready for starting.

There was no moon and a smell of rain in the air. Pol understood enough of flying to know that what Ryderbeit was about to do required enormous skill and a fair measure of luck, even in a plane as manoeuvrable as a Caribou. He was not sure that he had entirely liked Ryderbeit — his politics had seemed dubious to say the least — but he now experienced a solemn sense of affection, even affinity with the man up there somewhere in the dark grey dawn, feeling his way down towards this narrow curving strip of light in the heart of the jungle, risking his life for an illusory fortune.

Pol was not a cynic; and in this moment he was conscious of the dead hand of guilt, as he stood watching the two pilots coming back at a run between the two rows of harsh acetylene flares. He thought of the other man up there — the Irishman, Wilde, who'd picked that ridiculous fight with him in Bangkok, and then been so willing to help save his life. He'd liked Murray Wilde. There was something vulnerable and compassionate about him — unlike that mad Rhodesian who'd do anything for the promise of money. And then there was the girl — and a French girl too. He supposed she had been vital — the whole plan had finally depended on her — yet Pol was unhappy about her. His own wife had been shot by the Germans in Nancy in 1942. Even for money this was no game for a girl.

They saw the plane a moment later. It came in low over the far hills, throttles cut, making a smooth purring sound above the jungle, its landing beacons blazing on as it made a slow turn out to the left, speed dropping still further, disappearing for a moment over the trees behind them — then wheeling back in an amazingly tight circle, all flaps down, the undercarriage sweeping past twenty feet above their heads — hands over their ears, feeling the draught of the wings, port engine cutting to a whirring splutter as the slender high-tailed craft, silhouetted hard against its own lights, drifted down over the curving flarepath, forward-beacons bouncing as it made the touch-down, both props roaring into reverse and slowing it to a halt in less than half the distance across the dam.

The two pilots nodded gravely; but there was no time to lose in admiration of Ryderbeit's flying skill. They turned to the heavy vehicles behind them, with Pol following the tall man up into the tip-truck which was parked with its back facing the dam. The short snub-nosed pilot had already started up the huge earth-moving machine with a shattering roar through the stillness of the morning. A moment later its caterpillar tracks were crawling out along the dam wall towards the Caribou. The truck, with Pol and the tall pilot, followed a moment later. Between the lane of flares they could just make out the plane's tail-ramp being lowered on to the muddy track.

Murray was the first to meet them, coming round the side of the earth-moving machine with his carbine slung across his waist, standing in front of the track as it drew to a halt. Pol clambered out with a tired smile. '*Félicitations,*' he called.

'*Salut!*' cried Murray, and they embraced. The tall pilot had already got out and was hurrying back with his companion, extinguishing the flares. 'It's all there,' said Murray. 'The whole damned lot! Don't you want to look?'

Pol forced another smile. 'I'll believe you. I don't like looking at too much money so early in the morning — it makes me nervous.'

Ryderbeit had switched off all the aircraft's lights and they stood under the headlamps of the two heavy vehicles. Ryderbeit now appeared at the top of the tail-ramp with his M16 in one hand, waving at Pol with the other and shouting, 'Where are the bloody pilots?'

'Putting out the flares,' said Murray. Ryderbeit nodded and skipped down. '*Salut Monsieur Charlie!*' he cried with his abominable accent: 'Not a bad landing, hein?'

'Magnificent,' said Pol.

Jackie and No-Entry came round and joined them, and Murray introduced Jackie with a slightly stilted formality. Pol bowed, unconsciously touching his kiss curl and stepping back on his tiny feet with an absurd modesty. '*Enchanté, madame!* Perhaps you would prefer to wait inside the hut until we are finished? Only —' he paused — 'there is a dead man inside.'

She shrugged. 'There are also two dead men in the plane, monsieur.'

Pol turned with his hand held out to No-Entry. '*Enchanté, monsieur.*' The Negro merely nodded. 'Perhaps you would like a drink?' Pol added. 'My pilots will do all the unpacking.'

'I'd like to meet these pilots,' Ryderbeit broke in. 'But Holy Moses, I'd like a drink too!'

Pol chuckled and took his arm, beginning to steer him back towards the hut. 'The pilots are both new to Air U.S.A., *mon cher Sammy*. Their names are Ribinovitz and Taylor. Taylor is the short one,' he added, nodding at the two men coming back down the darkened dam. 'He doesn't talk a lot.'

'How much are we paying them?'

'One hundred thousand dollars each — what we agreed.'

Ryderbeit sneered: 'Two bloody lucky new boys! And the kickers?'

'They're down at the airport.'

Ryderbeit stopped and looked at his watch. 'Light's coming up. Sorry, Charlie, the drink'll have to wait.'

'You don't want any?' Pol said, frowning.

'I'd like to help deliver my babies first — then I'll drink all the booze in Asia!'

'I'll stay and watch too,' said Murray.

'Me too,' said Jones softly.

Pol stood for a moment looking at all three of them; then shrugged and took Jackie's arm, waddling back with her through the half-light to the hut at the end of the dam.

'He seems in a big hurry to give us a drink,' Jones murmured.

'He's half-drunk already,' said Ryderbeit, turning as the pilots came up to them.

'Hi!' the tall one called. 'That was a great landing you just made there, Mister Ryderbeit! I'm Jo Ribinovitz. This is Chuck Taylor.'

They all shook hands. 'Mind if I see your I.D.s?' said Ryderbeit.

'Sure thing!'

Ryderbeit glanced at the familiar blue Air U.S.A. cards, each bearing a photograph with a just plausible likeness to its owner. He nodded and handed them back. 'Just that I've grown a little suspicious in life, Jo. So you're both new to this game?'

'We're new to nothing,' Ribinovitz laughed. 'We're old hands.'

'Where were your last jobs?'

'Flying oil surveys over Alaska — goddam it! We quit a month before BP hit. Just our luck.'

'Well your luck's in now, Ribinovitz baby! So let's get on with movin' the baggage.' Ryderbeit was still holding his M16 as he leapt up the tailboard, signalling to the thick-set Taylor who had already climbed back into the cabin of the caterpillar truck, with its digging scuttle wrenched up so that the steel teeth came just level with the top of the ramp.

Taylor manoeuvred the machine slowly but with skill. Murray guessed that he had once worked with a construction company — or that he must have been putting in some pretty stiff practice recently. Then he looked up at the man's face, stolidly watching Ryderbeit's signals from under those huge curling eyebrows — and there was something oddly, uncomfortably familiar about those flat features with the loose mouth and little button nose. They began to nag at him, like the memory of that crooked-faced *boy* at the Continental Palace giving the wrong directions to the *cyclo-pousse* driver — Jackie's mysterious phone call on the same day — the rocket attack and the Red Alert — even Pol, the usually jolly twinkling Pol who'd even seemed so curiously subdued, almost sad when they'd just met. And now that blunt slack-mouthed face. Where the hell had he seen it before? — or one very like it? Was it all part of a pattern? They had seized the plane, taken off and escaped, dropped their paper-chase far to the south, and were now landed safely on the dam. Yet something, indefinably, was wrong.

He heard Ryderbeit shouting, 'C'mon soldier, put a shoulder to it!'

He joined Ryderbeit, Ribinovitz and Jones at the top of the ramp, and they moved back behind the piles of money, lifting the top plywood raft and shifting it inch by inch towards the open vent. When it was just over halfway, it toppled up like a seesaw and the two-foot-square packages, with their wiring now cut, trundled down into the earth-moving scuttle below. By the time they had unloaded half the first pile the scuttle was full, and Taylor signalled them to halt.

They were dripping with sweat as they stood at the top of the ramp, watching the scuttle slide back, hydraulic pistons hissing as the whole machine ground round on its axis, swinging the great load of dollars out over the dark pit of the reservoir and back again, the scuttle-arm lifting and opening, dropping the load of black packages into the ten-ton truck.

The whole operation took just three minutes. The light was coming up fast now, the reservoir covered in mist like steam off a saucepan, the jungle above rising in cobwebs of cloud.

The scuttle was coming round again, as they put their weight against the next stack of dollars, heaving the plywood raft over the edge, standing back and watching once more. Another three minutes — at about a million dollars a second.

Ryderbeit sighed. 'Beautiful work, eh?'

'The best I ever did,' said Jones.

Ryderbeit looked at the tall slant-eyed Ribinovitz. 'Where are you from, Jo?' he asked suddenly.

The man smiled. 'Brooklyn.'

'A good Polish Jew, eh?'

The man stared at him, poker-faced. 'Yes, I'm a Polish Jew.'

'I'm a White African Jew,' said Ryderbeit. 'Pleased to meet you.' They shook hands for a second time. 'What sort o' plane are we flying?'

'C 46. All cleared for take-off and weather.'

Ryderbeit nodded. 'You know where we're landing?'

'Small place just outside the Burmese border. It's as secure as anywhere. We'll hole up there for a couple of days, then arrangements'll be made to move to a secret rendezvous. Only Pol knows the exact plans.'

The skuttle was swinging back again and they started on the next load. For most of the time they worked in silence, watching the sky grow light and grey and empty. Pol appeared only once, moving none too steadily as he called up to them, 'The Cambodians have ordered an air search of Tonle Sap lake! They've found the dead American.'

My God, thought Murray, they're working fast. And in less than four hours. They must have an agent down there on the fishing-beds. Which meant the Cambodians were getting greedy too. He wondered what the international rules were in a game like this. Findings keepings? 'Where did you hear it from?' he called back.

'Phnom Penh. You forget, my dear Murray, that I speak Cambodian.'

'Anything out of Wattay?'

'Only that all air reconnaissance have been alerted. You're nearly finished?'

'We're nearly finished,' Ryderbeit snarled, heaving the last sledge of money into the scuttle. 'And a lot of bloody help you've been!' he muttered in English. 'Gettin' soused with Mrs Conquest, I s'pose?'

The last packages rolled out of the Caribou's tail. Ribinovitz jumped down and ran over to the tip-truck. The yellow scuttle swivelled round for the last time and dropped its load into the back. Ribinovitz started the engine and climbed aboard, driving forward this time, fast down the dam wall to the shelter of the high trees beyond Donovan's hut. Taylor followed more slowly in the earth-moving machine.

Murray, Ryderbeit and No-Entry did not wait to watch. They had turned back into the Caribou. All loose objects not already dumped in Tonle Sap were to be secured; tail-vent up, front and rear doors closed. Ryderbeit was the last to leave, having turned the undercarriage at a hard right-wing angle, all brakes off.

The bulldozer was now grinding along the wall towards them — pug-faced Taylor again at the wheel. Ryderbeit looked grave, almost glum. He had a love of aircraft as other men do of certain animals. He did not like to see a good plane destroyed. Taylor brought the bulldozer up very gently until its broad mud-polished shear was jammed up against the raised tail-door, pausing for a moment while he changed gears, the bulldozer shifting on its massive caterpillars, heaving now against the body of the plane, tilting it, then shaking it forward with its undercarriage churning mud, sliding it sideways towards the edge. The water level had risen perhaps thirty feet since Murray had last seen it, but it was still a long way down. Another bump and the right-hand wheel was within a foot of the drop. Essential that it should go down intact — nothing torn off, nothing that could float up and betray them.

The bulldozer drew back a couple of feet, grunted with a belch of smoke, then rammed the tail head-on, driving both wheels over the edge, following through as the belly of the plane crunched down on the slimy edge-lifting it up like a broken toy, one wing heaving itself into the air with a splintering crack of alloy, holding still for perhaps two seconds. Then the huge pyramid tail-fin with the Treasury markings swung up; there was another slow crunch of metal, the whole machine wobbled on the edge and suddenly cartwheeled down the wall, hitting the surface with a long splash. They could just see its roof rocking in the darkness below, settling very slowly, its nose the last to go — a blunt black-painted nose bobbing up like everyone's favourite dog — then sinking back under the deep lapping water, into silence.

'How long till the oil comes up?' asked Murray.

'With nothin' broken,' said Ryderbeit, 'it might be a day — perhaps two or three. There's always a little, but nothin' to see from the sky.' He glanced up at the grey ceiling of sky, then back at Taylor, who was already reversing the bulldozer back down the dam. 'He knows his job, that boy. You have to hand it to old Pol — he can sure pick 'em!' (Sure, thought Murray: perhaps too well.) 'I just hope the bastards can fly,' Ryderbeit added. 'But whatever else you may say o' the outfit, Air U.S.A. doesn't hire duds.'

Murray made no comment as they walked back down the now deserted dam to the hut. Jackie came out to meet them, standing stiffly with cheeks flushed, eyes turning slowly towards Murray. 'Did it go all right?'

'Fine. How's Pol?'

Pol came out beaming, the second bottle of Johnny Walker half empty in his hand. 'Have a drink, my dear Murray!'

'Gladly.' He took a quick pull and Ryderbeit grabbed the bottle from him, swallowing from it as though it were water.

'Flyin's over for today, soldier!'

Murray nodded. 'We've still got a lot of work to do before we get that money into a nice Swiss bank, Sammy. Come on, let's get aboard.'

CHAPTER 3

In the back of the truck, behind the great stack of crumpled black waterproof packages, lay a pile of empty triple-sackings marked in stencil: '*Donated by the United States of America.*' While Ribinovitz drove down the steep winding track towards the *Route Nationale Treize* into Vientiane, Murray, Ryderbeit and No-Entry began stuffing these sacks full of dollars. Pol and Jackie were riding in the Land Rover behind with Taylor at the wheel.

The three of them worked frantically, despite the swaying, bouncing floor; and by the time they reached the highway, less than half the money had been stowed away. Already the cloud was lifting and they saw two L 19 spotter-planes circling like moths, coming down slowly from the direction of Wattay airfield. Murray wondered what they'd be able to see when they got over the dam? Just a few heavy track marks in the mud? While in about a couple of hours' time a surprised Lao guard would saunter up on duty, to find his round-eyed boss lying dead from a heart attack.

Now that they were down on the flat again, the work became easier. No one seemed to be astir as they drove fast down the straight narrow track between the rice fields and the little open houses on stilts, with water buffalo snoozing up to their ears in water. By the time they reached the edge of the airfield all sixteen sacks were bulging to the neck and sealed with wire; and the three of them sat panting, limp and wet with exhaustion.

They drove on to the field through an unfamiliar, unguarded gate, far out in the corner near where the Ilyushin bombers lay rusting in the long grass. It was still too early for much activity, but there did seem to be a lot of small aircraft moving about in the middle-distance — probably more L 19 'Bird-dogs' on special reconnaissance duty. Murray tried to look for them. He felt that hazy, heightened excitement that comes with drinking on an empty stomach and no sleep.

The plane was drawn up at the end of the first runway. A big, solid, oil-streaked C 46 — its rice cargo already being loaded from a forklift by a team of Laotians in baseball caps. The truck drew up about fifty feet away, just behind the Land Rover from which Pol climbed out, carrying the shotgun in one hand and his plastic bag of Johnny Walker in the other. 'Ça va?' he called, stepping back for Ribinovitz and Taylor who were breaking into a run towards the rice-loading team.

'What happens now?' said Murray.

Pol chuckled and handed up another bottle out of the bag. 'It's all under control, my dear Murray!' He suddenly sounded more cheerful. 'These sacks will be loaded with the others. The flight is all in order. The weather excellent.'

'Excellent,' Murray echoed, as Jackie got out of the Land Rover and stood smiling at him. He smiled back, listening to a small plane whining up into the grey morning.

Over by the side door of the C 46 Ribinovitz stood towering over the crew of Laotians working the forklift. The man in charge had started to jabber in a confusion of pidgin French and English; but Ribinovitz cut him short with what sounded very much like Lao. The man nodded and gave a shrill order to the driver of the forklift, who started to back his vehicle, empty, away from the loading-door in the plane, round to the rear of the tip-truck. Ribinovitz had already hurried back and let down the rear-flaps. The forklift stopped exactly opposite them. Murray watched and thought how easy and simple it all was. Perhaps just a little too easy, too simple. He began to open Pol's new bottle of whisky, watching in a kind of daze as the two flat spatula forks rose on their pistons to the level of the truck floor. The driver edged forward, sliding the forks deep under the first half-dozen sacks, lifting them a few inches, then reversing slowly, carrying them over to the door of the C 46 where the kickers had now appeared — wiry little men in spotted camouflage who began to wheel the rice-sacks up the roller-tracks into the hull of the aircraft.

Murray went over and stood beside Jackie, glancing down at her hard swelling breasts — calculating that if each of the packets of fifty-dollar bills under her dress contained two hundred and fifty bills, those two breasts at this moment were worth twenty-five thousand dollars. Meanwhile, over by the plane, the next load of sacks was being pushed aboard — a couple of hundred million dollars, at least. Perhaps it was the hard light of day, or just the Johnny Walker, but he began to feel a dull sense of futility.

He said quietly, '*Jacqueline, chérie!*' — leading her away from the others who were all busy watching the operation over by the plane. 'Why don't we just walk away — slowly — now? Over to the main gates and back into town. We'll take the ferry and be in Thailand in an hour. We've got our passports. Our visas are valid. We can be in Bangkok by tonight — if we hurry and make the morning train.'

She had turned and was staring at him, her eyes bright and puzzled. 'Are you drunk?' she said suddenly.

'A little.'

'You're mad!'

'Not mad, love. Practical. Let's get out while the going's good. We only have to walk over there to the gates.'

'Dressed like that!' Her laugh was more a snort of scorn; and he looked down — at the M16 still slung across his waist, the baggy fatigue pants, the big clumsy combat boots yellow with mud from the dam.

'I can change in town. You can buy me some new clothes.'

'*I* buy you clothes? While you run out — when everything's going so well!'

'It's going too well, Jackie. The alert and then the attack together — that phone call you got before our lunch at the *Cercle* in Saigon.'

'I don't understand. What's all that got to do with us now? We've got the money, haven't we? We've got fifteen hundred million dollars — and now you begin complaining! And it was all your plan in the first place. I just don't understand you.'

'It was my plan. But other people are taking over now. It's no longer in my hands.'

'What other people?'

'I don't know, Jackie.'

She looked at him, slowly, almost brutally, no tenderness or understanding now in those big dark eyes. 'You want my money?' she said, touching one breast. 'You can have it all. But not me. I'm not running.'

He looked wearily back at her, listening to another tiny plane taking off far across the field. 'Listen, Jackie. With twenty-five thousand dollars we can start all over again. You don't even have to get rid of your husband now — thanks to Sammy.'

She wrinkled her nose with a sly little smile as she took his arm. '*Viens, tu dis des bêtises!* All nonsense! You talk as though we're going to be caught. By who? By those little spotter-planes up there? What are they going to find?'

Ryderbeit came over, drawing on a cigar and grinning hugely. 'Well children? Oh what a beautiful morning — and everything's coming our way!'

Murray smiled bravely back. 'When's the take-off?'

'In about ten minutes. Ribinovitz has just gone up to start the props.'

'You're happy about those two boys, Sammy?'

Ryderbeit shrugged. 'Well, if you're happy about Pol, then I'm happy about the pilots. They've done all right so far. Why?'

'No reason,' said Murray. One of the C 46 engines grunted and swung to life. The forklift was moving back for the last load now. Taylor was climbing up through the cabin door. Murray suddenly felt very, very tired. I've had too much bloody whisky, he thought: too much whisky, too much worry. I should be like Ryderbeit, enjoying a king-size cigar at five-thirty in the morning. Or like No-Entry Jones — cool and calm and able — a man who can roll with the punch. He looked at Pol, who had come over to share the Johnny Walker with Ryderbeit, both drinking from the bottle. Jackie had lit a cigarette and stood quietly watching.

Perhaps this is the moment of truth, Murray thought — or the moment before the truth. The misty airfield with the dead brown Ilyushins in the grass beside them and the little 'Bird-dogs' droning up half a mile ahead; while less than twenty yards away was a planeload with fifteen hundred million dollars in rice-bags.

Ryderbeit yelled, 'Right, children, all aboard!'

CHAPTER 4

Murray was half-asleep in his hammock-seat when the plane took off. He dreamt of a tomb of black water where the corpses of two pilots floated slowly about in the casket of a sunken aircraft — of a chateau in France with tall stone walls and a row of Citroën police cars drawing up at the gates — the officer saluting graciously, apologising to madame for the inconvenience…

He woke to see Ryderbeit embracing each of Jackie's well-stacked bosoms, shouting between kisses, 'It'll be the biggest balloon ever built, darling! Cruising speed of over a hundred miles an hour — and a gondola big enough for three hundred people. Bars, casino, nightclub, sunken baths, bedrooms with gold-leaf for wallpaper…' He looked across at Murray and laughed. 'You'll be on the maiden flight, soldier! You and Jackie and Charlie boy here, and we'll be flyin' anywhere you like to go. Though I have to be a bit careful where *I* put foot, on account o' my troubles. Most o' the time it'll just be flyin' — nice and gentle like, over the Alps, Himalayas, Andes — just where you say, soldier!'

Pol sat opposite them, solemn-faced with the shotgun on his knees and the whisky bottle between his feet. He raised a smile when he caught Murray's eye, and Ryderbeit shouted, 'What about you, Charlie? What are you going to do?'

'I shall get drunk,' said Pol. 'Then maybe I shall find an alias and creep into Les Halles at four in the morning and find a bottle of Montrachet and two dozen oysters.' But there was no joy in his voice, no light in his eye. Perhaps he was just tired too.

'Where are we?' said Murray. It was nearly an hour since they'd taken off from Vientiane.

'Another ninety minutes,' said Pol.

'And what about you, No-Entry? What great plans have you got now you're a multi-millionaire?' Ryderbeit yelled.

The Negro, who had been dozing behind his dark glasses, stirred up in his seat. 'I'm a modest man, Sammy. I'll buy meself a farm maybe — somewhere like in Spain or Mexico where I can breed animals and have a pool-room and a gymnasium, with maybe a boxing ring where I can train a few young fighters. Just strictly a quiet life for me, Sammy.'

Murray fell asleep again. And this time his sleep was heavy and dreamless, unbroken even by the violent jolts and drops as they climbed into the high mountains. Only once, when he was on the point of waking, did he have a sudden electrifying image. He saw the pilot Taylor, with his slack mouth and button nostrils, at a diplomatic reception in Vientiane, wearing shelves of epaulettes on a dove-grey uniform that hung badly on him as though it had been made for a nobler generation...

He woke in a panic. Ryderbeit was shouting at him, 'We're goin' down, soldier! Fasten your seatbelt, no smoking, we hope you enjoyed your flight and that Air U.SA. has seen the bloody last of us!'

Murray twisted his head, watching through the small round window the clouds racing up towards him, suddenly gone, and he was looking at the ground, tilted on its side like a lime-green wall, with the white thread of a road running across it, joining a town — just a jumble of huts next to a complex of runways looking like criss-crossed strips of Elastoplast. He swallowed hard to clear his ears, holding the metal rungs under his seat, his M16 still laid across his lap, catching Ryderbeit's eye and seeing him wink and give the thumbs-up sign. The plane flattened out, both engines going strong, flying down low now over rice fields drawn across with fine lines like freshly-cut turf, the edges of the fields dotted with sultana-shaped trees that reminded Murray of those trees they stick on architects' models.

All around was an amphitheatre of dark hills streaked with rain. There were planes — small bat-winged jets — lined up on the runways in front of a camouflaged control tower. Pol suddenly unfastened his belt, stood up with his shotgun and started to sway clumsily down between the rows of sacks towards the pilot's cabin.

The plane bumped down a moment later, and Ryderbeit snapped his belt free and stood up, even before they stopped. Murray was shouting above the roar of the reversing props: 'It's a bloody big airport they've chosen, Sammy!'

But Ryderbeit had already bounded to the open side-door and was peering out, while the plane slewed round to a halt. Murray got up and stood beside him. From the ground the place looked less formidable: a grey Asian town, with the rain splashing off the tarmac. Ryderbeit leapt out, his M16 in his hand, with No-Entry Jones right behind. Murray waited to give Jackie a hand down. Once outside he looked round and saw no sign of Pol or the two pilots. The engines behind them came to a stop. There was a sudden weird silence, broken only by the hiss of rain.

They began to walk together, out across the tarmac towards the control tower. As they did so they saw a number of men coming towards them. Small men in uniform — drab and grey-green like the landscape — flat, short-peaked caps, skeleton-handled machine-pistols in their hands.

Ryderbeit stopped and swung round. 'Where's old Charlie?' he yelled.

Murray grinned unhappily and shook his head. 'Charlie's out there in front,' he said, still walking. Even through the rain he could read the name on the control tower; and now, as he took Jackie gently round the waist and held her tightly, he recognised the framed photograph above the door of the building — the frail, wispy-bearded features of the little man who had once worked as a pastry cook in a London hotel and was now known as Uncle Ho, Hero of the People.

Ryderbeit had seen it too and just stood with his hands helpless round his M16. The soldiers were coming closer — fanning out in two groups, one towards them, the other round towards the C 46.

'Dien Bien Phu,' said Jackie softly, with a strange reverence, reading the name on the control tower.

Ryderbeit turned, his gun dropping limply on to the wet tarmac. 'We're in North Vietnam,' he muttered. 'Fuck!'

A NOTE TO THE READER

Dear Reader,

If you have enjoyed the novel enough to leave a review on **Amazon** and **Goodreads**, then we would be truly grateful.

Sapere Books is an exciting new publisher of brilliant fiction and popular history.

To find out more about our latest releases and our monthly bargain books visit our website: **saperebooks.com**

Printed in Great Britain
by Amazon